SLEIGHT
OF HAND

Anne Marie Becker

COPYRIGHT

This is a work of fiction. Names, characters, places, and incidents either are the product of the author's imagination or are used fictitiously, and any resemblance to actual persons living or dead, business establishments, events, or locales is entirely coincidental.

DEDICATION

For Tim. Always.

ACKNOWLEDGMENTS

I want to acknowledge the constant and unwavering support of my family, including my husband and three beautiful kids, and my extended family. You all mean so much to me.

Also, I am fortunate to have a fantastic team of writers and editors who make both me and my books better. Deborah Nemeth, you're one of the best editors on the planet. Emme Adams, thank you for the final read-throughs, and strengthening this book even more. Kim, June, Rita, Di, and so many other writer friends, your input and encouragement while brainstorming and editing have been invaluable. Andrea, you're family, friend, and fabulous beta reader all rolled up in one. How did I get so lucky?

And to my readers, thank you for your emails and reviews. Your support means so much.

To all of you, I extend my heartfelt gratitude.

Other Books by Anne Marie Becker

MINDHUNTERS SERIES

Only Fear

Avenging Angel

Deadly Bonds

Dark Deeds

Acceptable Risk

End Game

REDEMPTION CLUB SERIES

Stacking the Deck

CHAPTER ONE

The hairs on Emily's arms stood at attention, the first sign that trouble had just walked through the door. She placed a beer in front of a customer as her gaze traveled across Legacy Lounge, searching for the source of her apprehension.

She rounded the long bar and walked among the clusters of comfy chairs and intimate cocktail tables that formed a semicircle around the stage, where a band was setting up for the Saturday evening entertainment.

Fingers curled around her hip and she whirled on the owner of the wandering hands.

"Hey, baby," he said, looking up at her with a lopsided, obviously inebriated grin. His hand slid around to cup her ass.

She gently removed his appendage from her rear and placed it back on his beer bottle. "Keep your hands on what you purchased."

His gaze swept over her. "How much?"

"More than you could afford."

The two friends at his side guffawed and slapped him on the back, defusing the tension and giving her a chance to slip away.

The feeling of being watched stuck with her, but it wasn't coming from the amorous drunk. The cause of her unease was something bigger. Dangerous.

She reached the wall opposite the stage. Here, tall booths afforded more privacy. A woman flagged her down, while simultaneously laughing at something her date whispered in her ear. His eyes, however, were on the woman's other assets. Her clinging red dress gaped at her bosom, just short of indecent exposure, revealing a black lace bra. There was a cunning edge to her gaze that put Emily on alert as she stopped at their table.

"Another drink for me and my friend," the lady in red said.

Emily spied her cocktail waitress taking orders at the other end of the lounge, and then eyed their empty wineglasses. "The same?"

"How about it, sugar?" The man's eyes had taken on a glaze of lust and alcohol that would doubly impair his judgment as he addressed his date. "More of the same, or should we go for something different?"

"How about champagne?" the woman purred.

"Whatever you want." The man's wedding band caught the light as he reached out to toy with the ends of the woman's long, brown hair. His fingers casually brushed the sides of her breasts. Her ringless hand slid farther up his thigh, squeezing lightly and distracting him as her other hand shifted to the man's pocket. She had a light touch and had made a wise selection. He was an easy mark, and wouldn't make a fuss if the woman took advantage of him, lifting his wallet. Filing charges would require admitting that, though a married man, he'd been here with an escort. He'd risk everything.

It's none of my business what they want to do in a dark corner. But it was her bar—at least, she was the manager. Someday she'd have her own place. Still, she took pride in keeping her patrons happy. If the woman started causing trouble, Emily would get rid of her. In the meantime, maybe the man would come to his senses.

She turned to fill their order.

"And don't try to fool us with the cheap stuff," the woman called after her.

The barb to Emily's pride was the final straw. She swung back to their table. "May I speak with you a moment?" she asked the woman.

The woman didn't spare her a look. "I'm a little busy."

"Trying to make a living—the illegal way."

That got the woman's attention, and her hand stilled on her mark's crotch, but her other hand slid into her purse—with his wallet, no doubt. "I don't know what you're talking about."

"I'm quite sure you do." Emily leaned over the table, getting in the woman's face but keeping her voice low so as to not disturb the other patrons. "Get out of here and don't ever come back."

"Hey!" The man seemed to finally realize his fun was about to end, with no clue that Emily was helping him dodge a bullet.

"If you're still here in—" Emily glanced at the clock behind the bar. "—thirty seconds, I'm calling security. The next call I make will be the police."

The lady in red looked at Emily with a boatload of irritation and a modicum of respect, and disengaged herself from the man.

"What the hell?" The man's glare turned to confusion as his escort slid out of the booth, pulling the strap of her purse over her shoulder.

Emily stopped her with a hand on her arm. "I'd better not see you in Legacy Lounge again."

Without a word, the woman sashayed through the archway that led from the lounge into the enormous, glass-domed rotunda that formed the hub of the sprawling Legacy Hotel and Casino complex. The man rose as if he'd go after her, but stopped when Emily tossed his wallet on the table.

"I believe this is yours," she said. While distracting the woman with a hand on one arm, Emily's other hand had been occupied retrieving the wallet from her purse. Distraction was the key.

The man gaped, scooped up his wallet and mumbled a thank you before taking off.

Emily smiled with satisfaction. As manager and

head bartender at Legacy Lounge, troubleshooting of this variety came with the territory. Especially when the bar was an offshoot of a hotel and casino, where people's inhibitions were already loosened, inspiring them to take all kinds of chances. Then again, this was Las Vegas, and risking everything was not only encouraged, but expected.

The perfect environment for a conman—or conwoman—to thrive.

But dispensing with the lady in red and returning to her post behind the bar didn't dispel the feeling of trouble waiting in the wings, watching. The prickles of sensation ricocheted along her skin as if a lightning storm was about to hit. Her gaze resumed its perusal... and landed on a cowboy hat that lay at the far end of the bar.

Apprehension tightened her chest. She had an unnatural weakness for a man in a black Stetson—one man, in particular.

It can't be his.

Almost reluctantly, her gaze moved from the hat to the long, tanned fingers clasped together beside it. Her attention continued in an upward trajectory, past a broad chest and wide shoulders clad in a black T-shirt. Those shoulders had often held the weight of the world. A coil tightened in her abdomen as memories flooded her.

Crap. She knew that grin—a sinner's smile that didn't belong on a supposed saint. His dark eyes twinkled as her gaze met his.

Adam Wilde. Trouble. That explained her gooseflesh, and the sense of impending danger. It had been eight years since she'd last seen him in physical form, but he'd taken over her dreams since she was eighteen.

She ignored the warm, languid feeling that came over her limbs and pulled on her poker face as she made her way to his end of the bar.

"Nice work handling Miss Scarlet." His chin jerked

toward the archway where the woman had disappeared. "Then again, you always could spot a con." His gaze narrowed. "Or maybe she's one of yours?"

"I don't run cons anymore, and I don't allow criminals to take advantage of my customers."

"Your loyalty is touching." His head swiveled to take in the crowd. "Not sure they deserve it, though."

Defensiveness locked down her muscles. She had to force her jaw to relax in order to send him a stiff smile. "This is a classy place. Not like what you're used to."

Memories lit eyes so dark and deep they were like volcanic glass. "Not like what *we* were used to." They'd both spent way too many late nights hauling their fathers' butts home from dive bars. His intense gaze shifted from her to his surroundings, taking in Legacy Lounge's dark wood bar, which echoed the wooden beams of the ceiling. Cobalt blue tablecloths and platinum tea lights decorated each table, giving the bar the touch of elegance the hotel and casino had become known for. Adam was probably trying to reconcile the Emily Moore he once knew—the scrappy tomboy in secondhand clothes and skinned knees—with such luxurious surroundings.

But for all its finery, Legacy Lounge was still a bar. And that was one place she had always felt comfortable. Except for the occasional ass-grabbers and flirts, most customers typically only wanted an ear to listen and a hand to pour, and perhaps the occasional sympathetic smile or supportive word.

They didn't take anything from her. Not like Adam had. The reminder of her naïveté had her mind slamming the door against unwanted memories.

"I shouldn't have brought up the past," he said, as if reading her mind. "Now, you look like you've seen a ghost."

"For a second, I thought I might have." He'd been as good as dead to her for years. Not a call or a text. She arched a brow, using nonchalance to disguise the torrent of feelings that threatened to sweep her away. Still, she couldn't help noticing the tired lines around his eyes and mouth. Something worried him. *Damn it*, she absolutely did not care. "What are you doing here?" Her words came out sharper than she'd intended.

"Maybe I just want a drink."

She raised an eyebrow. "You sure you trust me to make you a drink?"

"You have no reason to harm me this time."

"I didn't have a reason then, either. I was protecting you."

"At least you stick with your lies." So he hadn't forgiven her.

She shrugged as if his words didn't still have the power to hurt her. She'd need every inch of the tough-girl armor she'd been developing her entire life if she was going to stay strong. "And you're still holding a grudge."

"I suppose you did offer me some recompense." He'd dropped his voice, but his eyes simmered with an alarming amount of anger and... desire. That was a surprise.

She *had* offered him more. So much more. *Everything.* And he'd said no. His rejection had shredded her eighteen-year-old heart. But now his eyes were conveying a different message.

She hid her confusion by turning to fill a glass of water, giving her a chance to recover her wits. She set a cardboard coaster with the Legacy logo—a stone pillar with a celestial background—and the water in front of him.

"That was another life," she said. "I've moved on." Just like the phoenix tattoo, in brilliant reds and oranges that wrapped around her shoulder, she'd risen from the flames, born again. The phoenix reminded her to soar above it all. Her other tattoo, the delicate weaving of an intricate, chain-link pattern around her wrist, was like a cuff, anchoring her to reality. Reminding her of the shady roots she struggled to bury before they reached up and strangled her, but that would forever be a part of her. Of who she was.

But Adam had known her before and wouldn't be convinced by declarations that she'd moved on. His next words disabused her of any notion that he'd forgiven her for her past transgressions. "You tease a man for that long and he begins to expect some kind of payment. And after so many years, there'll be considerable interest tacked on."

Adam didn't touch the glass of water, drinking in the sight of Emily instead. She still had that inner fire that drew people to her, but he would guess she was also still walking on the wild side, flipping life the middle finger. Which meant they were still on opposite sides of the fence, especially now that he worked in law enforcement.

So what the hell was he thinking, asking for repayment of a debt he'd said he'd forgiven and a humiliation he'd tried to forget? His actions were suspiciously like... *flirting*. Hell, he didn't do flirting. Direct and to the point was his usual *M.O.*

On the other hand, his reminders of her past transgression and his poor handling of it kept her temper up. She'd never been able to walk away from a fight. He needed her to stay, to talk to him, even if it was via an argument. If anyone knew where Tanner Wilde was, it was Emily. Growing up in Kingman, Arizona, those two had been the dictionary illustration of *thick as thieves*.

Physically, she'd changed. Time had shaped a beautiful young woman into an enticing twenty-six-year-old. Her features were more defined, honed to a sharp sexiness that held more appeal than it should. Her body was still lean and fit, but her curves had filled out in all the right places. As a tomboy, she'd spent most of her youth with her long blonde hair pulled into a ponytail through the hole of a ball cap.

Now it was cut in a sassy bob with a blunt edge that swung against her chin and brushed against her lips when she leaned forward to serve a drink. His skin had erupted in goose bumps as he'd watched, as if her hair was touching his skin. Her eyes, the same golden brown as drizzled wild honey, still held a mix of streetwise intelligence and fuck-off toughness that hid her vulnerability. He'd always been drawn to that. To her. Like a good whiskey, her potency had only strengthened over the years.

With a skill born of years of practice, he shuttered his reaction to her and gave her a lazy smile. Not that she was buying what he was selling.

Suspicion narrowed her eyes. "You here to drink or not?"

Not. But ordering a drink was one more way to force her to acknowledge him. He picked up a laminated cocktail menu and perused its contents. "What the hell's a Redemption?"

"House specialty drink. Vodka martini with curacao and some fruity stuff thrown in. It's pretty and sweet." She smirked. "Takes a manly man to ask for redemption."

"Give me a beer." He wasn't feeling that manly— yet. Seeing Emily again had testosterone and adrenaline pouring into his system as if someone had opened a damn floodgate. Or as if his brain had identified a threat. "Whatever you'd recommend."

She set a bottle of a local microbrew in front of him and moved away to serve other guests. He took the opportunity to observe his environment, and her. The band tuning up onstage created an electric atmosphere. Or the heightened sense of anticipation could be due to the way Emily ran her turf like a crime boss, directing the waitress and loading up her tray, accepting payment and mixing drinks, all while conversing with patrons—and avoiding Adam. Her quiet efficiency was surprising. The girl he'd known had been wild, not wanting to be tied down by anything or anyone, and certainly not desiring any lasting responsibilities.

Back when they were teens, Emily had kept up with his brother, Tanner, who was her age, two years younger than Adam. Adventurous, she hadn't minded getting into trouble, so she and Tanner had gotten along famously. Or infamously. Half the time she'd instigated the escapades. The other half she'd been saving Tanner's hide.

Adam was betting she still kept up with Tanner and could lead Adam to him.

After serving everyone else in the room, she made it back to his end of the bar. "Can I get you anything else?"

"Information." Was that a flash of disappointment in her eyes?

"I figured as much. About?"

"Tanner."

"Haven't seen him." Her words were curiously abrupt. Was it the truth, or was she protecting Tanner?

"When did you see him last?"

"A little over a week ago."

Around the same time Adam had received an anonymous envelope with a typed note that Tanner was in danger, along with a picture of Tanner's apartment—ransacked—and a torn playing card. Adam hadn't been able to reach his brother by phone. The strange warning, combined with a lack of communication with Tanner, had rocked him to his core and he'd wrapped up his caseload the best he could to take personal leave and come to Las Vegas. But Tanner was nowhere to be found. Filing a missing person's report at the LVPD, retracing Tanner's credit-card trail and phone records—which had both gone quiet over the past week—hadn't given Adam anything to go on. It was as if his brother had simply disappeared.

Emily turned to leave and he scrambled for a way to keep her with him, to open her up. Hell, maybe he'd order that fruity drink. He could use a little redemption right about now—and he'd get a chance to watch Emily's tats ripple as she created the concoction. The phoenix at her shoulder, revealed by her black, sleeveless button-down top, nearly took flight every time she shook a shaker or dug in the cooler for a bottle of beer. But he wasn't here to drink.

"You're busy," he said. "I should settle my tab while you're here."

She turned back to him. "That'll be eight dollars."

Having just taken a sip, he nearly choked.

"Problem?" The guileless, wide-eyed look she sent him was promptly ruined when she pressed her lips together in an attempt to hold back a laugh. At the sight and sound of her usual mischievous self, something light and feathery brushed across his insides.

"Talk about a racket." He took out his wallet and fished for a bill, his thumb brushing the torn playing card he'd tucked inside. He laid down the twenty and, after a moment of indecision, pulled out the half-card and laid it on top.

Her attention flicked from the card to his face and her laughter faded.

"What?" he asked, watching her carefully.

"Nothing." She moved to turn away, but his hand snaked out to grab her wrist.

"It's something. You recognize it?"

Her gaze met his and shimmered with distrust and... *fear.* She pointedly flexed the hand he still held within his grip and he released her, trying not to notice the softness of her skin as the pads of his fingertips slid along her wrist.

"What do you know about this?" He picked up the torn half-card, a three of spades, and flipped it between his fingers. The backside displayed the bottom half of the Legacy logo, a marble pillar on a celestial cobalt blue background. When he'd seen the playing card that was clearly from Legacy, he'd suspected Emily was a part of this—whatever *this* was. Tanner had told him months ago that she worked here. Had she mailed Adam the anonymous note along with the photo and this torn card?

No, she'd been surprised to see him. He hadn't been joking when he'd said she looked like she'd seen a ghost. But she was adept at schooling her expressions and hiding her feelings. Still, what kind of coincidence was it that she worked at Legacy, and he'd received a card from here? And what was so frightening about a torn card, anyway? He laid it on the bar again.

Emily licked her lips nervously. She glanced around to see if anyone was paying any attention to them. They weren't. He'd been eyeing the crowd just as much she had been. The mirror behind the bar gave him a fantastic vantage point.

"Emily?" he prodded, concerned now. Just what was Tanner into?

"It's a marker from the Redemption Club. And you'd be smart to put it away. Now."

The scent of victory—much like the vanilla-and-whiskey scent of Emily's skin—created an adrenaline surge. "*Redemption*. Like the drink on your menu?"

She shrugged, but the look she shot him said she wouldn't be providing further clarification. The connections between this place and Tanner's disappearance were growing stronger, but how did the pieces fit together? Despite several days of leaving messages on Tanner's phone and searching the places where Tanner had recently used his credit card or tagged on his social media page, Adam hadn't heard from his brother and nobody had seen him in the past week. Apparently, Emily hadn't, either. His concerns were growing by the second.

"Where did you get it?" she asked, eyeing the card like it was an unpredictable dog that might bite.

"Someone sent it to me, along with a picture of his apartment, which looked as if a tornado had hit, and a note that said Tanner's in danger." He ran his thumb along the jagged edge.

"Put it away." She'd dropped her voice and covered his hand with hers, hiding the card. Her gaze shot to their joined hands, and the worry in her eyes told him she was thinking of the card beneath, not the zing of electricity flowing between her skin and his. "Don't show that here—or anywhere, for that matter."

"So Tanner *is* in danger? Do you know what the card means?"

"Yeah. And I'm guessing you don't or you wouldn't be so casual about this. What you're doing is the equivalent of walking into the lion's den and poking the beast with a sharp stick."

He leaned forward until his nose nearly touched hers. "Maybe I want the lion to come after me. He may already be after my brother."

She huffed. "You two are more alike than you'd ever admit."

"Me and Tanner?"

"You think you can take on a criminal organization without any repercussions or backup?" Her opinion of his judgment was obvious by the incredulous look she shot him.

"Criminal?" Redemption Club was an illicit group?

"You don't want to go up against them. They'd eat you alive."

He bristled at her lack of confidence in his skills, but she might not be aware he was a detective. "Don't worry about me. I can handle myself."

"I didn't mean it as an insult. It's just that you're not the type to walk the line between good and evil. Despite your black hat, you've always been firmly planted on the good side. You've made that very clear." Again, memories of the past stood like a tall wall between them.

"And Tanner?"

She met his gaze. "We both know he's walked that line—and poked the lion—many times." As had she.

Once upon a time, Adam had as well. "Maybe I'm tired of being the good one in the family."

She dismissed the idea with a laugh that hit him square in the gut and pulled away, releasing his hand. "You're not cut out for the dark side."

"And Tanner? Is he cut out for this club?"

"If that marker's his, it's already too late. He's made his choice." Her eyes were troubled.

"I'm worried. He hasn't answered my calls for the past week, and hasn't been to his place in days. It's like he's disappeared. I've even filed a missing person's report. Why wouldn't he call me if he needed help?"

"Would you have come?" Accusation frosted her tone.

Guilt pierced him but he shoved it away. He was here now, wasn't he? "What about you? Why weren't you there to rescue him this time?"

She flinched at the hint of indictment in his words, but he was truly curious. Emily and Tanner had been a dynamic duo ever since Adam could remember, running small-time cons together. They came by the lifestyle honestly. Emily's father, Howie Moore, and his father, Frank Wilde, had once been more than drinking partners. They'd been partners in crime, modeling the pattern of troublemaking that seemed to be hereditary, typically tied to running scams and abusing whatever substance was handy. Apparently, Emily had chosen to embrace her inherent wild streak, moving to Sin City, working in a bar, adding tattoos and multiple piercings in the form of little silver studs that marched up one ear like sentries.

And he still found her sexy as hell.

"Who says Tanner's in trouble, anyway?" she asked. "He's a big boy. Maybe he just needs time away."

"Any idea where he might have gone?"

"For all I know, he's hiding out in his apartment. Maybe he didn't feel like answering the door."

"He's not there, but the place had been cleaned up since whenever that photo was taken." And he'd been staying there for the past couple days, lying in wait—when he wasn't checking out Tanner's last known locations.

"What, did you commit a B&E?" Her mouth curved in a wicked smile that made certain parts of him tighten with appreciation and longing. "Now who's breaking the law?"

"Found the spare key. I had to make sure he wasn't inside, hurt or something." But finding nothing was almost worse. "I need your help, Em."

Some of her hard edges softened at the use of her childhood nickname, but she didn't seem overly worried about Tanner, which gave Adam hope his brother was okay. It also dashed his hopes, because she obviously wasn't willing to be disloyal to his brother to soothe Adam's concerns. "I'm sorry, but I can't help you."

A customer from the other end of the bar shouted across the noise and music. "Hey, baby, you going to get that cute butt over here and fix me a drink?"

Adam stiffened, ready to verbally flay the man for his derogatory remarks, but Emily didn't seem shocked or offended.

"I have to work," she told Adam, and then glanced back down at the torn three of spades. "Stop asking questions about the Club and go back to Phoenix. Tanner will be fine. He can take care of himself. He's had to ever since you left."

Ignoring the jab, he tucked the card back into his wallet, frowning when she visibly relaxed. Whatever this Redemption Club was, it was clearly bad news. "How about dinner before I leave? For old time's sake." He had no intention of leaving town before this case was solved and Tanner was safe, but maybe she'd actually accept his invitation if he appeared to be giving her what she wanted—even if it annoyed him that what she wanted was for him to disappear from her life again.

Wariness flashed in her eyes. He understood the value of caution, but he didn't like that the carefree Emily he'd once known was so guarded, especially against him. He'd imagined her smile and laugh so many times over the years, had even ached for them. He wanted their easy friendship again.

"I have to work late," she said.

"After, then. Midnight snack? Nightcap? Early breakfast?" He could see she was about to refuse all offers. "I really do think Tanner's in trouble, and not the type he can talk his way out of this time. He needs me. He needs *us*."

A furrow formed between her brows and her gaze went to his wallet, where the card was now tucked away.

He grabbed a cardboard coaster and leaned forward to snatch a pen out of her breast pocket.

"Hey!" She pressed her hand to her chest, which only served to draw his attention to the soft mounds beneath her shirt. She'd left the top couple of buttons undone and the hint of the swells beneath had his throat going dry. He took a quick swallow of his beer and started writing.

"This is the number for my cell." He slid the coaster toward her. "Call me. For Tanner's sake, if you won't do it for mine." Leaving his unfinished beer, the pen and a twenty on the bar, he walked out through the archway and into the rotunda with its fifty-foot-high glass dome centered over a fountain. The sun was setting, so the slice of desert sky visible above was pink, purple and orange. Constellations were etched on the glass, and colorful panels along the edge of the dome echoed the cobalt and magenta theme that had been evident in Legacy Lounge. He prayed to the heavens beyond for patience, and strength.

There was only so much of his past he could take at one time. Emily was a concentrated dose of memories of the life he used to live, a reminder of the infamous family reputation he'd tried hard to leave behind as he carved an honest future for himself. Unfortunately, his current mission wasn't going to be a help-and-leave-in-one-day type of job. And Emily would just have to accept that he was here until he got things done.

CHAPTER TWO

The parking lot at the Legacy Hotel and Casino complex was enormous. Adam cursed the mid-summer heat as he crossed the pavement, stopping short as he reached his car. "Do I know you?" he asked the man leaning against the trunk.

"Not yet." Tall and lean, the man was probably in his late thirties. He unfolded his arms and stuck out his hand. "Will Remington." He had a quick smile with a hint of geek, but behind his glasses, his eyes were sharp. "Special Agent in Charge Will Remington, to be specific." He pulled out his badge and flipped it open.

"FBI?"

"At your service." He chuckled. "Actually, I need you to be at my service."

"For?"

Remington dropped his voice. "Taking down Redemption Club. We need someone with both inside and outside connections. Congratulations, you fit the bill."

Adam shook his head, wondering if he'd stepped into an episode of *The Twilight Zone*. "Maybe you'd better start from the beginning."

Remington gestured to Adam's car. "Perhaps we could talk as you drive." When Adam hesitated, he sent him a disarming smile. "It'll help your brother."

"How do you know him? Or is this because I filed a missing person's report?" But why would the FBI, not the local police, approach him?

Remington simply stood by the passenger door

with a raised eyebrow. Right now, Adam supposed the stranger was more likely to give him answers than Emily was. Besides, he had his pistol beneath his seat. So he unlocked the doors.

Once they were on the road, Remington spoke again. "Where were you headed?"

Adam cast him a sidelong glance. He'd been about to canvas the casinos Tanner, a professional poker player, had been known to haunt, but he had the feeling the FBI agent had something else in mind. "Maybe you should tell me, since you know so much. And you haven't answered *my* question yet."

"I've been watching your brother for about a month now. He's landed himself in the middle of a mess and seems to be taking full advantage of it."

"Sounds like Tanner." He always could make the best of any situation.

"You recently received a package," Remington stated, not asking for verification.

Adam slid him a look. "Was that you?"

"I felt it was time to involve you."

"Using scare tactics? Threatening my brother isn't the way to ingratiate me to your cause."

"Oh, that wasn't the FBI's work in his apartment. The guys who did that were part of the Club. But I figured sending the picture, and the card I found in your brother's apartment, was the quickest way to get you here fast. You had to see for yourself how serious this is."

"And how serious is this?"

"That torn card means your brother has ties to the Club, that he went to them for a favor at some point. Because it was a three of spades, a relatively low value, we don't think he did anything like kidnapping or murder—"

Adam stiffened. *Murder?*

"—But he must have done something to piss them off. Now that their people are after him, I'm hoping maybe he'll finally be willing to help the FBI take them down."

Adam gripped the wheel tighter, his attention on the freeway as his brain sorted through his emotions. "Is he okay?"

"He dropped off my radar after the Club did that to his place, but I think he's okay. He's hiding. My sources indicated the Club is still hunting him, which means he's still alive."

"Why involve me?"

"You know him better than anyone, and I need to find him."

Adam bit back a grimace. Those were nearly the exact same lines he'd used on Emily to gain her assistance.

"With his talent for becoming whoever he needs to be," Remington continued, describing Adam's brother's skills as a con artist in a tactful way, "Tanner can disappear indefinitely, if he wants to."

Adam was well aware how difficult it would be to find Tanner, but he was reluctant to involve others in his search until he knew what the hell was going on. "Is he wanted by the authorities?"

"The FBI wants to talk to him."

"Forgive me, Agent Remington, but if he hasn't done anything illegal, why should I help you find him?"

"Oh, I didn't say he hadn't done anything illegal. But Tanner could cut a deal if he helps me land a bigger fish. I think he's got his hands on something valuable. He may not even recognize its value—or the danger it puts him in."

Or maybe Tanner was aware of the danger, especially since someone from Redemption Club had apparently searched his apartment, which was why he'd gone underground. "What valuable object are we talking about?"

"A ledger, Detective Wilde."

"Some kind of accounting book?"

"Exit here," Remington directed, ignoring Adam's curious gaze.

He took the exit, which led to a populated area. Still, he'd remain vigilant with this so-called agent. "Where are we going?"

"An educational field trip."

After following Remington's directions, Adam pulled up in front of a federal prison. He arched a brow. "What kind of education did you have in mind?"

Remington grinned. "There's a prisoner I'd like you to talk to. Tristan Floyd is a known member of the Redemption Club. Violent son of a bitch, too. Murdered several people without blinking. Perfect recruit for the Club." Remington's tone was matter-of-fact, as if he dealt with this type of person all the time. Adam had run into some stone-cold killers over his years with the Phoenix Police Department, but he hoped he never ran into enough of them to take it all in stride.

"And he's talking? If this club is as powerful as I've heard, he'd be stupid to go against them."

"Not if he's offered the right deal."

"You offered this *violent son of a bitch* a deal?"

"For the information he has, yes. This Club barters in murder and other illegal acts. In order to survive, the group needs people who enjoy doing evil or thrive on greed. And making arrests is all the more difficult because the person who commits the crime is rarely tied to the victim. Plus, the Club retaliates against narcs in a vicious way. All kinds of alphabet agencies want to take this organization apart, but the infrastructure is sound."

"Who's the ringleader?" Adam asked, ready and willing to go straight to the top.

"The current theory is that the leader was Finn Tucker, now deceased."

"There have to be others who would step up to the plate. It's a Club."

"Exactly." Will's eyes sparkled as he led Adam inside the building and checked him through security. "Tucker's friend Ryan Stone was a suspect for a while."

"But no longer?"

"We can't get close enough to the guy to find charges that'll stick. His lawyers—and he can afford the best—spun it so he was just the innocent best friend of the real perpetrator and our case fell apart. Besides, the Stone family is like royalty around here— and in many places in the world. Robert Stone, Ryan's dad, owns Stone Corp, which is a conglomerate of several businesses ranging from a cruise line, to a film production studio, to a worldwide chain of fancy hotels that includes Legacy Hotel and Casino, right here in town."

At the mention of the familiar locale, a chill went down Adam's spine. Yet another tie between this mystery and Emily. "Hard to get close to people with resources like that." And yet, if anybody could do it, Tanner could. Scamming people was his specialty, and he would have seen outsmarting Ryan Stone as a special challenge.

"Nobody will flip on the Club. Membership is a closely-guarded secret and investigators who get somewhere have been known to back away when something bad happens to them, or they disappear or end up dead." Remington grimaced. "The Club's reach is long, and those members who could tell us about the organization are guilty of something." He sent Adam a look. "Which is why we need your brother. If he has the ledger—and Tristan says he does—then he has the key to bringing down Redemption Club."

"I'd love to help you, but I don't know where Tanner is." And if Tanner had crossed a secret group with vast resources, he'd be better off staying hidden until he could go to the authorities. "Do you have any proof he even has this ledger? Sounds like all you have is a con's word."

Remington's grin was without amusement this time. He opened the door to an interview room where a man in an orange jumpsuit sat on the opposite side of a thick window. "Tristan says he had the book delivered to Tanner as Finn Tucker's last request. He says your brother plans to go against the Club, and bring down Ryan Stone, but I think Tanner's unprepared for the risks he's taking. As long as he has that ledger, he has the means to make some serious trouble for a lot of dangerous people."

The walls pumped with heavy bass as Ryan Stone watched Brenda snort a line of cocaine off his glass coffee table. She leaned back into his leather couch with a satisfied smile.

"That's the stuff, baby," she said. "I've missed this."

He draped an arm over her shoulders, tucking her against him as his palm found one of her D-cup breasts. They were fake, but that didn't bother him. No matter what the world professed about inner beauty, it was appearances that counted. And money. And power.

He was close to having all of the above. So close that he lay awake at night, imagining how he'd rule his world. He'd be fucking awesome at it. But there were loose ends to tie up first.

Brenda pressed her red lips to his and he tasted the expensive champagne they'd consumed earlier. When she pulled away, her eyes were wild, her smile vacant. "We should do this more often," she said.

He wished. Tonight, he could jack up the music. There were currently no other occupants on the penthouse floor of Legacy Hotel and Casino. Six luxury suites, and three were spoken for by his half sister, Ivy, who managed the Legacy Hotel and Casino and worked insane hours; their father, Robert Stone, who was currently traveling for business but didn't often stay here anyway, preferring his mansion on the south side of town instead; and Ryan. The other three suites, at ten grand a night, were currently empty.

His body ached with desire—for Brenda's lush body, but also for the booze and drugs. But he abstained. He'd pop an oxy later, when his work was done. First, he had business to conduct or he'd be out on his ass, penniless and pathetic.

A Stone wouldn't let that happen. His dad, while emotionally absent, had attempted to instill a kickass work ethic in his children. As a teen, Ryan had started cataloguing what he'd come to call his Stone Rules. And one of those rules was *Business comes first, always.* That discipline would serve Ryan well as he carried out his plan—a plan that was currently being thwarted by a rogue Club member. That would end tonight.

"You found Tanner?" Ryan asked. "He'll be there tonight?" His hand clenched Brenda's breast as she stiffened against him, giving away the answer. Even through her drug haze, she must sense his frustration. "It was your only job." When she'd shown up at his door, he'd figured the job was done.

She pressed closer, shifting her hand down his chest. "I'm sure he'll turn up. He loves a good card game."

"He'd better." The monthly poker night for Redemption Club members started in a couple hours, and Ryan needed Tanner to be there. The prick had disappeared several days ago, dodging the men Ryan had sent to rough him up. Searching his place had yielded no answers—and no ledger. Since then, Tanner had gone underground.

Then, a few days ago, Tanner had sent a message via a mutual acquaintance that he'd decided the only way Ryan could regain the ledger was to win it fair and square. It burned in his gut that he was expected to win back what was rightfully his. But he'd tried for weeks to take down Tanner and locate the ledger. He would have killed the asshole the moment Ryan got his hands on the book—which, obviously, Tanner knew. The guy was crafty, and had successfully evaded Ryan's men and Brenda's surveillance. This poker game, where the stakes were high and they both could get what they wanted, was the only way to lure him out.

Brenda's hand slid lower, reaching for the button

on Ryan's pants. He caught her fingers and squeezed until she gasped. "Don't mistake tonight's generosity for leniency," he growled. "If he doesn't show up, everything ends. We'll have nothing, including these private parties you enjoy so much."

Brenda tried to shift away and gauge his expression, as if uncertain of the degree of his anger. Her knuckle popped beneath his grip. She whimpered and began spouting excuses. "I've been watching his apartment religiously for a week. He hasn't been there. I figured, with the game tonight that time was up. I can find you another poker player. I have contacts." He hadn't told her about the ledger, or that Tanner had the only thing Ryan wanted.

"It has to be him. Where else have you checked?"

Her brow knitted in confusion. "You told me to watch his place."

Ryan let go of her breast to pinch the bridge of his nose with his free hand. *Jesus.* "I told you to find him at any cost."

"I figured he'd have to come home eventually."

"Not if he's on the run. You fucking idiot." He sliced his free hand through the air so sharply that Brenda flinched, thinking he was about to strike her. Her fearful reaction appeased him. He released his grip on her hand and shoved her away. "Would you go home if you knew I was looking for you, knew that I suspected you'd double-crossed me?"

Brenda gnawed on her bottom lip and glanced at the table as if she could use another hit. "No. But maybe there's someone else?"

"There's no one else," he roared. "Tanner has what I need. He's supposed to bring it to the game tonight as his stake, but he must have gotten spooked. Damn it, someone talked!" Tanner must have found out that, once Ryan had what he wanted, he planned to get rid of the bastard for good. A threat like this couldn't be ignored, and Tanner couldn't be allowed to live to tell others how he'd strung Ryan along, or Ryan would lose all credibility in the Club. He kicked the coffee table over, spilling the contents onto the floor, and glared at Brenda.

Brenda's eyes widened. "It wasn't me."

No, she probably wasn't smart enough to put together a plan to betray him. Besides, Ryan gave her free booze and drugs.

"I can help with that frustration, baby." Her words were liquid heat as she scooted closer, pressing into him in all the right places. Her hand slid his zipper down and slipped inside, stroking him. She had some serious skills in that department.

"The only thing that will help is finding Tanner." And regaining the ledger. And then killing Tanner and anyone else who tried to come between him and his destiny. The Redemption Club was his, and his alone, but he needed the ledger that detailed all the members and what they owed, or he had no power.

Seeing that he was no longer aiming his anger at her, Brenda seemed to relax. "I didn't see Tanner, but there were others at his place the past few days."

Ryan scowled. "Why didn't you tell me earlier?" Probably because she'd been too focused on the blow and champagne.

Brenda looked confused. "You asked if I'd seen Tanner."

"Well, who the hell *did* you see?"

"Earlier in the week, a woman, a blonde I didn't recognize, stopped by briefly. Then a couple days ago, a guy shows up. Looks a little like Tanner. Dark hair, strong shoulders. Handsome, especially in that cowboy hat." Her stroking increased as she talked about the man and Ryan put a hand on her wrist to stop her, even as his body protested. *Business comes first, always.*

"But it wasn't Tanner?" Could he be working with someone to betray Ryan? That level of betrayal was unthinkable, but lately Ryan had had his hands full with people wanting a piece of his pie. And someone was hiding Tanner. People didn't just disappear in this town—not without leaving a trace that Ryan's capable Club members could find.

"I'd guess they were related. Same swagger and dark eyes, you know? The guy's been back and forth for the past few days, staying there at night. That's one reason I thought Tanner could be inside. But today, after the guy left, I was able to sweet-talk the landlord into letting me inside. Tanner wasn't there."

"And the woman?"

"She only visited once. She let herself in."

"She had a key, too?"

"Yes. She was pretty. Maybe Tanner's girlfriend? That should be worth something, right?" She glanced hopefully toward the cocaine that dusted the rug.

"We'll see." He nudged Brenda aside and went onto the balcony that overlooked the desert outside Vegas, which was cast in a warm orange glow by the setting sun. On the opposite side of the hotel, the neon lights of the Strip would be winking on. The heat of the July day was still uncomfortable, but the balcony was private as he dialed Tanner's number. A look back showed Brenda on her knees on the carpet, trying to scoop the powdered drug back onto the now-righted coffee table, her focus wholly on getting high.

As before, his call went directly to Tanner's voicemail. Perhaps threatening the people important enough to have keys to his apartment would ensure he brought the ledger tonight.

"You're out of time," Ryan said. "You requested this damn poker game. If you fail to show tonight, and bring what I asked for, I'll take my payment in the form of your hot, blonde female friend. Or someone in your family. Sooner or later, I'll get to somebody you care about more than yourself."

Emily was still a little shaky as she let herself into her apartment around one-thirty in the morning. She blamed her jitters on the triple shot of espresso she'd consumed on her dinner break, around nine o'clock, but she'd never been good at lying to herself. The memory of Adam's piercing gaze, which had burned holes through all of her defenses, had stuck with her all evening.

She tossed her keys and purse onto the tiny kitchen table and sighed as Calliope jumped onto the counter to purr her greeting. She scratched the calico under the chin. "You're not supposed to be up there. You know that." Like her owner, Calliope was a rebel at heart and enjoyed breaking the rules. But even when she'd skirted the law, Emily had limits she didn't surpass, and one of those included messing with the Redemption Club.

Her thoughts went to the torn card in Adam's wallet. Her worst fears had been realized, and she was suddenly glad she'd kept her boundaries in place and hadn't let Tanner drag her into this mess. Only desperate or deviant people turned to the Redemption Club for favors. In exchange, the unthinkable was sometimes demanded as repayment. Working at Legacy, she'd seen and overheard enough about the Club to know she didn't want to be beholden to them.

She pulled a water bottle from the fridge as she recalled a conversation she'd had a month ago with Tanner, when he'd approached her about the con.

"Something just fell into my lap, Em. It's got potential for a huge payoff." The thought of a new conquest lit Tanner's dark eyes.

"Not interested." She turned to stock the bar. "You don't want to mess with them."

"So you've heard about the Redemption Club?"

She looked around nervously. "Don't talk about it here."

Tanner laughed. "What? Like it's Fight Club or something?"

"Worse. I've heard some people end up in prison. Or dead."

"Or rich."

She wished her warning had been enough to put him off the potential of a large score, but it had probably only heightened the appeal.

"And now Adam has a debt card," she told Calliope, wishing saying the words aloud would reduce their power. It did no good. She still shuddered with worry for him. And for Tanner. She'd gone to check on him earlier in the week, as he hadn't been returning her calls. But he wasn't home. At the time, she'd shrugged his silence off, attributing it to their little falling out. Now, however, she feared Adam was right to be worried.

She filled Calliope's food and water bowls and warmed up leftover takeout Pad Thai for herself. Sitting cross-legged on the couch with her late-night meal, she listened to the cell phone messages that had piled up in her inbox while she'd been at work.

The dean at the local community college was contacting her about the gaming class she'd taught last spring, wanting to verify she'd be teaching the popular course again in the fall. And there was a message from a woman named Gladys at the memory care center where Emily's mother lived since a car accident a few years ago. The residents there received treatment or rehabilitation for memory issues or long-term brain injuries and Emily had met many of them during her weekly visits. Gladys asked Emily to stop by and update her computer software, then teach her how to use it.

Another now-legit side job that had sprung from her skills as a con artist. Emily had once been the one to send out a virus, then conveniently swooped in to *fix* it—for a price.

She'd gone legit in the past couple years, trying to rebalance karma by volunteering at the memory care center once a week, teaching basic computer skills to the residents, and sometimes the staff, and hooking them up on social media if they so desired. All for free.

Even her bartending job, for which she did accept payment—a girl and her kitty had to eat—was aimed at realigning the karmic scales. No matter what Adam thought of her, she had a sense of justice. In fact, there were some things she'd like very much to set right. She just had a different way of doing things.

At the sound of Tanner's voice on the next message, she froze.

"Hey, Em. I need a favor." He laughed in disgust and she could envision him shoving a frustrated hand through his dark hair. "When do I not need something? Jesus. I'm sorry. I'm a horrible friend. You deserve better." There was a manic note beneath the self-recrimination that had Emily setting aside her food.

No, not mania, she realized. *Fear.*

After fifteen years of shared antics, she'd only heard him this way once before—and he'd had good reason. That time, she'd come to his rescue, though it had cost her Adam's friendship.

He blew out a breath. "I need to see you, at least one more time before... Can you meet me at our place tonight? Don't tell anyone. I'll be waiting." He hung up.

Before what? God, was he in danger? Was he suicidal? That didn't sound like Tanner at all, but then, he hadn't been acting like himself for weeks.

Damn. His call had come in at ten and it was nearly two in the morning. Their usual place, a tiki-style dive bar on the old Vegas strip that was just quirky enough to feel inviting, was open until 4:00 a.m. on a Saturday night—rather, Sunday morning. How long would he have waited for her, or was he still waiting?

She tried calling him on his cell phone, but again there was no answer. Nor did anyone pick up at his home number—not even Adam. She hung up without leaving a message.

He'd sounded so scared. And there was nobody else to help him. Unless...

She paced for a moment, glaring at her phone on

the counter. After Adam had left the bar earlier, she'd tucked the coaster with his number into her apron pocket. Later, she'd transferred the number to her cell before she'd clocked out for the night. *Just in case,* she'd told herself. It was only prudent to have it—and wouldn't Adam Wilde be shocked to hell and back to see Emily Moore making a sensible choice?

But Tanner had often lamented his brother's holier-than-thou mentality. And his message sure as hell hadn't mentioned asking his brother for help.

Out of loyalty to Tanner, she wouldn't call Adam, no matter how worried he'd seemed. Besides, maybe Adam had found his brother and talked to him already. If so, that might be the reason behind Tanner's message to her. He probably just wanted to talk things over, use her as a sounding board. Adam stirred up all kinds of things for Tanner, who'd never felt like he'd measured up to his older brother's standards.

Join the club.

CHAPTER THREE

Did the woman never sleep?

Adam was dog-tired, but Emily was his best chance at finding Tanner, who could possibly be inside her apartment with her right now, possibly with some legendary ledger that both Special Agent in Charge Will Remington and lowlife murderer Tristan Floyd believed was in Tanner's possession. So Adam sat in his car in her parking lot, peering up at her second-floor apartment through his windshield, at two in the morning.

Floyd had related how the red leather-bound ledger, full of documented evil deeds, had fallen into Tanner's hands after Finn Tucker's death two months ago. And now several people—on the right and the wrong sides of the law—would do anything necessary to get their hands on the book. No wonder Tanner was in hiding.

After his visit with Floyd, Adam had promised Remington he'd be in touch if he learned anything and returned to Legacy to follow Emily home from work. She was his only lead at the moment. Besides, he was concerned for her, too. His gut told him she was somehow involved in, or at least knowledgeable about, whatever had prompted Tanner to disappear. Remington had indicated that the Redemption Club was a secret organization, and yet Emily seemed to recognize the significance of the torn card and its connection to Legacy Hotel and Casino. She knew more than she was willing to share. Adam needed to change her mind.

He checked his phone, but there were no messages from her or Tanner. His boss, on the other hand... He listened to the latest voicemail from Chief Jimenez as he stared up at Emily's apartment.

"The victim is sticking to his story that you cuffed him, then pushed him to the ground and put your knee on his neck," Jimenez said. "I'm sorry, Adam, but with the conflicting stories, it'll take a while longer to sort this out. It's probably a good thing you're on leave. Some distance might help."

The victim.

It was such bullshit. He didn't know how the drug dealer he'd arrested had come by the injury to his back and neck, but it wasn't from Adam manhandling him. Adam hadn't touched him other than to cuff his wrists and put him in his car.

Adam deleted the message. He was sick of the whole thing. Trumped-up allegations, stemming from Adam getting too close to arresting the ringleader of a drug trafficking group that had connections to the Mexican drug cartel, had forced him to sit behind his desk for nearly a week. The supposed victim's lawyers were dragging everything out while keeping Adam from pursuing the investigation.

A shadow crossed behind one of the thin curtains. Damn, she worked long hours. He'd sensed an underlying fatigue in her eyes earlier that evening. Emily always had been one to push her limits to the max, to test the boundaries. She'd been a ball of energy, one that could either consume and destroy, or rejuvenate and motivate a man.

He could use a bit of rejuvenation in his life.

The sudden thought shocked him. It shouldn't have. The memory of her smile had haunted him since the day he'd left. Her lips had always seemed built for sin, but now her body had attained womanly curves, slim and toned in some parts, fleshed out and inviting in others. Just the right blend to entice any man. But her smile... that sarcastic tilt of her lips had always felt as if it were made just for him.

She was one of the reasons he'd had to leave his life in Kingman. She'd tempted him to abandon all his good sense and follow her over the cliff. At the time, that had been scary. Hell, it still was.

Annoyed with the direction of his thoughts, he took a gulp of his lukewarm coffee to refocus. He wasn't here for Emily, wasn't looking for a relationship or even a fling. He was here for Tanner. Over the past week, he'd checked the jails and hospitals, but Tanner hadn't been arrested or injured. Which meant he was either hiding because he was a hunted man—wanted by whoever wanted the ledger and knew he had it—or he was already dead. The latter was unthinkable. For all of their differences, Tanner was still his baby brother.

Emily's apartment door opened, jerking him out of the past. He bumped his elbow on the door and muttered a curse. With quick, purposeful strides, she crossed the parking lot to her car. Where the hell was she going, alone, at this hour? There was only one person he could think of who could lure either of them out into the night at this hour—Tanner.

As she pulled out onto the main road, he retrieved his Stetson from the passenger side and started his car. He reached under his seat to assure himself his pistol and badge were there, at the ready. Something told him there was trouble ahead.

After a short drive, she pulled into a public parking lot near Fremont Street, the popular downtown tourist destination. There were plenty of people walking around, probably relieved that the summer heat, finally released from the concrete's tight hold, was dissipating. Something about her earlier poor reception of him told him to hang back a bit, to watch and wait rather than approach her.

At the unmanned kiosk, she slipped a bill into a slot to pay for her parking space. As she headed to the sidewalk, not bothering to glance about, worrying him

as to her sense of personal security, he retrieved his
gun and put it in the waistband at his back, hidden by
his untucked shirt. The badge, he shoved into a pocket.
The moment she was almost out of sight, he hurried to
pay, too, then followed her as she made her way down
the famous Fremont Street pedestrian mall.

A dome-like canopy stretching 1500 feet down the
mall's length hosted the Viva Vision light show during
the evening hours. The canopy was dark at this late
hour, though people still gaped upward at the zip lines
and casino lights, or clustered around doorways as
shouts of victory and dinging of buzzers ricocheted
when someone hit a jackpot. Farther down, the iconic
neon cowboy affectionately known as Vegas Vic waved,
marking the position of the old Pioneer Club.

But Emily observed none of that. She walked like
a woman on a mission, and he couldn't help but admire
her long legs and the feminine sway of her hips. She
wore the same black jeans, ankle boots, and button-
down sleeveless top she'd worn at Legacy Lounge, but
had pulled her light hair into a short ponytail that
bobbed as she walked.

She didn't look back. Not once.

Later, he'd give her hell for her failure to observe
her surroundings.

The thought gave him pause and his next steps
slowed before he spurred himself onward. He was
assuming he'd have another encounter with her beyond
tonight. If she led him to Tanner, her part in this would
be over. He wouldn't need her any longer, and she
would be safer if she remained uninvolved. Unless she
was already involved.

Maybe he'd stick around a few days to make sure
Tanner was back on the straight and narrow and take
the opportunity to check up on Emily, too. After all,
he'd once been a close friend. He was allowed to care
about her, whether she wanted him to or not.

His blood beat thick and fast at the thought of
more face time with her. He enjoyed her wit. And the

way she drove him completely nuts. Damn, he must be crazy. He'd only been back in her life one day and he was already losing his common sense, just like before. He was already forgetting why he'd had to leave eight years ago.

Several yards ahead of him, Emily turned into a dive bar with a turquoise-and-yellow neon sign that said Pete's Paradise. The neon palm tree's coconuts blinked in sequence. She hadn't had enough of the bar crowd at work? Maybe she'd become an alcoholic like their fathers. Working in a bar could do that to a person. Genetics could do that to a person. Hell, being friends with his brother probably did that to a person.

He took a few steps inside and stopped, giving himself a moment to survey the lay of the land. His body prickled with awareness before he even heard her husky voice against the back of his neck.

"Looking for someone?"

Emily was pleased she'd been aware enough, despite her preoccupation with getting to Tanner, to observe Adam following her in his car. Who else did she know who wore a cowboy hat while fighting crime? Only Raylan Givens in *Justified.* Come to think of it, Adam and Raylan shared the same confident swagger and slow, sexy smile.

Only, Adam wasn't smiling as he turned to face her. "As a matter of fact, I was looking for you," he growled.

She planted a hand on her hip. "You found me. Again. Careful, or I might think you're stalking me." And damn, the thought of him wanting her that badly sent a shock of anticipation through her. She was a freak, still addicted to him, hungry for any little crumb of attention he'd toss her way.

"You didn't appear particularly worried. A woman walking alone at night should be more careful."

She matched his scowl. "What do you want now?"

"Same thing I wanted earlier." His gaze dipped to her lips, but quickly refocused on her eyes. The slow, unsteady prancing in her chest became a gallop.

"Help finding Tanner," she said, more to remind herself than to state the obvious. "This might be your lucky night. He left a phone message earlier and asked me to meet him here." She gestured to the bar, which was dim except for the pops of bright color from neon accents. The theme was tropical, complete with fake palm trees and booths with false roofs that gave the impression of grass huts. There were a few customers, but it wasn't a crowd by any means. "But it's obvious he's not here now."

He scowled at her. "Why didn't you call me right away?"

She fluttered her eyelashes at him. "You think little old me can't be out alone at night?"

"Not with the likes of my brother, if he's running with the crowds I'm afraid he's running with."

"I used to be that crowd." She huffed out a laugh, then sobered. He'd voiced her deepest concerns.

"Which is why I think you're the key to finding Tanner."

She glanced around, checking if anyone was close enough to overhear, then pinned Adam with her gaze. "It would be best if you just dropped this. You're only putting yourself in danger." He arched a brow, but didn't look prepared to back down. She straightened. "But you already know that." Now who was holding out on whom?

"You seem to know an awful lot about this *secret* Club. Have you had personal dealings with them?" He was watching her carefully. "Maybe you even work for them, or owe them a favor. Perhaps finding Tanner is repayment. I can't think of any other reason he wouldn't tell you where he's gone."

Her heart sank that he could believe she'd trade her soul to the devil so easily. She made to push past him and walk out, but he grabbed her arm.

"Or maybe you're hiding him." He cocked his head at her and she looked away. His dark eyes saw too much and her barriers were weak around him. Only a few hours ago, he'd crashed into her life again and she was already feeling like the naïve girl she'd once been rather than the cautious, capable woman she'd become. "But why would you feel the need to hide him from me?"

She went on the attack in an attempt to regain some ground. "You never understood your brother, did you?" *Or me.*

Anger tightened his expression. "You're the only person who ever understood him. And right now, I need that kind of insight, need to think like him. I wouldn't be here otherwise." *Ouch.* "I have to find him, fast. If you've got any other information—"

She spread her arms wide. "Search me. I'm an open book."

He grinned wryly. "Right."

Her gaze swept the few people who populated the bar. "You and I have the same information regarding your brother's current whereabouts."

His eyes narrowed on her. "Only because I followed you."

"I would have called you after I found him." Maybe. "He said he wanted to meet here, so I figured I'd make sure it was okay with him before I notified you. But his message was left hours ago and I didn't get it until I got home. He obviously didn't want to wait. Not sure why he didn't try to reach me at work." *Or just meet me at my apartment.* He had to be hiding from someone. She wasn't sure she wanted to know who. He could even be a fugitive from the law. She gnawed on her lower lip and looked back at Adam in time to catch his attention there.

He quickly looked away.

"This isn't just brotherly concern, is it?" He'd been gone way too long from Tanner's life to suddenly come swooping back in. "Who do you work for?" Last she'd heard, he was getting a degree in criminal justice. Their hometown had gotten a good laugh at that one— a Wilde descendant on the other side of the law for once. Had he become a lawyer?

"I'm an officer of the law."

"A policeman?" *Shit.* Tanner hadn't said a word. Then again, speaking of Adam had become taboo between them for many reasons.

"Detective."

She sucked in a breath and slowly blew it out. Part of her was intensely proud of him. The rest of her was even more wary.

He scowled. "This is why I didn't tell you."

"What?"

"The invisible wall you just erected between us."

She forced her muscles to relax, even if her brain couldn't. "Force of habit, I suppose." She'd spent a lot of years dodging people like him, people in authority. Her parents had cultivated a sense of suspicion and self-preservation that she couldn't easily discard. "What does a Phoenix detective want with Tanner?"

"This has nothing to do with my job. It's a family matter." But he wasn't meeting her gaze. "Let's talk to the bartender and waitresses. If they don't know anything, you can try calling Tanner again."

Fine. She didn't want to know his deep, dark secrets anyway. It would only suck her back into that world. "I'll talk to the bartender if you'll use that unfathomable charm of yours on the waitress." He grunted at her sarcasm but moved toward the woman who was serving a table in the corner. When she realized she was watching the way his jeans hugged his ass, she spun on her heel with an exasperated groan and headed for the bar.

"Haven't seen you in a while," the bartender said as she approached.

She returned his smile. "Hey, Rick. How are you?"

"Can't complain. Business has been great. Summer heat makes them thirsty." He sent her a wink.

"Bet it's been the same at Legacy."

"I'm definitely seeing an uptick in business. Have you seen Tanner lately?"

"He was in earlier. Stayed awhile but left about an hour ago. You two supposed to meet or something?"

She sighed. "Yeah, but I didn't get his message until I got off work. He didn't happen to leave a note or anything, did he?"

"Nah. Sat in the corner. I was surprised he didn't sit at the bar like you usually do." A crease formed between Rick's bushy gray eyebrows. "He didn't want to talk, either, just wanted to sit and watch the door. Seemed nervous."

"Thanks. I'll have to catch him later, I guess."

Nervous? Tanner was low-key and relaxed most of the time, though he'd seemed to be in a heightened state of alertness over the past couple weeks. She'd chalked it up to their strained relationship and hadn't brought it up. But even when he was in one of the high-stakes poker tournaments, he was cool and collected. It took a lot to rattle him—much like his older brother, whose outward calm hid the coiled tension within.

She glanced across the bar to see Adam chatting with the waitress. He was all easygoing smiles and inviting posture, leaning toward his interviewee to gain information, but there was a sinewy toughness beneath the charm. Deep down, he was wound so tight she thought he might snap like a guitar string. The devil in her was curious to strum that string, to push a little bit and see if she could break him. *Naughty Emily.*

He caught her watching and something flared in his eyes, igniting an answering fire in her belly, especially when his gaze held hers as he walked to her side.

"Any luck?" Adam asked.

"He was here but left about an hour ago."

He nodded. "The waitress said the same. Said he nursed the same beer for a long time. Kept checking his phone. Finally got a call and left soon after." He looked around as if he'd spot another clue as to where Tanner had gone. Worry lines furrowed his forehead, and fatigue tightened his mouth. Emily resisted the temptation to smooth a fingertip over them. He straightened. "Let's check a few more places around here. Then I'll walk you to your car and follow you home." She opened her mouth to reject his offer, but he stopped her. "I insist. And if you hear from Tanner again, contact me. Right away, Em. It could be a matter of life or death."

Ryan drove through the quiet, gated neighborhood south of downtown Vegas. His car could practically drive itself to Blake Toll's home, since Ryan had been coming here once a month for a couple years now. Poker night was for Club members only, and limited to participants of his choosing. Typically, he chose desperate members who wanted to earn back their freedom or barter for darker deeds than they could repay—and frequently ended up owing the Club even more.

Another Stone Rule: *Take advantage of every weakness.* Desperation was certainly a weakness. Ryan had experienced a dose of it himself lately, and it didn't sit well in his gut—mostly because of another Stone Rule. *Take out the competition.* If his father knew his own son had become competition, that Ryan hadn't destroyed the ledger and ended the Club as he'd promised—that he had, in fact, pursued illegal Club activities with renewed gusto despite being under the scrutiny of the LVPD—Ryan might as well be in hiding with Tanner. But the defiance had added a new element to his pursuits. It had heightened the experience, and he wasn't about to shut it down because of one guy who thought he could ruin him.

He focused on that positive energy as he walked through Blake's front door without knocking. Tonight, Tanner would be the desperate one, looking for a way out of the mess he'd put himself in. If he'd simply handed the ledger over to Ryan a few weeks ago, as requested when Ryan learned Tanner had received it, they could have avoided all of this. He still didn't like that there was an element of chance, no matter how small, in this poker game. But Blake, an even better poker player than Tanner, had convinced Ryan he could manipulate their mark.

So far, Blake had been right. As someone who knew both Ryan and Tanner, he'd offered himself as an intermediary. Tanner's ego would be burning for a rematch after losing big-time to Blake two weeks ago. The opportunity to win his money back, as well as maybe keep the ledger, was supposed to be too great a lure for Tanner to resist.

And once Ryan had the ledger, Tanner would be fair game. He reached into his pocket and gripped the handle of his gun as reassurance the night would play out as planned. Before he entered Blake's game room, he let go of the gun and smoothed a hand over his clothing. Appearing in control was just as important as being in control.

What most people would have made into a library or den, Blake had converted into a recreational area of a different type. The green-felt poker table was the focal point. Blake loved cards, and some said he had a gambling problem—a problem the Club had been happy to help him out with by extending him credit at Legacy.

Take advantage of every weakness.

Blake looked up with a grin as Ryan entered. "I do believe it's time to up the ante," Blake said to the other two men at the table, who had alternating looks of anticipation and fear as Ryan took his place in the fourth chair. "How about it?"

"That's what we're here for," the younger man said, but he couldn't meet Ryan's eyes.

The rush of power that came from Ryan's position of authority made him grin, and they relaxed marginally. He gestured to them. "Please go ahead and finish your hand." Besides, it would give him the chance to observe their game play. Another Stone Rule: *Know your enemy.*

In the Club, each member had a code name to protect their anonymity when at gatherings such as this. The older man in the fedora, codename Slick, was holding his own, slightly ahead, judging by the number of chips on the table in front of him. He owed the Club for taking out a business partner of his who'd been embezzling money—and sleeping with Mrs. Slick on the side.

The younger guy, codename Bubba, couldn't be more than twenty-one. But physically, he was a beast and would make a good candidate when they needed muscle. Bubba had asked the Club to pull some strings to change his college grades so he could remain on the football team and so that he could graduate next year. Relatively small stuff, but Ryan would try to double the guy's debt. After tonight, Bubba would owe the Club something along the lines of murder.

At the conclusion of the hand, Blake sent an arched eyebrow toward Ryan.

"I'm waiting on one more, but we can settle the other accounts," Ryan said, pulling out the torn cards he'd brought with him. Slick's, and Bubba's. Their real names were on the torn cards as well as the dates they incurred their original debts. In keeping with Club procedure, they had retained the other halves of the IOUs. At least Ryan didn't need the ledger to conduct that part of Club business. "I assume you know that if you win, your debt to the Club is considered settled. However, if you lose, you double down."

Bubba's eyes sparkled with a mixture of hope and greed that made Ryan's stomach flutter. God, he loved this. He feasted off the power he held in his hands. It filled him up, made him whole like nothing else in his life had. With one call, he could ruin either of these men. Their crimes were laid out in the ledger with their signatures—

He glanced toward the door, but his true mark had yet to arrive. He needed that ledger.

With renewed vigor, Ryan tackled the card game, quickly dispensing of Slick and Bubba as planned. Slick left with the other half of his card, as Ryan intended. A man with his mentality would remain loyal to the Club and likely come back for another favor. He might even recruit new members for them in the business circles he ran in, and expand Ryan's empire.

Bubba, sadly, would remain in debt—doubly so. He now had a second debt card in his pocket—one with a higher denomination. Bubba left with his head hanging low, and a hole in the wall where he punched it after signing the latest torn card.

"I'll pay to have that fixed," Ryan told Blake. After all, the man had been a faithful servant of the Club, discreet and reliable. And Ryan could afford to be generous. He stood and stretched.

"You're not giving up, are you?" Blake said, glancing at his watch. It was nearly two in the morning.

"I never give up." His threats hadn't been enough, but if he could locate the hot blonde who had keys to Tanner's apartment, there was hope. "It doesn't appear our other guest will show tonight." The gleam in Blake's eyes indicated he believed otherwise. Before Ryan could question him, the doorbell rang.

Blake rubbed his hands together and grinned. "Looks like we're in for more excitement."

"Just be ready to act as intermediary. I need that ledger, or there's no more Redemption Club." Blake had promised he'd win the ledger back if Ryan was having any trouble holding his own in the game. Either way, he'd walk away with the damn ledger.

Ryan answered the door himself. Tanner, dressed in black slacks and a black dress shirt unbuttoned at the collar, a briefcase in his hand, stood in the doorway. Apparently, the man's survival instinct had finally kicked in. He would still kill him as payment for the years he'd taken off his life over the past two months, but he was feeling a bit more charitable now that the ledger was almost in his hands. He eyed the briefcase and smirked. "About time you showed. Thought you might back out of the poker game *you* set up."

Tanner's expression hardened. "I considered it, but you've left me with little choice, especially when you've stolen my life and then threatened my friends and family. That's a chicken·shit move, by the way."

Ryan shrugged. "You play the hand you're dealt, and since you disappeared and I couldn't be sure you'd show tonight, you didn't leave *me* much choice."

"Ransacking my place, looking for the ledger, was one thing. But when your guy on the police force pulls me over and threatens me, I figure it's time to lay low."

"You could have just handed him the ledger."

"And you'd have let me go?" Tanner laughed. "Right. The ledger is my only bargaining chip. At least, with this poker game, I have a chance to win— assuming you'll play fair. If you don't, I'll make sure the entire Club knows how you conduct business, and the danger you and Finn Tucker put them in by not securing this book." He lifted the briefcase.

Ryan struggled to hide his annoyance. "I think we can all leave happy tonight, if you play your cards right."

"You have the money?"

"It's inside." Satisfied things were finally turning out how he wanted, Ryan grinned to himself as he led Tanner to the game room.

"Blake." Tanner exchanged a handshake with the other man. "Good to see you again. Thank you for arranging this, and for your patience."

Blake chuckled. "You're the guest of honor. We've been waiting for you." He winked at Tanner, and Ryan felt his anger rise. Whose side was Blake on? Then again, Blake was the charming type. Perhaps he was lulling Tanner into a false sense of confidence before they took everything from him. He gestured to the briefcase. "I'll verify the goods."

Tanner set the case on the table and pulled out a crimson book. The edges of the pages were soft with age, the leather worn from twenty-plus years of handling. Ryan's father had started the Club decades ago—before he chickened out when the heat was on. Ryan had come across the item in his father's things years ago, on a break from college, and he and his best friend had picked up where Robert Stone and his cohorts had left off. Like a tradition passed from generation to generation, except that his father hadn't known what Ryan was doing behind his back.

Blake flipped through the book. With a nod to Ryan, he laid it in the center of the table. "I think we have something to bargain with."

Ryan's hand slipped into his pocket and stroked his gun. He could shoot Tanner right here, right now, and be done with it, but he'd wait and see how this played out. He could end up walking out with the ledger, the chips, and bragging rights that he'd beaten poker champion Tanner Wilde in a poker game. Besides, he should wait until he didn't have a witness. Or better yet, have a Club member perform the act as repayment of a debt. Perhaps he could even get Tanner to gamble more and owe the Club again. Apparently, Finn had decided to grant Tanner the other half of his playing card, signifying he'd repaid his debt, when he'd given him the ledger—all for Tanner helping Finn stab Ryan in the back from the grave.

Tanner cocked a brow at Ryan. "And you brought what I want?"

Ryan laid a briefcase full of Legacy poker chips, as well the torn card Tanner had requested, the one with his father's name on it and a date from several years ago, on the table. "Another debt paid off—though I'm not sure why you'd bother. Your father's dead."

Tanner's mouth tightened as if he'd tasted something bitter. "Consider it tying up loose ends."

"And a million dollars in Legacy poker chips to be cashed at the casino." If Tanner somehow won and disappeared again, at least Ryan would find him when he cashed in the chips. "Quite a haul."

"A pittance in comparison to what possession of the book is worth," Tanner reminded him, tapping the ledger. "Or maybe you'll win the entire pot." His smirk indicated he believed that possibility was a long shot.

"Maybe I will. Especially, since I'm going to let my pinch hitter play in my stead." Ryan gestured to Blake.

Tanner froze. "That wasn't the deal."

"I believe you said we'd play one hand to determine the winner of the pot. You didn't say who had to play the hand."

"That's unacceptable."

"Actually," Blake interrupted, sending Ryan a significant glance. "It's a moot point. I want in. On my own."

"You want to play for yourself?" Ryan laughed in astonishment even as he felt the blood heat his cheeks. Blake would dare to go against him? "This is a joke, right? With what buy-in? What could possibly be of similar value as a million dollars in chips or control of the Redemption Club?"

Blake retrieved a folder from a drawer in a table along the wall and slapped it down on top of the ledger. "Evidence you blackmailed your father for most of this past year."

Ryan's chest ached from holding back his rage. He glared at Blake. "Why would you do this? You had everything you could want." He'd practically been his right-hand man since Finn's death. Again, Blake shot a knowing look to Tanner. *Traitors.* "You're working together? I thought you were enemies."

"We may have led you to believe that to serve a greater purpose." Blake shrugged. "He who has that book has the ultimate power, right?"

"Over the dark side of Vegas, at least." Tanner's dark eyes sparked with determination.

How long had he been plotting to overthrow Ryan? Perhaps he and Finn had been working together for months, before Finn's death.

Blake chuckled. "And he who has this folder has control over Ryan Stone, one of the richest men in the country. At least he would be if his daddy decided to let him touch his share of the money."

"You're going to regret this," Ryan promised them both.

Blake's grin only widened. "Figured this pot was too sweet to pass up. Tanner presented me with a great deal a few weeks ago."

"You gave me no choice," Tanner said, obviously choosing the same words they'd exchanged when he'd arrived. "You made it clear in your threats and your actions that I shouldn't go to the police, couldn't trust anyone on the LVPD or anywhere in Vegas, so I found other ways to ensure my safety."

"He'd heard from Tristan Floyd that you'd been blackmailing your dad and figured that I had the means to get the proof," Blake added. "He set about to lose to me in that poker game a couple weeks back. We figured you'd agree to this poker game if we set it up right. Oh, and he's been staying in my guest house ever since your people came after him." The final nail in Blake's coffin, but he didn't know it yet. Ryan would make him pay. "Are you ready to play the hand? Or maybe you should just forfeit now."

Ryan glared at them as a cold calm slid over the hot rage roiling inside. They'd changed the plan on him, but his father would say: *Only the adaptable survive.* There was only one way he could be certain Blake and Tanner would remain quiet and keep his secrets.

One of Ryan's favorite Stone Rules. *Eliminate enemies using force and finality.*

CHAPTER FOUR

Emily let herself into her apartment and gave Adam a thumbs-up from the window to indicate she was safe inside. His car pulled away as she let the curtain fall back into place. It was nearly five in the morning, but attempts at sleep would be futile. The sun was already poking up from the horizon and she was amped up after spending hours by Adam's side, searching Fremont Street for Tanner—to no avail.

So, despite emotional and physical exhaustion, she went straight to the bathroom and filled the tub, pouring in several capfuls of bubble bath. Maybe she could finally quiet her brain, soak her tired feet and catch a few quick hours of sleep before she had to return to work. If she had Angela open the lounge for her and cover the lunch hour, she wouldn't have to go in until midafternoon.

She stripped out of her clothes and sank into the hot water with a blissful moan.

She cracked open one eye as she heard a meow, and connected with Calliope's green gaze. "What do you want?"

The cat perched on the side of the tub, eyeing the bubbles as if they were her archnemesis.

"I fed you earlier."

"Then she'll soon be a fat kitty because I fed her, too," a male voice said from the doorway.

Emily lurched up in surprise, but sank back down into the bubbles as she realized the motion would expose her very naked, very wet flesh. "What the hell,

Tanner? Were you lurking in my closet or something?"

Dressed in blue jeans and a plain white T-shirt, he leaned against the doorjamb. His dark hair was on the long side of short. His jaw sported a couple days' worth of beard growth, and his familiar, teasing grin didn't quite reach his eyes. "Something like that. I was waiting for you and fell asleep on your bed. I didn't peek, if that's what you're worried about." His eyes flicked to the bubbles and right back to her face, like a gentleman. A gentleman who'd let himself into her apartment, and her bed, and now her bath.

Outrage made her cheeks flame, but they were quickly doused by relief. Her friend was whole, and apparently healthy. "Why didn't you just call me back? Jesus." She'd left him a couple messages—one after realizing she'd missed his earlier voicemail, and another after she and Adam hadn't located him at Pete's.

"I find it more rewarding to do the unexpected."

"Or you're afraid someone is listening in on your calls."

He shrugged, looking like the teenage Tanner she'd followed into trouble without a second thought. "Or that," he said lightly. But his brown eyes conveyed a different message.

Exhaustion. Fear. And, she worried, guilt.

"Figured you'd rather see for yourself that I'm good." He gestured the length of his body. "See? *Good.* Now you can stop calling."

"You're the one who called me to meet, sounding like doom and gloom, remember?" Irritation nearly had her climbing from the tub to throttle him, but modesty kept her in place. "Go wait in the living room while I get dressed and we'll talk. Have you eaten?" His cheeks had taken on a pale and slightly sallow look, now that she looked past the whiskers. "I can make you a sandwich."

He shoved a hand through his hair. "Em, stop trying to take care of me. I'm a big boy. And I'm not staying. I wasn't even supposed to come here. There are people after me, and I don't know who I can trust." He looked toward the living room as if he might have been followed. "Except for you. But when you didn't show up earlier…"

"I just came back from Fremont Street. I'm sorry I missed you. Just let me—" When she moved to get out of the tub, he held out his hands.

"Really. If you get out, I'll take off."

She sank down again, sending him her fiercest scowl. "The vanishing act is getting old."

"I thought I had it all under control, but everything went wrong. I really fucked up this time." Every muscle was tensed for a fight, and it reminded her of Adam's grave words.

It's a matter of life or death.

"You know Adam's been looking for you, too," she said.

His gaze whipped back to her. "He talked to you?"

"He stopped by Legacy to see me today. Guess he ran out of other options, since you're apparently ignoring him—and me."

"I got all of your messages. Saw his car at my place, too. He's been making himself at home."

"But you didn't talk to him? Didn't bother to call either of us back?"

His eyes twinkled with a hint of the old mischievous Tanner. "I'd much rather disturb you during bath time." He sat on the edge of the tub and drew a finger through the bubbles nearest him, by her knee. Leave it to Tanner to use flirting as a defense. Her mind drifted to the memory of Adam trying to flirt with her at Legacy Lounge to soften her up. He'd obviously been less experienced in the tactic than Tanner, but Adam was by far the more successful when it came to Emily—probably because he'd long ago worked his way into the deepest part of her heart and made himself at home.

She pulled a washcloth from the side of the tub to

cover her chest, not that Tanner could see anything. But if the bubbles started to disappear...

"How is he?" His question surprised her, as did the knot of emotion she heard in his throat. He'd always looked up to his older brother as an invincible god, but he didn't talk about him much since Adam had taken off for Phoenix. She realized now that she hadn't been the only one to feel abandoned by Adam's departure.

"He looks good," she admitted. "Same stubborn streak, though."

Tanner grunted. "That's unavoidable. It's in the Wilde DNA."

"Yeah, I can see that. Did you know he's a detective?"

"I heard something to that effect." And he hadn't shared that information with her? He'd probably thought he was protecting her.

"Which brings me to my next question."

Wariness flashed in his eyes. "What might that be?"

"What the hell does Adam want with you? Why does he have a torn Redemption Club card that he claims belongs to you?"

"He... what?" He stood and shoved his hand through his hair. "Both of you need to stay out of it."

"*You* got us into it, whatever *it* is. Might as well let me help. Break the Wilde stubborn streak and let me in. What the hell is going on?"

"I need to go away for a while. I've already stayed too long. I just wanted to tell you not to worry."

"Too late."

He ignored her reply. "And, I wanted to warn you to be careful."

"Me?"

"Someone who's not so nice may have mentioned something about going after my hot, blonde friend." Who he clearly believed was her.

"Why would this no-name person do that?"

He held up a hand and she was surprised to see it

was trembling. "It doesn't matter. I'll take care of everything. I just need time."

"Is this related to the Club?"

"The less you know, the better. If something happens to me—"

She straightened, clutching the washcloth to her chest. "Tanner, so help me God, you'd better—"

"I've got evidence that you can bargain with to keep you safe, if necessary. It's hidden away."

"Where? What?"

"An SD card."

A memory card, like from a camera? What had he been taking pictures of? "If this card is so important, why not make a copy of it or put it somewhere safe?"

"I did, and it is. You'll find it in a few days, when I'm ready. I need to take care of some things first, and if all goes well, you won't even need the evidence."

"Bullshit. Cut the cloak-and-dagger stuff."

"We all have secrets." He bent to pet her cat. "Even Calliope."

"This is *me*." Panic was clawing at her ribcage with razor-sharp nails. He was talking as if he was still in danger. As if *she* might be in danger.

"If you knew what was on the card, if anybody even knew it existed, we'd be dead. Besides, I don't know who I can trust. Let it go for now. It'll all be clear in a few days, I promise."

Only because his expression was tortured did she relent. "I'll do what has to be done to help you. You know that. But damn it, talk to me before you leave. At least give me an idea what this is about." When he gritted his jaw in reluctance, she softened her voice. "We'll get you a lawyer, if you need one. Or a counselor."

"I can't trust anyone."

"Adam, then. Surely, you can believe your brother has your back. He always has, when you really, truly needed him. We'll get you whatever you need to face whatever's going on. Please don't disappear again." She heard the desperation in her plea and pressed her lips together to stop the flow of words.

Not since she'd been eleven, and her parents had been about to leave for another long cruise to work some con, leaving her alone to care for herself, had she begged anyone to stay.

And not since she'd turned eighteen and had implored Adam to take her away with him had she begged anyone to leave.

Asking for what she wanted hadn't worked in the past, and she was damn sure it wouldn't work now.

Tanner smiled softly. "You always were a sucker for defending the underdog."

She scoffed. "You're no underdog."

That brought a flicker of his normal good humor to his eyes, but it was quickly extinguished. "Watch yourself with Adam, okay, Em? Let him help you, but don't let him all the way in." He knew what she'd gone through before. The hurt and rejection. What she'd become, and how her life had been ripped apart by external forces while her defenses had been low.

After the turmoil of the past twelve hours, her emotions were still percolating too close to the surface, threatening to break through the tough skin she'd carefully cultivated over the years, so she lashed out with sass. "Fuck that. You'd better watch *your*self. Because if you leave me right now without any other explanation, I'm going to hunt you down and kick your ass, Tanner Wilde."

Tanner shook his head. "You can't help me. Not with this. There might be some things that come out over the next few days. I need you to believe in me. I need to know someone out there does. I'm going to be laying low, but I need you to remember the man I am, and not who the cops or media will say I am."

Cops? Media? Her heart pounded.

"Don't trust anyone," he added.

"You know I won't let anyone use me."

He laughed softly. "I know. You're a tough cookie,

but these guys would gobble you up. Watch for that SD card. Consider it insurance." His gaze was intent again. "Promise me."

"Tanner, of course I'll believe in you. You've always been like a brother to me." She was ashamed when her voice broke. Why couldn't the people in her life trust her to help them? When had she ever disappointed them? Despite how hard she tried, somehow she was never enough.

He strode forward and bent down to press his lips to her forehead. "I care about you, too. You're like family, Em." He swept a fingertip through the bubbles on her arm, just below her phoenix tattoo. "Bubbles look good on you."

He straightened and turned to walk out. That was when she caught sight of the dried blood. Dark and crusty, it was a splotch just below his ear, toward the back of his neck. His own, or someone else's?

He was out of the room before she could process the sight and find her voice. "Tanner!"

The sound of the front door closing was all she heard. Another man had walked out of her life. Another *Wilde* man, at that.

Emily never did get to sleep, and when she walked into Legacy Lounge at the tail end of lunch hour, she was running on caffeine fumes and a Peanut M&M's-induced sugar high. At least they contained a modicum of protein.

Despite what she'd promised Tanner about being patient until he was ready to reveal whatever evidence he possessed, she'd searched her apartment but hadn't found a memory card. Then again, Tanner had told her she wouldn't receive it for a few days. Maybe he was having it delivered. She'd like it on a silver platter, alongside his head. She was still steaming that he'd run out on her. When everyone else in their lives lied or betrayed them, they'd vowed to be there for each other.

Always.

And he'd left.

Damn the Wilde men, anyway.

She tied the black apron that was her Legacy Lounge uniform around her waist. Sundays typically generated lighter traffic, but the bar was surprisingly packed and there was a nearly electric buzz in the air that made the hair on her arms stand on end. She could read people and situations, a valuable skill in a con artist, and this crowd was expectant, waiting for something big to happen.

"What's going on?" she asked Angela, who was behind the bar, mixing a pitcher of margaritas.

Angela shot her a harried glance. "Thank goodness you're here. I could use a break."

"Bigger crowd than usual. Is there some event today that I forgot about?" Emily surveyed the customers as she gathered empty plates and glasses from the bar and put them in the bin to be washed.

"No special event. Must be the murder."

Emily nearly dropped a glass as she whirled to face Angela. "Murder?"

"You didn't hear?" Angela moved closer and dropped her voice. "Blake Toll was found dead in his home."

"*The* Blake Toll? The flashy poker champion?" The guy was infamous for playing the worldwide poker circuit, always wearing the bling he'd accumulated in the form of rings, bracelets, and necklaces, from his various tournament wins. He was also known for throwing his money all over Vegas, especially in Legacy, since he was a friend of Ryan Stone. In fact, Tanner had come up against Blake a couple weeks ago in a local tournament right here in the Legacy private game rooms. Tanner had been excited, telling Emily the guy's card-playing skills were legendary, and enjoying the challenge of studying the man's tells and playing style. Afterward, he'd become sullen when he lost a small fortune to Blake and then complained to everyone within earshot that the whole thing was rigged.

Her heart skidded to a halt as she recalled the splotch of blood she'd seen on Tanner's neck. Her skin went hot and itchy.

"They say it was pretty gruesome," Angela continued, unaware of Emily's inner freak-out. "Blood everywhere."

"But why would his murder increase traffic *here*?" Emily asked.

"Apparently, his body was covered in over a hundred thousand dollars' worth of Legacy poker chips. *Bloody* chips. What kind of sick message do you think the murderer was trying to send?"

"I don't know." She was afraid she didn't know anything for certain anymore.

For the next hour, Emily went about her work, but her mind was filled with Tanner and his early morning visit. He'd indicated the cops and media might slander him. Is this why he'd seemed so nervous to the staff at Pete's? Had he been about to commit murder? And if she'd received Tanner's message earlier, would she have been able to prevent the despicable act? But he'd implied he was innocent of any wrongdoing, had told her not to believe what she'd hear in the coming days.

Between serving customers, Emily searched her phone for news on the murder, but there was precious little information, other than that the great Blake Toll appeared to have been murdered following a card game in his home. Police were currently searching out the other players who'd been there. She worried Tanner was one of the people they were looking for.

She considered calling Adam, who had to have heard the news by now, as well. Each time, she stopped herself when she recalled Tanner's warning. People could be watching her, hoping to get to him. The last thing she needed to do was drag Adam into this mess, too.

"That new band you booked is packing them in,"

Ivy Stone said, derailing Emily's train of thought. Her business suit was crisp, yet the skirt showed off her long legs. The royal blue of her attire reflected Legacy's color scheme, but contrasted with her green eyes and glossy ebony hair to perfection. Always so well put together, Ivy could have been a porcelain doll.

"Thanks," Emily said. "It's bringing in local clientele, too." She scanned her boss's face for signs of strain and saw that makeup hid dark circles under her eyes. "Late night?"

Ivy looked at her sharply, but then sighed. "Guess you've heard the news."

"About the murder? Apparently, word is getting around." They both eyed the crowd.

Ivy released a disgusted laugh. "Nothing like bad press to bring the thirsty—the bloodthirsty—out in droves."

"Or, like you said, it could be the band." They shared a wry smile.

"Could be," Ivy murmured. "But the police were asking for every possible way Blake Toll could be connected to Legacy. He participates in tournaments here regularly. You may even have met him, having tended bar at a few of them."

"I've heard of him and did see him at a game a couple weeks ago." At the same tournament Tanner had played in. It was only a matter of time before police connected Tanner to Blake. "Is there a suspect in custody?"

"Not yet."

Emily released a relieved breath and forced her lungs to draw in more oxygen. "Any leads?"

"Not that I've heard, but the LVPD hasn't actually been friendly toward my family, or the casino, since the incident in Arizona two months ago." She was referring to the discovery of several murders that had shed light on the existence of the Redemption Club. The torn playing cards found among those involved had the Legacy logo on the back.

"I thought all of the suspicion died down when the investigation didn't turn up any concrete connection to Legacy." The cards could have been used by anyone, after all. The decks with the logos were sold in the hotel gift shop.

"Doesn't mean they aren't still looking for a way to bring us down. Answering police questions took up most of my morning. Press releases and damage control took up the rest. We're experiencing a surge in business that should be a wonderful thing, but it's perpetuating a negative image. Word got around about Blake's body being covered in our casino chips, and now they've become a keepsake item." Ivy glanced at the bottles behind the bar.

"Sounds like you could use a drink," Emily guessed.

She shook her head. "Later. I'm just doing my daily rounds. You really have done a great job here. Keep up the good work. And if anyone starts asking questions, direct them to me."

CHAPTER FIVE

"The LVPD found a body," Special Agent Remington said when Adam answered his call. "A man named Blake Toll, who has connections to the Redemption Club as well as to your brother." As he explained how Toll's murder was sending ripples throughout the poker community, the news was sending tsunamis through Adam. His brother's alleged involvement with an illegal crime group was now connecting him to murder.

"Blake was seen with Tanner just a couple weeks ago at a poker game at Legacy," Remington continued. "Tanner lost a large sum of money to him and then sulked in the bar, proclaiming to anyone who'd listen that he'd been cheated. Those are fighting words in the poker community. You still haven't seen or heard from Tanner?"

"No." Adam had to squeeze the word past a tight throat. His brother was out there somewhere, scared and on the run, wanted by the law—or worse, a murderer. And for some reason—probably stubborn pride—Tanner didn't think he could come to Adam for help. "If you want me to help find him, I need all the information I can get."

"Would a look at the crime scene help?"

"You can arrange that?"

"I can."

"Give me an address and I'll be there."

A short drive later, Adam was admitted into the gated community where Blake Toll had lived. The

LVPD officer manning the gate gave him directions to Toll's home, where Remington greeted him at the door and led him down a marbled foyer. If the furnishings and artwork were the real deal they appeared to be, Blake Toll was a highly successful poker player.

"The LVPD has been working with the FBI, since Redemption Club has a foothold in all sorts of criminal endeavors in Vegas," Remington explained. "My specialty is audits, and the money laundering in the Club is what first brought me on board. Poker tournaments, such as the ones Blake Toll played in, are a great way to shift money around without arousing suspicion."

"So you've been watching Blake Toll as well as Tanner."

"Yes." Remington grinned. "I watch everyone I can, including Blake's widow. She's been known to frequently travel abroad, purchasing expensive art and jewelry."

"And spreading the money around."

"Investments, she says. I was interviewing her just now. I'd love to hear your impressions." Remington led Adam into a drawing room furnished in a mash-up of modern and gilded antique pieces that turned Adam's stomach. Still, everything looked expensive and luxurious.

"I'm sorry for your loss, Mrs. Toll," Adam told the woman as he took a chair opposite where she sat on the couch. "I'm Detective Adam Wilde."

"Thank you." She aimed a brief smile his way, then dabbed at her eyes with a tissue. "Please, call me Selina." She was young, probably just a shade older than a college graduate. She had the appearance of a trophy wife, from the toned body revealed in tight-fitting spandex to the gemstones and diamonds adorning her neck and fingers.

"We were talking about Blake's friends," Remington prompted her with a warm smile. "The ones who attended Blake's monthly poker games. Do you remember any of their names, or could you describe them for us?"

Adam had finally obtained his brother's cell phone records that morning and discovered several calls from the Blake Toll residence over the past two weeks. Likely, Remington already had that information, and was looking for more confirmation that Tanner was a friend of Blake's.

Selina shook her head, her blonde curls dusting her shoulders. "Blake usually treats me to a girls' weekend once a month, on his poker nights. I don't know who attends. Besides, he sent me on an extended trip this past week. I just got back this morning." Her gaze shifted to the door, and Adam guessed she was thinking about what she'd discovered when she'd returned home.

"Did you ever see Blake with this man?" Remington brought up a photo on his phone. It was one of Tanner's social media pages, with his professional poker player profile. The woman's gaze shot to Adam, clearly noting the resemblance.

"I've seen him," she admitted. "He was here last week, just before I left on my trip. They were arguing."

Adam's gut clenched, but he didn't dare interrupt.

"About?" Remington prompted.

"Blake was excited about the game, and the other guy was a downer. Blake couldn't stop talking about how he'd have the whole world in the palm of his hand."

"But Tanner didn't agree?" Adam asked.

"I got the impression he wasn't happy about whatever they had planned. He said something about going to the police instead. Blake told him the police couldn't be trusted. I remember being curious, but that's all I heard, and Blake doesn't like it when I ask questions, so I shrugged it off."

"Was there anything else?" Remington asked.

"Something about a ledger being the key to his future," she told them both.

Remington's gaze met Adam's before turning back to Blake's widow. "Did you see this ledger?"

Selina shook her head. "No."

"And nothing seems to be missing? You checked his safe?"

"It's completely empty. I don't know if anything was in there before his... murder." She let out a shuddering breath.

After a few more quick questions, Remington thanked Selina and gestured to Adam to follow him outside the room. "This doesn't appear to be a case of the wife lashing out or a robbery. My money's on one of the guy's poker friends."

"I'd like to see the crime scene," Adam said. Remington nodded and led the way. He dismissed the crime scene team, asking them to wait outside for a moment.

In the den, the copper-penny smell of blood, mixed with the acrid odor of spent ammunition, stung Adam's nostrils. His gaze landed on the bloodstained area of carpet next to an overturned chair. Blake Toll's body had already been taken to the coroner's office.

"Preliminary estimates put the time of death around three in the morning," Remington said.

Adam had been with Emily at Pete's Paradise. The waitress and bartender said Tanner had left the bar around one, and that he'd seemed nervous before he received a phone call and left. The phone records Adam looked at a few hours ago showed that the call had come from Blake's residence. The FBI and police would surely be requesting Blake's phone records, if they hadn't already. Adam sure hoped his brother had an alibi, because the case against him was looking grimmer by the minute.

Remington gestured to the wide area of bloodstained carpet. "The victim was shot three times. Spatter analysis and angles of entry seem to indicate the initial wound was inflicted while the victim was seated, and the other two came after he was on the ground, where the body was found. The blood pooled around him."

"Weapon?"

"None was found, but bullets were .45 caliber. And surfaces had been wiped, so no usable fingerprints."

Adam walked around the card table, surveying what was left of the scene. There were no bloody footprints either. If the murderer had acted out of rage, he'd been lucid enough to know how to avoid leaving evidence, which suggested a professional, or at least someone familiar with murder. A deck of cards and poker chips were scattered across the table, as well as on the floor, with blood on those closest to where the victim had died. "So this looks like a dispute over cards." Or was it staged? Things weren't always what they appeared. "Is there surveillance video?"

"Only at the community gate. I've got people analyzing it now."

"Suspects—besides Tanner?"

"The video surveillance is being examined for who came and went, but the prevalence of Legacy chips had police talking to the Stone family already. Ryan Stone has been known to associate with Blake, including staking him in a couple big poker tournaments."

"Maybe he was here last night," Adam suggested, hoping there was a strong lead besides Tanner.

"If so, the LVPD and FBI are going to be taking things slow and methodical. We don't want him to fall through the cracks. Besides, anybody could have used Legacy chips, but why would they?" He gestured to the floor where a few chips lay. The sight of the logo reminded him of Emily and the coasters at the bar. Had she heard about the murder, and Tanner's possible tie to it? As a Legacy employee, she probably had, but she certainly hadn't called Adam about it. Her stubborn silence grated on him.

"There were even more found on the body. Most of the chips were worth one thousand dollars each. The rest were in a briefcase, left open on the table. They were already collected as evidence. All told, about a million dollars' worth."

"The value of the chips alone indicates whoever committed the murder didn't do it for the money," Adam pointed out. "If it had been a crime of greed, the murderer would have taken the chips. As you said, anger was the more likely motive."

Remington slid him a sideways glance. "I have to point out that your brother was reportedly angry with Toll. Lost a lot of money to him a couple weeks back."

"If it were Tanner, and he'd lost so much money, then why leave the chips? It's just as likely one of the other players here last night was equally angry, or more so." Adam couldn't remember Tanner losing his temper so easily—especially during a game, and especially to the point he would kill someone. "Blake was notorious for flaunting his wins, and his skills, as well as running his mouth as part of the head games he played against his opponents."

"And we'll question all of the people who were here last night, once they're identified. But it would help if I could bring Tanner in, keep him safe while we seek the truth."

"I'm doing my best to find him." But he'd be damned if he'd turn his brother over to the FBI, the LVPD, or anyone else until he knew who to trust.

Remington studied him a moment, as if sensing his reluctance. "I hope you're willing to work with me, because the LVPD is determined to pin this on your brother. They've been looking for a scapegoat ever since Ryan Stone's lawyers made them look bad for accusing him without enough evidence."

Adam felt tingles of apprehension. "I get the feeling you might be worried someone on our side of the law is impeding the investigation, or at least blind to the alternatives."

"Your gut isn't necessarily wrong." Secrets danced in Remington's eyes. "It's almost as if the direction of the investigation is being steered away from Ryan

Stone and toward your brother."

"A mole within the LVPD?"

"That's one reason the police are cooperating with the FBI. Anything's possible when the Redemption Club, or the Stone family, is involved." Remington gave him a sympathetic look. "If you find your brother, get him to come forward and tell his side. If he has the ledger, I'd hate for the Club to find him first. They have a different way of dealing with traitors, and if Tanner's gambling with the ledger, he'd most definitely be considered a traitor."

Only problem was, his brother wasn't answering Adam's calls. If he were Tanner, possibly scared and on the run, where would he go? The answer came to mind immediately. He'd run to the one person who'd always been there for him, the one who'd been blind to his misdeeds since childhood. *Emily.*

Late in the afternoon, Ryan was still enjoying the most amazing sleep, courtesy of an oxycodone and several glasses of champagne, when a light shove against his chest had him opening his eyes.

"There's someone at the door," Brenda muttered, her blonde hair disheveled as she leaned over him.

She'd been just what he'd needed to celebrate taking down a double threat. Blake Toll had proven himself a traitor, and had been dealt with appropriately. Tanner would take the fall for Blake's murder. Tanner would be killed—his death made to look like a suicide—before the truth came out. And Ryan would be free to live and run Redemption Club as he saw fit. Life was good.

Ryan had thought that if anyone was going to be murdered last night, it would have been Tanner Wilde. But things had worked out. Ryan had been adaptable, and now he had everything—including the ledger, which was safely stashed in his suite's safe, and the folder that showed Ryan's Swiss bank account had received deposits in the exact amounts his father had paid in blackmail over the past year. Now, nobody held anything over Ryan, and the Club was completely his. He intended to keep it that way.

The knocking on the door of his penthouse suite grew louder. He'd know that crisp, impatient knock anywhere. He sighed.

"Stay here," he told Brenda, brushing his fingers across her bare nipple and giving it a light pinch. He swung his feet out of bed and pulled on his jeans, leaving them unbuttoned as he moved to peek through the peephole. Long dark hair, vivid green eyes, and a face that was classically beautiful despite the scowl that marred it filled his field of vision.

He swung the door open. "Dear sister, to what do I owe the pleasure?"

Ivy pushed past him on three-inch heels and stood in his living room, her scowl deepening as she took in the three empty champagne bottles and two glasses, one with bright red lipstick, then his unbuttoned jeans and bare chest. "Sorry to interrupt, but Dad and I have been dealing with some serious shit all day. I wouldn't have woken you at—" She glanced down her nose at her wristwatch. "—five o'clock in the evening if it weren't important. I'm surprised the police haven't been knocking down your door yet. Or Dad, for that matter."

The police, he'd expected. But at the mention of his father, it was his turn to scowl. "When did Dad get back?" He'd hoped to have a couple more days to celebrate before dealing with him again.

"Just a few hours ago. He cut his trip short and flew back to help deal with this. There was a murder linked to the hotel last night, and somehow the police think you knew the victim, were maybe even with him last night. They want to talk to you."

He pretended concern. "Murder? Who?"

"Blake Toll. Please tell me you know nothing about this."

He scrubbed a hand across his jaw, adopting a look of shock. "I was with Blake last night, but I wasn't the only one."

"And when you left his house, he was still alive?" Her eyes narrowed, daring him to admit to wrongdoing. She'd fucking love that, for him to get reamed and shut away in prison for years. She'd always enjoyed being the perfect one in their father's eyes.

"Of course," he lied. "He was there with one other guy, and they were still playing poker when I called it a night. There was some tension between them, but... murder?"

"Did you use Legacy chips?"

"What? No."

"Legacy chips were found all over the murder scene. Nearly a million dollars' worth. It was as if someone wanted to point the police in our direction."

Shit. He'd expected some heat, which he'd made plans to redirect—right onto Tanner Wilde—but Tanner must not have taken the chips after Ryan had left the scene. That was a surprise.

"Anybody you know who can validate what time you left?"

As if on cue, Brenda walked out of the bedroom wearing nothing but a short silk robe and a smile. She padded over on bare feet and tucked herself against his side.

"I suppose you have your answer to that." Ryan placed a kiss on Brenda's upturned lips. "I had more pressing matters to attend to. I returned home around two·thirty. We were up all night celebrating, so we slept in today."

"Celebrating what?"

Well, she had him there. "Life." And his renewed lease on it.

Ivy muttered something under her breath and turned on her heel. Her hand on the doorknob, she whipped back to face him. "I suggest you answer the LVPD's questions as soon as possible so we can clear this up. The longer this story stays hot with the media, the more damage it could do to the hotel."

The fucking hotel. Everything was about Legacy, and protecting their father and all of his holdings, so that one day, they might inherit a piece of Robert Stone's *legacy*. And the asshole was barely closing in on sixty, so that inheritance could be forty years from now. Their father would probably outlive them just for kicks. Or donate every penny to some obscure cause. He had a twisted way of using people, including his own progeny, for his own amusement and to his own ends.

Another Stone Rule: *People are a resource to be exploited.*

And yet Ivy continued to do his bidding. Pathetic. Neither of them would ever measure up to their father's insane standards. Years ago, Ryan had decided it was time to make his own mark on the world. When he'd discovered his father's ledger and the barter system he'd come up with, his destiny had become clear. He'd pick up the reins and succeed at the only endeavor where Robert Stone had failed.

"I'll set up an interview with the LVPD right now," he said to appease Ivy. "I'm sure this is a onetime thing. Besides, once I tell the police the name of the guy who last saw Blake alive, the heat will be off of us."

"Who?"

"Tanner Wilde. That's who they'll want to talk to." But Ryan would have him killed before he could reveal anything important about the true events of last night. In fact, the guy might already be dead. Ryan couldn't kill him last night. Two dead bodies would definitely throw suspicion Ryan's direction, especially if Slick or Bubba were questioned and decided to mention that when they'd left, Ryan had been alone with Blake.

But if it was made to appear as if Tanner killed himself from the guilt overload, or was shot in retaliation by one of Blake's friends... Well, there'd be nobody left to tell the truth. Tanner would take the fall, and he wouldn't be alive to dispute it. Blake and his blackmail threat were squashed. Ryan would be free and clear to resume his Redemption Club activities, with the ledger in his possession.

He looked toward his phone as he realized he hadn't heard from Bubba. The man was supposed to have tailed Tanner from Blake's house and staged Tanner's suicide. Ryan needed confirmation of Tanner's death like he needed his next breath. If Tanner was still alive, it could ruin everything.

CHAPTER SIX

The FBI's Vegas office was quiet on a Sunday evening, but there were a few agents hard at work. Within Remington's cubicle, Adam leaned closer to the computer screen to view the footage the FBI had obtained.

"The camera at the main gate captured four cars that entered Blake's gate code that night," Remington said over his shoulder. "We're tracing the vehicle registrations now, but one of them was obviously Ryan's yellow sports car. The police and our agents are trying to track him down now to interview him."

His heart sank as, when the time stamp recorded one forty-eight in the morning, Tanner's car drove up. "That's my brother."

Remington's expression was grave. "I know you're confident he's innocent, but the evidence does seem to be mounting against him."

"I've been retracing his steps over the past couple days—as much as I can from what I've found of his credit card history prior to his disappearance—and there's been no sign of him. He's been acting more like the hunted than the hunter." Tanner was a resourceful individual and knew how to make ends meet in all manner of ways. For all Adam knew, his brother could be deep in a con, posing as a house sitter or squatting in an unrented apartment. Both were things he'd done in the past to survive under the radar. However, there was one curious purchase on a recent credit card statement. A small microphone and camera, the kind that could be easily hidden away, had been purchased a couple weeks ago. It gave Adam hope that maybe Tanner had a plan.

"What about Emily Moore?"

Remington's question jerked Adam out of his mental distraction. "What?"

"I know she's a friend of your family's."

"How?" A surge of protectiveness made the word shoot out like a bullet. Remington simply slid him a knowing look. "She's been on your radar, too?"

"For months," Remington admitted. "After all, she and your brother have a long history together."

Damn it, Tanner. He'd dragged her into this mess. "She's not hiding him."

"You're certain? It wouldn't be the least of the offenses she's committed on his behalf."

Adam was as certain as he could be about anything when it came to Emily. "I'm keeping my eye on her, too."

"Her name's in the visitor log for Tristan Floyd. She saw him once, not long after he was arrested two months ago. Why would she have reason to visit a murderer?"

Adam hid his shock. The woman was definitely full of secrets. And Adam was tired of waiting for her to reveal them.

Sunday had flown by as the crowd enjoyed the local band and Emily kept the customers satisfied. Cleanup began around midnight, after the band packed up and only a few stragglers remained. Unfortunately, the return of a normal late-night pace freed Emily's mind to return to thoughts of Blake's murder, Tanner, and how she hadn't yet called Adam to tell him she'd seen his brother just hours after Blake was killed. Surely, he'd heard about the murder by now. Could he defend Tanner if the police started looking his way?

After checking that the remaining customers had

what they needed, she ducked into the storeroom. The twelve-by-six, windowless room was lined with shelves of extra glassware, bottles of alcohol, boxes of coasters and cocktail napkins, and other supplies that filled the space from the door to the desk area that served as her tiny office. Opposite the desk, there was a small cot where she sometimes grabbed a quick nap.

She made the call she'd been attempting to make all evening, reaching Tanner's voicemail yet again. "Call me ASAP. I mean it, Tanner. I'm worried about you, and I'm not sure I can keep my promises."

"Promises?" Adam's wide shoulders filled the doorway. Though there were several feet between them, his dark eyes caged her in. Under the guise of straightening some papers on her desk, she turned away to hide the sudden flare of guilt that she was sure had reddened her face, and to recover from the usual stutter of her heart whenever she saw him.

After a deep breath, she turned back to him with a frown. "Eavesdrop much?"

"You pick up some of the best information that way." He was carefully analyzing her expression, which she struggled to keep neutral when the sight of him sent emotions careening throughout her body. He stepped a little closer. "You heard from Tanner?"

How much to reveal? She thought of the mysterious, possibly nonexistent memory card, and her promise to Tanner. And her promise to herself, to keep her distance from whatever Tanner was involved in, as well as from Adam, out of a need for self-preservation. But Tanner was in danger, and by his own admission, she could be, too. Without sleep, she was tired of fighting and her defenses were down.

She sighed. *Forgive me, Tanner.* "Yes, I heard from him. And I think you're right about him being in trouble. But you're wrong if you think he murdered Blake Toll."

His jaw hardened. "I don't think he did."

"So you believe he's innocent?"

"I make decisions based on fact, not emotion." The look he sent her said he believed she, on the other hand, let sentiment guide her. That he was right didn't keep her hackles from rising. He stepped further into the small room, suddenly engulfing her whole world. "I'm not the bad guy here. I want to help. Where is he?"

"I don't know. But he says he's okay." He'd looked okay, but Emily didn't want to share that his brother had been in her bathroom last night. Let him believe that Tanner had simply called to check in.

"When was this?"

"Right after you followed me home."

Adam scowled. "Nearly twenty-four hours ago and I'm just now hearing about it?"

"He said he was okay," she repeated. "He doesn't need our help."

"But you don't believe him, or you would never have shared this much with me." The tinge of sadness and regret in his eyes indicated he wished things were different, that she felt comfortable opening up to him. Why would he care?

He surprised her by closing the remaining distance between them and reaching out to tuck a strand of hair behind her ear. The gesture was so tender and intimate that for a moment she couldn't breathe. His fingers lingered, lightly tracing the curve of her outer ear, lined by little metal studs.

She bit her lip. Something was definitely wrong. Maybe murder.

Adam sat on the desk and ducked down to look her in the eyes, and apparently read her thoughts. "Was Tanner involved with Blake Toll somehow?"

She fought to keep from caving under his scrutiny. And from inhaling any more of his familiar, heady scent. It was messing with her mind, and her loyalties. "I don't know." Except that Tanner had lost a large sum of money to Blake.

"But it's not outside the realm of possibilities."

She sagged. "No. I've been trying to reach him, but I'm not sure my messages are getting through."

"Probably not. He discarded his phone."

"What?"

"I tried to use it to locate his position. It's been disabled. He's not using his credit cards or anything that would lead us—or the police—to him. It looks suspicious, Em. And I think you know why. I think you've been worried about Tanner for a long time, and that's why you went to the prison to talk to Tristan Floyd."

She went completely still. If he knew about Floyd, he might know about other things. "How do you know about that?"

"I talked to him, too, since you weren't willing to talk about Redemption Club. He told me about the ledger that was passed down to Tanner when one of the Club members betrayed Ryan Stone. But I found out later that you'd visited him, before Tanner even had the ledger. Why?"

Because she'd wanted to see the ledger for herself.

She'd heard rumors of its existence. If she'd known it had been given to Tanner, the past couple weeks might have gone down differently. But she wasn't ready to tell Adam everything, especially when she didn't have proof. And once she found proof of who had attempted to kill her mother in that car wreck... Well, she might never be ready to share that information.

Adam was watching her expectantly, waiting for her answer.

She went with the story she'd concocted weeks ago. "I helped put Tristan behind bars a couple months ago, when he used my bar to conduct business for the Club. I had heard rumors about a ledger, and had hoped to help authorities recover it and remove the stain the Club was putting on Legacy. I didn't know anything about Tanner's connection to it. If I had, I would have insisted Tanner handle things differently. I certainly wouldn't have wanted him to be in danger."

His possession of the ledger would have changed everything, had she known weeks ago. Could the contents of the book be on the SD card he was supposedly going to leave for her?

"He could have avoided trouble by turning the ledger over to authorities. I have to wonder why he didn't." It was clear he thought Tanner's motives were impure.

"You think he's trying to extort money from whoever wants the ledger."

"It appears he's choosing to put himself in danger, probably for the chance of a financial payoff rather than trusting us to help him do the right thing." And Tanner was putting her in danger in the process, but Adam was unaware of his brother's early-morning visit. And she needed to see that ledger—or a copy of it—before the authorities took it away forever.

She pressed her fingertips to her closed eyes. "There's got to be another explanation. I've heard the Club has members everywhere. Maybe Tanner didn't know who to trust." He'd certainly hinted as much.

He stroked a hand down her back. "We don't always see the truth when it comes to people we care about."

She stiffened, at first with surprise at the comforting gesture, and then with anger as his words registered. He was implying Tanner would lie to her, and that was the biggest irony of all. Adam had been the one to break her trust, and her heart.

He's here for his own reasons, not for you. Never for you. She had to keep that thought always in her mind.

She was hiding something. Adam caught the flashes of guilt and disappointment across her features as he asked about Tanner. And he'd bet his last dollar she knew more than she'd admitted. Maybe Tanner had even given her the ledger to keep hidden. Or maybe he'd hidden it at her place without her knowledge. So when she returned to the bar to finish out her shift without telling him anything important, he went by her apartment to poke around.

He stomped down the guilt, telling himself he was doing this for everyone's safety. Later, Emily would be grateful. As would Tanner, when he cleared him. Tanner was impulsive, but murder? No. He couldn't see that, especially not one so vicious. But he could totally see him being in the wrong place at the wrong time, somehow wrapped up in a troubling situation.

He jimmied the lock and let himself into her place, then took a moment to take in his surroundings. The air held the same light vanilla-and-whiskey scent that seemed to cling to her skin, and he found himself inhaling deeply. A smile tugged at his lips as he took in the quirky but efficient décor, an illustration of her personality. Little decorative boxes filled one shelf, a collection of fantasy figurines, including jeweled dragons and phoenix carvings, comprised another. He knew there must be a story behind each object, even if it was simply that it made her smile. He found himself wanting to know those stories.

With only an hour until she got off work, he moved on to checking cupboards and closets for anything hidden away. A long-haired calico followed him wherever he went, perching nearby where she could watch him with silent disdain. There was nothing unusual in the kitchen, and he lingered near a side desk where she had two computers and a shelf full of an intriguing mix of books on computer science and casino gaming and gambling strategy before moving on to the bedroom.

No sign of a man anywhere, which meant no sign of Tanner, but also no sign of a boyfriend. That made him curious, and happier than it should. *She's not for you.*

He moved on to the drawers, swallowing hard as he picked through her underwear and other personal items, carefully replacing everything he picked up. It had been a long time since he'd had the inclination to appreciate a woman's wardrobe, but with Emily he was oddly envious of each piece of lace or scrap of satin that had the privilege of clinging to her skin.

Conscious of time slipping away and annoyed with himself, and the lack of answers—or a ledger—he continued on to the bathroom. A towel rack held a purple towel, and when the urge to press his nose to it and inhale her sweet scent struck him, he clenched his fists and pivoted on his heel, walking back to the kitchen. He jerked the trash from beneath the sink and saw only grounds leftover from Emily's morning coffee. Someone had taken out the trash overnight.

He let himself out of her apartment and went down the steps. If Tanner had stopped by last night, either before or after Adam had seen Emily safely back to her apartment, what would he have done next? If he'd been involved in Blake Toll's murder, he would quite possibly have gotten bloody. The crime scene had certainly indicated a violent, unplanned crime.

But if Tanner had been covered in blood, he'd need a safe place to clean up and change—and dispose of the evidence. Somewhere away from his own home, away from Adam and the eyes of the FBI, LVPD, or Ryan Stone's men, where nobody would think to search.

Adam was standing at the community Dumpster, pulling on latex gloves, before his thoughts caught up to his feet. At this late hour, there was nobody to observe him. He lifted the lid, shined a flashlight inside and rummaged around for a moment. A trash liner that matched the ones from Emily's place caught his attention. He ripped a hole in it, shined his flashlight inside and muttered a curse. Bloody clothing and another towel—a purple one that perfectly matched Emily's from her bathroom—filled the bag. He didn't touch the contents, but could see black slacks with a tag that indicated they were Tanner's size. The flashlight illuminated several dark spots. Blood.

Fuck.

He dialed Remington, who answered on the first ring.

"I found something," Adam reported before he could think twice. He had to trust someone if he was going to solve this murder. His gut told him Remington was on the up-and-up. "I want your promise you'll keep it quiet, at least for now. I don't want the media or the possible LVPD mole to catch wind of it." He hoped they'd keep the circus, which was already pronouncing Tanner guilty, out of this for now. The last thing he needed was his brother burrowing deeper into his hidey-hole. "If you can do that, I'll owe you one."

"What'd you find?"

"Bloody clothing and towels. I think it's related to Toll's murder."

"You think the murderer left them?"

"I didn't say that." An ache was beginning to pound against Adam's temples. "But they might be related, yeah."

Remington's silence told Adam just what he thought about that comment. "Tanner?"

"Just get over here. I want *your* people, people you trust, to analyze them." He sighed, knowing in his gut that his brother was into something deep and bad. And whether he'd meant to or not, Tanner had made Emily an accomplice. The same trash bag he'd stashed the clothing in held discarded mail addressed to Emily. Or maybe she was consciously involved. He squeezed his temples. "Got the official coroner's report yet?"

"No, but I got confirmation there were three gunshot wounds. One to the chest and two to the head after the guy was on the floor." *The blood.* "Whoever did this was cold, man."

"It wasn't Tanner." But even Adam heard the lack of conviction in his voice.

Remington sighed. "Help me find another suspect, or evidence pointing to Ryan Stone, or I'll have no alternative but to launch a manhunt for Tanner Wilde.

He could go down for murder."

Murder. His baby brother was going to be accused of a violent crime that could put him away for years, maybe decades. Tanner had done a brief stint in juvie, and a couple of minor infractions since, resulting in minimal jail time, but this... This would be bad and Adam wasn't sure he could bail him out this time, let alone save him.

He glanced at the clothes. He wished he could face his brother and decipher the truth for himself, because the evidence sure didn't look good.

Especially if the clothing could be linked to Tanner *and* to Blake. And to Emily.

CHAPTER SEVEN

After a few hours of sleep, Adam spent Monday morning visiting every friend and poker cohort of Tanner's he could find, most from his brother's social media page. A few of them had mentioned Emily had also been looking for Tanner for the past week.

He saved the interview that had the potential to do the most damage for last. Adam told himself it wasn't because he was worried about Tanner's guilt, but because it might generate more leads he could pursue that afternoon.

But as he interviewed the poker player known as Ruiz, a brown-haired, bronze-skinned man who must spend as much time in the gym and tanning beds as he did in the poker rooms, Adam had a bad feeling he was about to learn something that could further hurt the people he loved. Two weeks ago, Ruiz had been one of the eight players who'd gathered for a private poker tournament at Legacy. Tanner had been another of those players and had lost a small fortune to Blake Toll.

"He cheated," Ruiz said from across his dining room table. Behind him, a hutch displayed a strange mishmash of poker trophies and religious icons. Gamblers were not without their superstitions.

"Tanner cheated." Adam repeated the words, but they didn't sound any saner than before. If his brother had cheated, he'd have won—that much Adam knew about Tanner's skills. They talked every few months, usually about safe topics like weather and sports, but

Adam had followed his brother's career and triumphs via the Internet. Tanner was good at what he did. While Adam had hoped Tanner would eventually choose a different, safer method of making money, at least he'd selected a legal means.

"Everyone else was out except Tanner and Blake," Ruiz said. "It was down to the two of them, with nearly two hundred thousand in the pot."

"I'm sorry, but if he cheated, why did he lose?" Tanner had always excelled at manipulation. Maybe Blake had also been swindling the group.

"I didn't say he cheated to win."

Adam sat back as the possibility rolled through his mind. "He *wanted* to lose?"

Ruiz smiled wryly. "Crazy, right? He must have had a reason."

"So if he wanted to lose, the rumors of him throwing a tantrum afterward were... what? An act?"

"I guess. Maybe he was looking for a heightened rush? Gambling was more of an art to him than a desire to make money."

"He craved the challenge." That sounded more like the brother Adam knew. In fact, their falling out, the event that had led to Adam leaving home eight years ago, had involved a particularly risky challenge that Tanner hadn't been able to resist. Like Houdini, his brother was constantly trying to test and prove himself.

Ruiz nodded. "And maybe that's why he lost to Blake. Throwing a game with that much at stake would have gone against every instinct I have. For him to do that would have been like an award-winning actor trying to mimic a bad actor."

"But he did it."

His grin flashed. "Nobody else noticed his sleight of hand, man. That was the beauty of it. And I kind of like the dude, so I didn't say anything. Besides, he walked away the loser, so I figured karma ironed it all out in everyone else's eyes." Ruiz leaned forward. "But I know he threw that game."

Perhaps Tanner's losing was meant to hook the big fish for a bigger score. To get an invite to Blake's house, where he could win his money back, and then some. If that bigger game had gone wrong, would Tanner have killed Blake? Or was someone else involved?

"How did he manage it?" Adam asked.

"We had a private bartender at the event. She slipped him a different deck of cards during a break. I'm guessing the deck was dirty, the cards marked. I don't think anybody but me saw her do it, but that was because I couldn't take my eyes off her." Ruiz winked.

He straightened, his internal sensors going off. "Was she a blonde with a couple of tattoos, by any chance?"

He grinned. "Yeah. She was the memorable sort, but I guess you already know who I'm talking about?"

Yeah, he knew her. He'd dared to hope she'd stopped running cons with his brother. Dared to believe people could change. She'd even told him she was walking the straight and narrow, avoiding Tanner and his scams. But that poker game had only been a couple weeks ago, and connections between Emily and people Tanner had visited and places he'd been continued to pop up. First, Legacy, then Tristan Floyd, and now Blake Toll.

He tried to ignore the disappointment that twisted inside his gut. Adam could never fully trust Emily. Obviously, her loyalty was still to his brother.

Legacy was filled with an odd vibe as Emily walked in through the employee entrance and made her way through the rotunda. People went about their normal business, and there was no obvious reason to feel the way she did, so she chalked it up to guilt making her feel out of whack.

She was still keeping things from Adam. She hadn't told him about Tanner's mysterious SD card, which she hadn't found despite turning her apartment upside down. She hadn't even told Adam that Tanner had been to see her, in person. With blood on his neck.

She said a quick hello to the hostess, who pointed toward the bar.

"He's been waiting for you for half an hour," the woman said, her appreciative and curious gaze sailing over Emily's shoulder and homing in on the lounge.

Without turning, Emily knew who was waiting for her. Her body was already tingling with awareness. Steeling herself for another confrontation, she thanked the hostess and turned to face the next round of questioning. Surely he'd found out about Tanner's recent exploits, and her involvement in them, by now. Adam was nothing if not thorough. She'd spent entirely too much time over the years fantasizing about him turning that kind of dedicated interest to her, and her body.

She sighed and shook the image from her mind, though he looked especially dark and sexy today in jeans and a soft short-sleeved Henley. But the set of his jaw told her he wasn't there to seduce her.

Damn. She'd hoped Tanner would have shown up to talk to him by now and explain everything—while keeping her out of it. Apparently, she wasn't that lucky.

His dark gaze burned with intensity, but gave none of his thoughts away, as usual.

"Can I help you?" she asked.

"I suspect you can, but you won't." Something dangerous glittered and crackled in the air between them, so Emily resumed walking, heading to the storeroom so she could drop her purse and get to work. The lounge opened in half an hour and she had stocking to do and orders to place.

"Just come out and say what you're thinking," she said, sensing he had followed. "I'm tired of the games."

"Good," he said from right behind her. "So am I. That's why I'm here. I know you know things." When she stopped abruptly, he nearly mowed her down from behind.

His hands went to her hips as he steadied them both. "What's wrong?" he asked, his anger turning to concern as he realized her attention had suddenly shifted.

The space seemed tiny with his broad chest and long legs fitted perfectly against her backside. But that wasn't what was creating the odd sensations.

"Someone's been here." She moved to the desk, needing some distance to sort out what she was thinking and feeling.

"Okay, Goldilocks, who's been sitting in your office chair?" Adam moved to look over her shoulder. Surprised by the hint of humor she heard in his voice, she turned. Too late, she realized that put them chest-to-chest, her nose too close to his bare neck and the fabulous smell that was Adam's unique scent.

She sidestepped and eyed the trashcan under the desk. "There's an empty can in here."

"And that's unusual because…?"

"I don't drink energy drinks, and neither does Angela or any of my staff." She arched a brow as Adam waited patiently for an explanation. The guy could wait out a sloth. "Guess who *does* drink energy drinks—this particular brand—on a regular basis."

"Tanner." For the first time since she could remember, he cracked a genuine smile, and her heart flipped over in her chest.

"Yes."

"He was here, safe." He blew out a breath of relief and some of her tension melted. Whatever Adam's motives for finding Tanner, love and concern ranked high among them. She should have told him she'd seen Tanner in person, and that he'd appeared unharmed. But if she mentioned it now, it would break the fragile bond of trust they were beginning to rebuild. He'd just come back into her life, and she was realizing she didn't want him to run away again. Yes, he would leave and go back to his normal life when Tanner was found, but she didn't want him to leave like he had before.

"He must have made a duplicate of my key without my knowledge," she said. A transgression she'd make him pay for later.

"With Ryan and the police looking for him, he's either stupid or desperate."

"He's not stupid."

He frowned. "So that leaves desperate. Why come here?"

The only reason Emily could think of was that he'd wanted to talk to her. Or leave something for her. A note, maybe. Or the SD card. Had Tanner finally left her the evidence that would clear him? She glanced around but didn't see anything else out of the ordinary. She'd have to wait until Adam left before doing a more thorough inspection.

As she reached for the trash to see if there were any other oddities, Adam grabbed her hand. "Don't."

She tried to ignore the messages zinging from her hand to her naughty parts, but apparently they'd decided to avoid the pesky filter in her brain, which would have nipped her reaction in the bud. "Why not?"

"Don't disturb anything. He may have come here to sleep. If Tanner knows you know he's been here, he might not come back."

"Unless he was looking for me." She looked pointedly at their joined hands and he immediately let go as if he were shooting dice against a craps table. "What now?"

"Can you contact your staff and ask if anyone saw him?"

"Sure, but I'd bet he was smart enough to get in and out of here while he could without being seen." She just hoped he'd gotten some sleep. He'd looked exhausted last time she'd seen him, and sleep deprivation wouldn't make for good choices. But the cot and its blankets appeared untouched.

As Adam followed her from the storeroom, her gaze went to the doorframe, searching for the telltale symbols she and Tanner had once used as a communication method. So she was distracted when she suddenly came up against a solid male chest.

"Whoa!" said the man to whom the chest belonged. *Mason.* He sent her a smile full of straight white teeth as his hands came up to her arms, putting a little distance between them but keeping her close. "I was looking for you."

Another pair of hands—Adam's—reached around from behind to pull her away, as if sensing a threat. But she stepped away from both of them, leading them away from the cramped storeroom and into the bar area. She took in Mason's attire and her grin widened until the apples of her cheeks hurt. "You're the Samson half?"

"Samson half?" Adam's tone indicated his irritation at being left out of the loop.

"Maybe you should introduce us," Mason said, quirking a brow at Adam's piercing look.

"Mason Gray," Emily said, "Meet Adam Wilde."

"I'm performing in the Samson and Delilah skit." Mason gestured to the gladiator-type outfit that showed off his muscular thighs and chiseled chest. "It's a two-person version of the show in Legacy's big theater. This shorter version features a seductive dance that will be all the more intimate when we're performing it on the small stage, here in the lounge." He winked at Emily. "Glad you could arrange for this extra show each week."

"I'm hoping it'll increase midweek business." She turned to Adam. "Mason's really good." She could have sworn Adam growled, but she had to be imagining it. "Adam Wilde is an old family friend."

Mason's glance moved to Adam, then back to her, his smile widening. "We should catch up on the latest. It's been far too long."

"I'll call you," she said, wanting to close the subject quickly, especially with Adam listening.

"I'll look forward to it. I've missed our time

together." Mason surprised her by leaning forward to kiss her cheek and then sending her a significant look before walking away, his muscular thighs flexing beneath the edges of his gladiator-style skirt. Their relationship was a whole lot more complex than she was ready to explain to Adam—not that she owed him an explanation. But he had observed their exchange with interest and a scowl that could eclipse the lights of Vegas.

"Old family friend, huh?" Adam asked.

"How would you have described our... relationship?"

He didn't seem prepared to answer, instead shooting her another question. "Are you dating him?"

"What?"

"He obviously likes you, and you two seem close."

"I may have met up with him a few times." She could tell him that, while attractive and intelligent, Mason could never measure up to the man she'd always wanted—Adam—but he wouldn't like that. That would be too much of an emotional connection.

"But you're not a couple?" He watched her closely, and she sensed her answer was important to him.

"No. Wrong time, wrong place, I suppose." The story of her life. "Why are you here, Adam?" She couldn't keep the tiredness from her voice. Every man in her life seemed to want something from her and gave little in return.

He glanced at Mason, who had joined his partner, dressed as Delilah, on the stage. But Mason's gaze continually drifted to Emily. "Maybe we should talk in the storeroom," Adam suggested.

Emily led the way, again trying to ignore how Adam seemed to overtake the space, and her senses as she closed the door. "You clearly have something you wanted to talk to me about today. I believe you said something about knowing I know things, or whatever."

"I heard about the game where Tanner lost big to Blake a couple weeks ago."

Emily nodded. "It's no secret. Tanner came in here, complaining about the loss afterward. I suppose that makes him a stronger suspect in Blake's murder."

"I also heard that you were there, that you helped Tanner cheat." He stepped closer, but she didn't step away. His eyes scanned her face, and she sensed a need within him—not just the usual chemistry he'd always denied, but a need for her to tell him the truth. A need to trust her. He took her hand and pulled her closer, then cupped her face so she was looking into his concerned, regret-filled eyes. "We were once friends, too. Tell me what's going on. Don't shut me out, Em. What am I missing?"

She tried to ignore the flames of desire licking the inside of her belly, but couldn't resist breathing deeply and filling her lungs with his clean masculine scent. She wanted to tell him, wanted him to come closer, both physically and emotionally. She also wanted to distract him from his questions.

The heat in his eyes clashed with the hard set of his jaw, reminding her that whatever this chemistry between them, he was fighting it, trying to shut *her* out.

She slid her hands up his chest, uncertain whether it was to hold him at bay or tug him closer. His heart beat strong and steady against her palms. She wanted to make it race—to see if she held the kind of power over him that he held over her.

Do it.

She'd learned to silence the devil on her shoulder over the years, but when it came to Adam, she was inclined to listen to her naughty side. She leaned forward and pressed her lips to his jaw. He went completely still before pulling back just enough to look into her eyes, his dark brown gaze searching. But he didn't pull completely away, didn't reject her.

"What are you missing?" She repeated his question, surprised at the huskiness of her voice and the thickness in her throat as she laughed. "So, so much."

"Show me." His eyes flickered with need. "Make me regret walking away."

Time seemed to slow. Her heart thumped harder, her blood pumping thick and languid as he stood stock-still, waiting for her to make a move.

She leaned into him, nipping at his chin before sliding her arms around his neck. He shivered but didn't stop her, so she continued, threading her fingers into the thick dark hair at the back of his head. With the lightest of pressure, she bent his head to hers. Her mouth met his halfway and the warm, sweet taste of him touched her tongue. She traced the seam of his lips, and he sucked in a breath, parting his lips and letting her in.

She took her time, savoring the slow build, the rare vulnerability he was showing her. He pressed her body to his, one arm locked around her waist and the other around her back as if she'd try to get away. The taste of him took her back a thousand years—or just eight—to their first and only kiss.

He let his tongue dance with hers, a slow waltz at first, and then suddenly, as if his passion had been kept on a short leash and she'd sliced the tether, the pace became a tango that had her head spinning.

A minute later, when the dance suddenly ended, she was off balance. His lips left hers and his arms dropped away. Breathing as if he'd just finished a brisk walk, he took several steps back.

"That shouldn't have happened," he said.

Stunned, both by the intensity of the kiss and the abrupt shifts in his mood, she could do nothing more than stare and try to catch her own breath. For a moment, she thought maybe she'd heard him wrong. Her pulse was hammering in her ears.

A moment later, raising her chin as if daring him to reject her, she found her voice. "You wanted to know what you'd been missing."

He shoved a hand through his hair, looking

uncharacteristically uncertain. "And now I know." With those cryptic words, he turned and left.

The breath whooshed out of her and she sank to the edge of the desk. She took a moment to calm her anger and frustration, as well as her reaction to Adam. Thankfully, she had ten minutes left until opening, and much to do to occupy her mind.

With shaky hands, she searched the storeroom for any sign of a message or SD card left by Tanner. Seeing nothing around the desk, cot, or shelves, she examined the doorjamb again and found the tiny pencil marking, not even a quarter inch high, that had caught her eye just before she'd run into Mason. Near the place where the deadbolt could slide shut was a tiny octagon.

Stop. Danger.

Transient people such as hobos and gypsies sometimes used symbols and markings to indicate locations and occupants were dangerous or an easy mark, or any number of things. She and Tanner had developed similar codes and symbols they employed when running a con. Signs that meant a location was safe, and others that meant not so safe.

She eyed the symbol and snatched up a pencil from her desk to put her response. A tiny checkmark indicated she'd received his message, in case he came back. She added a tiny eye with a hash mark through it. *Stay hidden. Don't be seen.* Tanner shouldn't come back here.

And she couldn't go back, either. Not backwards with Adam, or into more trouble with Tanner. It was time she look out for herself first.

CHAPTER EIGHT

Ryan paced his dad's office, wishing he were anywhere but here. He'd normally spend a gorgeous day like today having lunch out by the pool. Robert Stone's office had an entire wall of windows that overlooked the pool area and its ten-foot waterfall and lush surrounding gardens, which were a level below. Cool marble was in abundance there—the stairs, pillars that were Legacy's trademark, and a fountain with white-and-cobalt-blue tiles that continued the Mediterranean theme his father so loved.

From here, at night, the lights of the famous Las Vegas Strip were like a neon rainbow set against the velvet black sky. But in the bright light of late morning, the water shimmered, the palm trees danced, and the carefully manicured blades of grass were a crisp, cool green. Bikini-clad hotel guests lounged at cabanas and along the rim of the pool, which was already sun-warmed on this hot summer day.

And Ryan was trapped here, awaiting his father's judgment.

Next door, Ivy's office had a similar view, befitting the manager of the entire Legacy complex, which included a thirty-floor hotel, 90,000-square-foot casino, theater with shows six nights a week, and a five-star restaurant. Ryan had once had an honorary office down the hall, but it had been a pittance in comparison. And when he'd failed to succeed as the vice president of special promotions, the space had been repurposed to suit someone who—in his father's words—actually did some work around here. Ryan hadn't been fired so much as encouraged to disappear quietly into the night.

Or into his suite on the thirtieth floor.

Ryan was a failure in his father's eyes. He and Ivy existed to carry on the Stone legacy, and to feed Robert Stone's ego. Most days, Ryan could convince himself he didn't care what his dad thought of him. But part of him cared very much. He'd tried to drown that part in alcohol, drugs, and extravagant parties.

In the end, the Redemption Club was the only thing that had saved him. Running it made him feel unique and powerful. There, he earned the respect he deserved. There, he was no longer just the son of Robert Stone. He arranged for murders, drug deals, revenge plots, money laundering. He got shit done, illegal stuff that would chill most *average* people to the bone.

He should be out there soaking up the sun by the pool or cutting a swath through the crisp, cool water. A typical Monday. Instead, he had to deal with the shit-storm that had followed Blake Toll's murder. After Ivy's visit to his suite yesterday, he'd volunteered to meet with the LVPD to answer their questions. He'd been sure to act appropriately troubled about the death of a friend at the hands of another friend. The oxycodone he'd popped right before the interview had helped him appear tired and depressed.

And it had helped him remain relaxed and calm when he'd received news that Tanner had disappeared before Bubba could stage a suicide. Ryan had called Bubba immediately after leaving Tanner with Blake's dead body, and Bubba had followed Tanner's car as he'd exited the neighborhood gate, but he'd lost sight of Tanner almost immediately. Which meant the only other man alive who knew what had happened at Blake's was still out there, a liability. Had Tanner gone to Ryan's father with the truth? Is that what this sudden summons was about?

His pacing continued, faster now as he smothered his anger and fear. His father would be here any moment, and Ryan had to appear unconcerned and confident. He poured himself a glass of water from the sidebar, testing his hands to be sure they weren't shaking, and wishing he'd taken another of his pills this morning to steady his nerves. At the sound of his father's Italian loafers clicking against the marble in the lobby, and his voice speaking to his secretary, Ryan carefully set down his glass and straightened his tie. He'd dressed up, uncertain what this meeting would yield. Based on history, his father could be preparing to issue anything from a stern warning about all-night poker games to an arrest warrant.

Ryan's least favorite Stone Rule: *Spare the rod, spoil the child.*

Robert Stone strode in with barely a glance, as if he had more important things to do than take time for his only son. His hair, still more pepper than salt, was carefully combed and his tie perfectly knotted. His appearance should be perfection, since he paid his staff handsomely to keep him dressed in the latest men's fashion and styled to look less than his fifty-eight years. But anger radiated in his stiff movements as he took a seat behind the immense desk that had once belonged to a famous billionaire. His father liked to brag that he'd won the monstrosity in a card game just after Legacy opened.

He finally lifted his gaze to Ryan's and arched a brow. "Take a seat."

Full of nervous energy, Ryan would rather pace. Besides, sitting would give his father the upper hand. Still, defiance wouldn't get him anywhere when he wasn't sure what kind of mood his father was in, so he sat. "What is this about?" His fear came out as annoyance, and he instantly wished he could call the words back as his father glared at him.

"Did I drag you out of bed too early?"

Ivy must have blabbed that he'd been in bed late yesterday. Ryan held his arms out to his sides. "I'm gracing you with my presence, aren't I?"

His father's lips pressed tightly together and his

expression hardened. "And I'll grace you with some advice."

"Oh good, more Stone Rules," he muttered under his breath.

"Don't push me, especially after your latest stunt." His mood was now dialed to pissed. That, Ryan could deal with. It was when his father was quiet that Ryan didn't know what he was thinking.

"I've had a bad couple of months, what with my best friend's death—"

"That asshole Finn Tucker tried to blackmail me."

Ryan gauged his father's expression and found no hint that the man believed anyone other than Ryan's ex-best-friend had been responsible. Apparently, killing Blake had silenced that leak. Ryan had burned the file the moment he got home that morning. Tanner was the only other weak spot. "Which makes what he did to you—and to me," Ryan reminded his father, "all the more painful."

His father suddenly sprang out of his chair and circled the desk to stop in front of Ryan. He bent down and peered into Ryan's eyes, then straightened. "You stopped taking the pain meds?"

"I told you I would." And he had, at least for today.

"So you're completely healed?"

"Only a scar to show for the whole mess." The bullet to the chest had taken Ryan down for several weeks, but the best doctors and nurses his father could buy had overseen his recovery. Still, the scar would always be there, a reminder of his friend's attempted betrayal. A caution never to trust anyone, even someone you'd known most of your life.

"We'll call the plastic surgeon when you're ready." Robert Stone couldn't abide by imperfection, especially in his offspring. He waved a hand as if dismissing the issue and returned to his chair. "I'm impressed you were able to see things through."

Ryan's chest swelled with a sudden burst of pride, but his father's next comments deflated it again.

"And then you went and got involved in another shady incident." He tapped his fingertips together. "What did you tell the cops about the night Blake Toll was murdered?"

"The truth. That I'd sensed something going on between the two men." The police had assumed he'd meant tension and Ryan hadn't disabused them of the theory. "And that when I left his house, there were only two players remaining, Blake Toll and Tanner Wilde." One of them had been dead, but that was another bit of information he'd withheld. "The police are looking elsewhere for answers. Our family's reputation is secure."

His father looked thoughtful for a long moment before speaking again. "I'm going to offer you a job at Stone Corp. People are expecting my son to take my place someday."

The brief flare of pride at his initial statement quickly dissipated. "We don't want to disappoint your faithful admirers." He crushed his disappointment, reminding himself he'd rather live off the cash cow than work for a living, anyway. But the sting still hurt. That his father still had the power to make him feel less capable than an infant hurt even more.

His father scowled. "I've been keeping tabs on you, seeing if you did, indeed, disband the Redemption Club as we discussed."

Ryan had expected his father's distrust, which was why he'd limited his Club activities. But totally disband something he had spent years cultivating? He hadn't been able to bring himself to do it. "I hope you've seen that I've ended that part of my life."

"It certainly seems that way."

"I don't see why we had to get rid of it at all."

His father arched a brow. "We?"

"It was your brainchild, after all." Decades ago, his father and two of his father's cohorts had set up the Redemption Club to make money and amass power. It had worked well for them, but they'd closed up shop when the cops were getting too close to the truth, and when danger was coming too close to their families. "It was a really great idea."

"And there's a reason we nixed it. Besides, you told me you burned the ledger, so there's no record of markers to call in. Unless I'm mistaken?" His gaze was piercing, but Ryan knew better than to flinch. He'd learned this Stone Rule well. *Never show your cards.*

"There's no other record of Redemption Club exchanges or loans." But the ledger still existed, and Ryan intended to use it to stockpile his own wealth and climb the ranks in society.

"Good. You don't need the Club anymore." More likely, his father was jealous that Ryan had been successful at running it.

He grinned at the thought of finally accomplishing something without his father's help. That was likely what was bothering the great Robert Stone. "I also don't need a job here. I certainly don't need you or Ivy babysitting me."

"Your behavior reflects upon me. Months ago, you were almost implicated in several murders, and now another murder leads cops to our doorstep?" His father shook his head in disappointment. "You'll be watched even more carefully now—and not just by me. Your actions threaten to tarnish Legacy and my reputation. And *that* is unacceptable."

"You have Ivy to polish your image issues. She'll shine under this scrutiny. She's already getting kudos from the media and the LVPD for her cooperation. I hear she even offered a reward to whoever provides information leading to the killer."

While their father's empire was vast and diverse, the Legacy Hotel and Casino had been the start, and the heart, of it all. Ivy ran the establishment for their father like a stoic sea captain expertly steering the course. Sure, on occasion Ryan had resented how easily it came to her, but she was all work and no play. Ryan's destiny was far different.

"She shines because she listens to me," his father said. "It's time you did, too. You'll be working under my close supervision. When you prove yourself, I'll consider moving you into a position of real power."

Fuck that. He already had a position of power—of *real* power. Annoyed with his father's controlling behavior, Ryan covertly palmed his phone. He'd received a text from Bubba twenty-three minutes ago, saying there'd been no activity at Tanner's place except for another man coming and going. Probably the same man Brenda had described, who looked similar to Tanner. Unlike Brenda, Bubba was checking other locations. It was only a matter of time before Tanner ran out of options. Ryan held all of the good cards.

Maybe he wasn't so different from his father after all, except that the senior Stone was currently droning on about building a legacy, about stock portfolios and an upcoming board meeting at his hotel in the Cayman Islands.

And Ryan needed to be somewhere else. He looked up from his phone. "Can you have Megan send me the necessary information in an email?" Their secretary handled everything, anyway. He moved to the door, ready to make an escape.

His father frowned. "Where are you going?"

"You're not the only one with business to attend to."

Green eyes that matched his own pierced him like shards of emerald. "It had better be legitimate business and not another party or poker game. I just spent a fortune on lawyers, PR people, and other specialists you don't even want to know about to sweep your last couple screw-ups under the rug. You're being watched." Controlled rage shook his father's voice, making Ryan's breath freeze in his lungs for a moment. Maybe his father did know more than he was letting on. "And that's all the more reason why you should be focusing on a legitimate job. If I find out you're working on another illegal venture behind my back, heaven help you. Because I won't."

Ryan's sister saved him from having to lie again.

Ivy knocked before entering and looked up from the paper she was carrying just in time to avoid bumping into Ryan. "Oh, hello." Her gaze swept over him, taking in his suit and tie. "Should I come back later?"

Their father came around the desk. "Your brother was just on his way out, though I think we should all set up a time to celebrate."

"Celebrate?"

"Ryan's coming on board. He'll be working with us. Closely supervised, of course."

Ivy's gaze, devoid of emotion, moved back to Ryan. She'd always been the hard worker in the family. He wondered how she felt about this, but they'd never been the type to share deep thoughts, let alone feelings. Ivy hid those well. Part of that skill came from having a famous, award-winning actress as a mother. Ryan's mother had been Robert Stone's first wife, a debutante without any useful skills to speak of. She was content to live in Europe, ignoring her motherly duties most of Ryan's life, living off her significant divorce settlement.

"Really?" Ivy said, arching a sleek, dark brow. "I thought you..." Her words drifted off and she shook her head. Her wide mouth curved in a smile that didn't reach her eyes. "Welcome aboard." She reached out to shake his hand, and then changed it to an awkward embrace.

"Thanks, sis." He strode past her and was nearly out the door before he turned to face them, walking backwards as he grinned. "Have *our* secretary set something up. I think you're right. I have a lot to celebrate."

And when he found Tanner and snipped the final loose end, he'd be golden.

Monday was going from bad to worse as Adam

pulled into the parking lot. Blazing heat surrounded him, biting at his ankles and baking his shoulders as he exited the car and climbed the stairs. At least cool air conditioning awaited above. It was that promise of relief from the midafternoon furnace that kept him moving forward.

The coroner's report had come in and confirmed what Remington had already presumed about the scene of Blake's death. Crime of passion. And there were plenty of witnesses to state how passionate Tanner had been about losing to Blake. Adam hoped to hell that the blood on the garments he'd turned over to the lab wouldn't come back as Tanner's or Blake's, but his hopes were plummeting as the hours went by without a word from his brother.

To top it off, Adam's lawyer in Phoenix was having trouble getting a court date from the judge. It appeared the bogus case was never going to be settled and Adam would be doomed to a desk job indefinitely.

But the worst of his mood was due to the unwanted cravings he couldn't shake, even though the subject of his desire clearly wasn't the woman he'd thought her to be. Emily was keeping things from him about Tanner, and possibly lied about going legit. Plus, she might be dating a man in a gladiator costume.

But he hadn't misread Emily's passionate reaction to their kiss. She'd softened toward him, coming to life in his arms. Hell, he'd felt more alive in those few minutes than he had in the past few years.

And he'd had to end it. She clouded his judgment, made him want things he couldn't have. Not with a woman who couldn't be totally honest. A woman like that had already ripped his family to shreds once. He'd be stupid to put himself through that kind of pain again. Sidney Wilde, a mother and wife who'd grown tired of chasing after two active sons and a rowdy husband, and had left town when Adam was eight. They'd never seen or heard from her again. He wouldn't let Emily manipulate him the same way, yet he needed a strategy for getting answers from her.

Hoping to wash the sour taste of regret from his mouth, Adam had just snagged a beer—at least his brother kept those in good supply—from the fridge when a knock sounded at the door. He sighed and set aside his beverage. His strides quickened as he realized it could be Emily seeking him out. Maybe she'd reconsidered his request for information and was finally planning to come clean. Or maybe she wanted to continue what he'd broken off in the storeroom. He had half a mind to let her change his attitude.

His hope died as he opened the door to a man who looked to be Tanner's age, but with a polish to his smile that hinted at the cocky kind of confidence Adam detested. Plus, he was dressed in a suit that was probably worth several months of Adam's detective salary.

Ryan Stone.

He recognized the man's face from the Internet search he'd done after talking to Tristan Floyd. Ryan, the son of Robert Stone, CEO of Stone Corp, looked to someday inherit an international chain of luxury hotels, as well as other travel and entertainment businesses such as cruise ships and Stone Studios films. The high-wattage smile aimed at Adam was even stronger in person than in the online photos.

"Can I help you?" Adam leaned against the doorframe, blocking Ryan's curious gaze from seeing the inside of the apartment.

"Is Tanner here?"

He arched a brow. "And you are?"

"Ryan Stone." He flashed those perfect white teeth again.

Too bad Adam was immune to charm. "Doesn't ring a bell."

"I'm a friend of his." The guy's gaze shifted again to Adam's shoulder, which still blocked his line of sight.

"He's not here." And he had the sense Ryan had more than a *friendly* interest in his brother.

Remington's warnings about the man rang in his head. Besides, Ryan didn't seem like Tanner's usual choice in companions. Tanner preferred people with grit, friends who were loyal and... *real*. His thoughts briefly flitted to Emily and her tough-girl attitude.

Still, it wouldn't hurt to get to know the heir to the Stone throne, especially since Ryan was so eager to get a look at Tanner's apartment that he was practically oozing charm.

Adam shifted out of the way and invited Ryan inside. "Tanner could be back any minute. Come in and wait, if you want."

Ryan hesitated a second, then stepped over the threshold. "Thanks. Are you related to Tanner? You have the same look."

Though his immediate reaction to Ryan's probing was annoyance, Adam grinned amicably. "We're brothers. Beer?"

"That'd be great."

The open-concept layout of the apartment allowed him to watch Ryan from the kitchen as the guy surveyed the living room, trying to look casual. What was he hoping to find, the ledger? Adam had already been over the place with an investigator's trained eye. Several times.

But the thought that Ryan didn't have the valuable book, and that Tanner might still have it, made him grin. His brother was smart enough to recognize a bargaining chip. This particular chip might save his life.

He handed Ryan a beer and sat in a chair at a ninety-degree angle so he could observe every expression, every twitch or flinch. "So, how do you know Tanner?"

Ryan shrugged. "We've been friends for a couple years. He plays in poker tournaments at my casino." His chest puffed with pride at the mention of Legacy.

"And which casino might that be?" Adam played dumb. That stance typically worked with a man like

Ryan, who wanted to be the smartest person in the room.

"Legacy."

"I was just there this weekend."

"With your brother?"

"No. He's been really busy. I've been playing tourist, just seeing what's new since the last time I was in Vegas."

"You're not from around here then?"

"Just visiting. Legacy's a fancy place."

That evoked an easy grin. "Yeah. *Fancy*. My sister's responsible for most of that. She's high class all the way."

"Must be tough to let her have all the glory. And your dad? I think I heard about Robert Stone. He heads some multibillion-dollar corporation, right? Must be hard to fill shoes that size."

Ryan's expression soured. "Yeah, well, sometimes it's better to find a new pair of shoes to break in."

"Sounds like a healthy attitude. Heard there was a murder loosely linked to Legacy yesterday. The cops stopped by here, asking all kinds of questions about where Tanner was, who his friends are, his phone records, et cetera. I told him there was no way he was a murderer. Had to be one of the other people who'd been there."

Ryan narrowed his eyes at him. "I'm sorry, but I don't think I caught your name."

"Adam."

"I don't think Tanner mentioned his brother would be visiting... or that he had a brother." Ryan was fishing, but Adam didn't bite. "Are you a professional poker player, too?"

"Nah. I don't go looking for trouble half as much as my brother does. In fact, I try to avoid it at all costs." He tipped the beer bottle to his lips.

"I wish your brother shared the same view." Ryan met Adam's gaze with all the sincerity of a concerned friend. "It's no secret he knew the murder victim. And nobody's seen him since Blake's death. Unless...?"

More fishing. Tanner would have seen right through this guy, so why wouldn't he turn over the ledger to the police and be done with it? Ryan had to have something on Tanner, or had convinced him he couldn't trust anyone—not even Adam.

Rather than reply, Adam took a long pull on his beer and waited him out.

Ryan glanced at the door, then at his watch. "Were you expecting him soon?"

Adam shrugged. "He comes and goes as he pleases. As for the murder, I believe the phrase is *innocent until proven guilty.*"

"I'm sure, if he came forward, he could clear up this mess quickly." Ryan leaned forward, elbows on knees, the picture of earnestness. "I'm happy to lend him my team of lawyers. In fact, he should come to me first and we can assemble the team, come up with a strategy before he talks to the police."

"I'm sure Tanner would appreciate the offer, but he has enough friends and family who would help him out."

"Has he already turned to any of these friends?" Ryan asked, trying too hard to seem casual about it. "I heard about a sexy blonde he's been seen with."

Shit. *Emily.* Normally, she could handle an egotistical jerk like Ryan Stone with both hands tied behind her back. But if this guy was the leader of the Redemption Club, and she was in his sights, she might be out of her depth.

Ryan walked to the kitchen with his empty beer bottle. Adam couldn't help but notice how the man's gaze swept his surroundings as he moved to the recycling bin below the sink. *There's no ledger here.*

"Hope you find what you're looking for," Adam said.

Ryan nodded. "Thanks. I have to get back to work." According to Adam's research, Ryan hadn't worked an honest day in his life. "Let Tanner know I stopped by, would you? And if you're ever at Legacy, tell the front desk to contact me. I'll buy a round to repay you. That goes for Tanner, too, of course."

"Very generous of you."

A moment later, Ryan's footsteps sounded on the stairwell as he descended to the parking lot. From the window, Adam watched the canary-yellow Ferrari peel out of the parking lot, narrowly missing a woman with her arms full of groceries.

Prick.

He made a call to Emily, but she didn't pick up. Not surprising, considering she wasn't exactly excited to have him hanging around, asking questions and basically using her to get to Tanner.

"Leave it at the beep," Emily's voice said when her voicemail picked up.

"Hey, it's me. Adam." He rubbed a hand down his face, feeling like an idiot as he left the message. "Just wondering if you've seen or heard from Tanner yet."

And if you knew about the bloody clothes in your Dumpster, or that Tanner used your place to dispose of evidence.

Or if you've been thinking about our kiss as much as I have, regretting that it ended.

"Oh," he continued, "and we're not the only ones hoping to find him. Ryan Stone was just here. Said he's a friend of Tanner's, too. Anyway, he may come your way asking questions..." He stopped. What could he say? For all he knew, Emily was a friend of Ryan's. He really didn't know her world, or who she ran with anymore. But if Ryan was looking for a blonde who'd been hanging out with Tanner, the best guess was Emily and it was only a matter of time before Ryan stumbled across that information.

He sighed. "If you have any problems, call me, okay?"

She'd never come to him for help. He hung up, feeling even more frustrated than he had before Ryan's visit.

CHAPTER NINE

"How cozy." Ryan shook out his cloth napkin and draped it across his lap as he surveyed his father and sister. "I can't remember the last time we did something like this."

"Dinner?" Ivy asked, waving the waiter away before he could refill her champagne glass. Likely, she was going back to work after a quick toast. She worked constantly, which was probably why they were having dinner in the Legacy restaurant. Sure, it was a five-star, world-renowned steak-and-seafood establishment, but Ryan would like them to have taken a little more effort in celebrating his new job.

He shrugged off the disappointment. He had plans to party with his friends later, anyway. "Share any meal."

His father frowned over the rim of his dirty martini. "Don't be sarcastic. We see each other a few times a month."

"You have to admit, it's been a while since this family has gotten together to celebrate—just the three of us, anyway."

Robert Stone was notorious for his social events and grand parties, which were almost weekly, and his children were expected to attend, but they rarely interacted as a family. It didn't really matter, since Ryan enjoyed the benefits, meeting celebrities and influential businessmen, imbibing the free-flowing alcohol and recreational drugs, more than he valued family bonding time. Ryan had never seen his sister party, though she was always present when their father required it. The elder Stone seemed to think it reflected well on his image to have his kids doting on him, and appearing successful.

His father scowled. "Are you trying to provoke me? We're here to celebrate."

"Ah, yes. I've finally been deemed worthy of rejoining the family business. However, I haven't heard the details of the position yet. Maybe I'll turn it down." At his elbow, Ivy sucked in a breath. He grinned.

"How's your Italian, son?"

Fuck, no. His father wasn't going to banish him to Europe. He had too many irons in the fire here. And Adam Wilde had been toying with him—trying to make him think he was simply a tourist and Tanner could walk back into the apartment at any moment—when he'd filed a missing person's report. He had already put a private investigator to work digging up information on the guy. "I was thinking something a little closer to home."

"And I was going to suggest running one of our boutique hotels in Tuscany. Beautiful area."

"I know. But it's not my cup of tea, or glass of *vino.*"

Ivy's guarded green gaze was watching their byplay. She was probably worried Ryan was gunning for her job. She'd run herself ragged trying to get their father's approval and had to be exhausted and frustrated by the lack of recognition, but there was rarely a crack in her cool veneer.

His father's lips twisted in a wry grimace. "Yes, I'm sure that quiet corner of Italy would be too sedate for you."

"Exactly." Ryan took another sip of champagne, letting the bubbles dance on his tongue before he swallowed. He'd have to remember to ask for the same superior vintage when he celebrated with his friends in the lounge after dinner.

"Which is why it would be such a good place for you to go right now." His father raised his eyebrows in silent warning. "At least until things die down here."

"That's all been handled. I was cleared of any wrongdoing before, and I will be again." Blake was dead now. And any moment, Tanner would be eliminated. Ryan would be free and clear to take the whole pie instead of settling for a slice.

"Yes, but now there's Blake Toll's murder." He held up a hand to halt Ryan's objection. "Even if you're innocent, your name was connected to it. Best put some time and distance between you and any other nasty rumors. You could visit your mother."

"Wouldn't she love that?" He set down his glass with more force than was necessary. A distant relative to European royalty, his mother was likely gallivanting with her latest boyfriend. She was the perfect portrait of a spoiled divorcée, and a cougar, to boot. She didn't give a rat's ass where Ryan spent his time, as long as he was out of her hair.

The lines bracketing his father's mouth tightened. "Then go do the tourist thing."

"Or I could stay here and you can keep a close eye on me, make sure I don't get into any more trouble."

Beside him, Ivy's brows were drawn together. "What am I missing here?"

Their father ignored her question, his gaze intent on Ryan. "What are you angling for, exactly?"

"I think I should take over Legacy." Ryan ignored Ivy's sharp intake of breath. He glanced about the restaurant. "You and Ivy can train me, and move on to bigger and better things. Besides, the atmosphere is just my speed, and hospitality and charm are my forte. I learned from the best." And he could continue to handle Club business here.

His father seemed to consider the proposition. He was probably tempted to be rid of the albatross around his neck that was his only son, but Ryan was betting that being able to keep an eye on the progeny who was notorious for getting into the kind of trouble only a rich playboy could find, and keeping him out of the tabloids, was too tempting to pass up.

"I'm not playing babysitter," Ivy said into the silence. "I have enough on my plate." Her gaze softened a bit as it fell on Ryan. "I'm sure you'll find the right place within Stone Corp, but it's not here." Despite her Ice Queen reputation, his sister could be such a Dolly Do-Right sometimes and was a peacekeeper by nature. More than once, she'd come between Ryan and their dad's ire to smooth things over.

Their father sat in contemplative silence, downed his martini, and rapped his knuckles on the table once as if to punctuate his decision. "He stays, at least for a few months while we see if he can prove his worth. Ivy, I'll send you on a tour of the various Stone Corp holdings. I've been meaning to do that for a while, anyway. When you return, we'll know better what suits each of you."

"Then it's settled," Ryan pronounced. He tipped his champagne glass to them in silent salute before tipping the final drops to his lips. Victory tasted sweet.

His father's look was chilly, but Ryan felt a moment of triumph. Ryan had his old man over a barrel and his dad knew it.

"No," Ivy said. Her hand shot out to grab their father's, but she quickly recovered herself, jerking her hands back into her lap. "I mean, I've already got things under control here. Last quarter was our highest profit margin yet. I'm good at this. I know Legacy. And I'm already grooming someone to take over full management of the lounge."

"Emily?" Ryan asked, envisioning the sexy blonde bartender. Though she wasn't as perfect as his normal stable of girls, he wouldn't mind sampling her. "Does she have a business degree?"

"Do you?" Ivy shot back at him.

"Yes."

"On paper, maybe. But only because Dad's money

bought you some leeway when you were barely making the grade."

Anger and bitterness soured the champagne on his taste buds. "It's better than no degree at all."

"Emily has a head for business."

"And no reason to be put in a position of power in a *family* company. The place is called *Legacy* for a reason."

Their father held up his hand, halting any further arguments. "My decision's been made. Ryan will give it a go for a couple months and you'll learn more about the rest of Stone Corp."

Ryan grinned and raised his glass. "I'll toast to that."

On her evening break, Emily was about to close herself in the storeroom for a quick nap when Ryan Stone entered the lounge with a blonde bombshell plastered to his side and two male friends trailing behind. She recognized the men from other times they'd been in. They were Redemption Club cohorts.

A chill of foreboding ran over her skin. She thought back to the phone message she'd received from Adam earlier that afternoon, warning her Ryan might come by, asking questions about Tanner. And Ryan had reportedly been at Blake's the night of Blake's murder, same as Tanner had. Had he been the reason Tanner had warned her not to trust anyone? Still, the man was part of the family that employed her, and she couldn't afford to be rude.

When Ryan saw Emily, he grinned widely and extracted himself from his date to come over to the bar. "Should have figured you'd be here tonight. You work just as hard as my sister." She took that as a compliment, though he seemed to intend it as a criticism. "I have good news."

Judging by his grin, she wasn't sure she believed him. "Really?"

"Bring a couple bottles of your best champagne and five glasses to my table and we'll toast together."

His breath already smelled like he'd been drinking, but she didn't argue. She'd known Ryan for the couple years she'd worked at Legacy, but they weren't exactly friends. In her capacity as bartender, she'd served him and various groups of people he'd been intent on impressing enough times to know who he was deep down. He was a charmer to the core, but that core was rotten. She suspected he was running the Redemption Club after his best friend's death. When she'd visited Tristan Floyd in prison he'd hinted that Ryan was at the helm, but had been afraid to name the important names that could get him killed, even behind bars. Which meant Ryan had to be looking for the ledger, too. Which meant he was looking for Tanner.

As she returned with his order, Ryan introduced her to his friends—Brenda, Mike, and a hulk of a man named Bubba—as she poured them a round. "Stay for a few minutes," he insisted.

"I really should get back," she said, wishing the bar were busy enough to keep her away. Unfortunately, it was a slow Monday night.

"You can't miss the toast." He unwound his arm from around the big-bosomed blonde and nudged her over to make room. Brenda didn't look happy to be pushed aside. He patted the seat on the other side of him. "It involves you."

"Me?" Reluctantly, she sat and accepted a glass of bubbly.

Grinning, Ryan raised his glass and gestured to one of his friends, who looked confused. "I can't toast myself," he snapped with sudden irritation.

Sitting opposite them, Mike cleared his throat. "To the new manager of..." He looked uncertain. "Of something within the Stone Corp umbrella."

Ryan's scowl turned back into a grin. "Looks like that something will be the entire Legacy complex. I'll be your boss." He winked at her and she hoped he couldn't hear the churning of her stomach. He was going to run the place—a place she'd worked so hard to build into something great—straight into the ground.

She took a sip of champagne and attempted a smile of congratulations as the others praised Ryan. Brenda pressed close and turned his face to plant a kiss on his lips.

Emily's confidence sagged as she put a few inches between her and them. Ryan Stone was an arrogant ass. And quite possibly the most cunning, evil son of a bitch she'd ever come across.

The sip of alcohol soured her near-empty belly. "Speaking of work, I really should get back behind the bar. Break time's over."

"Don't want to disappoint the boss." Ryan caught her and rubbed a thumb over her wrist. She fought the urge to yank her hand away.

Brenda was staring at her, but not with the jealousy Emily expected. Her expression was one of sudden recognition. "Do you know Tanner Wilde?" she asked. The whole table went quiet and Ryan's interested gaze swung between Brenda and Emily, awaiting her answer.

Emily licked her dry lips. "Yes, I know him." Brenda exchanged a significant look with Ryan, and Emily was certain she mouthed *the blonde.*

"How well do you know him?" Ryan asked.

She shrugged and decided Ryan didn't need to know everything—future boss or not. "You came in with him a couple times. And I was the bartender at that private poker game a few weeks back. I may have chatted with him on a break."

"And other than that?"

None of your damn business. But saying what she wanted would only arouse more suspicion and maybe land her in danger. Thankfully, several guests chose then to come in and head for the bar.

She stood. "I have to get back. Enjoy your celebration." She walked away before Ryan could stop her again, but his thoughtful gaze followed her.

Was he the reason Tanner was hiding? She supposed she'd have plenty of time to get to know Ryan Stone better—as her boss. And to watch for more signs that the Redemption Club was rebooting again. Emily had hoped that the loss of the ledger would slow it down, but it appeared Ryan wasn't letting anything stop him. Ryan used to have semiregular gatherings here. Those had ended after his shooting, but men like him lived for the rush of power. She'd bet everything he planned to get the Club going again.

The more she thought about Ryan's potential new position as overlord of the entire Legacy complex, which would only make him more untouchable, the more unacceptable that arrangement became. Her anger built until she put Angela in charge of the bar and decided it was time to make a move.

When Adam ran into Emily in the enormous rotunda that formed the hub of the hotel and casino complex, she was running on a full head of steam. He couldn't get Ryan Stone's odd visit, or the reference to Tanner's *blonde friend*, out of his head. Despite his confusion over the kiss they'd shared, he needed to see her. But she clearly had other matters on her mind. He gripped her shoulders and turned her toward him when she tried to charge past. "Hey, what's wrong?"

"Ryan Stone says he's my new boss."

"Ryan talked to you? Didn't I warn you to stay away from him?"

"Hard to do when I apparently work for the man." She muttered a curse as she pulled away and headed toward the check-in desk.

He kept pace with her determined strides, trying not to notice the way her short skirt showed off her long legs. "Where are we going?"

"*I'm* going to talk to my real boss, Ivy Stone." Ryan Stone's half sister. Adam had yet to have a personal introduction to the woman and wouldn't mind seeking her out now, but he didn't want Emily to burn her bridges in a moment of hotheadedness. She needed a moment to breathe.

"You sure you want to go in there angry?"

She didn't respond until they'd circumnavigated the check-in area and reached the empty hallway beyond that led to the main offices. She surprised Adam by jerking him to a halt and shoving him up against the wall.

Her eyes blazed with anger and hurt. "Just because you can keep emotion out of every facet of your life doesn't mean it doesn't belong there. Ivy's a friend. This mess with Ryan came out of left field. She'll understand why I'm angry, and she'll hear me out. She won't bail on me. So don't impose your restrictions on me." The final sentence was spoken with a couple well-placed finger-jabs to his chest.

He grabbed her hand and stroked a thumb across her wrist, feeling the rapid staccato of her pulse. "I don't deny that feelings have their place. But I can see how much this job means to you. I don't want you to blow it." As he spoke, he caressed the fingers he'd captured, and her shoulders relaxed slightly. But the inferno in her eyes continued to blaze. "And I don't want you to become Ryan Stone's enemy."

She jerked her hand away from his. "You never had an ounce of faith in me."

She continued down the hall, not pausing to see if he followed. He probably shouldn't, and at first, he was so shocked by her statement that his feet wouldn't move. This was between employer and employee—or between friends, as Emily put it. But he couldn't bear to see her get hurt. He'd do everything in his power to avoid that.

And then there was his primary mission of helping Tanner. Meeting Ivy Stone now could give him a leg up later, if he needed her cooperation. So he followed.

Ivy's dark head came up sharply as they entered

her office. Her irritated expression fell away, replaced with concern as her gaze scanned Emily's face. "You already heard?"

Emily planted her hands on the desk and leaned forward, causing the edge of her skirt to rise up along the back of her smooth thighs. "What the hell, Ivy? I at least deserved to hear this news from you, and not be sideswiped by it."

Ivy nodded. "I planned to stop in tonight before closing time." Her curious gaze shifted briefly to Adam, but Emily demanded her full attention. "And then I couldn't get away." She gestured to the paperwork on her desk. "Dad threw another large party booking at me last minute."

"And how many times have I helped you out with those?"

"I'm sorry, okay? It was out of my hands. And yes, I should have been the one to tell you. I didn't expect Ryan to go waltzing in there so quickly. But I really don't think anything will change, especially in the lounge, since you have things under control there. In fact, given Ryan's history of avoiding work at all costs, I doubt he'll be more than a figurehead."

"How long has this change been discussed behind my back?"

Adam resisted the urge to reach out and touch Emily, to attempt to calm her. She had every right to be upset. And he had no right to touch her. Frustration gnawed at him with little pointy teeth.

Ivy sighed and pressed her manicured fingertips against her closed eyes. "I didn't want any of this. It happened so fast."

He was surprised to see a crack in the woman's icy reputation, and misery as Ivy opened her eyes again.

Emily straightened, sensing the genuine distress in her friend. Casting aside her own anger, she blew out a breath and propped a hip against the edge of the desk. "What happened?"

"It's just so odd," Ivy said. "Suddenly, my father's

intent on bringing Ryan into the family business."

"Why is that odd?" Adam couldn't resist asking, which drew both women's attention to him.

"This is an old friend," Emily explained to Ivy, not sounding thrilled to have him there. Adam wasn't too thrilled, either, at constantly being introduced as her old friend, but it was better than annoying jackass. "He's in town to find his brother."

He stepped forward and extended a hand across the desk. "Adam." He left his last name off the introduction in case Ivy connected him to his brother's name. Earlier that day, Tanner had formally been named a suspect in Blake's murder. Besides, he didn't know how much Ivy could be involved in her family's side business. Did she help run Redemption Club? Emily seemed to trust the woman, and was usually a good judge of character, but he'd watch and decide for himself.

Ivy slid her cool, slender hand into his, her grip strong. "Ivy Stone." She sent another curious glance between the two of them before answering his question. "Given his history and playboy reputation, my brother doesn't exactly inspire confidence in his business acumen. Then again, he's never been interested enough to apply himself. But he might make a good manager, especially since he can be very personable when he wants to be."

"Then maybe he should start at the ground floor and work up to manager," Emily suggested. "Running this ship is more than just being a people person. He could be a host at the restaurant, or even wait some tables. Or book the talent. Or he can be a doorman."

"He'd see that as—" Ivy stopped suddenly.

"Beneath him?" Emily's lips twisted.

Ivy met her gaze with one filled with regret. "I tried to talk him into going to Europe, as my father suggested... Or maybe I can persuade him to take on the Malibu hotel. He loves it out there by the ocean and it's a brand-new project we're launching."

Emily sighed. "I don't think he plans on going anywhere. And now that he knows I know Tanner—"

Alarm prickled along Adam's spine. "He'll have to go through me before he hurts you." The women seemed just as surprised as him that he'd spoken. He quickly covered the display of emotion with a justification. "I'm certain Ryan's uncharacteristic career move is about my brother. Ryan's looking for Tanner, and he thinks targeting Emily will help him find him."

"Tanner? Tanner Wilde is the brother you're here to find?" Ivy asked, shocked. Just as quickly, the shutters came down over all emotion, turning her expression to stone.

"There's something more than Blake's murder going on here," Emily said. "And I'm afraid it all connects to your brother."

"And do you know Tanner?" Ivy asked Emily.

"He's a friend."

"The police are looking for him."

She shrugged. "I don't know where he is, but I'm damn well not going to volunteer information. And taking over Legacy isn't going to ingratiate Ryan to me."

"No, I can see that." A smile tugged at Ivy's lips. "But why does he care about finding Tanner so badly? He should just let the police handle it."

"That's what we'd like to know," Adam said. "He even tried to convince me Tanner is a murderer."

"Could he be? I mean, he's your brother. Maybe you're not entirely objective."

"I could say the same to you, Miss Stone." Adam sent Ivy a pointed look, but she met his gaze evenly, her tough exterior impermeable.

Instead of replying, she returned her attention to Emily. "I'll do everything I can to keep an eye on Ryan and keep him from making any significant changes in the lounge, unless they're for the better. Unfortunately, part of this deal means I'm going to be traveling for a couple months."

"What?" Emily shook her head. "They're shipping you off? You do such a good job here."

"My father wants to give Ryan a shot at learning the ropes. I'm supposed to work on the bigger picture for Stone Corp, at least for a bit." Ivy didn't seem excited about the opportunity, and Adam got the feeling the Stone men were manipulating her along with the rest of them. "Try not to worry. I'm guessing Ryan will grow bored with the whole thing and turn the helm back over to me within a couple months."

"Just long enough for him to undo all of my hard work." Emily's face fell, but she straightened her shoulders. Adam wanted to punch Ryan for taking this source of pride away from her.

"I'd appreciate you keeping me posted about any further changes," Emily said. She turned and walked out.

Adam sent a last look at Ivy. The woman was staring blankly at Emily's retreating back. Her mouth opened as if she might say something else. Instead, she promptly shut it again and picked up her pen, already returning to work.

Adam caught up to Emily after they'd passed the secretary's desk, empty at this late hour, and reached the deserted hallway that led to the check-in area. He grabbed her arm, turning her to him. "Emily, this will all get sorted out—" *Shit.* Her eyes were glistening and she was biting her lip. "Don't cry." He started to tug her into his arms but she put her hands on his chest, keeping some distance between them.

"Don't," she bit out between gritted teeth. "I'm okay. Besides, you don't do emotion, remember?"

Ah, hell. He tried to pull her closer but her elbows locked, arms straightened in resistance.

"I mean it, Adam." She pressed her trembling lips together for a moment. "I'm not going to do this. Not with you."

"With who, then? Tanner's gone." He was

surprised and annoyed to find jealousy rear its ugly head. The rush of hot anger had him releasing her arms and stepping back. Which was just as well, since she looked as if he'd slapped her. And she thought he didn't *do emotion*? Everything was emotion when he was with her. That's why he kept his distance. Why couldn't she see that she was his one weakness?

"I can take care of myself. I don't need Tanner, or you. I'll deal with Ryan Stone my way." She squared her shoulders, steeling herself to face the world.

As she walked away, Adam hung back, giving her the space she seemed to need. She didn't want him to be her white knight. And he shouldn't want her to want him that way. Emily was right. It would be best if he kept his distance, because he didn't do emotion well—not when it came to her.

CHAPTER TEN

The next morning, Adam went over every item within Tanner's apartment again to see if he'd missed something that Ryan had been hoping to find when he'd stopped by. Adam had hoped the activity would stop the replay in his head of his last conversation with Emily. And the pain in her eyes.

She'd been hurt. She didn't want his help. He didn't want to get emotionally involved.

And yet, he couldn't stop thinking about her. Now that Ryan was her boss, she'd be caught in the middle, especially if Ryan realized she was a link to Tanner. Who had the ledger now? Tanner?

It was enough to make his head hurt.

Unfortunately, as he checked his email on his phone, his heart sank. He couldn't leave Emily alone any longer. Remington had forwarded him the preliminary DNA analysis on the bloody clothes and towel, and the blood types were a match for both Tanner and Blake. Another nail in the coffin, though the final DNA testing wouldn't be available for several weeks yet.

Tanner was running out of time. The moment he was found, he'd be under arrest, or possibly killed, if he'd crossed Ryan Stone. And Emily could now be linked to Tanner around the time of the murder.

He snatched up his keys and shoved his hat on his head. Though most of the rest of the world was already heading to work on a Tuesday morning, Emily didn't work banker's hours. He hoped to catch her at home.

A few minutes later, he stood at her door but she didn't answer his knock. He knocked again and the sound of movement came from within, along with a soft curse that curved his lips.

The door swung open and a scowling Emily greeted him. "Can I help you?"

"Yes, I think you can." *Especially if you know CPR.* Jesus, his heart had stopped. She was wearing a T-shirt with a rock band emblazoned on it and thin cotton sleep shorts—and, he was fairly certain, nothing underneath. He swallowed hard. "You always open the door like this?"

She glanced down, her eyes still bleary with sleep. "Nothing you haven't seen before."

But before, it hadn't been quite so curvy. And there had been so much standing in their way. That he was forgetting those barriers showed just how weak his defenses against her were.

"Besides, I don't have to get out of my PJs on my day off. I think that's written in the rulebook somewhere." She turned and shuffled back inside, nearly tripping over the calico that had followed him as he'd examined her place the other night. Thank goodness Emily wasn't a dog person, though the glare the cat was shooting him wasn't exactly inviting.

He closed the door behind him and followed Emily to the kitchen, trying not to admire her heart-shaped ass. Oblivious to his sudden discomfort, Emily fiddled with the coffeemaker, which gave him a moment to observe the bare length of legs that ended with toes painted a glittery ruby red.

He was hit with the sudden image of those long legs wrapped around his waist, her ankles locked together against the small of his back... He cleared his throat. "I was hoping to catch you before you left for work. Sorry I woke you on your day off." Especially when he spied the hint of dark circles beneath her eyes.

She shrugged. "I don't sleep much, anyway."

"Insomnia?" She'd frequently had it as a teen, and couldn't sleep more than a few hours a night. Except for those few times just before he'd left town, when the three of them—Emily, Tanner, and Adam—had gone camping in his backyard. She'd usually arrive unannounced, looking so alone that it had made his protective instincts surge to the forefront. She'd never talked about what made her feel that way, but in her sleep, she'd let down her guard and roll closer to him. She'd once admitted that she'd never slept better than when she'd been camping with them, and he'd wondered if it was because she fitted perfectly against his side. Those nights, Adam hadn't slept so well. But they'd been worth it to be close to her.

She seemed about to share something with him but shook her head instead and turned away.

"Were you replaying the scene with Ivy?" he finally asked. Or was she thinking about how he'd admitted he avoided emotional entanglements?

She hesitated a moment longer, then leaned back against the tiled counter, her hands gripping it as if for support. "I let Tanner down." Regret darkened her expression, as if she instantly wished she could recall the words. "And I'm about to again."

He held his breath, wondering if she was finally going to let him in. He didn't have to wait long. As if she needed to unburden her conscience, her next words came out in a fast spurt.

"I lied to you. I didn't just speak to Tanner the other night, I saw him. And it's been haunting me ever since."

Let *him* down? *What about me?*

Though her expression was one of tortured guilt, his heart lifted as she confessed what he'd already suspected. Perhaps they'd made some strides toward trust. "I know Tanner was here that morning." *I let myself into your apartment and looked at everything from your underwear to your trash.*

She met his gaze and frowned. "Really?"

"Why didn't you call me right away that night, the moment you saw him?"

"Tanner asked me not to." Her cheeks reddened. "And I was indisposed."

The air seemed trapped in his throat. She and Tanner had been close for so long that it was only natural things would go that course between a charming, good-looking man and a beautiful, spunky woman. Logic didn't prevent jealousy from slamming into his chest with the force of a Mack truck, finally releasing that air in a whoosh. "You and he...?"

Her eyes widened. "God, no. He's like a brother. I was in the tub when he decided to grace us with his presence."

"Us?" He nearly choked again.

She bent down to stroke her cat's back. "Me and Calliope."

She hadn't slept with Tanner. Judging by her shock at his assumption, the possibility had never even crossed her mind.

He shouldn't feel relief. He had no hold on her, no right to feel possessive. But that didn't stop the feelings that puffed up his chest. In a way, she'd been his since he'd met her, since the first time he'd held her in his arms, even if she'd been asleep and unaware of her vulnerability at the time. He'd always looked out for her, often from a distance, often without her knowing.

And she thought he didn't do emotion.

"For me, it'll always be you." She'd told him that the night she'd bared her soul.

And he'd thrown her words back in her face. *"You don't know what you want. Christ, I don't know what I want. But it isn't..."*

"Me?"

"Family." He shook his head. *"I've seen what family is. I don't want that. I'd rather be alone."*

He'd left the next day to pursue a future—alone. One that didn't include the burden of continually bailing out his dad, raising his brother, who was finally old enough to take responsibility for his own decisions, or taking on a wayward teenage girl who needed more than he could give.

What had Emily done after he'd left? How long had it taken her to move on? She had to have found some other man, loved some other man—real love, not the teen version she'd professed for him—in the years since he'd left. But her place didn't reveal signs of anyone's personality but hers. Bold colors seemed to bloom as the sun rose in the sky, filling the windows on the west side of her apartment. It was a tiny place, but somehow seemed bigger with signs of her brightness surrounding him. Still, he caught a sense of loneliness from the woman before him.

"What did Tanner want?" he asked.

"To warn me to be careful, and to say good-bye. I didn't call you right after because he left so quickly that it didn't matter anymore. You wouldn't have been able to stop him." She set a full mug of coffee in front of him and cupped her own, lifting it to her lips. His eyes tracked its progress.

Adam's gaze shifted to the open door to her bedroom, and then to the bathroom, which was also open. "So he hasn't come back?"

She pursed her lips, clearly irritated by his question. "No. Hasn't tried to reach me in any way, either, even after I told him we were both here to help him. You *are* here to help, right?" There was a world of emotion behind her question.

"Of course. Did he say where he was going?"

She sent him an incredulous look. "Why yes, he looked fine, Adam. So sweet of you to ask."

"Christ, woman. Does everything have to be an argument with you? You're the most prickly female." He sighed and backed down, since she was on the defensive now, her back straight and shoulders rigid. "I figured he was okay or you would have called me." He'd assumed she'd known nothing about the bloody clothing or she would have alerted him. His eyes narrowed. "You *would* have called me, right?"

She gave a casual, one-shouldered shrug. "I'd have thought about it. There was something that made me think he might not be okay, but I shrugged it off—until I heard what happened to Blake."

He muttered a curse. "What was it?"

"There was blood on Tanner's neck."

"Blood?" Across from her, Adam went totally still. "You said he looked okay."

"It was only a drop, and I don't think it was his." She gripped her coffee mug tightly, wishing this could be a normal morning off, just her and Calliope lounging around. Adam had told her that he didn't do emotion. She couldn't be around him without feeling something, so any further contact between them was doomed. But until he found Tanner, he seemed determined to dog her steps. "And then I heard about the murder."

"Talk to me, Em. I can help him." The tenderness in his tone surprised her, but she couldn't cave.

"You're a detective. One of *them*. You say you're here to help Tanner, but justice will always come first with you. It always did." It was one of the reasons she'd chosen to help Tanner rather than Adam that fateful night, and as a consequence, she'd lost her friendship with Adam.

"Justice is important, but it's not up to me. For what it's worth, I don't think Tanner's a killer."

She frowned. "You'd be the only one. Tanner had motive and opportunity. The police are looking for him. *You're* a member of that brotherhood." It was a conflict of interest if ever she saw one.

He gave her a guarded look. "I'm also Tanner's brother. I'd like to hear his side first."

"I'm afraid not even you can swoop in and be his hero this time."

He muttered another curse and tossed back a gulp of coffee as if it could burn away his frustration.

"What was that?" she asked, hiding a smile. She was getting to him—or Tanner's avoidance was—and she couldn't deny a tiny bubble of satisfaction.

"I think the murderer—possibly Ryan Stone—is setting Tanner up to take the fall for Blake's murder, and he'll come after you, too, if he knows Tanner was here after the murder. Tanner probably knows who the real killer is, and that killer might think he talked—to you."

Her bubble popped. "Nobody knows he came here except you."

"How do you know nobody followed him? What you and I believe about his innocence won't matter if he doesn't step forward and defend himself. And now he's dragged you into it."

"There's nothing to tie him to me. He was very careful about that. Even warned me to protect myself. He wouldn't put me in danger." Her words trailed off as he shook his head.

"Maybe not consciously. Tanner's car was recorded entering and leaving Blake's neighborhood around the time of the murder. I found bloody men's clothing—identical to what Tanner was wearing, and in his size—in your Dumpster, just out back. In the same garbage bag was a purple towel that matches those from your bathroom."

"What?" Her head swam and, not trusting her wobbly legs, she moved to a chair and sank into it. "You... I..." She sorted out her Molotov cocktail of feelings and went with anger. "You searched my trash?" Because he'd obviously expected to find something. Because he'd suspected all along that Tanner had come to her that night.

And then another thought hit her. "And my apartment? You were here?" How else would he have known what kind of towels hung in her bathroom?

He shrugged as if it was of no importance that he'd broken into her place. He sat down in the chair opposite her and leaned his elbows on his knees so he was meeting her gaze. "I had a feeling Tanner would have come to you for help. You're all he has."

If she was all Tanner had, and he'd turned away from her, where would he go now? "He has you."

"He doesn't believe in me like he does in you."

"Because he thinks you don't have faith in him." She stopped as Adam looked away. "You do have faith in him, right? Or were you just blowing smoke to get me to talk? Surely you don't believe the guy who took in any stray puppy or befriended a lonely kid is capable of murder."

Adam held her gaze for a long moment. "We're talking about the same guy who played shell games on the playground to get the other kids' lunch money and eagerly played wingman for our father whenever he needed a partner. Besides, whether or not he's capable of murder isn't the argument. He could have been framed. My guess is Ryan Stone wants to get rid of Tanner so he can have the ledger. And with the way you said he was celebrating last night, Tanner might already be—"

"No. Tanner has to be alive."

"The best way to stay that way is to hand the ledger over to the authorities. He's choosing money and power over what's right."

She shook her head. "I just can't imagine he'd choose the same path that destroyed our families." Her father had landed in prison. Adam's father had died a couple years ago, in debt and alone. Judging by Adam's grim expression, his thoughts were traveling a similar journey as hers.

She softened but resisted the urge to reach out and lay a supportive hand on his arm. Instead, she clutched her mug tighter. "Your father didn't have the support Tanner has. Tanner has friends and a big brother who's always looked out for him."

"Didn't have much choice." Because their mother had walked out on them and their father had never really been there for them. No wonder Adam didn't do emotion. He'd had to be the practical, responsible one from an early age. "But I could have done more. I could have tracked down Mom. Kept Dad out of the bars..."

Oh, Adam. "No, you couldn't have. You were ten years old. Tanner was eight. You did what you could."

He rubbed a hand across the back of his neck. "Let's get back to Tanner. Did he give you any idea where he would have gone, where he's staying? Did he have clean clothes? Did he look fed? Unharmed?"

"He looked okay except I could see he was worried—and except for the spot of blood he must have missed." When he'd cleaned up at her apartment, involving her in this mess, making her an unknowing accomplice. Anger threatened to rise up and she forced it down. There would be time to lose her cool when they found Tanner and cleared him of the charges. "I think he was truly shaken by whatever went down that night. I don't know how else to describe it. He's scared, Adam. And he said good-bye. I tried to make him stay. He'd been staying here off and on before—" She stopped as she realized she'd just revealed that she'd once again been holding out on Adam.

He sighed. "It's okay. I know your allegiance is to him, and I figured he had the help of friends to disappear so thoroughly. I just wish I knew how to gain your trust." His hand reached across the distance to clasp hers, squeezing lightly, just enough to send her pulse skittering, before he pulled his hand back to scrub it over his unshaven jaw. "Why won't he let me help?"

"He's stubborn, like someone else I know." She smiled when he met her eyes. "And he cares what you think about him."

That seemed to shock him. "Why the hell should that matter?"

"He's always idolized you. You're like a god to him. You changed your wild ways and found a way out, a respectable life."

It was good that Adam had rejected her and left

all those years ago. She'd probably have become a burden to him. And he wouldn't have complained because once Adam Wilde made a decision, he stuck by his choice.

She swallowed more caffeine to drown the self-pity that was rising to the surface. Work was usually her answer for loneliness. Too bad it was her day off. She could climb back into bed once Mister Tall, Dark, and Brooding left. Except then her thoughts would be full of him. Hell, her place already carried his scent.

"You could have that, too," Adam said. "You could make whatever life you chose."

"What makes you think I'm not living the life I've chosen?" Her heart cracked just a little bit that he thought she hadn't already been trying to walk the straight and narrow. He didn't even seem to have the faith to ask her about her life. "You think you always know what's best and that I'll always choose what's worst, but you don't know me. You assume things, but you don't really know my heart." Except her heart *had* made bad choices. It had once chosen Adam.

He gripped her shoulders and waited until she met his gaze. "I know you're loyal to Tanner, but I need you to tell me if he contacts you. For his sake."

His steady gaze made it very clear he wasn't letting his own emotions get tangled up in this. It made her want to rattle his cage, to push his buttons, to shake him until she discovered his limits. *Some* kind of reaction, to show she wasn't a nobody. To prove she could affect him.

But that meant she still cared about Adam Wilde.

Which made their fragile alliance just as dangerous to her as it was to him.

CHAPTER ELEVEN

"How can he just disappear?" Ryan wanted to throw something. Or punch a wall. Better yet, he wanted to shove his fist through Tanner's face—if only they could find him.

Bubba shrugged. "The guy's good. I've been asking everywhere you said, and I really think he must have skipped town."

"That takes money, and he's not touching his credit cards or bank account." But he'd left the Legacy chips at the murder scene, so he must have some source of income, or somebody supporting him.

"Maybe he hitched," Brenda said, then stretched and went to refill her mimosa glass from the room service cart he'd ordered for brunch, as if the conversation already bored her.

"Or maybe someone else killed him, or took him and is torturing him for information," Bubba suggested.

The thought that Tanner could be telling some stranger his secrets turned Ryan's belly cold. But the authorities would have been knocking on his door again if Tanner had talked to them. And Ryan's sources would have alerted them if something had happened on that front. So far, the LVPD had no clue what was going on under their noses.

For once, he was glad Tanner had a cunning mind. If he was evading Ryan, then there was a good chance he was hiding from everyone else, too. It gave Ryan time to find the weasel before he popped his head out of his hidey-hole again.

"I don't know what the big deal is." Brenda studied the champagne bubbles rising in her glass. "You have the ledger, right? So it's your word against Tanner's—*if* he even chooses to go to the police. You shouldn't have anything to worry about."

Ryan shook his head. How could she not understand? "It's the principle of the thing. If I don't make an example of him, I'll lose the respect of the rest of the members of the Club. *Actions speak louder than words.*" It was a Stone Rule.

"And if you put all your energy into chasing him and fail, those actions might send the wrong message." Brenda shrugged and ran a hand over his chest. "But I'm sure you know what you're doing, as always."

"I do." But she had a point. He turned to Bubba. "I'll give you a fifty-thousand-dollar bonus if you bring me Tanner by tomorrow."

Sometimes money spoke louder than words.

Adam had been surprised by Remington's request to meet for lunch at a sandwich shop near his FBI office.

"Did you hear something more about the clothing?" Adam asked, wondering what this meeting was about. They'd eaten half of their sandwiches and Remington hadn't brought up anything related to the investigation.

Remington grimaced. "Like I said, the DNA testing will take time. I've put a rush on it, though."

Adam wasn't sure he wanted those results, but they'd test for gunshot residue on the sleeves, too, and maybe, if they didn't find anything, it would clear his brother of the shooting. "I appreciate you not giving out Tanner's connection to the clothing."

"I was glad to—for now. The media's done enough to make this murder investigation a circus." Remington wiped off his fingers with a napkin and settled back in his chair. Maybe they'd finally get to the issue. "So Emily's coming clean with you now?"

"Seems that way." There were still secrets behind her eyes, but they'd made some progress. And then he'd fucked it all up by questioning her honesty and intentions.

"But no sign of the ledger?"

"I've searched everywhere I can think of, even at her place. It has to be with Tanner or Ryan."

"I came across some information this morning."

Adam waited, knowing by the man's expression that this wasn't going to be *good* information.

"It involves some things your brother was into back when he was young."

"Maybe you could be more specific? You must have pretty good connections if you got his sealed juvie records," Adam said, narrowing his gaze. What was Remington fishing for in Tanner's past?

"This was an incident just after juvie. He was eighteen."

Adam's stomach twisted. "He was cleared of all charges. Both him and our father."

"Still, the enormity of the attempt shows your brother's disregard for the law, and the lengths he would go to for money."

His irritation grew at the reminder of the past event that had shattered his family. "Not for money. He robbed the bank for my dad."

"And escaped federal charges." Remington shook his head. "Must have done some serious sweet-talking to beat the evidence they had on him."

"Must have."

"You think it was the Club that helped them get reduced sentences?"

Stunned, Adam leaned forward. "Why would you make that leap? I didn't even know the Club existed at the time."

"There's not even a small chance, given the circles your family ran in?"

Adam thought back. By that point in time, he'd withdrawn a bit from his brother and father. He'd been throwing his energy toward working hard, saving up and getting into college. "I suppose my father might have had dealings with them. He seemed to know every hustler, crook, and con within a thousand miles. But the bank heist was a different job than his usual small-time gigs." And he remembered thinking at the time that someone else must have spurred on the idea, maybe even have provided the information on the bank, hoping the Wilde family would do all the grunt work.

"So it's possible."

"I don't know how Dad got it in his head that he and an eighteen-year-old kid could take on a bank." And thoughts of that time inevitably brought back thoughts of Emily, and resurrected an old anger. She'd been the one to help Tanner drug him so that they'd be free to hit the bank that night. He'd known if Adam caught wind of the plan, he would have stopped Dad and him from even trying. "Why are you bringing this up now?"

Remington shrugged. "We never know what piece of information could spark an idea of where Tanner might be hiding, right? Maybe he has old friends he ran with back then who owe him? Or maybe he had a special hiding place where he'd stash the stuff he stole, and could have put the ledger there?"

"Maybe," Adam conceded. "But I don't know much about how he ran things, or who he would have trusted at the time." Except for Emily. She'd always been someone they could count on.

Emily hated seeing her father behind bars, but she was his only connection to the outside world, and to her mother. She sat at their usual table in the community room of the minimum-security prison. Luckily, Howie Moore's tax fraud charges were of the white collar variety and carried a light sentence that could be served among less hardened criminals.

"She's doing okay?" he asked. In the few years since her mother's accident, he seemed to have aged a decade. Emily scanned the lines on his face and frowned. "You still visit her often, right?"

"Mom's okay. No change. I see her every week." About as often as she visited her father. "What about you?"

"Absolutely fine." He smiled and the crow's feet deepened, yet somehow he seemed younger. It had to be the ever-present twinkle in his eye. The man was a natural-born charmer who could fool God into handing over the keys to the pearly gates. "I found out yesterday that I only have a few months left on my sentence because of good behavior."

"Good behavior? *You?*" she joked.

"Yep. I fooled them all." He winked. His teasing smile faded. "What's new with you? You seem to have a lot on your mind." One of the things that had made him a good con artist was his ability to read people.

"I've been thinking about Mom and the accident."

He frowned. "What brought that up?"

She shrugged. "Nothing special. Just thinking." And Adam Wilde had been a blast from the past.

"We'll probably never know who put out the hit. Could have been somebody your mother and I scammed. You've got to let it go, baby. Move on."

"I want to, but whoever cut her brakes, knowing she was going to drive to Sedona that day, almost killed her. What if they come back to finish the job?" The car had rolled off a steep embankment and she'd nearly died. If she'd been on a different part of the drive when they'd gone out, such as the scenic but winding road that cut through Oak Creek Canyon, she probably wouldn't have survived.

"It's been several years. And your mother's suffered enough. I don't think anyone will be coming after her."

"Maybe I need to know to put *my* mind at ease,

then."

"You still think the wreck is connected to the Redemption Club?" He shook his head. "I told you pursuing that was a waste of time. You've worked at Legacy for two years and it's yielded zilch." But he'd dropped his voice and looked around nervously. Obviously, he believed there was something to the power of the Club.

"Mom repeated the name several times in those first few days after the crash." It had been a couple years later when Emily moved to Vegas and was studying bartending when she learned that the Redemption Club actually existed. "There has to be some link to the Club. Maybe you guys accidentally conned a Club member and they took it out on you." Emily had another theory, but she wasn't willing to share it with anyone unless she had proof.

"If they're behind her accident, you don't want any piece of them. Just walk away. Find a job somewhere else. Besides, she was mumbling all kinds of things, slipping in and out of consciousness, memories jumbled..."

And then she'd slipped into a coma. When she'd woken several days later, she hadn't recalled the accident, or her ramblings, at all.

"Drop it, baby. No good will come of digging up old dirt."

It was the same argument they'd always had. Her father seemed eager to move ahead, to look toward the future, but she was afraid to let go of the past. It felt too much like giving up, and Emily Moore never gave up.

That night, Ryan was on cloud nine and reaching for a perfect ten. It was right there, within reach, especially since Bubba reported he might have a lead on Tanner. The guy really wanted that fifty-thousand-dollar bonus. The party writhed and pulsed around him, filling his suite with laughter and conversation. These were his people.

"No bartender this time?" Brenda asked with a pout. Perched on the arm of his living room chair, she slid a hand into the open V of his button-down shirt to stroke his chest.

"I think we can handle this ourselves." Besides, he no longer trusted Emily Moore to be his bartender at private events, let alone parties that included Redemption Club members. His sources had confirmed she was the bartender the night Tanner had been fleeced by Blake, and that Tanner had spent a brief time talking to her during a break. But his source had also reported that she'd served Tanner in Legacy Lounge later, when he'd been bitching and moaning. She'd pulled him aside, into the storeroom, to console him. And she had a key to the guy's apartment. Which meant she'd lied to Ryan, downplaying her connection to Tanner. Withholding information wasn't enough evidence to convict her of helping hide the man, but it was enough to make Ryan suspicious.

Someone changed the music to a song with a sultry voice and a slow, sexy beat, and suddenly the men and women around him were slow dancing. Actually, for some it was more like lap dancing. The Samson and Delilah duo who had been a smash hit in Legacy's nightly show had been invited, and they certainly knew how to move together. It was a turn-on, and he pulled Brenda into his lap.

The music suddenly shut off. Ryan ripped his mouth from Brenda's, prepared to chew someone out for the party foul. The words froze on his tongue as he connected with his father's frosty glare.

"Everyone out," Robert Stone shouted, the lines around his mouth white with barely suppressed anger.

The guests started to scramble and Brenda climbed off Ryan's lap. Clothing was righted and drinks and pills were plucked from tables as the suite emptied in less than sixty seconds. His father closed the door on

Brenda's sympathetic glance, which only fueled Ryan's irritation. He didn't need pity from anyone. His father was just being his usual asshole, domineering self. Ryan could handle him. He was better than his dad had ever been.

"You wanted to speak with me?" Ryan drawled, purposely resisting the urge to straighten his own clothing at his father's sweeping look of disgust. He refused to act ashamed of his behavior. He'd done nothing wrong.

"You must have a death wish," his father said. "Or a desire to live the rest of your good years in a prison cell. Partying when you're a prime suspect in a murder?" He eyed the remnants of drugs and paraphernalia on the table. "I'm not sure how you continue to afford these parties after I drastically reduced your monthly allowance."

"I saved up for a rainy day."

"Or you have an alternate source of income. Maybe you're still using the Club to make a little on the side?"

"If only I hadn't burned that ledger." Ryan was careful to maintain eye contact and not squirm. His father could detect deception a mile away.

"You sure you didn't make a copy of its contents first?" His father pulled an envelope from the inside of his suit and slapped it down on the coffee table.

Confusion now melded with anger and a sudden burst of anxiety. What was this all about? He couldn't dispel the image of a rabbit about to be ensnared in a trap—and Ryan was afraid he was the rabbit in this scenario.

Ryan reluctantly reached for the envelope, dreading whatever was inside. But if Tanner had sent a note to his dad about Ryan's blackmail, Ryan would probably be dead, or at the very least, evicted, so the contents couldn't be that bad. "Severance papers already?"

"Not yet, but if you don't finally do something right and resolve this situation, I'm done bailing you out forever. You'll be dead to me."

Situation? Ryan slid three photographs from the envelope. One showed the red leather cover of the ledger. In another, the ledger was open, showing his father's handwriting on one of the pages, to indicate the ledger's authenticity, he supposed. The third photograph showed a USB flash drive of some kind. *Fuck.* Now there were copies to hunt down, too? And Tanner had gone straight to the man who could hurt him the most. "I told you, I burned the ledger."

"So you said. But look closer." His tone was ominous.

Ryan took a closer look and saw the newspaper lying under the ledger in each photograph. Cold sweat broke out on his forehead. Prominently displayed was a headline from the *New York Times* and yesterday's date. But how? The ledger was in Ryan's safe in his bedroom closet. He'd put it there himself after returning from Blake's house.

"Read the back," his father ordered.

On the backside of the third photo, the one of the flash drive, was a handwritten, block-lettered message. *I have proof.*

He swallowed hard. Proof of what? Was it a digital copy of the ledger?

"Are you going to continue to lie to me?" His father stood so close his eyes could see every flinch of Ryan's expression, which was carefully neutral. "Because it's pretty fucking obvious the ledger is still intact. It's equally obvious someone outside of the family has it, and probably made at least one copy."

Ryan licked his dry lips. "Where'd you get this? They have to be fake." Unless someone had cracked the safe or digitally manipulated the photos to add in the *New York Times* image, these photos weren't possible.

"Someone sent it anonymously to my office. My *business* office, where Megan or Ivy could easily have opened it. It appears the pictures were ordered, printed and sent straight to me. I'm trying to dig up the name of the courier, and thus trace the person who ordered these, now. Unless you can tell me?" There was danger in his tone that told Ryan to tread carefully.

"There has to be a reason these were sent to you. What do they want?"

"They?"

"The general *they*." It had to be Tanner. He had to have manipulated old photos. There was no other explanation unless...

His gut churned as he recalled who'd verified the authenticity of the ledger Tanner had brought to the poker game. Blake. At the time, Ryan had no reason to believe his friend would stab him in the back, but shortly after accepting Blake's word that Tanner's stake in the game was legitimate, Blake had distracted him with the evidence Ryan had been blackmailing his father. A little sleight of hand from both Blake and Tanner, and Ryan could have easily been fooled with a lookalike. There was only one way to find out, but not while his father was here, in his face.

"There was no demand—*yet*," his father was saying. "Or maybe this person wants to create a rift in our family, so I'll get rid of you for them." A plausible scenario.

Ryan's calm façade was starting to crack under the pressure, and he straightened to firm his resolve. "I'm not betraying you," he lied.

"You were the last person, supposedly, to see the ledger, so who could do this?" He rapped his knuckles hard against one of the photos. Ryan imagined the fist plowing into his jaw and bit back a wince. "Give me a name." Doing so would be tantamount to Ryan admitting he'd lied to his father about everything.

When Ryan remained silent, his father replied with cold rage. "I know you didn't burn the ledger. You're a fucking idiot to think you can outplay me. If I weren't certain your mother had been too timid to cheat on me, I'd demand a paternity test. There's no way someone with my DNA would ever let something like this happen."

Ryan's defenses rose. Hadn't he run the entire Redemption Club for years behind the great Robert Stone's back? He'd handled things just fine. But he bit his tongue. Going head-to-head with dear daddy right now would only end badly for him.

"I can take care of this," Ryan said.

"You'd better. Get the ledger back and make this problem go away permanently, or I'll be forced to step in. Better yet, bring me proof that you have the ledger in your possession again. Friday night at the Henderson house. Bring the ledger and all copies to me there. I'll make sure we dispose of it this time. I don't care how you do it, what Redemption Club connections you have to use, or who you have to kill. Resolve this or I'll resolve it for you. And that may involve cutting my losses in a more drastic, permanent way."

Cut your losses. Another Stone Rule.

Ryan was suddenly certain that could include letting his own son go to prison, or maybe even killing him. His father valued his progeny, but if they became a liability, he'd dispose of them like any other threat— with brutal finality.

His father stalked out, and Brenda, who'd been waiting in the hall outside the suite, rushed in the moment the coast was clear. "Are you okay?" she asked. "He looked mad."

Ryan pushed past her and hurried to his bedroom closet, his fingers shaking as he punched the code into the safe.

He pulled the ledger from within, his hands shaking as he flipped it to a random page. The entries looked legit from a distance, but upon closer inspection they were a bunch of nonsensical words strung together. He'd been the victim of a bait and switch and he hadn't even known it.

"Fuck!" His roar filled the closet.

"What is it, baby?" Brenda's concerned voice came from behind him.

"Get out!" He whirled on her and she shrank back. He didn't need anyone to witness his failure. He stalked toward her, raising the ledger, and she turned on her heel and ran. He barely noticed.

This had to be Tanner's work. He was the only one who wouldn't immediately turn the ledger over to the police, but also wouldn't make an immediate monetary demand. After all, this wasn't about money. Tanner hadn't touched the pile of Legacy poker chips left at Blake's. The ledger was Tanner's life insurance policy, and his means of making Ryan's life hell.

He paced his bedroom, threw the ledger against the wall, and shoved his hands through his hair. This couldn't be happening. Tanner couldn't win. Failure wasn't an option.

He ran through his list of Stone Rules in his mind until he found one that he thought might work. *When in doubt, make a plan of action.*

A plan of action was what he needed. Step One would be calling Bubba and canceling the hit he'd put out on Tanner. He needed Tanner alive so the asshole could lead Ryan to the ledger. The real ledger.

But Tanner had proven an expert at hiding. Ryan had to assume that Bubba's so-called lead wasn't going to pan out. To lure Tanner out into the open, Ryan would have to hit him where it hurt the most. Restricting his ability to join in poker games around town clearly wasn't enough. But his family, his friends... A threat in that department had been enough to lure him to Blake's poker game. It would work again.

And then Step Two. Kill Tanner.

CHAPTER TWELVE

Wednesday had been another busy workday and Emily's nerves were shot by midnight. She felt eyes on her again, but this time she knew who they belonged to—unfortunately, not Adam, who'd been absent since their conversation yesterday morning. No, this time it was her new *boss* who was watching her.

Ryan had spent most of the next day in Legacy Lounge, asking her questions about the daily routine, chatting with customers, reviewing the entertainers slated to fill the stage for the rest of July. Thankfully, he hadn't brought up her friendship with Tanner. But Ryan's presence was more than him marking his new territory. Something dark lurked behind his gaze as it followed her. By evening, she was rattled. Like a predator, he watched and waited as she interacted with everyone around her. Was he hoping Tanner would show up and she would be the reason Ryan caught him?

Just before the lounge closed, Ryan disappeared, but Emily's peace of mind was short-lived. He returned to the lounge at closing time, carrying a briefcase, when she was alone. Her skin prickled with apprehension as he approached the bar.

"I was right," he said. "You do work long hours."

She wiped down the bar in front of him, wondering what he was after this time. "And I'm anxious to get home."

His gaze slowly traveled from her hand, up to her chest, where it lingered for a moment before his eyes met hers. "You have someone to meet there?"

"My personal life isn't any of your business." She

sensed he was trying to make her uncomfortable, to throw her off her game, but she wouldn't give him the satisfaction. "What did you need, Mr. Stone?"

"So formal." He smiled. "I'd prefer a more friendly relationship. It seems you have an admirable sense of loyalty to your friends. In fact, I'd like to buy you a drink."

"We're closed." Her gaze flicked to the briefcase as he set it on the bar and slid onto a stool.

"Good. Then you have no reason to refuse to join me. Champagne." He tried a charming grin.

She turned away to get one glass and a bottle from the mini fridge, then set the glass in front of him and popped the cork. Her stomach twisted as if it were effervescing, too. "Celebrating again?"

"Yes. And yet again, my good news involves you— not so indirectly this time."

She scowled. "Why don't you just come out and say whatever it is you're hinting at?"

"First, join me," he gestured with his drink. "I hate celebrating alone."

"Are you going to pay me for my time?"

"I didn't know you were that kind of woman."

Ignoring his teasing tone, she narrowed her eyes on him. "I'm tired, and I don't have any patience left."

"Why do you work here?"

Her heart leapt to her throat. Did he know she wanted to get her hands on the ledger just as much as he did? "I love the atmosphere, and it suits my skills."

"You're sure there's not another reason?" He clicked open the briefcase, reluctantly drawing her gaze to its contents. "You're sure it's not about finding this?" He removed the crimson book and laid it on the bar.

Her heart dropped back down from her throat to her stomach, but she forced herself not to react with so much as a flicker of fear or recognition. Tristan had described the book in great detail when she'd visited him in prison. Inside lay the answer to all of her questions.

Ignoring her dry mouth, she smirked and forced herself to meet Ryan's gaze. "Let me guess. You want me to go old school and start keeping the lounge's books on paper?"

He chuckled. "No. But you're right. It is a ledger." The listing of criminal acts and records of who owed what. Her fingers itched to reach out and yank the book from him. "It's for a secret society called the Redemption Club. You still don't recognize it? Your poker face is admirable. I believe you've heard of the Club, at least, and that you know how it works. After all, you know some of the people listed in here." He tapped his finger on the book.

Her gaze held his. "I may have heard of it."

"Then we can finally be open with each other."

"What is it you think I'm hiding?"

"Not a what, a who. Life's a game, and there are winners and losers. You have to decide which you're going to be, which friend you're going to be loyal to." He leaned closer. "I can be a very good friend, or your worst enemy."

Tanner. He had to be the "who" Ryan was looking for. And he wanted her to betray him. "Are you inviting me to be a part of the Club, to be on your side?"

"All you have to do is give up Tanner's location and the Club will owe you a great debt, perhaps the greatest. I'd pay you whatever you can dream up. Surely a savvy businesswoman such as you understands the power in that."

Just a peek, just a few minutes with the book, and she'd have what she so desperately wanted. Her heart was pounding so hard she could barely think. The answer she sought, the reason she'd pursued a job at Legacy two years ago, was in that book. How had Ryan taken it from Tanner? She didn't want to contemplate what might have happened to her friend.

She swallowed her fear and kept her game face in place. "You have what you need to run the Club. Why go after Tanner?"

"He crossed me. I have reason to believe he took some very sensitive information."

"So you want to make an example of him?" A chill ran down her spine, but she was hopeful that Tanner was away from here, safe.

Ryan twirled the stem of his champagne glass. "I'll enjoy making him suffer, especially after what he did to Blake." She didn't believe his lies for a second. "And then I'll enjoy getting to know his hot, blonde friend." His smug grin turned to a leer as his eyes took a slow crawl down her body.

She resisted the urge to cover herself. Or punch him. "My loyalty's not for sale. That's not negotiable."

He took a sip of alcohol. "Good thing for you I like my women willing. And I don't have to pay for them, though I do reward good behavior and excellent performance. We could both leave this relationship happy." He toasted her with his glass.

"There is no relationship. And I won't help you find Tanner. I don't need any *favors* from the Club. If you'll excuse me, I really do have to close up." She pushed away from the bar and stalked toward the storeroom, cursing her shaky legs. She'd nearly made it to the desk drawer, where she kept a pistol—just in case—when she felt him behind her. He reached out and grabbed her arm, spinning her around.

"I didn't dismiss you." Ryan's grin was gone, his eyes hard. "And I'm the boss now, remember."

How could she forget?

She took one step back, but her shoulder blades came up against a shelving unit full of supplies. There was no retreat that way. Her hands came up to press against his chest. Ryan didn't take the hint and give her space. Instead, he leaned closer and grinned. But something dark lurked in his green eyes. His breath carried the sharp, sugary note of fermented grapes.

The door was only a few feet away, but he blocked that exit. The pistol was too far in the other direction to get to it before he got to her. If she had to, she could knee him in the crotch, shove him to the floor, and make a run for it. It would give her some kind of satisfaction to do so. But she wouldn't get away for long and his revenge would be ten times worse.

He placed a hand beside her on the shelf, at the height of her breast, bracing his weight as he leaned in. He stroked a fingertip along her phoenix tattoo, exposed by her tank top.

She tightened her muscles against the shudder of fear and revulsion that tried to roll through her. "I was telling the truth. I haven't seen Tanner. I have no idea where he is."

"I suppose you understand the consequences of lying to the boss." Ryan's tone was teasing, but his expression had hardened.

"Why would I lie? And why would you go after Tanner? He's the killer, right, and you two are supposedly friends?" She forced a laugh. "Then again, it seems like your friends keep getting either murdered or involved in murder. First Finn, and then Blake. Now Tanner. And those are only the people I know about. If word gets around that dealing with the Redemption Club is tantamount to a death sentence, how long do you suppose you'll continue to have people coming to you, willing to trade illegal favors?"

Ryan's smile completely disappeared. "Be careful what you're insinuating. You may be beautiful, but you're replaceable. Maybe you just need to be put in your place." He leaned forward, the gleam in his eyes changing, their hard edge morphing to liquid heat.

She turned her cheek as he attempted to place a kiss on her lips. "I don't have a *place*."

He chuckled as he pulled back, then traced a fingertip along her jaw. "They're all easy when presented with the right deal."

"Deal?"

"Bring me Tanner and all copies of the ledger he has, and I'll make sure your parents are safe."

Her heart stopped for two seconds, and then beat

harder and louder against her ribcage. "My parents?"

"It's a tough choice, I suppose. Do you protect the people who raised you or the man you've been friends with for years? The smart move would be to cooperate with me. If a favor from the Club isn't enough payment for Tanner's location, how about the promise that I won't take out your disloyalty on your parents?"

"You couldn't..." But she was afraid he easily could. Her heart lodged in her throat and it was suddenly hard to swallow, or find words. But Ryan didn't seem to expect any. He'd threaten her parents? Karen Moore would be easy pickings. Since the brain trauma she suffered in the car accident a few years ago, she didn't even know what year it was. Howie Moore was locked in prison, but that wouldn't stop a man with Ryan's resources from getting to him, if he wanted to.

"They're getting older, and everyone knows that accidents happen, especially in an assisted living facility or prison. Institutions have such trouble getting good help these days." He smirked. "I see that finally got the wheels turning. I hope you make the right choice for all concerned. Friday night I'm hosting a little get-together at my father's estate south of town. Tanner needs to be there, with any Redemption Club property he's stolen from me. You bring me what I want, and you're free."

Her throat burned, knowing what would likely happen to Tanner after she was *free.* "No."

He ducked down to look her in the eye. "So you're choosing Tanner over your parents."

"Or I could go to the police with what I know—"

He grinned. "Try it. The Club has members everywhere. And then you'll find yourself dead, and I'll find Tanner some other way. He'll die, and for kicks I'll go after your parents, too. And then Adam Wilde." He sent her a wicked smile. "I know how much you care about him. It didn't take my private investigator too long to find out how close you are to the Wilde brothers. Seeing Detective Adam Wilde again after so many years must have been like a reunion. So sweet." But his tone indicated he thought it was anything but sweet. And Ryan obviously knew Adam worked for the Phoenix Police Department, too. If he perceived Adam as a direct threat, what would Ryan do? He'd take out both brothers. "Two days. Party starts at nine o'clock." He grabbed her chin and forced her eyes to meet his. "But I'll give you until midnight. See how generous I can be?"

Her stomach twisted but she held herself together as he walked away. The moment he disappeared from view, she slumped against the shelves.

Two days. How the hell was she supposed to save everyone she loved from ruin, and take down Ryan Stone, in two days?

Of the two men who could assist her, one was missing and the other was sworn to obey the law. She couldn't ask either to help her.

Dismayed to realize that her entire body was shaking, she took several deep, steadying breaths before pulling out her phone and dialing the memory center.

"I'm calling regarding Karen Moore," she said when the person on the line offered their standard greeting. "This will sound silly, probably, but I had a bad feeling. I wanted to check on her."

The night nurse on the other end offered to peek in on her mother, who was probably—*hopefully*—sleeping at this hour, safe in her bed. "She's sleeping," the nurse replied a minute later. "She looks to be fine. Did you need me to wake her?"

Emily released a breath. "No, thank you. I appreciate your help." After hanging up, she snatched her purse from the desk. Just in case, she'd drive by the center and check for herself. As for her father, she'd call the prison and check on him tomorrow—or maybe there was one thing she could do for him tonight.

There was another man she'd been avoiding, though he'd been leaving her messages for days. She hated to ask him a favor, but if she didn't return his call soon, he'd start to doubt her and then things would get worse anyway. So, before leaving the storeroom, she made another call.

"It's Emily," she said when his voicemail kicked on. "I may have something for you. But first, I need you to ensure my father's safety. Please check with your contacts in the prison and call me back ASAP."

When she emerged from the storeroom, the lounge was dark and empty, the ledger and briefcase, of course, gone. She walked the long hall to the service entrance that led to the employee parking lot. Thankfully, she saw no one, not even Ryan.

She drove through the parking garage reserved for guests and high-level employees, reassured when she caught sight of Ryan's bright yellow Ferrari. So, he hadn't immediately left to hurt her parents. Of course, he wouldn't do his own dirty work. He'd have someone from the Club do it for him.

Ryan had the ledger, but Tanner still had something to hold over him. The mythical memory card, maybe? And how much of this did Adam know?

Two days. She had precious little time to find Tanner and figure this out.

She breathed a little easier as her adrenaline rush faded and her thoughts cleared. Ryan wouldn't go after her parents tonight. He'd wait to see if she came through for him. Hurting her now would only make her mad, and he'd lose his bargaining chips.

Ryan had said no police, but Adam wasn't here in an official capacity, and going to Tanner's place wouldn't look suspicious. She was in over her head this time and could use Adam's expertise. Even Tanner had encouraged her to go to Adam if she ever needed help— as long as she kept her head and didn't let her heart take over.

Before she could talk herself out of it, she steered in the direction of Tanner's apartment—and Adam. She didn't care if he regretted their kiss, or seeing her again. Ryan was gunning for her family because of Adam's family. She'd become a target because of them. In a way, he owed her.

She knocked hard on Tanner's door. A moment later, Adam answered in shorts and nothing else. Her gaze traveled from his bare feet, over his muscled legs and the unbuttoned board shorts he'd obviously just pulled on, paused a moment to admire his bare chest and broad shoulders, and ended at his dark, ruffled hair. He'd obviously been sleeping while her life was falling apart.

"You okay?" he asked, his voice sleep-roughened. On her initial inspection, she'd skipped his expression, not wanting to see annoyance or rejection, but when she finally met his gaze, there was only concern. She was ashamed by the sudden, overwhelming need to fold herself into his arms, to feel his heart beat against her ear. She attempted to rally her defenses against her desires. They made her weak.

"Talk to me," he commanded, but she had no words. She was tired—of fighting all the unseen forces around her, of fighting to do the right thing, of fighting the temptation that was Adam Wilde. "Em?"

He dipped down to look into her averted eyes. With a muffled curse, he pulled her inside and closed the door, then gave one additional light tug on her hand. That was all the invitation she needed. She walked into him, and his arms came around her to hold her close. Her nose pressed against his throat, she inhaled his scent, letting it infuse her with calm.

CHAPTER THIRTEEN

Emily could lock her emotions down tight when she wanted to, and she wasn't into sharing with him. Adam got that. He really did. He was the all-time champion at keeping his feelings sealed away, so he wasn't one to judge. In fact, he'd done some strengthening of his defenses after the kiss they'd shared, telling himself he'd been an idiot to let things go that far. He was here to help Tanner, then return to his well-ordered life.

But, standing at his door, she'd looked as scattered as dandelion fuzz in the breeze. Her shaken composure struck him at his core, and he could see she needed someone.

No, scratch that. Emily Moore never needed anyone.

But Adam needed to be there for her. So he held her tight against him, trying to ignore how she melted into him, feeling like the missing piece of a puzzle he'd struggled to solve all his life.

"You look like you could use a hit of the strong stuff," Adam said when, a moment later, she stiffened and pulled away. No tears, but there was a hint of fear in her eyes. That couldn't be because of him. Anger, frustration, or even passion, yes. But never fear. Someone else had scared her, and he'd get her to spill the story one way or another.

"I vowed I'd never drink to bury my feelings," she said.

Because that's what their fathers had done.

His chest tightened. "I know for a fact you don't bury your feelings. You let yourself experience every single one of them." He moved to Tanner's liquor cupboard and brought down the bottle he'd spied earlier, setting it on the bar along with two shot glasses. "And I'll share another fun fact about Emily Moore: she likes to break the rules."

"You *want* me to break the rules?" she asked, incredulousness infusing her words. "You're the squarest person I know."

He winced because it was true.

She was watching him with distrust in her narrowed eyes. "Or maybe you just want to break *me*."

He'd never do that. He respected her, and her strength, too much. "I don't think anything or anybody could break you." Her eyes moistened and she glanced away. He'd like to know what or who was scaring her. And maybe five minutes alone in a locked room with the man who was causing her distress.

When she looked back at him, her expression was normal again, her shields up. She rounded the counter and took the bottle, studying it a moment before setting it down with a nod of approval.

"How about I play bartender for a while and you can unload your troubles? At least for however long I have until you close me out again." He arched a brow in challenge.

"You're the one who runs away."

"I'm not going anywhere tonight." He filled the two shot glasses and nudged one toward her. "What happened?"

She swallowed her shot before answering. "My new *boss* cornered me in the storeroom." The way she shuddered told him just how unpleasant that had been.

It didn't take a degree in criminal science or five years of experience with the Phoenix Police Department to figure out what might have gone down. A testosterone spike urged him to find Ryan and kick his ass, even as his training told him to be patient and gather every drop of information. "What did he want?"

"He says I'm supposed to bring Tanner to some

kind of party Friday night, along with whatever Club-related things he took from Ryan." Her worried eyes met his. "I think Tanner has a copy of the ledger. He's vulnerable." And so was she. Gone was the tough-girl exterior, the ramrod don't-touch posture he was accustomed to. He could punch Ryan Stone out cold for that alone.

"And if you don't follow through?"

"He said he'd destroy me and everyone I care about—my parents, Tanner, even you."

She was admitting she cared about him? His heart began a tap dance in his chest and he wanted nothing more than to pull her against him again and kiss her until all her worries were gone. Unfortunately, there were very real dangers to face first. "I don't want you alone with him anymore." He heard the steel and possessiveness in his voice, and forced himself to take a calming breath.

She scoffed. "He's now manager of the place where I spend nearly eighty hours each week."

"So spend less time there."

She rolled her eyes. Clearly, she wasn't willing to give up her job at Legacy.

"Or let me protect you."

"Not necessary. I can take care of myself. Anyway, I wanted to pass along that information about Ryan gunning for Tanner, and maybe you, too, and now I have." She was saying good-bye, but she made no move to depart.

"You can't leave me alone with this bottle." He sent her a grin. "Do you remember the first time we got drunk together?"

"Of course I remember." She picked up the shot glass he'd just refilled for her and held it up to the light. The liquid inside was the exact color of her eyes. "You and Tanner stole a bottle of your daddy's whiskey and we met at our special place." Her lips curved at the memory and something shifted in his chest, resettling more comfortably for the first time in years.

The abandoned shed at the back of the Wilde property had been a kind of fort for the Wilde boys, until Adam had outgrown kid games. It had also been the place the trio had spent many nights camping—which had been their excuse to avoid trouble with their parents. That particular night, when Tanner turned eighteen and their father honored the occasion by taking a swing at him, Adam had still been reckless enough to take Tanner out back with some liquid celebration of manhood.

Emily had shown up, wanting to wish her friend a happy birthday, frowned and fussed over Tanner's black eye and Adam's bruised cheek, and they'd all shared a couple hours of unfettered, inebriated escape.

He could still remember watching Emily do a shot. Sitting cross-legged on the blanket they'd put over the shed's dirty floorboards, she'd tipped her head to drink, and her blonde hair slid down her back until it reached her butt. In the light of the camping lantern, the sight of her had been more intoxicating than any drug, the triumph burning in her eyes more thrilling than stealing the alcohol from his father.

"You want me to go after Ryan?" Adam held her startled gaze as he angled his head back to take his shot, and then set the glass on the counter. "Better yet, let me have him arrested for threatening you."

She looked toward the door and grimaced as if Ryan stood there. "No. He told me no cops or he'd..." Adam's stomach tightened around the liquor, but she left off the end of her sentence. "Besides, he's my boss now. We can't upset him."

"Bullshit. *You* can't upset him. *I* can do whatever I want." And ever since Ryan Stone had waltzed through Tanner's apartment as if he were in control, Adam had wanted to ram a fist into the man's perfect nose. He was tired of dancing around the fact that Ryan Stone was very likely involved in the Redemption Club and Blake Toll's murder, no matter what his high-priced lawyers said.

Had Emily known before tonight what Ryan was truly capable of—or at least what Adam suspected he was capable of? After all, Tanner had warned her to stay away from the man. Of course, now that Ryan was the boss at her precious bar, it was unlikely she'd walk away.

One corner of her mouth tipped up. "I'd pay good money to see someone kick Ryan Stone's butt from here to the moon, or throw him into a hole to rot, but it wouldn't solve anything. And it might make things worse for Tanner, and for you. Wouldn't you get in trouble with the Phoenix PD for assaulting a suspect?"

"I already am."

"What?"

"In trouble for roughing up a suspect in my custody."

Her eyes went wide with disbelief, which made him feel better. Though he hadn't seen her in years, she knew how much following the rules meant to him. "They're crazy."

"That's for the courts to decide. I've been on desk duty for a few weeks, waiting for a court date."

Her hand touched his. "I'm sorry, Adam. I know you'd never do something like that."

"No, but for you? I might." She still had no clue what he'd do for her. One reason he'd left was because the intensity of his feelings for her had scared him. He reached out and tipped her chin up until she met his gaze. "It would be worth punching him in the face if it would make you smile."

"Now who's breaking the rules?" she asked softly, her gaze moving to his mouth.

Against his better judgment, but unable to stop himself, his thumb stroked the side of her jaw.

Heat flared in her eyes and her voice was velvet-soft when she spoke. "Careful. Touching me might lead to other things—things that will make you run away again. Besides, it's not like you really want me, not for more than a kiss."

She was so, so wrong. With her, he'd reignited an inner spark he'd been missing for a very long time. The same fire had always lit Emily from the inside, warming and charming anyone it touched. She was better now at hiding it, adept at suppressing the inner spirit when necessary, but he wanted to coax it to life again. Damned if he knew why. He'd be returning to Phoenix soon, hopefully to settle the charges against him for good, so he could make an even bigger difference in the world.

He dropped his hand, but he couldn't let her think she wasn't desirable—nor could he admit that he desired her. That would lead to pain when he left. "First of all, any man would be crazy not to want you."

She grunted, sending him a look that said she'd already questioned his sanity. "And second?"

"Second, I didn't run away eight years ago to hurt you. It was to protect you. Anything between you and me would very likely have consumed both of us." He was pretty sure, like an addict, he would never get his fill of her if he got a little taste. Addictions ran in his family, so he couldn't even allow himself a sample. Hell, kissing her had been enough to short-circuit his thoughts.

"So you're sticking with the story that walking out of my life after I'd professed my love for you was for my own good."

"It was." They'd both been too young for the kind of fierce feelings that Emily thought she had for him. Truth be told, he'd wanted her, so badly he was tempted to drop all his plans of being the first in his family to finish college, of pursuing a normal future, and run toward the unknown with her.

That she could make him give up all his dreams and hard work with a few words about love had scared the shit out of him. He couldn't rescue anyone else. Hell, at twenty years old, he'd still been getting his own head on straight. He couldn't be helping a wayward teen with her problems. Raising his brother had been difficult enough.

Besides, she'd been so sure of her feelings, so certain she loved him, and he hadn't believed her. She'd barely known him when he hadn't known himself, so how the hell could she love him?

Afraid. She'd called him afraid when he'd said nobody could be that sure about love. She'd said he didn't know what he was talking about because he'd never had someone love him like she'd loved him.

The only thing they'd agreed on was that getting out of Kingman, Arizona, and moving on was the best course.

"But that doesn't mean I don't regret the way I left," he said. Tanner had barely spoken to him afterward, and their relationship had never been the same. "I should have handled things better, let you down easier. But we're not going down that path again."

Emily's laugh was raspy with bitterness. He'd gotten to her emotions again. Fucked with her head. Not that he meant to. He never meant to. He only meant to use her to find Tanner, assuage his guilt or whatever else had driven him to come back to Vegas, and leave again. To his credit, he'd been pretty clear about his intentions. It was her own damn fault she'd let him close.

"Are you so afraid of taking a risk that you can't even take a minor one?" she asked.

He looked to the ceiling as if praying for patience or guidance or, hell, maybe a weapon. Emily would rather he shoot her dead now than drag her through what they'd been through eight years ago, again.

He tossed back another shot and heaved a sigh of pity that made her heart sink. She was thankful there was a breakfast bar between them, both to hold her steady and to keep her from facing a manslaughter charge.

His expression was pained, and when he spoke, it was as if to a child. "You wouldn't have been a minor risk."

She couldn't respond to that, as she wasn't sure what he was getting at.

"You and I were never going to work," he said, more gently. "You have to see that now, right?"

"Yeah, it's crystal clear." But only because he hadn't taken her seriously, hadn't given her any credit, hadn't... *Damn.* He hadn't loved her enough to trust her to make them work. "It's a moot point anyway, so let's find Tanner and take down Ryan Stone so you and I can get back to our normal, *separate* lives."

But it wasn't relief that darkened his eyes, it was regret and a touch of anger. "You know where Tanner is, don't you? You've been holding out on me."

"No." If she had, she sure as hell wouldn't be here with Adam, strolling down memory lane. "But he said he'd leave me evidence that would support his case."

His body language indicated he'd gone on high alert. "What evidence?"

"Some kind of memory card."

He shook his head in disbelief, the anger building. "And I'm just now hearing about this?"

"Don't get your boxers in a twist. I haven't found anything yet. I'm not even sure if he left it at all."

"The storeroom?"

"I'm sure he was there, but I didn't find anything he might have left." Except the symbol warning her of danger. And Tanner had been right on the money about that. "But I can help. I can work on the inside."

"No."

"I can get closer to Ryan, make him trust me. Maybe even make a deal with the Redemption Club."

"No," he repeated, more fiercely. "That won't help. It'll only hurt you. No matter what Ryan demanded of you, I want you to stay away from this."

She tried not to be hurt by his dismissal. *He doesn't know what you're capable of.* For that, she supposed she should be grateful. "Let me get this straight. You won't let me help, even though Ryan has demanded that I assist him? Even though it would help Tanner—your *brother*?"

He slid a hand through his hair in a gesture of frustration that was a Wilde family trait. "I don't want you hurt, and Tanner wouldn't either."

She laughed harshly. "You don't think I've learned to protect myself over the years? I've developed a skin so tough a rhino's horn couldn't penetrate it." *Most of the time.* "I certainly know how to protect myself against disappointment." *Unless it's dished out by you.* But she was going to work on it. She'd resist falling in love with Adam Wilde again if it killed her, and this show of bravado would hopefully insulate her until the real thing showed up. Besides, it was good to test one's fortress now and then for weaknesses.

"Any idea what was on this memory card Tanner was supposed to get to you?" He froze and looked at her. "Could it be a photo or digital version of the ledger?"

"Maybe. Once I get a look at it, I'll let you know."

"No."

"Your favorite word." When it came to her, anyway.

Shutters fell over his eyes. "All I need from you is Tanner's whereabouts. I'll take care of him and Ryan."

All I need from you. That about summed it up. He didn't need her, and she had to try like hell not to need him. Again.

Swallowing another dose of disappointment, she nodded. "I understand."

"Em." His voice held a note of warning, and he waited until she could control her anger enough to look up and meet his gaze. "The less you're involved, the better, especially if Ryan's watching you and threatening your family."

Why did he always get to decide what was best?

CHAPTER FOURTEEN

The next morning, the lack of sleep, the remnants of the whiskey, visions of the blood-red ledger and the torn three of spades, the argument with Adam, and her unpleasant encounter with Ryan continued to rattle around in Emily's head, lending fierceness to her pounding headache. It didn't help that Adam didn't trust her enough to let her help. Or that, when she left her apartment, he was sitting in his car in her parking lot. He'd followed her home last night, but it appeared he'd never returned to Tanner's apartment. In fact, it looked as if he'd slept in his car. To guard her, or to make sure she didn't make a move without his knowledge?

She ignored him, headed straight for her car and, after making a quick stop for provisions, drove to Oasis Memory Care Center. Adam followed every step of the way, but didn't approach her. It was already ninety degrees at eight-thirty, so she sauntered over to his car window and waited until he rolled it down.

"You may as well come inside," she said.

He eyed the building, which looked a bit like a two-story apartment complex. "You here on business?"

"Family business. Mom lives here. She was in a car accident a few years after you left. She hasn't been the same since, and never will be."

He studied her, empathy in his eyes. "I'm sorry. I hadn't heard."

"Anyway, if you want to come in, she probably wouldn't mind seeing you. That is, if she's coherent today, and able to recognize us."

He joined her as she walked to the entrance. "She doesn't recognize you?"

"On her bad days." She forced a smile. "But she has her good days, too. The brain damage from the accident created memory loss, and some symptoms similar to dementia."

He gestured to the two pastry boxes she carried. "Whatever you have in there smells delicious." His stomach growled on cue, and she sent him a wry glance.

"My mother's favorite." She'd brought iced cinnamon rolls, both because Karen Moore seemed to associate them with the ones they'd often made and it sometimes helped her remember her daughter, and because Emily could use the comfort food. "If you behave, you might get one."

"I always behave." But he shot her a wicked grin that, despite the heat, sent a shiver of delight across her skin.

At the reception area, she stopped to sign in.

"She'll be so happy to see you," the receptionist said, and then took an appreciative sniff from the box Emily gave her for the staff. "I think her previous visitor made her anxious."

"Previous visitor?" Emily was the only one who visited her mother. She glanced at the sign-in sheet and saw the name. *John Stone.* That was as vague as John Smith, but just enough to tell her exactly who had been here, or had at least sent an emissary. He'd signed out fifteen minutes ago after a brief visit.

Beside her, Adam swore under his breath and looked toward the parking lot, but they hadn't seen a yellow sports car, or anyone else suspicious. Ryan was probably long gone.

"He seemed so nice when he signed in," the nurse said. "But I guess your mother's having a rough day. She refused to eat anything. Having her daughter and her favorite breakfast should set her back on a good path."

"I don't want anyone else visiting her unless I've personally approved them," Emily said. "This guy actually might be out to harm her."

"Oh no," the nurse said, her hand going to her chest as she caught the fierceness in Emily's tone. "We'll certainly watch more carefully now that we're aware. We don't want anything to upset her."

As Emily walked with Adam to her mother's first-floor room, she explained. "Mom's mental condition is unpredictable. We never know what could set off her anxiety, or how that anxiety will manifest itself."

"So you never know what you're walking into." Adam's tone, and the look he sent her, was sympathetic. There were often days her mother didn't recognize Emily. On those occasions, Karen Moore could easily become angry and accuse her of anything from intruding on her privacy to being there to rob her.

As they passed the community area, Emily said good morning to some of the residents, who were about to begin their morning stretch class. Several stopped her and asked if she'd be working on puzzles or games, or teaching a computer lesson.

"You seem to know a lot of people here," Adam commented.

Suddenly uncomfortable with him seeing this other side of her life, she shrugged. "I'm here once or twice a week."

She felt his gaze on her as she knocked on the open door of the studio apartment before walking inside. Finding her mother curled up in an armchair, she set the box of rolls down on the coffee table and squatted to look into her eyes. "Hello, Mom. It's me, Emily."

"Emmy." Recognition lit her mother's eyes and Emily relaxed a little at the familiar nickname. Maybe her mother wasn't as bad off as the receptionist thought. Her mother's gaze shifted to the man behind her and her smile bloomed. "Frank! You came. I forgave you a long time ago, you know."

Emily's gaze met Adam's, but he looked just as surprised as her by Karen Moore's statement. Since the accident, however, her mother's thoughts and words were known to be muddled or downright wrong. She could be thinking of some falling out from twenty years ago.

Adam stepped forward. "No, ma'am. I'm Adam Wilde. But people say I inherited his good looks." He winked.

Her mother looked confused for a moment, clearly struggling with memories and Adam's placement among them. "Yes, I remember now. You're Frank's oldest boy." She frowned. "But you're so big."

Adam grinned. "I grew up. I was in town visiting Emily and thought I'd stop by to say hello."

"We brought cinnamon rolls," Emily said. "Shall I make some coffee and we can have breakfast together?" As she spoke, she stroked a soothing hand down her mother's shoulder. The arm had been mangled in the car wreck, but her mother had recovered most of the function in the rest of her body. A slight limp and the memory issues were the only other indication that she'd survived a near-death experience.

At her mother's nod, Emily went to the adjacent kitchenette to put on a pot of coffee. She kept up a stream of chatter about nonessential things that had happened over the past week—leaving out all the stuff about murder and death threats. She wanted to ask about the early-morning visitor but didn't want her mother to withdraw or become anxious again.

Adam was surprisingly helpful, keeping the conversation neutral and easygoing. Reluctantly, she admired his skill at making her mother smile. Then again, it was possible her mother thought he was his father, who'd been a longtime friend. Frank and her father had run many cons together throughout Arizona and Vegas. On occasion, her mother had helped.

After the coffee was poured and the rolls were

warmed and put on plates, Emily took a seat in the living room with her mother and watched as the last of the icy fear slowly thawed away. Emily didn't dare ask about *John Stone* now that her mother was relaxed and happy again.

But as their visit wound down, her mother surprised her by bringing him up. "A man stopped by."

"Oh?" Emily licked icing off her thumb and sent Adam a glance. He was watching her mother carefully.

"He said I should tell you to do what you need to do, or he'd be back."

"And you don't want him to come back?" Emily asked. Her mother shook her head vigorously and rubbed one hand along her other wrist. "Did he hurt you?"

"A little." Her mother looked alarmed. "I wasn't supposed to say that."

Emily was going to find a gun and shoot a bullet through Ryan's thick skull. Or remove his favorite part, from his pants. Or better yet, find the proof she needed to help Adam put him in a stinking prison cell for the rest of his measly, pathetic life. The man had preyed on the wrong family. Emily vowed then and there to teach him a lesson.

"You're safe now," she told her mother. "The staff has been told not to let him visit again."

"And I'll make sure to speak to the supervisor to reinforce that," Adam added.

She turned the talk toward happier times until her mother's anxiety had lifted again and she finished her cinnamon roll.

On the way out, Emily was so angry her strides outpaced Adam's. "I'll kill him," she muttered.

"Ryan?" Adam shook his head. "Prison would be a more painful punishment for a man like him. Speaking of prison, have you checked on your dad?"

"I have a call in to someone who can look after him." She pulled out her phone, but didn't see a return call from her contact yet.

Adam sent her a curious glance, but didn't ask questions. "I can have someone check, too."

She nodded, unable to refuse the offer when it meant additional security for her father. Though he'd made some serious mistakes, he was her father and she loved him. "I'd appreciate that."

They'd reached their cars and Adam reached out to stop her. "Thank you for letting me come with you today. I'm sorry I assumed..."

"That I was selfish and didn't care who got hurt?" She shook her head, subduing a sudden rise in anger at the same time. "Maybe now you'll stop judging me on who I was and the things I did when I was eighteen. A lot's happened in eight years."

He watched her for a long moment. "I'm sorry the past got in our way. I'm working on leaving it behind."

"And yet you won't trust me to help you investigate." He didn't reply and she sighed. "It's okay. I have my own irons in the fire."

His gaze darkened and the shutters that had been open between them since talking to her mother slammed closed again over his emotions. "Keeping secrets again?"

"A girl's gotta have a few." Her teasing fell flat, hitting the pavement and turning to dust between them. "I have some things to take care of at Legacy."

"I'm going to escort you to work—to make sure you get there safely," he clarified when she opened her mouth to argue. "I want to make sure Ryan's occupied with things other than terrorizing you." She actually appreciated that courtesy. "And then I'll leave you alone. But I don't want you to leave work without calling me. I'll follow you home tonight."

It was a relief to have someone watching her back, but also to have some time without Adam hovering. She needed time to plan. She had to find Tanner and the evidence he was supposed to leave for her. And she had to appear to give Ryan what he wanted without actually handing him her friend on a silver platter. And if Adam was insistent on pursuing Ryan, he, too, would have to be protected.

As she drove to Legacy, she decided she'd tackle the problem as she if she were planning any con—by gathering as much information as possible.

Emily was setting up to open for lunch when Mason, *sans* Samson costume, sank onto a barstool in faded jeans and a soft T-shirt. Thursdays were his day off from performing his act, as it was comedy night in the theater.

"Weird to see you out of uniform," she said.

He eyed her. "You duck me for weeks, and now you want to make small talk. What's going on?"

"This is the last time. I can't do this anymore."

He arched a brow. "Tend bar?"

She narrowed her gaze on him. "Can't *inform* anymore," she said in a lower voice. "Ryan's watching me like a pit boss and now innocent people might get hurt."

His eyes softened. "Your father. Though I'm not sure he's so innocent."

"In this case, he is. Is he okay? Were you able to connect with your prison contacts?"

"He's okay for now." Mason met her gaze.

She didn't like the concern she read there. "But?"

"He was in a fight in the prison yard this morning. Nobody will say how it started, or who's responsible. His attacker hit fast and hard, landed a few good punches, and then walked away."

She sank down on a barstool beside him, her legs suddenly weak. "He's getting treatment?"

"Yes. The wounds were superficial, bruises and scrapes. I've talked to the guards."

"Thank you for watching out for him."

He touched her fingers where they lay on her thigh. "And what about you?"

"I'm fine." And if she died in this mess, nobody

would miss her. Maybe her mother, a little bit, but she was trapped in the past most of the time. Karen Moore's memories seemed to stop in her mid-thirties most days, but she was happy and pain-free in those years. "Ryan wants me to bring him Tanner, and something related to the Redemption Club that Tanner apparently has."

"The ledger?" Mason asked.

"Ryan has that. He laid it right here on this counter."

"So close." Mason's jaw tightened. He'd been after the ledger for months now, too. "Maybe it's time I question him, do a search of his suite? The LVPD has been pussyfooting around him. They started to build a case against him as a suspect in Blake Toll's murder. But then another of the poker players, some guy who calls himself Bubba, came forward to say Ryan left with him, and couldn't have killed Toll. If you have anything on him that can get me a warrant, that info would be much appreciated."

"For an egotistical asshole, he's surprisingly cautious. He hasn't given me anything to implicate him, but I know he's guilty of a lot of bad things." She could feel it in her bones. "Besides, a warrant would put my parents in further danger. I'm not supposed to go to the cops."

"And yet you are."

She looked up to find him watching her, a baffled grin on his face, his head cocked to the side as if she were an inexplicable puzzle. "What?" she asked.

"I saw your detective walk you in earlier, so I waited in the casino area until he left."

Her detective. "You know about Adam?"

"I know he's not just the old friend you introduced me to. Sweetheart, in case you've forgotten, I make it my business to know about anyone who comes in and out of Legacy. It's my job." Mason Gray was DEA, undercover as a dancer at Legacy in order to gather information about the Redemption Club's drug activities. And because she had an inside track on the comings and goings at Legacy, Emily was his confidential informant.

Two years ago, she'd taken the bartending job to keep an eye on the Club when she'd gotten wind that they'd been involved in her mother's car accident. She was determined to find answers, which was why she needed the ledger. Until last night, she'd never seen the book, had started to wonder if it was a mythical object. Now that she knew it existed, she was aching to get a look at its contents. Whoever had ordered the accident, and why, was written inside.

As part of the deal she made with the District Attorney, she assisted with the DEA's investigation and, in return, her father would receive perks in prison that would make his life easier, as well as a reduced sentence.

"I thought having Detective Wilde here would be a benefit in this situation," Mason said. "He has the skills and the personal knowledge to help find his brother and the ledger. But I hadn't accounted for how he felt about you."

"He doesn't feel any way about me."

"Then you're blind. Anyway, it seems you've got several men vying for your attention lately. Just trying to figure out what it is about you that draws us," he teased.

She grimaced. "When you figure it out, let me know so I can stop doing it. By the way, what was that kiss on the cheek about the other day, marking your territory?" She batted her lashes playfully and dropped her voice to a sultry tone while leaning toward him. "You know I'm your CI, baby, and nobody else's."

His laugh was low, deep and sexy, another weapon in his arsenal. Too bad he didn't do anything for her hormones. "Yeah, right. The way Adam was looking at you... Let's just say he wants you for himself."

Yeah, Adam wanted her—to be *his* CI. Too bad there was only so much of Emily Moore to go around.

Lately, she was feeling spread a little too thin. "He's old news."

"Seems like he wants to be new news." Mason was looking into the mirror behind the bar, which reflected the archway that led into the rotunda and showed Adam heading their way. Mason's hand tightened on hers, where it still rested against her thigh. "Better tell me what you know, fast."

"Tanner communicated with me the morning of Blake's murder. I think he's left me some kind of memory card or flash drive, but I don't know what's on it. Haven't found it yet."

"You find it, you come to me immediately."

"And, in exchange, you protect my father. But I meant what I said. This is the last time. I can't do this, can't be put in the middle anymore."

After ensuring Emily arrived at the lounge safely, and bribing a hotel maid to check that Ryan was still in his suite and not out causing trouble, Adam had spent the past hour meeting with Remington and arranging for a guard to watch over Karen Moore at Oasis. Since he was in the area, he'd stopped by to let Emily know she had one less worry on her plate when he spied her with Mason. He watched from the arch that led to the lounge, seeing what they wanted him to see—a couple having a close, intimate conversation. Mason was even holding her hand, touching her thigh. But Adam wasn't buying what they were selling, the romantic image.

He'd seen Emily when she professed to love someone—to love *him*—and this wasn't it. Her posture and expression were all wrong. The memory of her declaration of love all those years ago, and what it had felt and looked like, was the only thing that kept him sane as he observed them.

Strangely, Mason's eyes were on his surroundings, watching Adam's approach, not on his love interest. Almost as if...

Adam's next step was hesitant, but he quickly corrected the stutter. The idea that had taken root grew into a fully formed hypothesis. Mason wasn't what he appeared to be. Observant, but seemingly casual gaze. Twitchy fingers ready to draw at a moment's notice, though he appeared unarmed. A layer of natural distrust beneath the welcoming smile.

If Adam were a betting man, he'd bet his last dollar that Mason Gray was law enforcement.

Emily watched Adam approach, but couldn't read his thoughts from his body language. His stride was fluid, his posture relaxed, yet he seemed to be in a state of readiness, his attention everywhere. It made her feel safe knowing he was on guard—until he came closer, and the power of his gaze pinned her like a wrestler. She quivered at the image of his body covering hers, pressing her into the mat...

"Am I interrupting?" His dark voice vibrated through her as if her nerves were a tuning fork—attuned only to him.

"Actually, you are." She turned her hand over on her thigh so she could interlace her fingers with Mason's. "Mason and I were just catching up and making plans. *He* wants to include me in his future." Beside her, Mason's lips curved in a slow smile.

Adam didn't seem upset by her implication that she was moving on, leaving him in her rearview. Instead, he turned to Mason and stuck out a hand for a handshake, forcing Mason to release hers to accept the friendly gesture. "I believe we met briefly the other night."

"The old family friend," Mason said, humor lighting his hazel eyes.

"That's me. And I always look out for my friends, even when they don't want me to."

Emily stood and moved behind the bar. "Did you need a drink, Adam? We don't open for a little while yet, but I can put something together *for an old friend.*"

"I don't need anything," he said, his gaze curious as it moved between Emily and Mason, probably picking up on things she didn't want him to see—like the fact that she wasn't interested in dating the other man.

"Boy, that's the truth," she muttered.

"What was that?" Adam claimed a bar stool one away from Mason, following the guy code that apparently dictated the appropriate amount of personal space between two territorial males.

She shrugged. "You don't need anybody. Easier to avoid those annoying emotional entanglements. Easier to walk away." She set a shot of whiskey in front of him.

"Not needing someone isn't the same as not wanting them." The heat in his eyes said he wanted her.

"And wanting them is a waste of time if you're not willing to take a risk to claim them." She held his gaze, aware that Mason was watching their exchange with great interest and a hint of a smile.

Adam shot the whiskey and grabbed her hand, tugging her to the end of the bar with him. "Your *old friend* needs to talk to you before you officially open. You'll excuse us for a moment, won't you, Mason?"

Would anyone rescue her if Adam throttled her? Because that's what it appeared he wanted to do. He pulled her along with him until they were in the storeroom with the door closed.

"Your caveman act won't intimidate Mason," she snapped.

"I don't give a damn about him." He turned to face her. A muscle in his jaw worked and his nostrils flared. She'd never seen him this angry, except when he'd found out the real reason she'd helped drug and cuff him to her bed for twenty-four hours. That day, he'd not only washed his hands of her, but of his own brother.

"Tell me you weren't just involving Mason in this mess with Ryan," he demanded.

Her eyes flicked to the strong column of his throat, unable to hold his angry gaze. "Okay. I'm not involving Mason in this mess."

He cursed and paced away a few steps, then returned to her. "How does lying come so easy to you?"

She stiffened. "You need to leave."

"He's undercover law enforcement, isn't he?"

Shock traveled through her limbs, all the way to her toes. "How could you know that?"

"He's got all the signs—watchful posture, shows up when it's timely, as if he got a tip to do so, and he's not all over you, though he pretends to like you. And you have that guarded look when you're with him."

She scoffed. "You have it all figured out, don't you?"

"Not all of it. Explain why he's hanging around."

"I don't have to tell you anything."

He crossed his arms. "Explain," he repeated. "No avoiding the topic. I'm tired of fucking around, Em. It's impossible to know who to trust here. What does he want from you—information on Tanner?"

Her own irritation rallied her. "You really think I would betray Tanner that way?"

His eyes clouded with confusion, battling with accusation. "I didn't, but people change. And you admitted you and Tanner haven't talked much in recent weeks."

"Friends can disagree. Why does everything have to be so black and white with you?"

"Shades of gray complicate things."

He hated complications. She knew that. Just as she knew she was one of those complications, and therefore he hated having to deal with her. "I didn't betray Tanner, or you. I mentioned the memory card, but that doesn't actually exist for the moment, does it? But it was enough information that Mason will continue to make sure my father is well looked after."

"You shouldn't trust him."

"I have to. He's been in my life a whole heck of a lot more than you have until recently."

"So your judgment's clouded."

She threw her arms up in the air. "Why do you never want to listen to my point of view?" She was tired of him ignoring her, dismissing her, treating her like a kid who didn't know what she wanted. What she needed. She jabbed a finger into his chest, meeting hard steel. "Trust requires a degree of openness. You need a lesson in opening up."

"And I suppose you're going to teach me?" His eyes glinted with steel and... curiosity. "You're probably the only one who can."

She was shocked to find herself suddenly pulled up against him. It wasn't cool steel, but hot passion she sensed from him. Her breath caught in her throat as his lips came closer to hers. She couldn't form a sentence or generate a coherent thought to save her life, though she was dimly aware that she should push him away, because it just might save her heart. When he'd left, his rejection had dampened her spirit. It had taken her a long time to heal those wounds. And in a matter of days, he'd broken through all her barriers again.

"You're too stubborn to teach." She wished her words had come out more forceful. Instead, they'd been a breathy whisper. Her breasts brushed against him as she struggled to maintain a regular breathing pattern.

His eyes sparked at the unspoken challenge behind her statement. "I was always more of a hands-on learner." One of his hands came up to sweep the hair from her cheek and cup the back of her head as if he'd hold her in place while he devoured her. Her body quivered at the gesture that was both commanding and tender. And entirely controlling.

Hell, no. If she was taking this insane leap, it was going to be on her terms, damn it.

CHAPTER FIFTEEN

"Up to your old tricks, I see." Emily stepped away from him.

Adam resisted the urge to reach for her again, though every cell in his body seemed drawn to her like magnets to the opposing pole. "Tricks?"

"Just like last time. Seducing me into confessing all, only to throw my feelings back at me when I've let my guard down. And then you leave. Well, I'm rejecting you first."

"This, just now, wasn't about getting away." Hell, he'd wanted to crawl beneath her skin.

"When hasn't it been about getting away? Leaving your brother, your life. *Me*."

He didn't know what to say, mostly because she was right. He'd left. And he'd do it again if he had to make the same choice. *Wouldn't he?* "I didn't want to leave."

"Bullshit." Heat and repressed anger flashed in her eyes. "You were looking for something better. Someone good. Someone *good enough* for you."

He stalked a few steps away. He couldn't stand that close to her while he thought about that time, and about the kiss they'd almost shared. About the ones they had shared. He was caught between two dimensions, and yet the end result was the same damn thing. Hopeless.

She didn't trust him now, and he couldn't blame her. They were both holding back, keeping secrets, but there was one thing he could give her—the truth about that time.

"Okay," he said. "So I wanted to leave, but not because of you."

"You're trying to tell me that my *declaration of love*," she practically spat the words, as if disgusted with herself, "had nothing to do with you leaving? It was just a coincidence that the day after I asked you to take me with you, you were packed up and gone without even a word of good-bye?"

He cursed. "You don't know what it was like for me, the pressure I was under."

She scoffed. "I believe I have some idea."

"From Tanner?" He crossed the storeroom to stand in front of her. "He only had part of the picture. Everything was falling apart around us. Our dad had lost all of our family savings and was drinking away what little else he made running his scams. He'd been depressed and withdrawn, lost in his own world like usual, but it had recently worsened. Tanner was finally eighteen but seemed determined, no matter what I said, despite all of my warnings about him being an adult who could face hard prison time, to pursue the same path our father did."

"So you bailed."

"I went away to finish college, to establish a career where I could set a good example and send more money home."

Her eyes flicked over his features, searching out the truth. He could see she needed someone to understand her, to be there for her.

You're not that man, his conscience whispered. But he suddenly wanted to be the guy Emily needed, the guy she could count on.

He shoved a hand through his hair, searching for the words to break through both of their defenses. "Tanner and I were arguing nightly." Sometimes about Tanner's friendship with Emily, and how he was continually leading her into trouble. "I couldn't stick around and watch him implode. The next arrest wasn't going to result in juvie."

Finally, something in her eyes softened. "I talked to him about that, too."

"Something worked. Whether me leaving took the pressure off, or you got him straightened out. That doesn't mean he won't go down for murder unless I—we—help him."

"Agreed. So we have to get past what happened between us that night so we can work together. We need complete honesty."

"And you can't bring outsiders into this. The Club has eyes and ears everywhere."

She leaned forward, mimicking his stance. "I'm not dating Mason. And yes, he's law enforcement. I'm his CI, and I have been for a couple months."

The thought of Emily passing along information to the authorities nearly made his jaw drop. "What agency?"

"DEA. A couple deals have gone down here at the bar, so he was watching the place. For the past few months, I let him know whenever something suspicious is going on."

"There's a rumor going around that there's a mole in the LVPD." Remington was FBI. How many other agencies were watching, waiting to take down Redemption Club? Was Ryan even aware how many eyes were on him? "If Mason Gray is an officer of the law, that still doesn't make him safe."

"One could say the same of you," she said.

He stepped closer. "You can trust me."

"I'd like to." She bit her lip. "But I'm pretty sure you're keeping things from me."

"One could say the same of you," he said, throwing her own words back at her, because damn it, she was right. There was something he'd withheld for years, one of the reasons he'd stayed away from her so long, and it weighed heavily on him. But he couldn't crush her with the truth.

Thursday turned out to be busier than anticipated, so Emily didn't have a lot of time to think about her conversation with Adam. After the last customer had left, she went into the storeroom and sank down onto the cot, just for a minute. Just one moment when she could forget her situation. But the small quarters reminded her of Adam.

He was always with her now, if not in body then in spirit. And he was expecting her to call him for an escort home. Part of her didn't want to see him again, knowing the risks she was taking with her heart. Another part of her very much wanted to see him.

It didn't matter, as she still had one more stop to make this evening—a special delivery that she hoped would give her valuable information in exchange. But on her way out, something caught her eye. A new graphite marking was sketched beneath the others. Tanner had been here again? Or he had sent someone to leave the message for her. She dropped to a crouch so fast her head swam. It was a tiny drawing of a house, and her initials. That had to mean there was something at her home.

With renewed energy, she pushed to her feet. After quickly closing up the lounge, she picked up the bribe she'd be delivering from the bar, made a quick visit to a restroom off the main rotunda and then walked past the Legacy offices and down a hall to a room she'd visited several times before, usually on a rare slow night when she was looking for some entertainment in the form of people watching.

Grinning up at the camera mounted high on the wall, she raised her offering and knocked on the door. A lock clicked open and she entered the room.

"Hey, Sal," she said. "How's life treating you?" She handed him the to-go cup of steaming fresh coffee she'd brought to butter him up.

The head of security looked up from the screen he'd been monitoring and his dark face split into a wide grin. He accepted the cup with a grunt of gratitude. "Can't complain, especially right now." He lifted the cup, and took the top off to take a big, appreciative sniff. "Just the way I like it." With a healthy splash of Bailey's Irish cream.

She perched on an empty chair, her eyes taking in everything. The large computer monitor on his desk showed a split-screen shot of numerous active cameras, rotating through various views of everything from the parking lot to the casino floor.

"What's up?" Sal asked. "You suspect another employee of doing long pours for bigger tips or something?"

"No, nothing like that. Just hadn't been here in a while and never had a chance to thank you for catching that thief."

Sal grunted. "I suppose he got fired?"

"Yeah. Thanks to your help, we saved a lot of money." They fell into a comfortable silence for a few minutes.

"Looking forward to the preseason games?" she asked, biding her time. "I heard the Raiders got a wide receiver in the draft." Just as it was important to know your marks while running a con, it paid to discover the details that made a difference in her coworkers' lives. For instance, Sal worked the late-night security shift on Thursdays and loved football. In particular, he loved the Raiders.

Sal launched into his optimistic predictions for the upcoming season—until he received a call about smoke in one of the public bathrooms. "I have to run, doll. But stay and people watch, if you want." He eyed his coffee with a longing look, and then took off, walkie-talkie in hand.

The door closed behind him and she leapt into action, slipping into his chair and inserting a USB drive into the computer. For a second, she thought about the evidence Tanner was supposed to leave for her, possibly on a drive just like this, but she quickly focused on her task. It wouldn't take Sal long to deal with the innocuous but effective slow-burning fire Emily had lit in a bathroom sink, but she only needed five minutes. With a few keystrokes, she found the files from the morning of Blake Toll's murder and downloaded them.

It was clear Adam wanted her help, but also wanted to keep her on the fringes of whatever investigation he was working. He thought it would keep her safe, but she was already in danger. Tanner had told her as much. She'd help Tanner on her own, get the ledger to the authorities, and Adam would be satisfied. Once Tanner was out of trouble, he'd leave, and then, when Ryan was behind bars and Ivy was back in charge, Emily would go back to her normal life. At least, that was the plan.

It was nearly two o'clock by the time she left through the service door and crossed the immense parking lot to her car. Her hand automatically went to the drive in the front pocket of her jeans, and her thoughts were on putting on a pot of coffee at home and viewing the footage. There had to be something of value that would help her find Tanner, and the SD card he'd left for her somewhere.

Vegas never slept, so the staff at Legacy worked in shifts. The employee parking lot was still half-full. As she frowned up at a broken streetlight near her car, she could hear Adam's chastising voice in her head. She was supposed to have called him for an escort home. Maybe she should have, but hopefully he was out finding things that could lead them to Tanner, and nobody had followed her thus far. Besides, she had less than twenty-four hours left until Ryan's deadline, and both she and Adam needed to be out looking for Tanner.

The heat had abated somewhat at this late hour, but it was still warm and her skin tingled as if the atmosphere were hugging her close. She could see her car several yards ahead when she heard running footsteps coming her way. She spun to face a dark blur, just before she heard Adam shout her name from somewhere in the distance. His voice registered alarm a moment before a body slammed into her, knocking her to the pavement between two cars. She kicked and elbowed as the man's body covered hers, and landed a few blows, if his pained grunts were any indication. The man's hand was going for her pocket when he looked over his shoulder and, with a muffled curse, suddenly leapt off of her. He took off just as Adam appeared in the space between the cars. He ducked when a gunshot sounded and the window of the car above them shattered.

"Close your eyes," Adam shouted, dropping quickly and laying his body over hers like a protective blanket as glass rained down on them. The tiny shards bounced and slid down her face and into her hair. Little pinpricks of pain along her bare arms told her she'd received a few nicks—but no bullet holes. The night grew quiet, and still Adam pinned her, shifting to redistribute some of his weight.

"What the fuck?" he muttered, but it was a whisper, and without heat. More of his weight lifted, and his hands brushed against her hair and cheeks. The tinkling of glass hitting the pavement told her he'd knocked more shards loose. "Emily? You can open your eyes now, baby. Are you hurt?" His hands continued to brush glass from her, but also traversed her limbs. "Did you get hit?"

"I'm not hit." She blinked a few times and looked up at him. His features were in shadow, the light of the parking lamp behind him blinding. Apparently, only the light near her car was out. Blood was slowly seeping from a small cut at his temple. She raised a hand to touch it but stopped, not wanting to infect it. "Are you okay?" He'd probably just saved her life, but judging by his expression, his typical confidence was shaken.

He leaned his forehead to hers and released a

breath. "Yes, as long as you are."

That seemed an odd statement, but they'd both just had the wind knocked out of them. She flexed some muscle groups, testing to make sure she hadn't broken or sprained anything. Thankfully, she was in one piece and could move all of her limbs.

Feeling her movement, he rolled into a crouch so the rest of his weight was off of her. "Let's get out of here. He might come back." The meaning of his words hit her and she struggled to sit up, feeling a bit battered as Adam got to his feet and scanned the parking area.

"Come back? You think he was aiming for me, in particular?" There was random violence in Vegas, after all, and maybe someone had been trying to mug her, hoping she'd just cashed in at the casino.

"I'm certainly not going to gamble with your life." He retrieved his hat where it had fallen a few feet away. A security vehicle turned down the lane and jerked to a stop in front of them.

"You okay?" the guard asked. "What happened?"

Adam quickly explained, giving a physical description of the perpetrator's height and build, though he couldn't provide much more. "I'm taking her home," he told the guard. "You should have her contact info on file. She's shaken up and the guy might still be around here somewhere."

The guard was radioing the information in—probably to Sal, she thought absently—as he drove away. She didn't object when Adam wrapped an arm around her and led her to his car. She didn't have the energy left to fight, and that scared her the most.

CHAPTER SIXTEEN

Adam observed Emily from the corner of his eye as he drove her home. She'd insisted on going to her own place, and he'd insisted on staying with her to keep her safe.

She was quiet, not wanting to talk about the incident. He thought about calling Remington, or even Mason, but he had to be smart. Who could he trust, and how much information did he trust them with? Besides, nobody would take care of Emily as well as he could.

Once they got inside her apartment, he pulled her closer so he could look into her eyes. She didn't appear to have a concussion, or any remnants of shock or anxiety, but he'd still like to murder the guy for the way he'd knocked her to the pavement and roughed her up.

"Are you okay?" he asked.

She nodded. "For the tenth time, I'll be okay."

He studied her another long moment before acknowledging that, in fact, she was looking calm—too calm.

"You can stay if you want," she said.

His body stiffened against the arousal her invitation evoked, even as his brain reminded him it wasn't *that* kind of invitation. Even now, he could see the fear lurking beneath the heat in her gaze.

Then again, an excellent way to dispel the fear after a close brush with death was to reaffirm life. When he thought about how he'd almost lost her, about how he'd been a few too many steps away to stop the man from tackling her, his heart had pumped harder than ever, his skin had gone cold with dread. He could have lost her forever tonight.

And he couldn't fool himself that it was because part of him felt responsible for her, since he'd been gone for so many years. Or that he was soothing his guilt because he'd broken her heart and he owed her a debt he had yet to repay.

No, this was different. He had feelings for Emily, and always had. He wasn't sure what to do with them, but they sure as hell weren't going away.

He tugged her gently toward the bathroom. "Let's wash those cuts."

She hopped up on the counter as he rummaged through her medicine cabinet and found the items he wanted. His hand shifted to her cheek to lightly trace a couple of the nicks and scrapes. Rage filled him again, and he choked it down.

She sucked in a breath at the sudden, intimate contact and smiled softly. "It's just a few scrapes— thanks to someone taking the brunt of the glass shower."

"Sorry about landing on you like that. I didn't hurt you too much, did I?"

"Hello? Again"—she leaned away and gestured to her body—"living, breathing. All of the rest are just superficial wounds." Her eyes scanned his face as he dabbed at the cuts with a wet washcloth. "I'm not sure if I thanked you. For being there tonight." As if to repay his medical ministrations, her fingers went to the nape of his neck and began to rub in soothing circles.

With his lowered defenses, her name was a whisper on his lips, escaping his usual censorship. Her hands skimmed upward until her fingernails dragged lightly across his scalp and her hands fisted in the hair that brushed his collar. She grinned impishly and the need to kiss her exploded inside him. "Just checking for glass," she said.

He suddenly needed to taste her again like he

needed his next breath. He closed the gap and let himself just feel. She seemed just as eager as him to lose herself in the kiss, using her new-found leverage to pull him to her mouth, tilting her mouth and parting her lips, making him regret what he'd denied both of them for so long. Damn, the woman could press all his buttons like no other person ever had. The good buttons, and the ones that drove him nuts.

Her hands continued to lightly massage his scalp as her lips claimed his. The twin sensations were just enough to make him tingle from head to toe. She was a woman who knew what she wanted, knew how to get it, and was loyal along the way—to the people she let past her barriers. That she was letting him in was oddly seductive.

His mouth slanted against hers as he backed her into the living room and followed her down onto the couch. His fingertips grazed her jean-clad outer thigh and stroked upward to her hip. Her soft moan told him she liked the contact, so he left his hand there as he focused on the wonderful feeling of her mouth under his. When she arched into him, he had to resist the urge to strip her naked, tug her to the edge of the counter and bury himself in her.

There were so many areas where they were on opposing sides, but in this one area, they'd always been in perfect alignment. Even if she had no clue that she had this power over his body, over his senses, and always had.

Eight years ago

Coming here had been a mistake. He had a bad feeling about it, especially when nobody answered his knock. He went back to his car and got his baseball bat from the trunk, just in case. His apprehension turned to worry when he turned the knob and found the front door of Emily's house unlocked.

She'd been alone here for the past week while her

parents worked a con on a cruise. He'd done what he could to check in on her, but in recent months, he'd started to pull back. He would be leaving for college soon, and the more time he spent with Emily, the less he wanted to leave to pursue his dreams.

"She sounded scared and I can't get there right now. Go to her as soon as you can."

Tanner's voicemail from ten minutes ago had indicated Emily was in some kind of trouble and they needed his help. So where was she? It hadn't taken him that long to respond.

He thought he heard whispers coming from the dining room. It almost sounded like arguing. With a shush, the whispers disappeared. He took another step, and another, his hands gripping the baseball bat so hard the handle had become slippery with sweat, until he rounded the corner.

"Surprise!" Emily popped up from behind the kitchen counter that divided the dining room from the cooking area. Tanner popped up beside her with a wide grin.

"What the hell?" It wasn't his birthday. Adam lowered his bat and surveyed the food and dollar-store decorations. The cake said *Congratulations*.

"We heard you were accepted into the criminal justice program at Arizona State," Tanner said, stepping forward to embrace him. His lean body felt tight with tension, at odds with the celebration he was trying to create, but Adam chalked it up to Tanner not wanting him to leave.

Emily took her turn hugging him. "We want to get on the good side of a future lawyer."

"Why?" Adam asked. "You think you'll need one?"

They laughed nervously at his jest. There was a weird vibe buzzing in the air, but he never knew what this pair was cooking up, so he just watched and waited. They'd tell him in their own time.

Tanner went to the fridge and brought back a pitcher of red liquid with... pineapple rings floating in it? "Hawaiian punch and vodka," he explained. "I tried to find something red and gold like ASU's colors. I call it devil juice, like the Sun Devils, you know?"

Adam chuckled, and the anxiety finally left his body. "I appreciate this, guys. I'm going to miss you. But I still have two weeks until I leave."

"Never too early to celebrate," Tanner said.

"Besides," Emily added, "this way it's a surprise." Her soft lips curved as she handed him a red plastic cup of the devil juice.

That was the last thing he remembered until he'd woken up in Emily's bed with one hand cuffed to her wrought-iron headboard with red-velvet-lined cuffs. Had they...?

He sat up suddenly, and then tipped his head back against the headboard as the room spun. How much had he had to drink?

The mattress shifted as Emily sat next to him. He knew it was her because the light scent of her vanilla lip balm floated his way and her soft hands cupped his face. "Adam? Are you okay? Please be okay."

When the spinning slowed, he cracked open his eyes again. They were both still fully dressed, so he didn't think he'd taken advantage of her.

Wait. He was the one who felt woozy—and had been taken advantage of. Drugged? Handcuffed? What was going on?

Emily's cheeks were flushed as she stroked his face, murmuring to him. "Oh, thank God. I thought maybe Tanner gave you too much."

He shifted his gaze without moving his head, but Tanner was nowhere to be seen.

"What's going on?" he asked, his voice croaky. He cleared his throat. "Where's Tanner?"

"He... left. Please don't be mad."

"Mad about what? What did you two do?"

"Tanner put a roofie in your punch."

"Son of a—" He jerked on the handcuffs. He could probably break them if he wanted, but he would hurt the wrist that was bound. It might be easier and less destructive to talk Emily into freeing him. She looked conflicted about the situation she'd helped put him in, anyway. Yeah, talking his way out of this might be the easier way to go. "You helped him do this?"

"I'm sorry," she said.

"If your apology is sincere, you'll let me go."

"I can't. Tanner said you'd kill him if you knew." His asshole brother probably didn't appreciate what kind of friend he had, that she'd face Adam's wrath to protect him.

"What's he up to?" He was afraid of what could be so bad that Tanner would drug him, would trap him like this... or that Emily would help.

"I can't tell you." She looked away and bit her bottom lip. It was plump and juicy and he wanted to taste her. She had to taste like vanilla, he decided. Or buttercream frosting. Something sweet and tantalizing that got your pulse racing but was bad for you.

He looked away, disgusted with himself. Maybe he was experiencing that syndrome where the prisoner falls for his captor. Except he'd started falling a long time ago and years of frustration hadn't broken the fall. He'd resisted his attraction to her, secretly wanting her but keeping his distance—when he could.

Giving in to temptation would be easier. But Adam had never chosen easy over right.

Her long hair was pulled back in some kind of twist that made the ends stick out in a playful way. Her shorts revealed long legs, tanned golden by the summer sun. They were folded under her now, cross-legged style, as her fingers fiddled together in her lap, showing her nerves.

"Let me go," he tried again. "I don't know what Tanner is worried about. And if he's in danger, I should be there to help him."

She glanced away.

"You don't know, either, do you?" he guessed, and then shook his head as she met his gaze. "You follow him blindly, and it's going to end up hurting you someday. He fucking drugged me, Em. And I'm his brother. The one who helps keep a roof over our heads and food in our mouths. If he can do this to me, how do you think he'll treat you one day?"

"He's scared of you."

He grunted. "He should be. I'll kill him if he tries another illegal stunt. He could go to jail now that he's eighteen. You both could. You were an accomplice tonight. In a kidnapping, and whatever else he's up to."

She paled but straightened, her steadfast loyalty to Tanner evident in her rigid posture. "He's the only person who's ever really cared about me."

"No." At his declaration, she looked at him sharply. "You've got me." Damn, a husky quality had entered his voice. Where had that come from?

She didn't buy it, though. Instead, she rolled her eyes. "You must think I was born yesterday."

"What? I've been there for you."

She took a moment to consider this, and her expression softened. "Yes, but only when you decided it was the right thing to do. Not because of me." A new intensity lit her expression and she scooted closer to him. Tentatively, as if expecting him to bite, she smoothed a hand down his face and laid it against his chest. "Your heart doesn't pound like mine does when we're near each other."

"What?"

"I've wanted you for months, and you've never made a move. Not even to kiss me. I know you had to have picked up on my hints."

Hell yes, he had. And he'd shot them down quickly. He didn't need another confused, temptation-driven person in his life, needing his support. His brother and his dad were enough.

But as much as he wanted to stay in Emily's bed and submit to his desires, he had to get to Tanner. Whatever he was up to was big, and probably dangerous, if he was chaining Adam up like this.

Besides, it was quite possibly Emily's plan to distract him with sexual tension. Two could play at that game.

He laughed low and deep, feeling her hand pressed against his chest every time he moved—and breathed in the scent that made him want to lick her from head to toe. "You and I are on different paths. You'll end up in prison at the rate you're going. You should stay away from my brother. In fact, you should get far away from here."

"Like you are?" Her expression turned earnest. "I could go with you."

"You would do that?" His free hand came up to cup her head and nudge her closer.

She stiffened in surprise at the sudden movement, but relaxed as his hand released her hair clip so his fingers could sift through the honeyed silk. She didn't move away, and their breaths were becoming shorter, intermingling as she leaned closer.

Her gaze dropped to his mouth, her eyelashes skimming her cheeks. She leaned closer. His breath stilled in his chest as their lips connected. It was a close-mouthed kiss, innocent in many ways. Even the taste of her lip balm was carefree and summery— *strawberries* and vanilla. How could he have missed the strawberries? A flavor for a girl, but her body melted against his like the woman she was quickly becoming, a woman who knew what she wanted. She straddled him, climbing into his lap, holding more of her glorious inches against him. His fingers clenched the bedspread beside his leg, resisting the urge to reach for her.

Remember the goal. Keep your head. Otherwise, you'll end up like the rest of your family.

And Tanner was in trouble. He had to get out of here and stop the idiot from whatever poor choice he was making now.

But then she let out a soft moan and parted her lips. She let him in, and suddenly he didn't want to leave. Ever. Sweet Jesus, the moist heat was his undoing. His hand went to the back of her head and angled her so that her mouth was better aligned with his. Her hips shifted, elevating the torture.

Drifting lower, his fingers went to cup her ass, and his good sense returned as he felt the denim of her back pocket—and the little outline of the key to the handcuffs. He let his fingers drift across the skin where her shirt had risen up, then down her leather belt, as if he were looking for a way to get beneath her clothes. Parts of him desperately wanted that and cheered his progress. Ignoring his desires, he slid his fingers into her pocket. She didn't even notice as he withdrew the key.

He let the kiss continue for several long moments, his mind half on the key and his duty to his family, and the other half on Emily, and how he was going to get out of here without hurting her.

When she pulled away a moment later, the moisture that lingered on her lips and the dazed look in her eyes stirred a tug of possessiveness, and a return of his protectiveness. He almost regretted what he had to do next.

She traced his lips and gave him a hesitant smile. "I've been wanting to do that for months."

He didn't know how to respond. He'd wanted that, too, but what they shared would never lead to anything lasting or good.

Her next words had him going completely still. "Would you take me with you? I wasn't kidding when I said I would go. I wouldn't be a burden. I can earn my own way—"

"No." His stark refusal obviously shocked her.

She blinked several times. "Just, *no?*"

He steeled his heart. "Look, that was a nice kiss, but don't go thinking it was anything more than that. I'll be a college student soon, and I need to keep my options open."

"We could be so good together," she whispered, unable to hide the hurt that roughened her voice. "I wouldn't be a burden. I can earn my own way."

His heart clenched, but he knew better. She was young. Naïve. He had things to do with his life. "You're thinking like a little girl."

"I'm thinking with my heart. I love you. I think I've always loved you. For me, it'll always be you."

God, her proclamation made his chest fucking *hurt*. But she didn't—*couldn't*—know what love was. She was barely an adult, for Christ's sake. "You don't know what you want. Christ, I don't know what I want. But it isn't..."

"Me?"

"Family. I've seen what family is. I don't want that. I'd rather be alone. Besides, what do you know about love? You lie and manipulate." He jiggled his handcuffed hand to remind her of the lying and manipulating she'd done just a short while ago. "I don't need any more of that in my life."

She went totally still, looking as if she'd been slapped. A second later, she was a blur of motion as she scrambled off his lap. Off the bed. Across the room. It seemed she couldn't get far enough away from him. She turned back as if she would say something more, but her mouth snapped closed and she fled.

But he'd gotten what he needed. He quickly used the key he'd liberated from her pocket to free his bound wrist. He'd rejected her. But he'd make it up to her later. He'd tell her he'd done it because he had to help Tanner, not because he wanted to hurt her.

But when he went into the living room, she was gone. He searched the small house, but she'd left. The bike she used to get around town was gone.

And the next day, when he found out why Tanner had needed him out for the count for the evening, their betrayal had been the last straw. He moved up his deadline, leaving for Phoenix the next day. And he never looked back.

Present day

Adam thought Emily would never forgive him, would never let him hold her like that again, after what he'd said and done eight years ago. But Emily's heart had always been generous and she was once again letting him in. He didn't deserve her. With a groan that was half pleasure, half frustration, he pulled back.

Her hands came up to cup his face so she could look into his eyes. "Why?" Her question had so many layers it could be a cake, but Adam knew what she was asking. Why had he suddenly decided to kiss her again—and again? She didn't trust his motives, and he couldn't blame her.

"Because I wanted to kiss you," Adam said simply, a hint of a smile tugging at his lips as she continued to stare at him. "Is that a surprise?"

"Frankly, yes."

Because he'd treated her like a bad hand, tossing her away. And now he suddenly wanted back in the game. "Maybe it's my turn to be full of surprises." His smile widened and she traced his curved lips with a fingertip.

"You don't smile nearly often enough," she said. "Never did."

Because he'd had to be the responsible one. And he had to now, as well. Someone had to figure out who had attacked her. He released a deep breath and let the last of his shaken nerves out. What if he hadn't been there, waiting for her to leave work?

He placed a quick kiss on her forehead and pulled away before he could be tempted to take more. "I think you should take a hot shower and clean all of those cuts." It would give him time to form a plan.

She ran a finger across the side of his neck, where he felt the sting of a small nick where glass must have cut him. Her gaze, still heated from their passion, met his. "You could join me."

His body tightened, yearning to do just that, but he had work to do. Besides, she could still be in a state of shock after tonight's events, and when they landed in bed together, he wanted it to be a mutual, clearheaded decision.

He reached into the tub to turn the water on. "Another time, maybe."

She frowned, but didn't argue. As she hopped off the counter, he let himself out, closing the door behind him but not closing out the thought of her stripping naked. His mind replayed the details of her attack as he made a call to Remington, who answered immediately.

"Emily was attacked tonight," Adam said. He gave Remington the man's description, though he'd only seen the figure from the back, and the guy had worn a dark hoodie.

"You think he's one of Ryan's men?"

"Maybe, but I'm not sure what the point would be. He needs her to be focused on finding Tanner and he's already scared her."

"Maybe she has something they want?"

Adam remembered how she'd been touching the front pocket of her jeans when she'd emerged from the building. Had she found the evidence Tanner was going to send her? "I'd also like you to check into a DEA agent named Mason Gray. I think he could be the mole working for Ryan. Can't get a good read on the man." Probably because his feelings for Emily got in the way of objectivity whenever he saw Mason with her. "Neither Emily nor I saw the attacker's face and I recently found out she's been reporting to Gray for months. Something about him seems off. He knows Tanner was going to leave something incriminating for her. Could be he thought she found it and intended on taking it from her."

"Good thing you're sticking by her. Sounds like she's in deeper than even you realized."

And yeah, as Remington stated, she was in deep. And she wasn't the only one. Adam wanted to drown in the woman. When he'd seen the dark shape coming at her at a full run... He shut down the memory quickly, knowing it would only get him agitated when there was little he could do about it at this time of night.

He hung up and turned, his gaze landing on Emily standing in the kitchen, still wearing the same clothes, her accusing gaze piercing him right to the core.

"Who was that?" Emily tried to control the slow burn that was turning her anger from simmer to boil. Adam deserved the benefit of the doubt after saving her tonight, but more secrets lurked behind his eyes, and lies behind his lips.

"I thought you were taking a shower." He put his cell phone in his pocket as if it could erase what she'd just heard.

"I decided to just wash my arms and face, since I plan on going back out. They were the only parts affected, anyway."

"You plan on going back out there tonight?"

"It has to be tonight. The deadline's in less than twenty-four hours and I need to find Tanner." And thanks to the house symbol on the storeroom doorjamb, she knew where to start looking. She'd planned on sharing the information with Adam, but he was keeping her out of the loop.

Adam must have heard the anger in her tone, because he tried a placating half-smile. She only glared harder. He'd given her name and told someone about her connection to Mason. He had the gall to tell her not to keep secrets, not to trust anyone but him. And here she'd deluded herself into thinking they'd moved beyond the surface level friendship to something deeper.

"That was an FBI agent working on the Redemption Club case," he finally conceded.

"And you went behind my back to call him." *You're keeping stuff from him, too.* She shoved her conscience to the ground and stuffed a gag in its mouth. He was using her. That wasn't the same as her keeping things from him. And the things she was keeping were to protect those she loved—including Adam. Besides, it was only a theory at this point. She needed the ledger to confirm her fears before she decided whether she'd share them with Adam. "I think you should go."

"I'm not going anywhere."

"I'm going to go get changed, and when I come back, I want you gone." So she could start searching for the SD card. She turned to walk toward her bedroom. She'd finish cleaning up and find Tanner on her own, as she'd intended. But Adam darted in front of her, stopping her exit before she'd even heard him move.

"I have a duty to resolve this investigation," he said.

"So do I. We're supposed to be on the same side here."

"I was going to tell you when I knew I could—" He broke off and looked away.

"When you could trust me?" She shoved him in the chest but he didn't budge. "I didn't ask for any of this. You've got your FBI connections to help you. You certainly don't need me."

"You're wrong." Adam arched a brow. "I do need you. I just don't want to."

"Then go. I'll let you know when I find Tanner. I'm sure it would be easier if we split up, each looking on our own." She tried to be nonchalant about *splitting up* while her heart was hammering in her ears.

"I'm not going anywhere. Not until I get a lead on Tanner and ensure your safety."

She crossed her arms. "That's how they taught you to do it at the police academy—just wait for leads to fall into your lap?" Of their own volition, her eyes flicked to his lap. In the split second between then and when she looked up again, he closed the gap between them.

His hands reached out and tugged her close. She tried to regain her stolen breath and step away from him, but his familiar scent—oh God, the memories that flooded her—had her entire body seizing up—right before a flood of happy tingles shot through her nerves.

He, apparently, wasn't so frozen in the past. In fact, he was suddenly on fast-forward, his fingers diving into her front pocket while her reaction time was seriously delayed. She attempted to swat him away as he located the flash drive with the surveillance footage she'd stolen from Legacy security on it and extracted it from her pocket.

"Speaking of information falling into our laps, what have we here?" He took a step back and held the drive up.

She wanted to curse him for using her body's natural reaction to him to manipulate her, but couldn't. That would tell him exactly how much she cared about him, and there was no way in hell she'd ever lay her heart on the table to be mutilated again.

"It's a flash drive," she said inanely, since he seemed to be waiting for an answer.

"What's on it? I'm pretty sure this is why you were attacked, so don't lie to me." He looked at the drive. "Must be some interesting stuff on here."

She shrugged. "Haven't looked at it yet. How did you even know I had it?"

"You told me Tanner would be giving you something you could view on your computer, which you would be on the lookout for. And when you walked out of the building tonight, you kept a protective hand over that pocket as you walked to your car. Which is probably why that man knew to attack you. I wouldn't be surprised if the purpose of the attack was to obtain this." He shook his head at her. "I thought you'd stripped yourself of all your tells ages ago."

She had. But Adam could always see more of her than she wanted him to see. "I didn't know anyone was watching."

He stepped closer, dropping his voice. "But they were. Who else did you tell about the possible existence of Tanner's memory card or drive? Anyone besides

Mason?"

She could trust Mason. Couldn't she?

There was no point in denying it. He was right. She'd been distracted. "That's not from Tanner."

His brows went up. "What is it, then?"

"Security footage from Legacy. I wanted to see for myself what went down the night of Blake's murder."

His brow crinkled. "At the hotel? What could it show that's related to the murder?"

"Maybe it'll show someone leaving with Ryan. Someone who could become another suspect. At the very least, I thought I could verify when Ryan returned that night, and whether he manipulated the footage to fit his story."

He frowned. "That's a long shot."

"But worth the attempt." She held his gaze, knowing they were talking about something deeper than an investigation. He'd never wanted to risk everything to be with her.

"And the item Tanner was supposed to leave you, the one he mentioned the night he stopped by to clean the blood off himself and found you in the bathtub?" His gaze flicked over her body and her skin heated. "You still haven't found it?"

She looked away before she could school her expression.

"Em," he growled the warning. "I need that evidence as much as you do. Tanner needs us to get it into the right hands, but I have to know what we're dealing with."

At the earnestness in his eyes, and the sight of the scrape on his temple, like a badge of chivalry earned while saving her earlier, she caved. "I haven't found it yet, but it has something to do with my cat."

CHAPTER SEVENTEEN

"Your cat?" Adam turned to the feline, who was stretched out in the middle of the kitchen floor looking for a cool tile to sleep on.

Emily jerked her head toward the bathroom. "Come with me." When he followed, she pointed to a spot on the doorjamb. "This is where Tanner was standing when I saw him last."

"Okay. And it gave you an idea?"

"He left a graphite marking for me at the storeroom."

"A message?" When she nodded, he shoved his hands through his hair, wanting to rip it out. "And you withheld that information?"

She shrugged as if it were no big deal. "A simple octagon, which means danger. Not valuable info. But tonight, there was another symbol. A house."

"Tanner was at the storeroom again?" *Reckless.*

"You're missing my point. The house had my initials. He was telling me it's time for me to find what he left me, and that it's in my apartment."

His gaze searched the bathroom and what he could see of the kitchen counter and living room, before moving to her pocket.

She shook her head. "I don't have it, if that's what you're thinking. But, look." She crouched and pointed to a symbol on the doorjamb. "By leaving those messages at work, and then the drawing of the house, he was telling me to look at the doorways here. He probably left this that night, before I came home."

"When he'd been cleaning up after a murder."

She grimaced. "Right. The point is whatever he wanted me to find was here all along."

He crouched beside her to study the symbol. A cat's ears and whiskers?

"Has to be Calliope," she said. "He even said something about Calliope looking like she had secrets." She pet her cat, her fingers moving along Calliope's collar. Not finding anything, she straightened and went to Calliope's bed in the window, next.

Adam began searching Calliope's food and water dishes. The cat rose to investigate, probably in hopes of a feeding. "You said Tanner wanted you to find this thing days later?"

"Yes." She pulled open a side table drawer full of cat toys and began sifting through them.

"Where's Calliope's bag of food?" If Tanner wanted Emily to find the evidence days after he disappeared, it was a possibility, and definitely worth a shot.

"Under the kitchen sink."

He spread out a trash bag on the floor and dumped out the five-pound bag of dry kitty kibble. A tiny, clear plastic case containing an SD card tumbled out at the end and lay on top of the pile. Beside him, Emily gasped and crouched down, staring at it for a few long seconds like it might bite her. She fished it out and hugged it to her chest, grinning at him. "This has to be what Ryan wants me to bring to him."

"Son of a bitch," he muttered. Calliope sent a meow their way and moved to sniff at the food.

She stooped to pet the cat, crooning to her. "Thanks for your help, baby."

Adam poured the kibble back into its bag. "She's a great secret-keeper, but I wish she'd told us this particular one earlier."

Emily filled Calliope's bowls as Adam cleaned up. Within minutes, they were settled on the couch with Emily's computer, waiting for the contents to load via her card reader. Was it a copy of the ledger? But if

Tanner had wanted Emily to have it to turn over to the authorities, why wouldn't he have done so himself, days ago? And why did he trust her to handle this instead of Adam?

He sent her a sideways glance. "Would you have called me if you'd found this without me?"

"If it will help Tanner, which he seemed to think it would, I would have handed it over." She reached out to touch him, tracing a fingertip along the corner of his mouth, surprising him with her tenderness. "Stop scowling. I like you much better when you're not disapproving of me."

He captured her hand before she could pull it away. "I don't disapprove of you. I never have." She was quite close to perfect in his mind, even with her flaws. "I'm angry I didn't think to search your place a little harder. I shouldn't have missed this."

"I missed it, too. Besides, you can't be right all the time." Before he could respond, she was frowning at the screen. "It's a video file." She clicked on it and Tanner's image filled the screen. "You were right. Tanner had a tiny camera on him. He said he made a copy of this, so he must have used my computer before he left."

Relief that Tanner might have evidence to clear this mess up, and clear him of murder charges, quickly outweighed Adam's disappointment that it wasn't a digital copy of the ledger.

Tanner's voice came through the speakers as the video showed him standing in front of a mirror. The camera recorded his reflection. "I'm wired for sound and picture. If anything happens to me, if anything goes wrong tonight, this will be my life insurance policy."

Beside her, Adam's entire body tensed and he leaned forward to get a closer look at Tanner. Of course, this pressed his arm and hip more snugly against hers. She tried to ignore the flush of heat that shot to those parts.

"Do you know where this is?" he asked, his attention entirely on the screen, where hers should be.

Bright turquoise paint and a mural of two palm trees and a hammock were painted on what looked like bathroom stall doors. "That could be the restroom at Pete's Paradise. I've never been in the men's room, but the women's restroom is similar."

On screen, Tanner read off a date and time.

"That was just an hour before we got there," Adam said.

Her spirits sank. If they'd only arrived a little sooner, they might have been able to talk him out of whatever this was. Her head was suddenly throbbing. As she pressed a hand to her forehead, Adam cast her a worried glance.

"He made his own choices, Em." He squeezed her knee in support.

She blew out a breath and nodded. There was nothing she could do about the past, but they could help Tanner in the present.

On screen, Tanner was checking that the tiny camera was hidden in a button on his black dress shirt and the mic in his lapel. He smoothed his dark hair and took a deep breath.

Adam cursed. "If he's recording himself, he had to suspect some bad shit might go down. I wish he would have come to me."

As if Tanner heard them, he spoke to his reflection again. "Ryan Stone demanded I attend a poker game at Blake Toll's home tonight. I tried to resist, tried to bargain my way out of this. He wants me to bring a ledger he insists belongs to him, but it was passed down to me by a dead mutual friend whom Ryan had betrayed. Ryan thinks he can use Blake Toll to win the ledger from me. But Toll and I, while acting like enemies, have become friends with a common purpose—knocking Ryan off his pedestal. We're working together behind Ryan's back to dismantle the

Club."

Adam grunted. "He could have just turned it over to the authorities."

On screen, Tanner grinned wryly into the mirror. "Adam, I know what you're thinking if you're watching this. Why didn't I just go to the authorities?"

Emily shot him a sideways look. "He's got you pegged."

"I refuse to let Ryan manipulate me, but he's threatened you, Emily, as well as Adam. And I know what happens to those who double-cross Ryan Stone. Him being behind bars won't stop him from taking revenge on those I love. Besides, Toll says Ryan has a mole within the LVPD. I don't know who to trust, so I'm doing this my way." Tanner left the bathroom and emerged in Pete's Paradise.

"Didn't you help Tanner cheat the last time he played Blake, only a couple of weeks ago?" Adam asked, a hint of accusation in his voice.

"I was the bartender. Tanner asked me bring in a deck of cards, but I didn't know what he had planned."

"It wasn't a con to lose to him, after all. Tanner and Blake were putting on a show for Ryan's benefit, so he wouldn't suspect they were working together for the past few weeks."

She shook her head. "I wish he'd told me what was going on."

"You were part of the act. He needed you to console him afterward, when he was supposedly ranting about his loss. Made it all look more real."

"It might also be because he knew I'd gone straight, and this was his way of keeping me out of it." She felt Adam's considering gaze on her and turned to look at him, defensiveness in her voice. "I've done a damn good job of living a normal life for the past couple years without scamming people, thank you very much."

"I was only thinking that he hasn't really kept you out of it. He's still dragging you into trouble after all these years, and yet you resisted for as long as you could." He smiled softly and a weight lifted from her shoulders. Maybe he could finally acknowledge the change in her, which meant maybe they could move away from the past. His words shouldn't mean that much to her, but they did.

Adam's gaze moved back to the screen, where Tanner must have paused the recording during his drive because suddenly he was walking up the steps of a high-class home. "That's Toll's place." At her curious glance, he explained. "That FBI guy on the phone? Remington was one of the investigators and invited me to the scene."

Tanner rang the bell and Ryan opened the front door. "About time you showed," Ryan said. "Thought you might back out of the poker game *you* set up."

"I considered it," Tanner replied. "But you've left me with little choice, especially when you've stolen my life and then threatened my friends and family. That's a chicken-shit move, by the way."

Ryan shrugged. "You play the hand you're dealt, and since you disappeared and I couldn't be sure you'd show tonight, you didn't leave *me* much choice."

"Ransacking my place, looking for the ledger, was one thing. But when your guy on the police force pulls me over and threatens me, I figure it's time to lay low."

Adam slid Emily a look. "There's been a rumor there's a mole within the LVPD. Guess now we know it's true."

"I'm getting a better idea of why he disappeared," Emily murmured.

"You could have just handed him the ledger," Ryan was saying onscreen.

"And you'd have let me go?" Tanner laughed. "Right. The ledger is my only bargaining chip. At least, with this poker game, I have a chance to win— assuming you'll play fair. If you don't, I'll make sure the entire Club knows how you conduct business, and the danger you and Finn Tucker put them in by not securing this book." Tanner lifted the briefcase into view of the camera. They hadn't realized he was carrying it.

Emily gasped. "No. He wouldn't risk bringing the ledger there." Yet, Ryan had possession of the book, so Tanner must have gambled and lost.

"You have the money?" Tanner asked Ryan.

"It's inside already," Ryan replied, gesturing to Tanner to enter.

Tanner followed Ryan to a room where Blake was waiting. Tanner and Blake shared a handshake. "Good to see you again," Tanner said. "And for your patience."

"He must have been late because he was waiting for me to meet him," Emily said. "If only I'd checked my messages sooner."

"You're the guest of honor," Blake said with a chuckle. "We've been waiting for you." Blake winked at Tanner.

"Look at Ryan," Emily said, pointing at the screen. "He saw that wink."

"And he looks livid," Adam said.

Tanner set the briefcase on the table, pulled out a red leather-bound book, and handed it to Blake, who skimmed through quickly and pronounced it worthy of a buy-in.

Emily shook her head. "This can't be right. He would never have risked bringing the real thing. If Blake and Tanner are working together, that could be a fake." She pressed a palm to her head. "That means the one Ryan showed me, when he threatened me, was probably the fake." She'd been duped.

"It doesn't change what we need to do," Adam assured her. "We still need to find the original. I'm hoping Tanner still has it and is using it to stay safe."

"His insurance policy," Emily murmured.

On camera, Ryan had opened another briefcase, this one full of Legacy poker chips, as well as a torn half of a playing card, on the table. Emily couldn't see the name scrawled on it, but froze as she heard Ryan's comment. "Another debt paid off—though I'm not sure why you'd bother. Your father's dead."

Emily glanced toward Adam. "Your father had a debt?"

Adam's jaw tightened. "It's not impossible. In fact, given the way he lived, I shouldn't be surprised."

Was this a piece of the puzzle she'd been trying to solve? She didn't have time to ponder it as the action on the screen continued. Tanner was arguing with Ryan that it hadn't been part of the deal to let Blake be Ryan's pinch hitter. And then Blake announced that he wanted a piece of the action.

"I want in," Blake said, obviously stunning Ryan. They couldn't see Tanner's expression.

Ryan laughed. "This is a joke, right? With what buy-in? What could possibly be of similar value as a million dollars in chips or control of the Redemption Club?"

Blake placed a manila folder on top of the ledger. "Evidence you blackmailed your father for most of this past year."

Adam sat back with a stunned expression.

"He's talking to Ryan," Emily said. "Ryan was blackmailing his father?"

"Certainly raises the stakes," Adam said. "And Tanner must have been counting on this additional piece of information to protect him from retaliation when he turned Ryan and the ledger over to the cops. But in exposing his knowledge to Ryan—"

"Blake and Tanner put themselves in even more danger." Emily's heart sank.

Ryan had wheeled on Blake. "Why would you do this? You had everything you could want." His gaze swung to Tanner next. "You're working together? I thought you were enemies."

"We may have led you to believe that to serve a greater purpose." Blake shrugged. "He who has that book has the ultimate power, right?"

"Over the dark side of Vegas, at least," Tanner said.

"And he who has this folder has control over Ryan Stone, one of the richest men in the country," Blake added. "At least he would be if his daddy decided to let him touch his share of the money."

Ryan appeared to be barely controlling his rage. "You're going to regret this."

"Blake had just signed his death warrant," Adam muttered.

"He probably only had minutes to live at that point," she agreed. "And Tanner's caught in the middle." Her gut tightened as she realized what would come soon in the video—unless Tanner and his camera had left before the murder. But she'd seen the blood on his neck.

Catching her grimace, Adam reached for her laptop. "You don't have to watch this next part." She shifted it out of reach.

"I need to know how this went down. I need every bit of information I can get to find Tanner and the real ledger. And help put Ryan away."

On screen, the card game had begun. Tanner dealt.

"What?" Adam asked, feeling her stiffen.

"I think Tanner just stacked the deck."

Adam's gaze whipped from the screen to her. "He's cheating? Do you think Ryan noticed?"

"I'm not sure." She watched the screen more closely.

Blake arranged his cards in his hand. "So I win this hand and I keep the ledger, the proof of blackmail, and a hundred thousand in Legacy chips." Blake chuckled. "Not a bad day."

"*If* you win," Tanner said. "Maybe you shouldn't count your chickens before they've hatched." There was a warning in his tone.

"I think he's worried Blake's going off-script," Emily said. "And I think the deck was stacked so Ryan couldn't win. He doesn't look happy with his hand." The trio played out the hand.

"I win," Blake announced as they laid their cards down.

"The fuck you did." Ryan pushed away from the table and stood. He jabbed a finger toward him. "You cheated. Nobody cheats me." He slowly rounded the table, aiming a glare at both Tanner and Blake. "You two are working together."

Blake leaned back in his chair. "Hard to cheat someone who's constantly changing the rules to suit himself. What about what happened to your best friend, who helped you run the Club? What about blackmailing your father? How is that not cheating? And you've consistently lied to Club members, letting them believe their secrets are safe with you when we both know they're not."

Adam's finger went to the screen, pointing to Ryan's hand, which was slipping into his pocket. "Blake doesn't even notice," he said. "He's too busy trying to preach to Ryan and gloat."

"You don't care about the lowly members, though," Tanner said. "You act like we owe you, but those people don't owe you a damn thing. They owe some fictional, illegal club."

"For very real acts that were committed at their request," Ryan said. "I'm not exploiting anyone. They knew the deal when they took it."

"Well, I, for one, value them," Blake said, grinning. "That ledger is like hitting the ultimate jackpot."

"That wasn't the deal," Tanner said, anger vibrating in his tone. "We're turning it over to the DA's office to let them sort out. I agreed to let you teach Ryan a lesson and hammer home that he couldn't win against the two of us, but that was it. No more Club."

"Think of the money we can make. The poor bastards in there will fork over millions to keep things secret." He turned to Ryan. "Or maybe your father would be interested in buying it from me. It was his book once, after all."

"Now who's being greedy?" Tanner bit out.

"You okay with this?" Ryan asked Tanner. "Your name's in there, your crimes recorded. You want a guy like Blake in charge of that information? There are other names—people who you might care about."

Emily glanced at Adam to gauge his reaction. "Do you know why your father was in there?"

Adam shook his head. "No clue."

Ryan had turned to Tanner, apparently deciding to target him as the more rational of the two men. "If you work with me, I can ensure nobody ever finds out why you or your father were in that book."

"He won't bite," Blake said, and Ryan spun to face him. "He's determined to do the right thing and turn you in." Blake clearly thought that was a crazy idea. "You and I both know that will never work. There are too many Club members who would rebel. Their deeds would become public record." His look turned sly. "Just as we both know there can't be two leaders of the Club."

"I'm the rightful leader," Ryan said. "And I can pay Tanner off to get the ledger, or trade him the blackmail evidence against me, so we each have something on the other. We'd be even... and cut you out completely. What I don't need is you when I have him. Especially when, with your history together, he has a motive for murdering you."

Blake's jaw dropped as Ryan pulled a gun from his pocket and a shot rang out. There was a flurry of motion as two more shots sounded and Tanner lurched across the table, trying to reach Ryan. But Blake was already on the floor, losing blood quickly. Tanner tried to get between a murderer and his victim, but the damage had been done. Tanner dropped to his knees beside the dying man, trying to press his hands to the wounds. "You're going to be okay. We'll call for help." But Blake wasn't okay. His eyes had already lost focus.

The sound of heavy breathing filled the recording for several long seconds. Tanner stood and whirled to face Ryan, who was gathering the ledger and the folder with the blackmail evidence into his briefcase.

"Why him?" Tanner asked, sounding breathless and angry. "Why not me?"

Ryan snapped the case closed. "Because you and I are more alike than you think. You'll do what you need to do in order to survive—and thrive." He left the pile of poker chips and the torn debt card with Frank Wilde's name on it. "Those are for you, in good faith. But I suggest you cash the chips and go far from here before the police come."

"I'm not the guilty one," Tanner said.

Ryan tucked his gun away as he laughed. "Obviously. But I'll make them think you are. And it'll be your word against mine. And remember that with this—" he tapped the ledger "—I can buy alibis, lawyers, even judges. A lot of people in high places owe me."

Adam cursed. "Ryan left him holding the bag."

On Emily's computer screen, Ryan walked out, leaving Tanner with a corpse, his father's torn card and a ton of chips.

The camera angle changed as Tanner turned to the table and with shaking hands, snatched up the half-card. He whirled back to the body, paused, and then scooped up a couple handfuls of chips and put them in his briefcase. The rest, he left scattered across the table or sprinkled over the body until they created a type of morbid burial mound.

"A statement," Emily said.

"He's trying to lead the police to Legacy," Adam said. And it had worked, but as Tanner was probably well aware, going up against Ryan Stone and winning was nearly impossible with the man's resources.

"That wasn't the plan," Tanner said, breathless as he spoke into the mic. "Blake was supposed to confront Ryan about the blackmail, and use that as our bargaining chip to ensure he wouldn't come after us. Going after the ledger himself wasn't part of the plan." He cursed long and fluently and scooped up the briefcase as the screen went dark and the mic went silent.

Emily frowned. "He's on his way to my place, to say good-bye."

"And to clean up," Adam reminded her.

"He's been all alone this past week, dealing with what he witnessed."

Adam uploaded a copy of the video to the cloud and saved it on her computer before removing the card, putting it back into its protective case and closing her laptop. "At least we have proof he didn't kill Blake. It's probably smart that he's hiding. He knows Ryan would destroy him whether he handed the ledger over to Ryan or the police. In the long run, Tanner's just as much a liability as Blake was."

"Whichever path he picks, he's somebody's target."

"Not true. He could have picked me." Adam had often hated his brother's choices, but the fact that Tanner didn't believe Adam would be there for him, no matter what, hurt.

"You can't protect him from the reach of the Stone family. I should know. Ryan visited my mother, had someone beat up my father. Nobody is safe, and I have less than a day to give him what he wants or more people will get hurt."

Adam put an arm around her shoulders and pulled her close until she let her head fall against his neck. "I won't let that happen." But even he was feeling the time crunch. It was already four in the morning. They had to work fast to figure out a solution. "Did you know he kept our father's special box? I found it on top of his refrigerator." He let out a harsh laugh that ruffled her hair. "It was this old tin where Dad stashed his take of whatever money he'd scored. It was usually empty. And yet, Tanner continues to believe he can beat the system, or beat Ryan Stone, or beat whoever or whatever is in his path."

Head still tucked against his chest so that he couldn't see her face, she interlaced her fingers with his and squeezed. "No matter what I said before, I'm glad you're here to help him. Tanner always thought you were stuck in a black-and-white world, that you couldn't see shades of gray, but I don't think that's true. You let us walk our own paths, even when you disagree."

Beneath Emily's cheek, Adam's heart beat steadily. When he responded, his words rumbled in his chest. "I understand why he made the choices he did, even if they weren't the choices I would have made."

Hope fluttered in her chest. If he was capable of forgiving his brother, maybe he'd forgiven her. "What are you going to do with the SD card?"

"Tanner probably wants us to use it as another source of leverage."

"Probably," she agreed.

"But I should turn it over to the FBI." He frowned.

Sensing his hesitation, she pulled away to look at his expression. "The man you spoke to on the phone?"

He nodded. "Special Agent in Charge Will Remington."

"Never heard of him. You sure we can trust him to do the right thing?"

He didn't look sure. His scowl darkened. "We're sure as hell not handing it to Mason Gray. We don't know any more about him than we do Remington."

"Okay. Besides, once we turn this recording over to someone, there are just as many things to implicate Tanner in multiple crimes as anybody else."

"Yeah, but it would clear Tanner of the murder

charge—and put the spotlight on Ryan."

"Still. We have to be smart about this. Ryan can get off any murder rap." She gestured to the card. "He's probably already thought up a defense to excuse that insane behavior. And you know his family's money and influence will count in his favor."

"What do you suggest?" His gaze was searching hers. That he'd listen to her, and recognize that her suggestions were credible made her fall for him all over again.

"Find Tanner and, together, come up with a way to make sure Ryan Stone is behind bars for good. I'm guessing Tanner's already been working on a way to clear himself and take down Ryan in the process."

"But how do we find Tanner? You said you don't know where he is. He hasn't been using his credit cards, so the best I can figure is a friend is hiding him."

"Or an enemy." Yes, it had been a long shot to get the security footage, but the more she thought about what she'd do, where she'd go, if she was a hunted woman, as well as the symbols Tanner had left for her in the storeroom, the more confident she became that her guess about his current whereabouts was correct.

She grabbed her flash drive, the one with the security footage, from the coffee table.

He watched her curiously as she loaded the files. "You really think there's something on the security footage?"

"It's worth a shot. If nothing else, it'll verify or dispute Ryan's story." She cued up a file. "He told the LVPD that he left when one of his poker buddies, Bubba, left, and returned to Legacy from Blake's around two in the morning, after he picked up his girlfriend, Brenda."

She scrolled through and fast-forwarded until she found the camera and timestamp she wanted. "That's him."

"At two-forty," Adam said. "And he's alone. That's a half hour later than he said, and without either of his alibis."

"But I'm sure he'll have an explanation, and someone to back it up later." She switched to a camera that monitored the front doors that led into the rotunda, and then began fast-forwarding again.

"What are you looking for now?"

"Without traffic, Legacy's about ten minutes from my apartment." She stopped the tape at about five-thirty. About fifteen minutes later, a man with gray hair and a stooped walk entered pulling rolling luggage. "That's Tanner."

Adam squinted at the screen. "No way."

"It wouldn't be the first time he used a costume to pull off a scam. Besides, I'd know his old man shuffle anywhere. And the luggage. That's mine." She shut her computer, grabbed Adam's hand, and pulled him to the door.

"Where are we going?"

"I think I know where Tanner's been hiding these past several days." She snatched up her purse and checked the cash in her wallet. "What time is it?"

"Why?"

"We need a bribe."

He shook his head as if trying to understand. "And the time of day determines the amount of the bribe? It's nearly four-thirty in the morning."

"Excellent. Chocolate truffle cupcakes it is."

CHAPTER EIGHTEEN

It was difficult to let go of his need to control the situation—or at least know the plan—but Adam let Emily direct him as he drove toward the Strip. He had no clue how chocolate truffle cupcakes had anything to do with the time of day, let alone how it would help them find Tanner. He was still trying to wrap his head around seeing his brother disguised as an old man.

"Right here," Emily said suddenly. "Pull over. I'll just be a minute."

After the twisted events of the past week, he wasn't all that shocked to find himself staring at the front window of a twenty-four-hour bakery. "Tanner's here?"

"No, of course not." She laughed as she got out of the car without further explanation. A couple minutes later, she returned with a small pink box that smelled like sugar and chocolate. His mouth watered.

"Let me guess. Chocolate truffle cupcakes?" he asked as she slid into the passenger seat. Behind her, dawn was just starting to lighten the sky, casting a purple-pink glow to her cheeks as she grinned.

"The best in Vegas. More important, they're Caroline's favorite."

Caroline? The name didn't ring a bell, but Emily clearly had a plan. "I hope you brought one for me."

She opened the box and swiped a finger across the top of one of the four cupcakes within, then touched the finger to his lips. He licked the frosting off and sucked her finger into his mouth. The taste and texture of sweet buttercream against her skin made him groan, but not as much as his need for her, which was mirrored in her eyes as she held his gaze. Her eyes dilated, her lips parted and her cheeks turned pink.

He released her hand and cleared his throat. "Where to next? Caroline's?"

She shut the box, not meeting his gaze. She seemed as affected by this new closeness between them as he was. "Legacy."

"I had a feeling you'd say that." All roads seemed to lead back to that place. But damn, he'd believed his brother smarter than to run a con right beneath the mark's nose, especially when the mark was wealthy, connected and had no conscience. Although he supposed there was something to be said for hiding in plain sight.

She used her employee access card to lead him from the parking lot through the service entrance. But when he would have turned toward the lounge, she grabbed his arm. "Not that way." She surprised him by heading straight down the hall that would take them to the main rotunda.

"You sure you don't want to be more inconspicuous?" he leaned down to ask. "Walking right into the enemy's turf, carrying a bright pink box is pretty noticeable, even at five in the morning."

"I'll protect you." She grinned when he grunted in response. "If these cupcakes don't do the trick, or if I'm wrong and it's not Caroline on duty, then we'll worry."

"Who's Caroline?"

"The gatekeeper at the front desk on the Friday morning graveyard shift, but she wants to earn her way out of those sucky hours."

"Via cupcakes."

"Chocolate cupcakes with truffle filling. And if the cupcakes don't do the trick, do you think you can remember how to flirt—if you ever knew how?" She arched an eyebrow at him.

He pulled her to a sudden stop in the long, deserted hallway.

"What—?"

He backed her against the wall and caged her in with his body. She held the box out to the side so it wouldn't be crushed as he leaned into her. Even through two layers of clothing, he felt her nipples harden against his chest. Her eyes heated to warm honey. He loved that his touch had just as much power over her as hers did over him, that he could make her go molten in an instant.

"I think I know how to distract when I want to," he said in a low voice. He cupped her jaw with one hand, stroking his thumb across her lips.

Mischief sparked in her eyes. "I may need more convincing."

A corner of his mouth kicked up at the challenge. Damned if she couldn't lighten even the most serious moments. Her lips parted slightly as if inviting him to sample their sweetness. So he did. He bent close, inhaling her for a moment before pressing his mouth to hers. His knee was wedged between her legs so that his body could align perfectly with hers. Her thighs squeezed around his thigh. His hand shifted from her jaw down her neck, and would have slipped lower to cup a breast and play with one of those perky nipples if he hadn't heard the clearing of a throat behind him.

A young man pushing a room service cart down the hall from the kitchen area toward the service elevator grinned as he passed. He looked like he might stop to give Adam a high five, but Adam turned his body to shield Emily from view.

He searched her face. Her skin was flushed, her lips plump and wet from his kiss, her eyes heavy-lidded. Yeah, he'd distracted her, all right. And himself, too. He was tempted to do some more distracting, but forced himself to take a step back once their audience had moved along.

She cleared her throat. "Okay, that was pretty good," she acknowledged, not looking entirely steady. She pulled the pink box in front of her body as if it were a shield.

"Pretty good?" He arched a brow.

"That technique won't work on Caroline."

He cocked an eyebrow. "You sure about that?"

She rolled her eyes. "Okay, so it might work, but I only need two minutes to get what I need from the computer. I'm certain between the cupcakes and hinting that they're her solution to better shift work, she'll be willing to work with me. The good news is there should only be her at the desk at this hour."

"And then what? How's that going to get us to Tanner?"

Her wicked grin had him wanting to press her up against the wall and sample her again. "You let me handle that. Wait here."

He'd tasted like chocolate buttercream. After leaving Adam by the bank of elevators, where he could observe without interrupting or distracting, she headed to the check-in area. Emily touched her smiling lips briefly before searching the rotunda. All was quiet here at this hour, the majority of hotel guests either sitting in the casino or sleeping in their beds. Nobody was paying any attention to her.

She stepped around the check-in desk and Caroline looked up from keying in a reservation from the Internet. "Hey, Caroline. Slow morning?"

She rolled her eyes. "The slowest."

"I was thinking about your... dilemma. You still want to change shifts?"

"Yes." She eyed the box. "Is that from Sweet as Sin?"

Gotcha. "Sure is. Only the best for this mission." Emily set the box in front of Caroline and opened it, hoping the sight and scent would entice her further. In the car, she'd given Adam the cupcake they'd already tasted and watched him devour it—after he'd given her several bites. There were three identical cupcakes remaining.

"Mission?" Instinctively, Caroline dropped her voice and leaned closer, mimicking Emily's behavior.

"I need your help with a covert operation." Drawing the woman into a sense of secret collaboration was the all-important step. Everyone loved to be inside the loop. And when poor Caroline had screwed up a massive convention registration last month, she'd been banned to the worst shifts and banished to outside the loop.

Caroline eyed her. "I figured something was up. You're not usually here at this hour."

"I made a mistake, and I need your help. I messed up a big liquor order, and with Ryan taking over as our boss, I have to make a good impression or he'll fire me."

Caroline nodded sagely. "I understand." She glanced at the cupcakes. "But how will these help?"

"They're his favorite."

"Really? They're my favorite, too."

"Small world," Emily said with an ingratiating smile. Of course, she had no clue what kind of cupcake Ryan preferred, nor did she care. What was important was that Caroline believed she wasn't alone, and that she'd get what she needed in this transaction. "Anyway, I thought I'd surprise him with a treat. Butter him up, you know? He likes surprises." Emily winked, again making Caroline part of the secret, in-the-know club.

"How can I help?"

"I don't have a key to his office, but I wanted to leave one of these for him to find. Figured after he got to the point later in the day where he couldn't stand not knowing who'd left it for him, I'd stop by and announce it was you and me who had the idea to deliver it—if you can help me get it to his desk. And one of them is for you, as payment for your trouble." Emily laughed as if this was all just some fun caper.

"And the other?"

"I thought you could leave it on Megan's desk. She

makes out the work schedules, right?"

Caroline's eyes widened and her lips curved. "Right." She looked around. "But I'm not supposed to leave the desk unattended."

Emily nibbled her lip as if that problem hadn't occurred to her. "You're probably not supposed to let me borrow Ryan's key, either. Tell you what. I'll watch the desk. Nobody's checking in at this hour, but if someone comes in during the few minutes it takes you to walk the cupcakes down the hall and leave them on their desks, I'll greet them and stall until you return. Sound good?" As she spoke, she removed a cupcake and napkin and set it on the back counter for Caroline and closed up the box, then pushed it into Caroline's hands. She wouldn't give the woman a chance to think—or, more importantly, to decide she needed to log out of her computer before she walked away. "Great. This should get us both in the new boss's good graces, as well as Megan's."

As Caroline disappeared, Emily went to work. She did a quick search for guests who'd checked in the morning of Blake's murder, around six o'clock.

Bingo.

Johnny Gondorff. She smiled at the tribute to Tanner's two favorite characters from the famous con movie *The Sting.*

Her grin slipped away and her jaw dropped as she clicked on the reservation details. Tanner was renting one of the six penthouse suites on the thirtieth floor. The suites were identical and three were set aside for guest rentals. The other three were occupied by Stones—Robert, Ryan, and Ivy. Robert Stone rarely used his, as he had a mansion across town, but he kept a suite for special guests of his choosing. But Ryan was nearly always in his suite, when he wasn't traveling. And all six were the epitome of luxury. Emily had once had the occasion to see the inside of Ivy's.

Tanner had been directly across the hall from Ryan for the past week? No wonder he'd been able to leave those symbols in her storeroom with relative ease. Still, he'd taken a lot of risks. Adam would not be happy.

She glanced Adam's way and he sent her the hurry-up signal that meant Caroline was probably coming back down the hall. Emily hurried to complete her mission. To give her an extra few seconds, he stepped in front of Caroline and asked a question. With one eye, Emily watched them, noticing the way Adam's shirt pulled across his chest, emphasizing the chiseled muscles, because his hands were tucked into his pockets. He laughed at something Caroline said, and had the appearance of a relaxed man out for some adventure and games, but there was a seriousness in his eyes. And questions. Always the questions.

A few more quick clicks and Emily slipped a keycard through the computer to code it. She erased her search terms and thus, any evidence of what, or who, she'd been looking for. Covertly slipping the keycard into her pocket, she stepped out from behind the computer and smiled in welcome as Caroline returned with the empty pink box.

"You were able to leave the cupcakes?" Emily asked.

Caroline looked flush with success. "Easy-peasy. I hope they do the trick. Thanks for watching the desk, and for the idea."

"No action here," Emily said. "Looks like it worked out for both of us."

After a hasty good-bye, Emily walked to the bank of elevators, but pretended to walk past Adam. She pressed the button to summon the elevator. "Is she watching?" she asked out of the corner of her mouth.

Adam grinned. "No. She's enjoying her cupcake." He followed her inside the car when the doors opened. She pushed the up button and slipped the keycard into the slot that allowed private access to the thirtieth floor.

"Are we checking in?" His tone was part teasing,

part hopeful.

"Actually, yes," she said. "I found Tanner."

"He's here?"

"Hiding where he could keep an eye on Ryan's comings and goings."

Adam pulled her to him and placed a celebratory kiss on her lips, releasing her before she could lose herself in it. "How'd you figure it out?"

"On the surveillance, when Tanner entered the front doors dressed as an old man with my purple suitcase, he looked as if he planned to check in. I used the time stamp on the video to search Caroline's computer for guests who checked in at that time. He used an alias, but I'm certain it's him."

His gaze moved to the button she'd pushed. "The penthouse suites?"

"His suite is right across the hall from Ryan's."

Adam shook his head. "Leave it to Tanner to push the limits of safety versus payoff... But how can he afford a penthouse unit?"

"I assume only he has the answer for that. I booked the suite adjoining his by telling the computer I paid cash. I figure we have a day before those who balance the books realize things aren't balancing and kick us out. And a day is all we need. This will all be over long before then." For better or worse.

It was nearly five-thirty in the morning and there was nobody in the hall as the elevator doors slid open, but Adam held her back before she could exit. "Cameras?"

She shook her head. "Guests who pay ten thousand a night don't want to be seen doing whatever it is they do. They want privacy. As do Mr. Stone, Ivy, and Ryan. But make sure Ryan isn't lurking in the hall." With the late hours he kept, she wouldn't expect to see him emerge before noon—if he was even home.

"Ten thousand?"

"Well, twelve, since it's the weekend."

"He must have taken it from the pile of chips at

Blake's. Little brother and I have to have a talk."

"Blake won't be missing it." She shoved her worries aside as she slid her card into the slot on the door of the suite adjacent to Tanner's—or, rather, Gondorff's.

"Is this his suite?" Adam whispered. His warm breath against her ear sent shivers of delight that tingled all the way to her fingertips, which longed to run over every hard inch of him.

"No. It's that one." She tipped her head toward the door several yards to their right. She hurried to open the door in front of her and pulled him inside. At any moment, Ryan could stumble home from a party or walk out of his room. She closed the door behind them and locked it, breathing a sigh of relief that they were safe and out of sight. And that Adam was by her side. For the first time in weeks, she had the feeling everything might work out okay.

Inside their suite, Adam studied the wall they shared with Tanner as if he wanted to push his way through it. "You think he's been holed up in there for nearly a week without leaving?"

"Yes, if he's being cautious." With Tanner, it would depend on how much Ryan riled him up, but she hoped he understood the severity of the situation and had stayed hidden. "Except when he snuck out to visit the lounge's storeroom. His room service bills certainly seem to indicate he's been there the whole time. I got a peek when I was searching on the computer," she explained when he shot her an amused look. "There's also a note in there that he's an eccentric, and instructions that the staff not bother him, and to leave any food deliveries outside the door."

"Smart." Adam turned in a slow circle to survey their surroundings. He let out a low whistle as he stepped farther inside and took in the gourmet chef's kitchen, vast living room with a marble fireplace, vaulted ceilings, and an entire wall of fifteen-foot windows that looked out over a deck with a private lap pool. Beyond that, a view of the Strip beckoned. "Are all the penthouse suites this luxurious?"

"Yes. And there are four bedrooms down that hallway there."

"Little brother's hideouts have improved over the years."

She huffed out a laugh. "Better than the old shed with a ratty blanket on the floor."

He met her gaze. "Oh, I don't know. We had some great moments in that shed."

"Hiding from life."

"And here we are, doing it again, except from much bigger threats." His gaze landed on the closed door that connected their suite to Tanner's. He turned back to her. "You obviously have some kind of plan, though it might be safer if we contacted some outside resources. We don't have to tell them where we are, but if we can get the ledger into the right hands—"

"You said yourself we don't know who we can trust. I need you to trust *me*. We'll come up with a plan we all can agree to." She worried Adam would walk away—or worse, turn her and Tanner over to the police or FBI—when he heard what she was planning. "Ryan Stone has vast resources. There's too much risk he'd escape any legal proceedings unscathed, and then come after those who wronged him." She held up a hand to stop the objection she could see forming. "He's done it before with Blake, and with others. Just ask Tristan Floyd. The guy fears every day that he'll be shanked if he lets down his guard. Ryan would come after us, or my parents, in a heartbeat."

"So what are you suggesting?"

"I propose we out-con him. But I could use Tanner's help, since you're not exactly a confidence man, and it may require some... unethical methods."

His slow grin sent a shiver of desire down her spine. "You must have forgotten how I grew up—in the same house, with the same father as Tanner." He sent her a mischievous smile that made her insides constrict with need. He reached out to touch her chin, nudging her mouth closed. "Like you said, some people perceive me as only seeing things in black and white. But there are pluses to believing in extremes. If I'm in, I'm in all the way."

CHAPTER NINETEEN

Emily knocked on the door between the suites in a precise pattern.

Adam's lips curved. "Our secret knock." He hadn't heard it since they were younger, hanging out in the shed like it was a secret clubhouse. "He might be sleeping or—"

She turned back to the door as the lock turned on the other side. In the next second, the door opened and Emily threw her arms around Tanner's neck. Wide-eyed, his brother caught her and pulled her close, soaking up the comfort she offered.

Adam had never struggled with a possessive streak. He'd always known Tanner was her close friend, just as Emily was Tanner's. Now, however, a twinge of jealousy was taking hold. Never mind that Tanner didn't deserve her comfort, that he had left her to deal with his mess in the outside world all by herself. Who Emily gave her love to wasn't for Adam to decide, especially after he'd thrown her declarations of love back in her face all those years ago. But she'd damn sure felt like Adam's woman after he'd had his mouth and hands on her.

It's not like that between them, his common sense whispered.

Tanner pulled away to hold her at arm's length. "Fuck, Em, how did you find me?"

She grinned. "It wasn't easy, but I followed the trail of clues."

His gaze met Adam's and they shook hands and

slapped each other on the back. "Are you sure nobody followed you?" Tanner asked.

"Nobody followed us." Emily's proclamation pulled Tanner's attention back to her. She cupped his scruffy face and searched his expression. "You're really okay?"

Tanner huffed out a laugh. "As okay as I can be for someone wanted for murder."

"We found the SD card. We know you didn't kill Blake. But why didn't you come to us for help?"

At the word *us*, Tanner's looked to Adam. "You're not here to turn me in to the authorities?"

"No," Adam said.

"So you're working together?" The incredulous tone was aimed at Emily.

She grinned. "Sort of."

Adam was irked to find possessiveness rearing up again. She *was* working with him. He'd told her he was all in, and expected the same from her.

Tanner stepped aside. "You might as well come in and catch me up. I have a feeling we have a lot to talk about. Starting with what dragged my brother away from rebalancing the scales of justice in Phoenix."

"I came to help *you*," Adam said, following Tanner into the living room.

"I'm not sure there's anything you can do, unless you know who in the Vegas area is more powerful than the Stone family and can be trusted to help us." Frustration clouded his eyes.

"An FBI agent named Remington sent me a torn card—your Redemption Club card, though I didn't know what it was at the time," Adam said. "It set me on this course to figure out what the heck the Redemption Club was. All I knew is it was connected to this hotel."

"Which brought him into the lounge," Emily said, smiling at Adam. His skin hummed with awareness— until he caught Tanner looking at them curiously. But Emily didn't seem to notice. Her gaze still on Adam, she laughed. "He came to interrogate me, since you weren't around to clear things up. He even tried to flirt to get on my good side."

Tanner's gaze narrowed on Adam as if he'd done something wrong. "Sorry about that. I was busy running for my life. Who's Remington?"

"He approached me about the same time I was trying to get answers from Em," Adam said. "Told me about the Club and took me to talk to Tristan Floyd, who filled in more of the picture. Remington's a forensic accountant, but his investigation led him to Ryan Stone and the Club."

"Well, whatever or whoever alerted you I was in trouble, I won't deny that I could use some help, but I didn't ever want you to be in danger."

"That's Ryan's fault, not yours," Emily said. Adam held his tongue. He was certain his brother hadn't meant to put her in danger, but the fact was, some of his actions had led Ryan to her, and Ryan had taken full advantage of Tanner's friendship with her.

Tanner looked genuinely remorseful. "You warned me about the high price of owing a debt to the Redemption Club. I thought possession of the ledger would be enough to protect me. I wish I'd listened."

"What did the three of spades mean?" Adam asked.

Tanner huffed out a laugh. "I wanted to buy into an exclusive game a few months back. A tournament with the best of the best. Finn Tucker offered to put in a recommendation and stake me if I gave him a cut of the winnings."

"The Finn Tucker who was believed to run the Club?"

"Yeah. I owed him for the hundred thousand he put up on my behalf. And I didn't win, so my debt was unpaid."

"Forgive me, brother, but you have a knack for getting involved with the wrong type of people," Adam said.

Tanner grunted. "We became friends after meeting

in the lounge one night. Shared a common interest in movie trivia, especially the ones with old con games, gangsters, or horror films." He laughed without humor. "That should have been my first sign to stay away, I suppose. Soon after he died two months ago, someone delivered the ledger to my door. Had a note from Finn inside indicating he had a feeling I'd know what to do with it. I wish I'd never met the guy." He shrugged. "And here we sit, in a prison of my own making."

"We'll get you out of this," Emily said softly, but with determination.

"No. *No,*" Tanner repeated more stringently when she looked as if she'd argue. "You have to go. I'll disappear again if I see you anywhere near here."

She looked stricken by the rejection and Adam had the urge to pull her into his arms. "You don't have to be an ass about it," he told his brother.

"It's not that I think you'd rat me out," Tanner told Emily with more tenderness. "But Ryan has ways of finding out things and manipulating people. He'll find your weaknesses and exploit them."

Emily frowned at him. "He already has. He's threatening my parents."

"Then you need to leave and never look back." His gaze moved to Adam as if blaming him for dragging Emily into this. Hell, maybe he had to some degree. But she would have come to Tanner's aid with or without him. "Whatever you think of me," Tanner told Adam, "I take responsibility for my own fuckups and try not to hurt the people I love."

"You didn't try hard enough," Adam muttered.

Tanner stared him down for a long moment. "Em, can I talk to Adam alone for a moment?"

She looked confused, apparently having missed the subtext going on between the brothers, but she got to her feet. "I'll order some breakfast and a pot of coffee from room service. We've got plans to make, and not much time to make them."

She went into the adjoining suite, shutting the

door behind her to give them privacy. Adam waited for the attack that had been brewing in Tanner's eyes. He didn't have to wait more than two seconds.

"What the hell, man?" Tanner jumped up and got into his face. He added a jab to Adam's chest for good measure. "You couldn't leave her out of this?"

"I needed her help—to find *you*." Adam moved out of jabbing range. "And you're the one who led Ryan to her doorstep. I've been there to protect her."

"That doesn't mean you fuck with her."

"There's no *fucking* going on." At his glare, Tanner relented somewhat, sinking back onto the couch. But when Tanner added a headshake, Adam knew his brother wasn't done.

"You decimated her last time you left."

Shock and anger rose up inside. "*You're* the one who put her in that position, asking her to help drug me and keep me cuffed to her bed until you and Dad robbed that bank. As if it wasn't stupid enough to commit a federal offense, you had her keep me in her bed when she and I were already fighting feelings for each other. You talk about me *decimating* her, but you were out committing a crime that could have put you and Dad away for years. You'd just turned eighteen, so there would have been no leniency in the court, especially with your prior record."

"You would have stopped us and probably gotten hurt."

"Damn right I would have stopped you." The old fury created a red haze that he fought to shake. Arguing about the past wouldn't get them anywhere. "You couldn't make a good choice to save your life."

Tanner shoved a hand through his hair. "There were other reasons I did that. I wasn't the first one to earn a Club card in the family, to have to repay a debt."

Adam went completely still. His heart may even have stopped beating. "Are you saying the bank robbery was repayment of a debt?"

Tanner put his head in his hands. "Shit."

"Tanner?"

"I didn't know at the time how deep this went."

"Talk to me."

"Dad owed the Club for something big. I didn't know what until years later, but I'd never seen him scared. Except for the times he was depressed, he was always so self-assured. But at that time, he wasn't just worried. He was petrified. He said people would come for him if he didn't succeed. That those people would come for us, too. They would make examples of his whole family to keep people scared of going against the Club. We all would have paid the price." Misery-laced eyes met Adam's. "You're not the only one who can protect the family."

"But you dragged Emily into it."

"She volunteered."

"What?"

"She knew I needed a way to distract you. She knew I was considering any number of ways to get you out of town, or knock you out. She was the one who suggested the milder roofie version. Shit, I wouldn't have hurt you, but she's the one who wanted to do it the most humane way possible. She didn't know what I was up to that night, just that it was bad—real bad. And dangerous. When she couldn't talk me out of it, she was afraid you'd get in trouble if she didn't stop you from coming after me. She was afraid *for you*."

"She really was protecting me that night?" And he'd treated her like dirt.

"Yeah. So don't act like I'm the only bad guy left in the family. I didn't rip her heart to shreds. You did that all on your own."

"I didn't ask her to tell me she loved me."

It was Tanner's turn to look shocked. "She told you that?"

Adam shoved a hand through his hair. "Christ, part of me thought it was a trick, another distraction."

Tanner's glower darkened. "And you just... left? With no explanation. Fuck, man. That's cold."

Apparently Emily had never shared the little details of that night with Tanner. For that, Adam was grateful, and he felt all the more protective of her and what they'd shared—even if he'd denied they shared anything at the time. "I didn't ask her to love me." It had scared the shit out of him, her blind profession of love. "She begged me to take her with me. She was young and didn't know what she wanted out of life. What was I supposed to do?"

"Take her with you."

Adam stared at him in disbelief. "That would never have worked. I had to get my own head together."

"You're assuming Emily would have been a lot of work, but she's always been the most self-reliant person I know." Tanner laughed without humor. "Or maybe you were afraid she wouldn't need you, wouldn't come to depend on you like the rest of us had. Then you couldn't play the martyr."

"And what about you? You walked away from her just a few days ago. That woman cares about you. She's bent over backwards trying to help you."

"She does that for all the people in her life. But there's only one person she's truly loved—at least, in *that* way."

Adam felt lightheaded and sank his head back into the couch cushion. "I didn't believe it, didn't trust it."

"It was there, if you'd only looked close enough." After a full minute of silence, Tanner's anger dissipated. "She's a CI. Did you know that?"

"Yeah."

"And do you know why?"

"I'm assuming it's to save your sorry ass."

Tanner nodded. "Now, maybe. But it started before that, when she was working on saving her dad's sorry ass."

Adam froze. He remembered Emily's dad as a boisterous drunk who spent money freely. It was part of the reason her dad and Adam's had gotten along so well. They'd been two peas in a pod. Or two drunks on barstools.

"And her mother's," Tanner continued. "And yours, too, in a way. Emily's thinking of everyone but herself, or her own safety. In exchange for information about the Redemption Club, the LVPD is promising not to press more charges against her dad, who's already in jail, or her mother, who's now incapacitated but had performed her share of swindles in the past. The memory care facility costs an arm and a leg each month. Mrs. Moore already lost most of her memory, so Emily's protecting what she has left—*without* running cons, though she could make ten times the money she makes at the bar."

Adam had seen firsthand how Emily cared for her mother, but her father had left her and her mother for an entire year before coming back into their lives and acting as if they should welcome him with open arms. At least, that's the impression Adam had received at the time. "Why should she risk herself to help her father?"

Tanner shrugged. "Why should she help any of us? Maybe she's a sap for an underdog. Or maybe when she cares, she cares with her whole heart. Her mother was decent, when she wasn't off for days on some adventure, which was nearly always. And her dad was into his moneymaking schemes. From the time Emily could walk, he'd use her in his cons, when he needed her. Didn't give her a choice."

Adam had been too busy working, helping raise Tanner, and bailing out his dad to notice the intimate details of Emily's life, and she'd never volunteered information. They'd connected by talking about dreams of the future, but rarely had she wanted to discuss reality. And in those later months, he'd avoided being around her much at all. She made him yearn for things he could never have, and she was much too wild to stick. Women didn't stick, period.

He'd had relationships in the past, but he'd made sure he never fell for the woman. Inevitably, the relationship would die and someone would be disappointed. That wasn't fair to anyone, so he'd purposely picked women who didn't expect much of him. And if they started to expect too much, he was gone the next day.

Fuck, maybe his super power *was* running away, as Emily had accused him of. Maybe he'd inherited that from his mother.

Tanner smiled wryly. "I should have done more to protect her. Her father got her wrapped up in his schemes and one time, it went too far."

Adam went utterly still. "What do you mean?"

"The mark got mad, figured out what was going on. Took Emily as collateral until her father would repay him, except her father didn't have the money. She called me that night, crying, when she finally got away."

Adam spoke through gritted teeth. It seemed every muscle in his body was too frozen to move. "What happened to her?"

Tanner laughed harshly. "Nothing, but only because she kept her head. Got the guy drinking and waited until he passed out."

"When was this?"

"She had just turned eighteen."

Right before Adam had left, then. That explained her desperate plea to let her come with him—to which he'd turned an unsympathetic ear.

"She refused to help her father anymore. He threatened and cajoled, but she refused. And he cut her out of his life. I didn't know all of this at the time... not until a few years ago, when Howie Moore got arrested for a big-time scam and went to prison. Then I dug the story out of her. We were drinking one night and she shared it all. I think there was other stuff, too, but she doesn't like to talk about it."

Other stuff. Bad stuff. And yet, Emily still stuck by her parents, risking herself for them.

Tanner put his heads in his hands. "God, I should

have been there for her, but she'd started pulling back, wanting to put our con days in the past. She'd even started bartending school. I was hurt, and gave her a hard time, but she remained my friend."

Adam knew the guilt he was feeling, because he felt it himself.

I wouldn't be a burden. I can earn my own way. Those were her words, the appeal in her lovely brown eyes, when she'd had him locked up in her bedroom.

"There's more." Tanner's eyes were haunted. "It involves our dad, and how he hurt her family. I'm not sure how much of it she knows."

"I remember Dad saying he'd lost his partner," Adam recalled. His dad had been morose, but not entirely broken up about it. Frank Wilde had been the eternal optimist and trusted there was always something better coming down the pike. Emily's father had seemed like the complete opposite. "I'd assumed Emily would be better off with her dad gone."

"He was only gone for a year, when she was seventeen. She may have been better off during that time in some ways, but then her mother partied more than ever. Em was pretty much on her own."

"That's about the time she started coming around our house more." It was also when Adam's attraction to her had reached an uncomfortable level.

"And when the debtors started coming around, insisting on being paid, she went to work. She and I started running cons. For the money."

"It's always for the money." Adam resisted the urge to grab his brother by the collar and shake him. "But it's dangerous."

"Yeah." He nodded. "Took me a while to realize that, huh? Anyway, after her mother's accident and father's incarceration, she got her act together. Started a new life. Went to bartender's school and started teaching."

"Teaching?" Adam frowned. She hadn't mentioned teaching.

"At the community college. A class on gaming, how to gamble, and all that kind of stuff." That explained the curious blend of books at her apartment. Tanner grinned. "Jesus, I'm so fucking proud of her. She's made her way with legitimate jobs. Not like me, huh?"

"The poker gig's legitimate, right?" Adam had judged his brother harshly his whole life, but he loved him. "I'm sorry I've been so hard on you, but you've never been a waste of my time."

Tanner released a harsh laugh. "Could have fooled me. I could see the disappointment in your eyes every time you bailed me out. And yet, you kept coming."

"That's only because I knew you were—*are*—capable of so much more. We can turn this around. For all of us."

Tanner shook his head. "I'll probably be in prison or dead when this is over. It may be too late for me, but I'd do anything for Em." He narrowed his eyes on Adam. "And I'd protect her from anybody who might hurt her. Even you."

"I'm not here to hurt her."

"And yet, you will."

He shook his head but couldn't bring himself to verbally deny it. "She and I are working together to help clear you of the murder charge."

"And after?"

"I go back to my sane life and she goes back to her crazy one." That's how he wanted it. It's how it had to be. He didn't want to hurt her, but her life and his didn't mesh. Except, he'd been making assumptions about her lifestyle and goals that apparently weren't true.

Tanner scoffed. "You're an idiot. Sanity is overrated. And it's not like she lives the *vida loca* anymore, anyway."

"She's still making choices that aren't level-headed."

"Like loving you?" Tanner shot a glare at his brother. "I can see the way she's looking at you again."

"And I see the way she looks at you," Adam shot back. He was shocked when his brother burst out laughing.

"It's about damn time." Tanner leaned over to slap him on the shoulder. "I thought I'd never see the day you finally showed some honest emotion."

"I get angry." Case in point.

"It's not anger. You're jealous," he explained when Adam simply looked at him in confusion. Tanner sobered. "Not that you have reason to be. We love each other like family, like siblings, always there for each other when the shit hits the fan. But no matter how much you want Em, you still won't stay. Not even for her."

"She can make her own decisions, Tanner. I don't have any power over who she chooses to care about. I certainly wouldn't have recommended she gamble on me, but we're all grown-ups." And grown-ups had jobs. Responsibilities. They had to make tough choices.

"But she leads with her heart instead of her head, and the heart isn't so smart when it comes to making decisions." Tanner stood and went to a cabinet next to the flat-screen television. He opened it and pulled out a red leather-bound book.

The ledger. "You do have it."

"I brought a fake to the game that night. Had it made when Blake and I discovered we had a common enemy and started formulating a plan. Ryan Stone was growing too powerful, too vengeful. Somebody had to stop him."

"And you elected yourself?"

Tanner shrugged. "Like I said, you're not the only one in the family with protective instincts." He flipped to a page and laid it out on the table, turning it so that Adam could see. "And this is what I'm trying to protect Emily from. I think you have a right to know why she's fighting so hard to get this ledger and take down the Club."

Adam scanned the page, which was full of entries

with dates from five years ago, names, signatures, card values and denominations, and favors traded. A familiar name caught his eye. *Frank Wilde.*

"That date is two weeks before the car accident that almost killed her mother," Tanner said when he saw that Adam had finished reading.

Jesus. Adam's chest tightened as he realized what this news would do to Emily. "Her mother wasn't the intended target."

"Our father wanted her father dead because he wanted Emily's mother, who was having an affair with dear Dad, all to himself." Tanner shook his head. "Karen Moore wasn't supposed to be the one driving down to Sedona that day, Howie was. Emily's mom almost died. In some ways, she did die, because she was never the same. Ironic how some things work out. And then Dad drank himself to death from the guilt of what he'd done."

"How much do you think Emily knows?"

"She definitely knows the Club was somehow involved in the accident. That's what led her to take a job at Legacy and why she's seeking the ledger. But I don't think she knows the who, what, or why of it all. And if she knew, she might never forgive our family."

CHAPTER TWENTY

After an hour went by, Emily figured she'd given the Wilde brothers enough time for their reunion. There was work to be done, and not much time to do it. Ryan was expecting her to meet his demands by midnight, which left them about seventeen hours.

She'd run a quick errand within the hotel and made a call to Angela to ensure she could take over running the lounge for the day. She'd ordered breakfast and taken a quick shower.

She was feeling human again as she wheeled the room service cart into Tanner's suite through the adjoining door. Both brothers looked up as she entered, their conversation dying on their lips. Their eyes were troubled, their expressions grim. She tried not to feel hurt or angry that they'd left her out. Maybe they'd simply wanted time to catch up or discuss Tanner's options.

And then her gaze landed on the red leather-bound book on the coffee table. She knew where the false ledger was, so this had to be the real one. And damn, she wanted a look inside, but not with Tanner and Adam so close by.

She clapped her hands together once, determined to change whatever subject was hanging heavy as a bloated storm cloud in the room. "I brought food and caffeine. It appears we already have the ledger, and the evidence Tanner recorded is in my purse, and of course we've located Tanner, which means I have everything Ryan Stone wants from me. Unfortunately for him, I'm not going to give him any of them, so what are we going to do to bring him down before he can hurt us?"

Tanner pushed to his feet. "*We're* not going to do anything. You're going to go back to your life and carry on like normal."

She huffed out a laugh. "It's far too late for normal. In fact, I'm pretty sure this *is* normal for me. Besides, Adam and I have reached an understanding and we're partners now. Or at least, I thought we'd come to an agreement." She tried to meet Adam's gaze but he was staring at the ledger as if it would disappear if he blinked.

"Jesus, Em, I thought you were smarter than this." Tanner looked at her with disappointment. "You'd let him take advantage of you *again*?" The heaviness in the room grew thicker and darker, like a living, breathing, *evil* thing. She could have sworn the same electrical current that generated lightning was making the hair on the back of her neck stand on end.

"He's not taking advantage." She jumped between them as Adam rose and the brothers looked prepared to bump chests in some masculine display. She shoved at Tanner's chest but he didn't budge. "And for the record, Adam never took advantage of me. He tried to do the right thing. And I take offense that you think I'd have *let* him take advantage. When have you ever known me to do anything I didn't want to do?"

Over her head, Tanner's hard gaze held Adam's a moment longer, before his lashes swept down and he met her eyes. "You're sure about that? Because last time—"

"I'm sure. I don't need you, or him, to save me." She could save her own damned self, and anyone else who came along.

Tanner scanned her expression and opened his mouth, looking as if he'd debate her words. But after a moment, he spun away and threw his hands up in surrender. "Fine. Have it your way." He stalked into the kitchen.

"He loves you," Adam said quietly.

She whirled to face him. "We've been friends forever. I know he cares."

Adam's dark eyes searched her face. "Why didn't you ever make a go with him?"

"We're too much alike."

"And?" He arched a brow. Damn, the guy could see right through her.

And my heart always belonged to you. She'd told him that. It was his choice whether or not to believe her. "And what does it matter? I'm not attracted to him in that way." She jerked a thumb over her shoulder. "Now are you going to stop him from lacing his coffee with whiskey at seven in the morning, before we can come up with a plan for tonight, or am I?"

The moment they sat down with their plates of food, Adam pinned his brother with a look. "I'll be running this operation."

Tanner nearly choked on a bite of pancakes. "What? No way." His eyes widened as he realized Adam wasn't kidding. Emily bit back a grin. "He's not serious," Tanner said to her, imploring her to help them find sanity.

She shrugged. "He told me if he's in, he's all in."

Adam grinned. "That's right. Besides, I'm guessing you don't have a better plan or you wouldn't be holed up here after nearly a week."

Tanner stabbed at another bite of pancakes. "I've set some things into motion that will hopefully protect us... and destroy Ryan's hold over anyone who owes him. I went over his head."

"Who's over his head?"

"His father. He's the only man Ryan's afraid of, though he likes to think he's not afraid of anybody."

"Sounds like you jumped from the frying pan and into the fire. Remington believes Robert Stone is just as responsible, if not more so, for the development of the Redemption Club."

Tanner grimaced. "Yeah, well, it didn't come to

anything. I sent Daddy Stone proof I had the real
ledger, figuring he would ostracize his defiant baby boy
or even turn him over in order to save Legacy from
further damage in the press. But Ryan wasn't sent
away or evicted or anything. I should have known that
blood would be thicker than water." He sent a sideways
glance to Adam that his brother didn't catch. No matter
what difficulties these two had been through, they were
still family. They'd always be there for each other.

"You're not seeing the bigger picture," Emily said.
"What does Ryan want more than anything? We figure
that out and we have the key to taking him down."

"The ledger," Tanner said.

She shook her head. "No. Power. Money. Status.
All preferably greater than what his father has. Those
are his weaknesses, and that's where we take aim." She
looked to Adam. "But we may have to bend a few laws."

Tanner scoffed. "We should do this without
Detective Justice."

Adam scowled at him. "You've always been my
number one priority. And you aren't the only one with
Frank Wilde's blood in your veins. He taught us both
how to run a con, and how to cheat. I know a few
tricks."

Tanner's brows went up.

Emily bit back a grin. "Okay, then. Here's what I
propose. We walk into the party and each target a
different area. Tanner, you have the most to lose, since
he wants you dead. You'll be flanked by Mason—"

Adam held up a hand. "Wait. We're not involving
outsiders."

"But we'll need backup. We're meeting Ryan on his
home turf."

Adam shook his head. "Too dangerous."

She crossed her arms and sat back. "You have a
better idea?"

"We continue to have private bodyguards watch
over your parents. Maybe even add an extra layer of
security. In the prison, we'll have to bribe some guards

to keep watch, maybe, but setting someone up at your mother's, someone we've vetted..."

"All in the next few hours?" Tanner asked. "How about we don't go to Ryan's party at all. We release his threats to the authorities. I've got his voicemails, though they're not very specific. But if something happens to us or Emily's parents, fingers would point at Ryan."

"*If?*" Emily gaped. "I'm not taking that chance. No, we have to look like we're going to bargain, as if we're going to give Ryan everything he wants, but fight for what we want. We take him down for good, by targeting those things I mentioned."

Adam lifted the pot to refill their coffees. "Okay then, hit us with your best ideas."

"Ryan demanded Tanner, and everything he has that's related to the Club. Obviously, he meant the ledger, and he probably knows about the memory card, or at least that there are copies out there. Tanner and I walk in—"

Adam arched a brow. "Not without me, I hope."

"You weren't invited, or expected. You being there will put him on guard. It's not like he'll let you bring in your weapons, anyway."

"I'm trained in hand-to-hand combat, too." He raised his hands at chest level and she had the fleeting fantasy of them on her body. She swallowed hard. "Besides, this is nonnegotiable. I'm team leader, remember?"

Tanner laughed.

"Right," Emily said to appease Adam. "You can watch our six then. But don't expect to get past the perimeter. He'll probably keep you out of the meeting room."

"And what will you be doing as I work crowd control among the party guests? How are you attacking item number one: Ryan's power?"

"By releasing the ledger to the media."

Tanner grinned. "Love that idea, except..." His

grin faded and he shot Adam a look.

"What?"

"I know people in the ledger who will be hurt if it became public." Tanner and Adam exchanged some nonverbal message that was lost on her.

"People who arranged for very bad things," Emily reminded them. "And did bad things in return. They deserve what they get."

"And their families?" Adam asked. "Do they deserve to be hurt by this?"

She bit her lip, her mind running through the alternatives. "We have to leak something, and make it look like Ryan can't control his Club. We take the Club away from him and that'll leave status and money. Maybe we choose a page or two that has a judge's name, or someone big and important. He screws them over and he'll never regain his reputation as a crime-boss-type dealmaker."

"Still not hitting him hard enough," Tanner muttered.

"I'm not done," Emily insisted. "Next, we go for status. I talked to Megan, his secretary, yesterday and he's had her send out some invites. Ryan loves his celebrations, and he must see tonight as a guaranteed success, because he's already invited some A-list people to be at his father's house. He probably wants us to take a walk of shame as we deliver the ledger."

"All the more reason not to attend," Tanner grumbled.

She ignored him. "Those guests are likely Club members. I can get a guest list from Megan and we can cross-reference the names with the ledger. I'm certain some of them will be in there. Maybe some of them have even ordered up crimes against each other, and we can expose some of those deals."

Tanner perked up. "Please let me read that list at the party. I volunteer for that job. We'll make Redemption Club *implode*."

Adam smirked, apparently on board with her plan

thus far. His gaze was filled with respect and a heat that warmed her belly. "And money?" he asked. "How are we taking that away from Ryan?"

"His money comes primarily from the Club—which we've already addressed with prongs one and two of the attack—but also from his father's fortune. We convince Mr. Stone to abandon Ryan and he'll be left out in the cold—which won't matter because he'll be in prison by then, but we need Robert Stone's cooperation, his agreement not to bail Ryan out this time, in order to totally do away with this threat."

"And how do we make a father forsake his only son, especially when Ryan's a chip off the old block?" Tanner opened the ledger to the first page. "I've had a lot of time to look through this thing. Interesting reading material. Judging by the oldest dates recorded, I'd say either Ryan was a prodigious ten-year-old, or someone from the previous generation started the Club. There's a gap of time when Robert Stone appears to have gone legit, but it picks up again about ten years ago. Ryan would have been about twenty-one."

"And probably thought he was invincible," Adam added. "If his father started the Club, he'd want this ledger as much as anyone. It's evidence against him, too."

"So we give him the ledger," Emily said. "Or we make him think we did."

Tanner sat forward. "We use the fake one. Do you know where it is?"

"I can get my hands on it. We use that to get our foot in the door and make another switch. With the three of us there, we can come up with some kind of distraction. When it's all over, we'll give the real one to the authorities." She looked to Adam. "I'll let you figure out who we can trust on that front."

"But how does that get Stone on our side, and not his son's?" Adam asked.

"We tell him his son was blackmailing and lying to him for years."

"We have no proof," Tanner said. "I've been trying all week to figure out how to recreate what was in that folder Blake had, but no luck."

Emily shot him an incredulous look. "We have the perfect proof. The recording you made of Blake's murder. In it, Blake offers up a folder full of proof as his ante."

"Stone wouldn't be able to deny what's before his very eyes, unless he thinks we manipulated the video. And all you see is a manila folder. How is that supposed to convince him we had proof?"

"We don't need actual evidence. I'm pretty sure the seed of doubt was planted in Mr. Stone's mind years ago. Ivy told me her brother's always looked for ways to show up their father. We nourish that seed and it'll bloom."

"Let's hope it blooms quickly," Adam said.

"And if we offer to destroy the ledger before his very eyes, so we can all see the evidence of Redemption Club is gone for good, we can all walk out of there alive."

"And we'll still have enough for the police to arrest Ryan because we'll have the real ledger," Adam said. "I like that."

"And there will be nobody to bail Ryan out this time," Tanner added. "I like *that*."

Adam's warm gaze met hers and he toasted her with his coffee cup. "Looks like we have a plan."

The sun was getting higher in the sky beyond the living room windows as they wrapped up their planning session. Their plates had been cleared, the coffee was long gone, and Emily had yawned four times in the past five minutes. Adam could use some sleep himself. There had been too many nights spent in his car, or not sleeping at all, and the suite next door had his choice of at least four huge beds he could fall into.

Adam stood and stretched. "As team leader, I

suggest we all get some rest before the party tonight."

"I've got an email out to Megan," Emily said, looking up from her phone. "I'm sure she'll send me the guest list by this afternoon. She'll assume I'm preparing to bartend for the party, as usual."

Tanner put the ledger back in the cabinet. They hadn't looked inside during the meeting, though Adam had caught Emily staring at it more than once. He didn't like keeping secrets from her, but this wasn't the time to tell her the truth about her mother's accident. He needed her focus totally on the plan tonight. And if she were angry with him or Tanner for this family secret, she might go off on her own instead. Inside, he cursed his father's choices for the thousandth time.

"Good thing we have blackout curtains," Tanner said.

"Just what every all-night gambler needs," Emily said, walking to the fireplace mantle. She picked up a remote and pressed a button. The blinds slowly slid across the fifteen-foot-tall wall of windows. A moment later, only the soft lights from the living room lamps illuminated the suite, giving the illusion of nighttime.

Behind her back, Tanner shot him a look. "There are plenty of empty rooms in my suite. I suggest you pick one." He held Adam's gaze a moment more, communicating a silent warning that echoed their earlier conversation. *Don't hurt her.* Tanner placed a quick kiss on Emily's cheek. "Sleep well." He disappeared into one of the bedrooms and the door clicked shut behind him.

The silence seemed to ring louder between Adam and Emily. For once, his brain and body were in sync, urging him to make a move, to tell her how he felt about her before the events of this evening went down and life returned to normal.

But the voice went quiet and everything calmed when she turned to him. She was smiling, relaxed and confident in their plan, and his heart shifted and fell a little farther down that slippery slope, clawing as it tried to gain purchase and failed.

Who was he kidding? His heart had always belonged to her, even if he hadn't wanted to recognize the facts. Today, he'd watched her strategize, carefully point out the pitfalls that could hurt them, and eagerly offer to put herself on the frontlines and take the brunt of the danger. He could no longer pretend that she was a teenager who didn't know what she wanted.

She was a woman, a warrior who would protect those she loved.

And she was nothing like his mother, who had abandoned her family. Emily was smart, dependable, fiercely loyal—and everything he wanted.

"What?" she asked, looking at him curiously when the silence between them stretched on.

"I think we've come up with a solid plan," Adam said. "I'm just... amazed, I guess."

She laughed. "That we can be that smart?"

He stepped forward and took her hand, bringing it to his lips. "That we could work together so well."

She grinned. "The con artists and the lawman. Maybe you're starting to see shades of gray after all?"

"My vision's definitely improving." He was seeing her more clearly than he ever had. Filled with a combination of exhaustion and adrenaline-induced confidence, he didn't want to fight his feelings anymore. "I see a woman I'd like to kiss."

Her gaze dipped to his lips. "I'd like you to do so much more."

CHAPTER TWENTY-ONE

She'd dared to show her cards, but would she lose again?

The risk was worth the payoff as Adam responded with an arched brow and a tip of his head toward the door that led to the other suite. *Their* suite. She realized she'd thought of it as such since the moment she'd programmed the keycard.

Something had shifted between them over the past few days, and she couldn't put her finger on it, but it was big. Powerful. And seductive.

She'd come to trust him with her heart. She knew, better than anyone, probably, how people could use and manipulate each other. Her trust had been totally shattered when one of the few people whom she trusted—really, there'd only been Tanner and Adam— had ripped her heart out of her chest and stomped on it. But he'd never intended to hurt her. He cared, in his own way. He might still leave when this was over, but she'd survived him leaving before, and she would again. She deserved a bit of happiness before he took her heart with him.

When she smiled her assent, he grabbed her hand and pulled her behind him, not stopping until they were inside the first of the luxuriously appointed bedrooms. He paused long enough to close and lock the door, then wasted no time pressing her up against it.

She gasped as his teeth nipped at her earlobe. His mouth continued a downward path, scraping lightly along her neck. His fingers circled her wrists and lifted them above her head, holding her prisoner. Not that she wanted to escape.

"I want you. All of you." His hot breath hitched in a way that matched her heart's ragged pace. He kissed her collarbone, dipping his tongue into the sensitive hollow, and she moaned.

"You have me. *All* of me." And he always had. "It's *your* turn to show *me* what I've been missing, what I've been fantasizing about for years."

He pulled away to look into her eyes. "That's a lot of pressure to put on a man." There was a teasing note in his voice that made her smile. Her black-and-white lawman had so many more facets than others realized. It was their loss, her gain.

"I think you can handle it. In fact, I'm betting on it." She leaned forward to catch his bottom lip between her teeth. He sucked in a breath, his chest rising against her breasts. Every muscle that clenched, every exhalation or tremor of desire within him, she felt.

Holding her body to his, he spun with her away from the door and backed her to the king-sized bed. He reached around to yank the bedspread and blankets down in one impatient movement. He straightened and covered her mouth with his again. His hands worked at the button on her jeans and then slid the zipper down as she did the same for him. They undressed in a flurry of flying fabrics until they were skin to skin.

He lifted her against him, and grabbed the back of her knees. She wrapped her legs around his waist, feeling the hard ridge of his erection so, so close to her core that she ached for him. She slid her body slowly over his, her nipples brushing against his chest, and he groaned.

His hands went to her butt. "Not yet, baby." He held her still, his hands massaging her as he settled in at her mouth, enjoying the play of tongue and teeth and lips until she was writhing against him.

"More," she urged. Her demand seemed to snap his control and he dropped her onto the bed, his body immediately following her down. She gasped as her bare skin connected with the fabric.

"Cold sheets," she explained when he looked at her with concern.

"I'll keep you warm." His body heat was such a sensual counterpoint to the crisp sheets that she gasped again, this time from pleasure. He caught her moan in his mouth. Her hands skimmed down his backside, holding him close. She wanted to feel all of him along all of her.

He ducked his head to explore her breasts. She bucked beneath him as his mouth found first one nipple, then the other, suckling them lightly, teasing and promising pleasure at the same time. She never wanted it to end. But the slow build—years of it—was creating an intense ache that would only be satisfied when he completely joined with her.

She wrapped her legs around his waist and nestled him closer to her body, to the spot that throbbed for him. He pressed urgently between her thighs and his hand went to her jaw, stroking down her neck. Then, everything went still. He'd stopped.

Stopped? She opened her eyes to find him looking down into hers.

"You okay?" he asked.

"Never better." She used the feet she'd locked at the ankles to hold him close as she ducked upward to nip at his jawline. *Keep it playful.*

His hands framed her face, holding her at a distance so he could read her emotions in the soft light.

"Are you going to make me beg, just so you can walk out again?" She unwrapped her legs and was about to roll him off her when his fingers tightened in her hair.

"I'm not going anywhere. I never want to leave, but I don't want to hurt you." With those cryptic words, he kissed her softly, as if sealing a vow, but the hunger could not be tamed—not after being denied for so long. The kiss became a heated fight for purchase, a primal claiming of each other.

He groaned. "You taste so sweet."

She laughed. "But we both know I'm not."

His hand slid down her stomach to find the spot that drove her wild. "I'm going to have to argue with you on that point." His finger dipped into her as his thumb slid against the bundle of nerves that had her arching into his hand.

Let him argue. It was what they'd always done best, after all—until now.

She was sweet, and spicy, and everything he'd dreamed of for so many years—when the dreams had slipped past his defenses and caught him unawares. He hadn't allowed himself the luxury of pretending anything like this could ever really happen.

And yet, it *was* happening. He'd looked into her eyes and been taken aback by the raw desire and... *more* that he'd read there. He'd nearly stopped, worried about the intensity of what he was feeling, about the emotions within that were mirrored in her body language and sighs of pleasure. Emotion. She'd told him he didn't do emotion, but this overwhelming need to be with her felt big. Important. On a different scale than anything he'd felt for anyone before.

Love? It couldn't be. Not between them. Not for him.

After all, they were still keeping secrets from each other. He could sense she held part of herself back, even as the rest of her was so hot and ready, pulsing with desire for him. That he would be given such a precious gift blew him away.

And that she would trust him with her heart. That was a whole different level of faith.

He spent several minutes paying homage to each beautiful piece of the puzzle that was Emily Moore before slipping on a condom and resettling between her thighs. He waited until her eyes were open, and held her gaze as he slid inside her, burying himself as she shifted to take all of him. Passion flared in her honeyed gaze, but she didn't look away, didn't hide who she was or what she wanted. That was Emily, always giving fully of herself.

His heart raced, beating only for her, but he forced himself to take it slow. She moved restlessly beneath him as he brought her to the brink, but he wasn't ready to end what he'd been waiting so long for. He laughed against her lips and used one hand to pin her wrists above her head.

"Not yet, baby," he said. "I've been waiting too long for this. We have all day."

He refused to think about what tonight or tomorrow would bring. She would probably hate him after he implemented Plan B—*his* plan—but it was for her own good. Instead of her saving others, he would save her for a change.

Her breath hitched and he knew she was close to the edge. Her body tightened and he released her wrists so that he could reach down between their joined bodies to rub the spot that would toss her over. He quickened his pace, letting her little gasps and soft sounds of pleasure guide him.

"Adam!" Her sudden shout, his name on her lips, her hooded gaze on his... She pulled him into the oblivion with her.

Minutes later, he'd pulled her against his side, her leg was thrown over his hips, her hand stroking slow circles over his heart as if marking it. He could have told her it was already hers, but there would be no point. They were on stolen time. They could shut out reality for a few hours, but it was lurking in the shadows, a force to be reckoned with. And there would be a reckoning, soon.

He intended to keep the threats away from their bed as long as he could. And he intended to do what he had to do to protect her, even if she'd come out of this despising him.

Emily blinked into the darkness. The blackout curtains had made the room seem like the dead of night, though it had to be the middle of the afternoon. Adam's body was tucked around her, his heat engulfing her as he slept. His chest rose against her back in a regular rhythm that indicated he was sleeping deeply.

Now was her chance. She couldn't wait any longer. She'd already waited years.

She slowly lifted his arm from where it draped over her hip. He moaned softly and tried to snuggle closer, but she slid to the edge of the bed and rolled to her feet. Without turning on any lights, she tiptoed toward the adjoining bathroom and removed a robe from the back of the door.

As she passed the bed again, Adam rolled over onto his back and said her name. She froze for a long minute, holding her breath. The rise and fall of his chest soon evened out again and she took a few hesitant steps forward before hurrying out of the room.

In contrast to the dim bedroom, the living room was as bright as the middle of the afternoon should be. Here, she hadn't drawn the curtains. Beside the couch, she dropped to her knees, sliding her hand underneath the furniture. A breath of relief whooshed out of her as her fingertips connected with the leather-bound book. Tanner had done an excellent job making a copy of the ledger. Of course, they knew the best forger in Vegas.

Earlier, while Tanner and Adam had been busy chatting without her, she'd taken the opportunity to sneak downstairs and break into Ryan's office and take what she wanted. Silly, really, that Ryan would think a locked drawer would keep people out. Then again, it wasn't the real ledger he kept in there. And, she'd consumed the fabulously decadent cupcake instead of leaving it for that undeserving bastard.

She scooped up the ledger and quietly cracked open the door adjoining the suites. No sign of Tanner.

Wincing when the hinges creaked slightly, she forced herself to stand still for a full minute until she was sure neither Wilde brother had heard and come running. When the coast remained clear, she entered Tanner's suite and moved to the fireplace mantel where the Redemption Club ledger lay.

The air conditioner switched on, startling her and setting off goose bumps. It also prompted her to move her ass. She didn't want to be discovered and have to explain what she was doing with two ledgers.

Switching out the forgery, she took the original back into the suite she shared with Adam. She was tempted to search out the information right then and there, but flipping on a light, or even being gone from Adam's side for too long, would be a risk. They'd woken twice already today, always reaching for each other as if they couldn't get enough.

Sex had never been this good, probably because her partners had never measured up to the standards she'd held them to. They'd never been Adam. Even without having known him in an intimate way, her heart had suspected what it could be like between them. Even so, she'd underestimated the intensity of the connection forming between them.

He's still going to leave you.

She slapped a hand over the imaginary mouth of the voice in her head. She had this moment, and sometimes you had to live for those few precious instants that made everything else worthwhile.

She crept back into their bedroom.

"Emily?" Adam's voice was a rasp. She could barely make out his form in the darkness, but he was rolling toward her side of the bed. Her empty side.

She ducked into the bathroom and shoved the ledger under the sink, placing some folded towels on top of it. "I'm here," she called softly. She climbed back in beside Adam, curling into his warmth.

"You don't need this." His sleep-roughened voice tickled her senses as his fingers found the tie on her robe and undid it. "I like you much better completely exposed to me. For me."

She did, too, and she stifled the tiny bit of guilt that reminded her she was hiding things from him. She'd make it up to him by giving him the rest of her. And she spent the next portion of the afternoon doing just that.

Emily woke from a deep sleep in which her limbs were languid, her blood pumped slow and thick through her body, and her skin still tingled from Adam's kisses. She stretched—or tried to.

As her arm resisted obeying her brain's command, she froze, her eyelids flying open as she jiggled her right wrist. It was trapped. An actual manacle overlaid the delicate chain tattooed on her skin. The other end of the handcuff was locked to the post of the bed, secured between the headboard and the frame.

She pushed into a sitting position. "Adam?"

She'd drifted off with her ear pressed to his heart, her arm rising and falling regularly where it rested on his abdomen. Her last memory was of his hand laid possessively across her hip, and how it had made her heart complete its landslide into the unknown.

She was in love with Adam Wilde. Again. Perhaps she'd never stopped.

But now? There was no sign of him. His side of the bed was cold. To add insult to injury, he'd handcuffed her as she had once done to him. She'd at least been kind about it, staying and watching over him as he'd slept.

Fool.

Her next thought was for the ledger and she looked toward the bathroom door. There was no way of knowing if the prize she sought was still hidden away. Not until she got herself out of this trap. She berated herself for letting down her guard, but shoved it aside. There was work to be done, and getting over this bump in the road would require all her energy. She'd channel her anger into finding a solution.

Her gaze searched the room, which was lit only by a slender part in the curtains. There was no answer when she called out his name. No sound at all except the air conditioner, which blew cool air against her suddenly ice-cold skin.

A glance at the clock told her it was early evening. The party would begin in a few hours. Like vampires, Ryan's crowd liked the cloak of darkness to blanket their bad behavior. Drugs, alcohol, murder... And Adam and Tanner were going to walk into that without her. At least they'd be somewhat prepared, as she'd forwarded Adam the email from Megan with the guest list the moment it had come through on her phone.

Not that Adam deserved her help.

She jiggled the handcuffs again, but they were high-quality police cuffs—not the velvet-lined ones she'd used on him. They weren't budging. Was this Adam's version of retribution, for when she'd chained him and kept him from interfering? She wasn't going to let him cut her out of this. That ledger held the answers she needed to resolve her mother's situation and move on. She only needed a few minutes to search out the entry.

First, she had to get free. She tugged on the manacle until her wrist ached, but the bed's frame was sturdy.

If she called for help, she had only a sheet to shield her nudity from whoever answered the call. But modesty wouldn't stop her from getting loose so she could be at that party. At the very least, she had to help Adam and Tanner. Except when she reached for her phone, it was, of course, no longer on the bedside table where she'd left it. Nor was the hotel's house phone, when it had been plugged in there just hours before. They'd accidentally kicked it off the table during a particularly enthusiastic moment in their lovemaking.

Lovemaking. A laugh squeaked past her tight throat, emerging as a pitiful croak.

Adam had unplugged and moved the phone across the room. She swung her legs over the edge of the bed and her toes brushed a slip of paper on the rug. Her name was scrawled across the top in Adam's handwriting. Using her toes, she scraped it across the carpet toward the bed until she could lean down and pick it up with her free hand.

Em, this is for the best. It's safer this way. Tanner understands that mine is the better plan, so don't count on him to save you. I'll send security to release you in a few hours, after it's all over.

All over, her ass. She was a part of this. She needed to be a part of this—for Adam's safety. And Tanner's. And her family's.

She'd show Adam that nobody could out-con Emily Moore.

CHAPTER TWENTY-TWO

The sun had reached the horizon and the Vegas lights were gradually switching on, the twinkles and splashes of neon growing in number as Adam waited. He couldn't prevent a smile as he thought about handcuffing Emily's naked body to their bed. God, he'd fantasized about that so many times.

His smile quickly faded. In the reflection on his side of the tall window, the door connecting Tanner's suite to his and Emily's was closed and locked. It was ridiculous to hope that one more barrier would be enough to make him forget what he'd done, and all that he'd just walked away from.

She was quite possibly awake by now, feeling betrayed and angry, but he couldn't think about her. He had a mission to complete, and then he could make it up to her. If she'd let him. It was very possible she wouldn't give him the time of day when this was over. And he couldn't blame her. He'd done the same to her for eight years, and he'd only punished both of them needlessly.

Then again, she'd forgiven him before. He'd do whatever he had to—hell, he'd chain himself to her bed and be his slave for as long as she wanted—if she'd give him another chance. He hadn't been ready for her all those years ago, but he was willing to take a risk. This bond, or whatever it was, between them was a force that wouldn't be denied. So maybe he should stop denying it.

"Daydreaming?" Rumpled and wearing only his

boxers, Tanner moved into his kitchen to pour a cup of the coffee Adam had set to brew. The look he sent Adam was half-incredulous, half-amused. "That smiling thing isn't like you."

"Maybe I had a good day." But his lighter emotions gave way to darker ones as he watched Tanner's gaze move over the open bedroom doors in his suite to the closed and locked door between the two suites.

Tanner's brows drew together. "Where's Emily? Does she have the guest list yet?"

"I have the list. And she's not coming."

Tanner straightened. "What?"

"I've removed her from the equation. I'm hoping you'll be reasonable and see that we both need to agree on this decision in order to keep her safe."

To Adam's surprise, Tanner only took a moment to consider the request before he nodded. "I'm glad you found a way. You didn't hurt her, did you?"

"Of course not." Not physically, anyway. She'd be steaming mad, though. Of course, Adam had experienced similar feelings of betrayal and frustration. He'd gotten over it. He could only hope she would, too. "She's otherwise occupied."

Tanner blew out a breath. "Okay then, how do you want to work this job now? Without Emily, I mean. The plan was to go in there as a trio. Who's our third?"

"I'll fill you in on the way. Grab a shower and get dressed." Adam would use one of the other bedrooms and bathrooms in the suite to do the same, and try his damnedest not to think of Emily so close by, naked and angry.

"What about the ledger?"

"That part of the plan stays the same. I'll need to borrow something to wear to the party, if you have anything." He didn't want to have to return to Tanner's apartment, in case Ryan was still having it watched.

"I should have something."

To survive the past week, Tanner had ordered clothing delivered from Legacy's men's boutique downstairs. The brothers were nearly identical in size. It might be a tighter fit across the shoulders, but at least he'd brought his ankle holster for his gun, so his shoulder holster wouldn't have to fit beneath a suit jacket.

"Good. Let's get moving." Before his brain listened to his heart and he went back to his bedroom to set Emily free.

"Damn it!" As another fingernail broke off, Emily uttered a few more choice expletives, all aimed at Adam and the entire Wilde family tree. Three of the five nails on her free hand were broken and jagged. Freeing the framing nail from the bottom of the nightstand with one hand was slow going. At least an · hour had passed since she'd awoken alone, naked and defenseless.

It had probably been forty-five minutes since she'd decided defenseless was a state of mind she'd rather not remain in. She'd kicked over the nightstand in her search for something thin that she could fashion into a lock pick. The wood on the underside of the table was unfinished, and one of the nails hadn't been hammered in straight. And so she'd spent the better part of an hour sitting on the floor, her cuffed hand resting on the mattress as she used her free hand to wiggle and scrape, working at freeing the nail, millimeter by millimeter.

She hissed as she discovered another sliver in the skin under the fingernail, and used her teeth to pull it out. Slivers and broken nails were a small price to pay for freedom. Adam, on the other hand, would have hell to pay when she caught up to him.

After another twenty minutes, she'd managed to wiggle some of the nail free. Her fingertips sore, she bent to take it between her teeth and tug. The nail gave a little more and suddenly it was free. She scrambled to the lamp she'd set on the ground before kicking the table over. Thankfully, it was a heavy stone base. She laid the nail against the corner of the nightstand and hammered at the head of it until the straight nail formed a ninety-degree angle near the tip. A homemade lock pick.

Pushing to her feet, she sat on the mattress and went to work on the handcuff.

A few prayers and mistrials later, the lock opened and the cuff slid from her wrist. Emily nearly cried tears of relief, but she blinked them back. There was too much to do.

She pulled on the robe that Adam had removed from her only hours ago and ran through the suite, checking every room. They were all empty.

She moved on to Tanner's suite, but the door that joined them was locked. She pounded on it for a moment, but stopped as the throbbing of her hand pulsed all the way to her bruised and bloodied fingertips. It was pointless. The brothers had to be long gone by now.

Back in her bathroom, she dropped to her knees, not caring that in her hurry, she bruised them. She reached into the cabinet under the sink and jerked aside the folded towels, releasing a puff of relieved breath as she spied the red leather. Adam hadn't found it.

But that also meant Adam might not know he had the fake ledger. In fact, since he hadn't come to her, demanding to know what she'd done with the real thing, he definitely didn't know the truth. And he had no reason to suspect she'd made the switch—because he trusted her. Although, not enough to let her help with the plan to take down Ryan, apparently.

If he went to Ryan with the fake, and Ryan looked closely enough, which was almost a guarantee after he'd been duped by Tanner before, he might even kill Adam and Tanner on the spot for double-crossing him.

Maybe Tanner would notice they'd been switched. But they'd had no reason to believe she'd done such a thing. And Adam had taken her cell phone, so she had no way of reaching him. She pressed her fingertips to her forehead, trying to see the phone number he'd scribbled down on a coaster for her, but she couldn't remember. *Damn it.*

Anger and hurt warred with worry as she thought about Tanner and Adam going up against Ryan Stone without her. Hadn't they trusted her to do her part?

At the very least, she could find the answer she wanted. But as she flipped through the ledger, she found no entry around the time of her mother's car accident. That couldn't be right. She flipped through a few more pages, scanning for her mother's name. Each entry had a few lines of details about the act, reason for the request, and which Club member had been assigned to the task, but she still didn't find the name she sought. And there were no other entries around that time, either. She ran a finger along the inside of the spine to confirm her suspicion. A page had been removed.

She scrambled to her feet. Back in the bedroom, she reconnected the hotel phone and called the one person she thought she could trust right now. While working to get free, she'd played out several scenarios in her head, and this seemed the most likely to succeed, and yet gave all of them the greatest chance of survival.

"Hello?" Ivy answered at her suite.

"Oh, thank God you're there," Emily said.

"You'd be proud of me. I'm taking the night off to pamper myself. I've decided I should start doing that at least once a week, like a sane person."

"Can I come over?"

"Sure. Are you on break?"

"I took the night off, too. I'll be there in two minutes."

"Two?"

Without explaining, Emily hung up and raced to pull on her shoes. She considered putting on her clothes from earlier in the day, but seeing them lying on the floor, where they'd landed when Adam had peeled them off her, her stomach twisted. She'd been at an all-time high just hours ago. Now, she'd crashed back to earth. Luckily, she was only going across the hall.

She tightened the tie on her robe, adjusted the collar and ran her fingers through her tangled hair as if it would make her look less bat-shit crazy. She winced at her forgotten sore fingertips. She grabbed the ledger and crossed the hall to Ivy's suite.

Ivy answered her knock immediately. "You weren't kidding about only being two minutes away." Her gaze surveyed Emily from head to toe, pausing for a moment on the ledger. "Or that you were taking the night off, apparently."

Emily looked each direction down the hall, from the elevator to Ryan's door just a few yards away. He was probably at his father's house, getting ready to greet his guests, but she still felt exposed. "Can I come in?"

"Of course." Ivy stepped aside.

Feeling better once the door was closed behind her, Emily followed Ivy inside, surprised to see her friend in her pajamas. "You're not going to the party?" Ivy often did the planning, played hostess, and entertained guests at her family's events.

"I begged off with a headache. Besides, this is Ryan's thing, not Dad's. And I'm supposed to be packing for that two-month tour of the company's holdings."

"Your dad won't be at the party, either?" She had been counting on speaking to the man.

"For once, Dad didn't seem to mind." Probably because he and Ryan had other events planned for the evening. Ivy hadn't reacted to the ledger, which confirmed Emily's belief that she hadn't known about Redemption Club, or her brother's involvement in it. "Can I get you some wine? We can make this a girl's night—"

"I would love that, but some other time."

Sensing the seriousness in Emily's tone, Ivy looked her in the eyes. "What's going on? Are you okay?"

Emily bit her lip, not sure how to proceed without hurting Ivy.

"Is this about Ryan?" Ivy sighed. "Has he done something inappropriate while managing the lounge?"

"It's so much worse than that."

Ivy pulled her to the couch. "Tell me what's going on." When Emily hesitated, Ivy squeezed her hand. "I know my brother's not usually a nice person. He puts himself first. And you wouldn't be the first person to complain to me. Tell me what he's done, and why the heck you're at my doorstep in a Legacy robe on your night off."

"How much do you know about a group called the Redemption Club?" Emily set the ledger on the coffee table.

Ivy frowned. "I know the leader was killed two months ago, and that he had some kind of deck of cards that was from Legacy. The police asked a bunch of questions, especially of Ryan, because he knew the guy. Never led to anything. I was just glad it didn't hurt the hotel."

"There's so much you don't know."

Sipping her glass of wine, Ivy listened as Emily caught her up to speed on the Club, the ledger, the different people who were after it, and the reason Emily had kept it for herself.

To her credit, Ivy didn't argue or leap to her brother's defense. She simply took it all in, and then asked, "How can I help?"

Surprised by her friend's easy acceptance, Emily shook her head. "I don't want you to have to take sides between your friends and your family."

"It's not your call." The businesslike Ivy was back in full force. "Protecting Legacy is what's important. That's my job. Besides, we all make choices and have to pay the consequences." Something like regret flashed in her eyes.

Emily got the feeling Ivy was referring to much more than Ryan's choices or the Redemption Club, but she didn't press. "Right now, you can help me make your brother take responsibility for his decisions. I think it's time to let your father know what's really been going on, and who's really at fault for Blake's murder. I don't want him to help Ryan escape justice."

Ivy shook her head. "I'm not sure that's possible. He'll get out of any kind of real prison time. If what you say about past events is true, you know what my father did to protect him from the last scandal. Dad's always believed in protecting his legacy, and Ryan, for all his faults, is part of that."

"I have a way to convince your father that protecting Ryan is the wrong thing to do." Emily told Ivy about the blackmail scheme Ryan had perpetrated on Ivy's father.

Ivy paled. "That's horrible, but not terribly shocking. Ryan's always looked out for himself first. If we show my father that Ryan's actions are hurting the family business, and that he had the audacity to blackmail his own flesh and blood, I think he'll choose to help you. What do you need?"

"First, I need to borrow some clothes. And some clippers or a nail file." Maybe she could repair some of the damage she'd done to her fingernails. "Second, I need more collateral. If I bring the real ledger to bargain with your father, I need a reason for him to let me go. I need to get into Ryan's suite."

"Why? I would think he destroyed the folder of evidence Blake had on him."

"Yes, but he's got a bunch of half-cards somewhere, and his safe is the most likely place. Those cards are just as important as the ledger. They signify debts to the Club, like IOUs."

"So you want to break into his suite and crack his safe?" Amusement and excitement lit Ivy's green eyes like light glinting off emeralds.

"It'll take some time." Time she didn't have. "But, yes. I need those cards to get us all—Ryan included—out of tonight's party alive."

Ivy grabbed her hand and pulled her up from the couch. "Lucky for you, I have the master key."

Adam turned down a side street and pulled his car into the driveway of a mansion whose immense yard butted up to that of Robert Stone's property. The sun was setting, turning the sky a fiery red, and reminding him of Emily's phoenix tattoo. Was she still in their bed, growing angrier by the minute? Cursing him?

He'd have to make it up to her when this was all over. Of course, he hadn't let her make it up to him for all those years he was angry. Maybe she would hold a grudge just as long. His chest tightened at the thought of not having her in his life, but he'd rather have her alive and well than caught in the middle of this and possibly killed.

But he wasn't done pissing off loved ones yet. There was one more person he'd sworn to protect.

In the passenger seat, Tanner looked up from the guest list he was studying on Adam's phone screen and straightened, his gaze on the house ahead. "This isn't Stone's place. Are we picking someone up?" Tanner still believed Adam was sticking to their original plan, which would require a third person.

"Something like that." Adam got out and removed the ledger from the trunk as Tanner joined him on the driveway.

"I haven't had a chance to look in the ledger and compare the guest list yet, and that'll take at least an hour. I don't like this. We're deviating from the plan too much."

"Plans change." He walked up the flagstone steps of the luxury home as the front door opened. A dark-haired man in an impeccable suit greeted them. "Will

Remington, this is my brother, Tanner Wilde. Remington's the FBI guy I mentioned," he explained.

"Good to see you in one piece," Remington told Tanner as he led them to a living room.

Mason Gray rose from one of the couches, his gaze going over Adam's shoulder.

"Emily won't be joining us," Adam said, answering Mason's unspoken question. "Tanner, I think you've met Mason Gray at the lounge."

Tanner nodded a greeting. "I didn't know you were Emily's contact until recently, though," he told Mason.

Mason smirked. "Good. Nobody was supposed to know."

"You trust these men?" Tanner asked Adam, doubt clear in his voice. "I thought we said no outsiders."

"Their credentials are legit," Adam said. "I told Emily no outsiders because I didn't want her getting further involved in this operation. But I've checked Mason and Remington out over this past week. Now that they've met, I'm sure they can't double-cross us without the other knowing about it and either agency raining hell on the other. Right?" he asked the two agents.

"Mason and I are prepared to back you up in order to take down the Club," Remington acknowledged. Mason nodded in agreement.

"We can trust them," Adam said. He'd also made a quick call to the Legacy security office after leaving Emily in their bed, and they'd confirmed that they'd apprehended the man who'd attacked her. The guy had several priors, including burglary and theft, but so far he wasn't talking to police. So Mason obviously hadn't been the one to attack her.

"I have to get something off my chest," Mason said, sliding a sheepish glance toward Adam. "In the interest of being totally open, that trouble down in Phoenix, with the suspect who's charging you with assault...?"

"Yes?" Adam asked, not sure he liked where this

was going.

"It seems Remington and I had similar thoughts at the time. Namely, that we needed you up here to gain Tanner's cooperation. I had a DEA pal set that story up. We didn't beat the guy up, either," he hastily added as Adam sent him a dark look. "A rival in jail did that to the perp, but we may have used the incident and convinced the guy to press charges—against you."

"Why the hell would you do that?" Adam yelled. He'd known there was something he didn't trust about the man.

"To help nudge you toward returning to Vegas." Mason shrugged. "I figured you could get information—like where to find the ledger—that we weren't getting elsewhere."

"So sending you Tanner's debt card and a hint that he was in trouble gave you the final push," Remington added, a thoughtful grin on his face. "Worked out well, since you were probably sick of the politics and desk work by the time I needed you up here."

Adam glared at them, relief and anger making his head swim. After embracing the anger for a long moment, he chose to let it go. They had a job to focus on tonight, and emotion would only cloud his judgment. Emily was right—there were times he didn't *do emotion*, but only when he couldn't afford to.

"We'll help you sort out the charges in Phoenix after this is over," Mason said. He smiled apologetically. "It won't hurt your career in the long run. I promise."

"Gee, thanks," Adam bit out. "All you had to do was get Tanner to call and I'd have dropped everything voluntarily." In his peripheral vision, Tanner stiffened. He was still angry about how Adam had changed the plan, but he understood they still had a brotherly bond that would overcome any challenge.

"Except we couldn't find Tanner to call you," Mason pointed out. "Which is why we had to pull those strings and push those buttons."

"Now that that's cleared up, let's get back to the job at hand," Remington said. "Since Ryan knows Mason from Legacy, and Mason managed to wrangle an invite to this shindig he'll go in as backup. Tanner will be safe here with me, as we discussed."

"Like hell!" Tanner's angry gaze sliced Adam to the bone. "I'm not staying here."

"You are," Adam said, his tone brooking no argument. "I've got the ledger and a flash drive— though your original recordings have been sent to the LVPD, DEA and FBI. Ryan Stone will have to be satisfied with the ledger, because that's as close as he's getting to you or Emily."

Tanner scowled. "And if I don't stay here?"

"I'll have to arrest you," Remington said, stepping closer.

"We've set up a deal with the LVPD and other agencies to drop all charges against you if you cooperate. You'll be in the clear, as long as you testify against Ryan when it comes time."

Tanner shook his head. "I wouldn't have thought you had this con artist side in you, brother. To go behind my back, and Em's? All of that planning was for nothing."

Adam smiled grimly. "I've always had it in me, I just chose to ignore it. But if being ruthless and cutthroat is what it takes to keep the people I love safe, that's what I'll become."

Ryan allowed himself one drink. There was business to conduct tonight, but the party had an excellent vibe and he deserved to enjoy it. He was on the verge of getting everything he ever wanted, and all that he deserved. The ledger. Tanner Wilde. The flash drive and whatever was on it. Ultimate respect and power.

Detective Adam Wilde thought he could handle him, but Ryan wasn't one to take orders. Adam had called earlier that day to set up a drop. The detective probably also thought he could get out of this without anyone getting hurt.

Ryan smirked. Once the man got here, there was no way Ryan could let him walk out. He'd been looking for the perfect bait to force Tanner out of hiding, and the bait was coming to him. He'd use Detective Wilde to lure his brother out, and then kill both of them. Tanner needed to die and his brother, as a detective, wouldn't let this go. They both knew too much.

His father had told him to snip any loose ends, and he intended to do exactly that. If he failed, and word got back to his father, it would be Ryan's ass on the line. Thankfully, he had seen little of his father this evening. The man had been irritated when Ryan initially told him he was hosting the party, but he'd relented when Ryan explained that having people around would make Tanner feel safer about bringing the ledger. Then the man had received a call and secluded himself in his home office for the past half hour.

Brenda slipped an arm around his waist. "We're still on for tomorrow?" They were flying to Mexico for a week on the beach. She deserved it for sticking by him during this mess.

He grinned. "Absolutely. Pack only bikinis. Little ones. You won't need anything else."

She laughed and kissed him thoroughly before moving outside to mingle. The Club members Ryan had invited tonight as a reward—and to subtly remind them that their debts weren't forgotten and they still owed him—were congregating mainly outside by the pool. He was itching to join them and relax.

He glanced at his watch. Adam was supposed to be here by now with everything Ryan had demanded. He wanted this over with. His future began tonight.

Bubba, who'd been invited as added security tonight, came up to him. "Sir?"

"What is it?"

"He's here. Adam Wilde just arrived."

CHAPTER TWENTY-THREE

The valet opened Emily's door when she pulled up in front of the opulent Stone mansion in Henderson, just fifteen minutes from the main tourist areas of Vegas. Tall palm trees dotted the desert landscape, but it was the large stone columns, reminiscent of a Greek temple and the Legacy logo, that drew the eye. They lined the front walkway, lit by blue- and magenta-colored floodlights.

She'd been here before—quite often, actually—but never as a guest. Usually, she was the bartender hired to serve people from all over the world who were deemed worthy enough to receive an invite to a Stone party, and came in through the side service entrance. Stone had lavish parties almost every week, when he was in town. It appeared Ryan planned to follow in his father's footsteps, though there weren't nearly as many cars lining the drive.

Her gaze searched the rooms as she walked through the house. Beyond the wide living room windows, more colored lights danced in the pool, a fire pit blazed, and the sounds of music and conversation vied for attention. Ryan apparently intended to mix business with pleasure tonight. There were several dozen people drinking, laughing, and even taking drugs in plain sight, but nobody saw her at the window.

And she didn't see Adam. Was he here yet?

She caught sight of Brenda laughing and mingling with guests under the misters that kept the patio cool in the dry desert heat. Everyone seemed to be having a great time, with no clue that deals were being made behind closed doors.

Instead of walking outside, she turned down a back hallway and knocked on the last door. It opened immediately.

"I thought I saw you coming up the walk," Ivy said, pulling her inside. "We've been talking." According to their plan, Ivy had gone in to talk to her father first to soften the blow.

"I assume you're the bartender I've heard so much about," Robert Stone said. He sat behind a large, ornate desk, surrounded by shelves of books and pieces of art. His den was like a museum, but a productive one.

"I'm Emily Moore." She set down the tote she'd brought with her. Stone's gaze automatically moved to it.

"And that's the ledger?"

"It is." She held his intimidating gaze. There was a reason Robert Stone was feared in the business world. He had a finely honed mind when it came to generating deals and managing or manipulating people, but he was also unpredictable. He had a reputation for ruthlessness if someone crossed him or reneged on a contract.

It would take someone like him to go up against Ryan.

His eyebrows, still more dark than gray, drew closer together. "Why come to me? It sounds like your business is with my son."

"He's threatening to go after my family. He already approached them before I even had the opportunity to try to do what he asked." She frowned. "I've heard you're fair. Hard, but fair. You have more respect in our community than Ryan could ever hope to earn—not with the way he handles, and bungles, things."

Stone considered this and gave her a humorless smile. "I'll admit he hasn't lived up to expectations, but he's still relatively young." The guy was thirty years old, certainly old enough to know better than to blackmail his own father.

Ivy stepped forward. "There's more, Dad."

"So you mentioned earlier," he said, gesturing to Emily to continue.

"I've recently learned that you were being blackmailed," Emily said.

He scowled but didn't deny it. "That's been cleared up. The man behind it is dead." He'd been led to believe that Finn Tucker had been behind the demands.

"That's what you were made to think, but it was your own son throwing blame on a convenient scapegoat. Ryan was doing the blackmailing all along."

His face reddened. "That's a serious allegation. Forgive me, but I'm inclined to believe my son's word over yours, Ms. Moore."

"I understand. And that's why I brought proof." She pulled out the copy of Tanner's video, which she'd downloaded onto another flash drive from the cloud where Adam had backed it up, and set it on his desk. "That's a copy of a video recording made the night Blake Toll was murdered by your son. It's all on there, including his confession that he was blackmailing you. Blake knew about Ryan's schemes. He had tangible evidence and Ryan killed him and took the proof. I'm not sure he's aware this footage exists."

Stone stared at the drive for so long, she thought he might not believe her, might not want to see the confirmation of his own blood's betrayal. A low, strangled growl filled the silence and it took her a moment to realize the tortured sound came from Stone's throat. He sliced a hand through the air. "Leave me."

"Dad." Ivy stepped forward as if she could console him, but he waved her off.

"Go. I need time. And I need to view this for myself."

Ivy tugged Emily toward the door, but Emily

hadn't been guaranteed her end of the bargain yet. She planted her feet and faced down Stone. "All I ask is that you consider what I've brought you today and make things right. Stop your son from continuing to drag us all down. With respect, if anyone I love gets hurt, I'm coming after him with what I know. I'm sure, as someone who wants to protect his legacy, you understand."

His eyes rose to meet hers, his expression solemn as he nodded once.

It was enough. Unlike Ryan's promises, Mr. Stone's word was as solid as... stone.

"You set?" Remington asked through the mic in Adam's ear.

"I'm waiting in the conservatory, where Ryan's guy left me, but no sign of Ryan yet," Adam replied. Exotic plants of all kinds filled the cavernous glass-and-stone-walled building, rivaling any botanical garden display. The pungent scent of moist earth, so incongruous to the dry desert that surrounded them, clung to his nostrils and tasted like dirt on his tongue. "I saw Mason by the pool." They'd arrived separately, so as not to arouse suspicion.

"Just lounging around," Mason replied on the party line, a grin in his voice. "But I'm nearby. The guy who took you to the conservatory is standing guard outside."

"He goes by 'Bubba.'" Adam said. "He's one of the poker players who'd been at Blake Toll's the night of the murder, but he'd left before Toll was killed."

"Ah, yes," Remington said. "I recall asking him questions. He was a staunch defender of Ryan's. Big son of a bitch, too."

"Just say the code phrase and I'll be in there," Mason said. *Power play.*

"And I can be over the wall separating the properties within minutes," Remington said.

"Just keep Tanner occupied and out of trouble," Adam said. That was a Herculean task in itself.

"I'm right here, brother," Tanner said in Adam's ear. "Remington's letting me listen in, in case I can help. Nice to know *someone* trusts me."

"Nice to know you don't hold a grudge," Adam muttered. "I can handle this." After all, he'd watched their father play games and manipulate people for most of his life.

"I'm sure you can do it all, but I know Ryan, and his tells. If he runs his hand down the front of his suit jacket, like he's smoothing the material, then he's nervous, and probably lying."

And a nervous Ryan was a dangerous one. "Thanks for the tip."

Someone opened the door and the sound of conversation and laughter drifted in. Stone's multi-acre property was vast, and the conservatory was in a more secluded, darker corner of the lot, but the pool was within shouting distance.

Ryan came down the stone path, eyed the bag Adam held, and grinned. "I'm glad you could make it, Detective Wilde."

Adam gritted his teeth. He'd known it was possible Ryan had the resources to discover his occupation, but he'd hoped it would remain a secret. Not that it mattered. The people he loved were safe, and the mission remained the same. Make the trade, get Ryan's confession on record, and arrest him and turn the ledger over to the task force.

"Me, too," he said. "But I'm not on duty. A simple 'Adam' will suffice." He was here as Tanner's brother and Emily's friend first. Once their safety was assured, he was here as an off-duty detective and concerned citizen. He wasn't sure when the shades of gray had become acceptable—probably when Emily had infused color into his life, softening all his hard edges—but the distinctions were becoming clearer. "Tonight, I'm here to bargain for everyone's safety."

"Alone?" Ryan cocked a brow. "Pretty confident in your abilities, especially when you don't have anything to make a deal with."

He lifted the bag with the ledger inside. "I have something you'd very much like. Two things, actually." He removed the flash drive from his pocket and held it up.

"What's on it?" Ryan asked, eyes gleaming.

"A recording of the night you killed Blake." Adam had the pleasure of watching Ryan go pale. "And a copy will go to the police if you don't leave me and my family and friends alone."

"That's never going to happen. You can't touch me, and I'll destroy you and everything and everyone you love if you don't bring me Tanner."

"So you can kill him?" Adam shook his head.

"He knows too much. Besides, he was part of the contract I made with Emily. He's part of tonight's deal."

"He doesn't have to be."

"It's him or you. I can't let you walk out of here. If you didn't bring Tanner with you, then you'll be bait."

For the first time, Adam felt uneasy. He wasn't worried for his own safety, but if Tanner was listening in, he might offer himself up to try to save Adam. "There's only one way this is going to end. As soon as you admit you've been running the Club all along, I'm walking out of here—with you in cuffs."

"I don't think you're in any position to make demands. In fact, I have a new bargaining chip. Caught her crashing the party just a few minutes ago." Ryan chuckled. "Although I suppose it's not technically *crashing* when I invited her."

Adam went still. He couldn't mean...

"Bubba's coming in," Mason reported through Adam's earpiece. "And he has Emily."

His heart stopped as the large, muscular man jerked Emily inside by her arm. Her eyes met his and went soft, then hard. Yeah, she was still angry, but there were more pressing issues at the moment.

Ryan laughed. "You should see the look on your face. Guess you weren't expecting your girlfriend to show up. And after all you did to try to keep her out of this."

No, he hadn't been expecting this kink in the plans, or the emotion it brought with it.

Emily pulled loose from Bubba's grip. "I thought this was a party. How about a game of Follow the Queen?"

Adam frowned, certain she was trying to tell him something, but what? *Follow the queen* was a term with which he was familiar, another name for a shell game in which the mark bet on which shell or cup hid the item in question. The cups were shifted around until the mark was confused as to the desired item's position. What was she hinting at?

Her gaze went to the bag that held the ledger. Was it not in there? He'd put it in there himself. He had to force himself not to pull the ledger out and examine it right then and there.

"I told you it was a ridiculous scheme," she snapped at Adam, surprising him with her venom as she stalked toward him. "Told you he's too smart to fall for it. And you thought you could play this game without me." She looked him in the eye with a hardness he'd never seen before. She was beyond angry, which chilled him. He'd much rather see her fiery anger or passion than this coldness.

"Em, I was only trying to protect—"

She cut him off with a jab of her finger to his chest. *God, her fingers.* He saw the bandages on the fingertips of her left hand, and the light bruises on her right wrist. His gut clenched. He'd done that to her.

"I told you a lot of things," she continued, ignoring his interruption. "You didn't want to believe any of them, especially eight years ago. I hope you believe them now, because they're all true."

Eight years ago. She'd told him she loved him and that she always would. His gaze connected with hers and he saw the plea there, the softening that only he could detect beneath the act. The weight on his chest lightened. This was a part of whatever con she'd planned. She loved him, and she wanted him to go along with her.

"I didn't believe you then, but I absolutely do now," he replied solemnly, wanting to reach for her and take her someplace where they could shut out the rest of the world. But he couldn't. Still, a flash of warmth entered her expression, just for a split second.

Ryan was watching their silent battle with great interest and a wide grin. "Well, well. Looks like I've caught you two in the middle of a lover's quarrel. Hand over the ledger and I'll let you two sort this out amongst yourselves."

Emily spun to face him. "That's it? Just hand it over and we're done?" She laughed, indicating her distrust.

"Well, there was one more thing, wasn't there? But once Tanner shows up—and I'm certain he will, because at least one of you has to mean something to him—I'll leave you two alone."

Emily pinned him with a look. "*Dead* alone or *living* alone? Are you going to try to attack me again next time I leave work?"

Ryan frowned. "Attack you?" He looked genuinely perplexed. Perhaps the perpetrator had just been the pickpocket Legacy security apprehended, but that would be a tremendous coincidence.

"Of course not," Emily continued. "You'd never do your own dirty work. You have a book full of desperate minions at your disposal. Or you will, if you get the book back."

Ryan smirked. "It's pretty clear I'm getting the ledger back. As for whether you live or die, I suppose that depends on whether you plan to cheat me like Blake and Tanner did."

"So you admit you killed Blake."

"If it'll make you happy, sure. You know I did. And

I'll kill Tanner, too, the moment I get my hands on him. And I will get my hands on him. Now hand over the ledger."

Emily looked up into Adam's face. "Was that enough for an arrest, you think?"

He grinned. "Should be."

Ryan's grin faded and his gaze shot to Bubba. "I thought you frisked him when he came to the door."

"I took his gun," Bubba said, shifting his weight nervously.

"You didn't check for a wire?"

"You didn't mention that," Bubba protested. For a beast of a man, he could cower like a mouse in the face of Ryan's anger.

Ryan pulled Bubba's gun from where the guy had it tucked in his waistband and pointed the weapon at Emily's head. Adam's gut clenched, but he didn't dare make a move other than to lift his hands into the air.

"Search him," Ryan ordered Bubba. The man moved quickly for a big guy, and he would find the hidden mic at any moment.

"Is this some kind of power play?" Adam asked, hoping the code phrase made it through to those listening in. Mason should be moving into a position to assist at this very moment. And just in time, too, because Bubba found the microphone a second later and ripped it off, then held it high triumphantly.

Ryan handed the gun to Bubba. "Keep this aimed at her."

He grabbed the bag from Adam and withdrew the ledger. At the subtle shake of Emily's head, Adam knew they were fucked.

Ryan was flipping through the book. "I'll take this while you send Tanner a message—" Ryan went still. His jaw tightened and his face mottled with rage. "What the hell? This is the fake." Ryan spun on Emily. "This was in my office. How did you get it?"

"It was easy, really." She shrugged as if she weren't looking down the barrel of a loaded gun.

Adam cursed her toughness even as he admired it. He shifted to the balls of his feet, preparing to close the distance and knock her to the ground if Ryan seemed ready to pull the trigger.

But Emily wasn't done taunting him. "You shouldn't leave your valuables behind a simple lock. Or in a safe, for that matter. For a crime boss, you don't pose much of a challenge."

Ryan grabbed the gun from Bubba.

Emily forced herself not to flinch. If she showed fear, if she didn't diffuse the threat, she could see that Adam was prepared to take a bullet for her and she couldn't allow that. "You might want to hold off on shooting me."

"Why would I spare your life at this point?" Ryan sneered. "You had your shot at working with the Club, and you chose to work against me. I'll find another way."

"I know where the real ledger is. If you harm either of us, every bit of evidence connected to the Redemption Club will wind up in the hands of the authorities. I wonder how your father and the rest of the Club's members will react when the police come knocking on their doors. They'll know you didn't take more measures to protect their identities. Little old me just strode right into your closet, cracked your safe, and voilà, everyone's exposed." She laughed. "Talk about skeletons in the closet. And I'm sure Daddy won't be happy that you kept all of that evidence in his very own hotel, endangering him and his entire empire. He doesn't seem like the forgiving sort."

Ryan grinned. "He'll forgive me. He did the same thing when he was my age, so he can't judge me. That would be like judging himself. A few calls from our lawyers and a payment to a handwriting expert and the ledger would be ruled a fake."

She held up a finger. "That might work, if I didn't

also have the box of half-cards you kept in your safe. They're in a neutral location now, but they'll end up in a police evidence locker if you touch us. And let's not forget Tanner has Blake's murder, and everything that was said that night, recorded for anyone to see. The only choice now is to turn yourself over to the police, confess all, and don't touch a hair on our heads. You may still escape prison time—if your father will show mercy and lend you his team of high-priced lawyers." She shook her head. "But I've heard he isn't the merciful sort—not when he's been betrayed. Besides, I doubt even your team of high-priced lawyers and experts can explain away so much damning evidence."

"There will be no lawyers," Robert Stone said from the doorway. "This ends here." He had the real ledger in his arms, and the flash drive with the recording of Toll's murder, in his hands. Mason, Ivy, and Brenda stood behind Stone. Bubba remained off to the side, looking like he didn't know which side to support.

"Dad, she's lying," Ryan tried, an appeal in his voice that nearly made Emily grin. Except that the gun was still aimed at her.

"Put the gun down," Adam ordered, using his most authoritative tone.

Ryan looked as if he'd forgotten he had it.

"Put it down, man," Mason said. "You're outnumbered. You don't want to face two murder charges, do you?"

When Ryan resisted, his father spoke up. "Drop it." His simple command was effective. Ryan dropped the weapon.

Emily stepped closer to Adam as he scooped up the gun. When he straightened, his free hand reached out to pull her against his side.

"Don't you ever take him on like that again," Adam whispered against her ear.

Her arm looped about his waist in quiet reassurance. "I won't have to."

CHAPTER TWENTY-FOUR

The skin on Ryan's nape prickled, warning him he was in deep shit. He smoothed his hand down his shirt, trying to hide his nervousness. His father wouldn't respect him if he showed weakness.

Another Stone Rule came to mind: *Even when you're not in control, appear that you are.*

He squared his shoulders. "I'll beat this, Dad. With the support of the family—"

"You're no longer a Stone." His father's words, said with such quiet finality, seemed to echo in the conservatory.

Ryan's breath whooshed from his lungs as if he'd been punched in the stomach. Behind his father, Ivy's eyes had gone wide.

"Don't you have packing to do?" He roared at his sister.

"She's staying in Vegas. I'll need someone to run Legacy."

That was *his* job, damn it. "Dad, you have the ledger. That's what you wanted. We can kick everyone off our property and call the lawyers. Everything will be back to normal by morning."

Stone ignored him, turning to Mason, of all people. What was Legacy's star dancer doing watching this private family moment as if he belonged here? "I have your word I'll be immune from prosecution for anything in this ledger if I hand it over and Ryan turns himself in for Toll's murder?" his father asked.

Mason nodded. "The District Attorney accepted

the proposal my agency offered. As long as you cooperate fully and help the DEA and other agencies apprehend the more serious criminals in there, Ryan will only be prosecuted for murder."

"DEA?" Ryan echoed. Mason was an undercover agent? His anger simmered, replacing the shame and rejection. He nurtured it.

Stone handed the ledger and flash drive to Mason and Ryan nearly leapt on the man. "I need a moment alone with my son," his father said.

"Dad, maybe we should—" Ivy tried to intervene, but his father had made up his mind.

"Just a moment alone," his father insisted. "Thank you for informing me about what's going on."

Ivy hesitated a moment, then turned to leave. Ryan's outrage surfaced. Where was her loyalty to her brother? Like a narc, she'd helped Emily turn their father against him and then abandoned the field of battle.

"We'll be right outside," Adam said. Emily trailed after him. Soon, only Brenda and Bubba remained with him and his father. Seeing he still had a couple people to stand with him, he found a spark of courage.

"I'm not sure what you've heard—" Ryan began.

"That you're bargaining with people linked to the various law enforcement agencies to get the ledger back. That, as usual, you're making horrible choices. You're acting cocky and letting power go to your head. You think that throwing alcohol and drugs around freely will buy you loyal friends, and you've made severe tactical errors."

"I got Adam and Emily here, didn't I?"

"But not Tanner, and he could do serious damage."

"I'm going to find him. It's just a matter of time. And I had the others in the palm of my hand."

His father arched his brows and glanced around. "You had nothing left to bargain with."

"I didn't need to bargain. I just need to get rid of them."

His father scoffed. "You planned to kill them, then? In the middle of a fucking *party?* How do you expect to do away with the threat if there are witnesses? I thought I taught you to always cover your bases."

Ryan muttered a curse. "I'm so sick of your stupid rules! You said to do what was necessary to set things right, and I'm doing that. I'm doing what's best for my business, as you always taught me."

His father jabbed a finger toward one wall of the conservatory, indicating the party guests beyond. "Those people aren't the kind of business connections that will help our company."

"No, but they're loyal to me."

"They're loyal to whoever has the ledger."

"I have personal connections with them you'll never have. True loyalty can't be bought." He held out a hand to Brenda, but she took a step away, closer to his father. What was going on here?

His father gave him a wry grin. "Brenda works for me. She's been spying on you for me for weeks. She's the one who told me about your dependence on oxycodone and your repeated fuckups. Let that be a lesson to you, son. Those people who seem so loyal will only stick by you until a better offer comes along. And you have nothing left to offer."

Ryan eyed the ledger. "Fine. I'll leave town until things calm down. I'll take that job in Tuscany for a couple months instead of here." And then, when he returned, he'd reboot the Club with his own damn ledger. A fresh start. It would be entirely his, not some castoff from his father.

"No." The single word was cold and final as it fell from his father's lips.

Brenda grinned, her expression one of someone about to watch a train wreck—and take great pleasure in seeing the resulting chaos.

"No?" Ryan asked. "You want me to work at Legacy instead?" Ryan nodded. That would work even better, once he was cleared of all charges.

"The hotel and casino are no longer *your* legacy. I meant what I said. You're no longer my son."

Once they were outside of the conservatory, Adam pulled Emily close and buried his face in her hair. "You just don't stay put, do you?" he asked, trying to lighten the mood to calm his frayed nerves. She wasn't supposed to show up tonight, let alone with Ryan's thug manhandling her.

Her shaky exhalation warmed his neck. "I'm sorry I couldn't just wait for you in bed, but if you think I'd take orders from you, you're crazy."

He'd almost lost her. He pulled away and planted a kiss on her mouth, feeling the last of her anger and fear melt away as she plastered herself against him, her hands fisting in his shirt as if she'd never let go.

He pretended to ponder her comment. "I think I am a bit crazy. Crazy for you."

She laughed. "You, Adam Wilde, are the farthest thing from crazy I've ever seen."

One eye on the door, he bent forward to speak against Emily's lips. "And you're the perfect amount. Except for the part about not pursuing the Redemption Club." He shot a glance toward Mason, who was near the corner of the conservatory, holding the evidence and talking on his cell phone.

"That was a promise I had Mason make. I said nothing about what *you'd* do in the near future."

He pulled away as Ivy approached. "I hope Dad breaking the news to Ryan in private will defuse the situation."

"News?" Adam asked, looking to Emily.

She shrugged. "I stuck to the part of our initial plan where we destroy Robert Stone's faith in his son. He won't be standing by Ryan anymore, and Ryan needs to know that so he won't feel confident enough to retaliate."

Ivy looked conflicted about that but didn't say anything. Ryan had made his own bed, and now he'd have to lie in it.

"My weapon?" he asked Bubba. The man pulled it from the back of his waistband where he'd tucked it and returned it to Adam. He still had Bubba's gun from when Ryan had dropped it, and the man looked at it hopefully. "Not going to happen. I'll be turning it over to the DEA."

"Just following orders," Bubba said, and moved off to join the other party guests. Apparently, he felt his job here was done.

"Don't go anywhere," he called after him. He could already hear sirens in the distance and saw Mason ending his phone call.

"I'd better get back in there and take Ryan into custody." Adam pulled cuffs from the snap pocket on his belt. He caught Emily looking at them with a half-smile. "Funny that Bubba never took these to be a threat. We both know how powerful they can be."

Her lips curved and her gaze heated.

Robert Stone was exiting the conservatory, as Adam headed to the door. A gunshot pierced the night and they both reflexively ducked. Adam looked back toward Emily, but she'd already hit the ground. Seeing his worried glance, she gave him a thumbs-up that she was okay. He got to his feet and ran inside the conservatory, entering cautiously, expecting more gunfire.

"Police!" he called. "Drop your weapon."

"I did," a woman's voice called back.

As Adam entered, his weapon raised, Brenda kicked her gun toward him along the stone path and put her hands in the air. There was a manic, satisfied gleam to her eyes.

"What happened?" Adam's gaze moved to Ryan's body where it lay on the ground, a shot to the chest and blood pooling on the pebble path beneath him. He rushed to pick up Brenda's gun and check Ryan's pulse.

He was already gone. "He's dead."

Robert Stone stood in the doorway, his shoulders sagging as he heard his words. He glared at Brenda. "What did you do?"

"I rid the world of the devil." Brenda laughed, but tears streamed from her eyes. "The bastard deserved it. His fucking *Club* was responsible for my sister's overdose. Prison would have been too good for him, and you weren't going to punish him, so I handled it. May he rot forever in hell." She spat at Ryan's body.

"Get her out of here," Adam told Remington as he appeared in the doorway and immediately assessed the situation. "Wait. Where's Tanner?"

"Once we heard your code phrase raising the alarm, he was very insistent about getting to you." Remington looked around. "I would have thought he'd be here by now. The LVPD's here and Mason was instructing them to divvy up the witnesses. Perhaps they detained Tanner along with the other party guests."

Stone's face was reddening, his breathing becoming heavier.

"I can take care of her if you want to get him out of here," Remington offered.

Adam went to Stone. "Why don't I help you find your daughter? Ivy will need to be told."

Having something to motivate him to action, Stone finally focused on Adam and nodded. "She'll be dealt with?"

"She won't get away with this," Adam promised.

As Remington cuffed Brenda and gave her the Miranda spiel, Adam led Stone outside and together they found Ivy standing with Emily. Beyond them, on the patio, LVPD officers were roping off the scene, keeping the party crowd back. Mason was nowhere to be seen. Stone was giving Ivy the grim news, anger and pain flaring in his eyes. Emily had a comforting arm around her friend's shoulders as the woman cried quiet tears.

Adam heard Tanner shout his name from the crowd on the patio. "Adam! Tell them to let me through. It's important."

Adam talked to an officer, who let his brother join him, Emily, and the Stones. He embraced his brother in a big hug, but Tanner's gaze was on the door of the conservatory.

"Looking for someone?" Adam asked. "Ryan's dead. The threat's gone." This didn't bring as much relief as Adam would have imagined.

"Have you seen Remington?" Tanner asked, his head swiveling to take in the dark grounds beyond the conservatory. "He took off after he heard Stone had the real ledger."

"Took off?" Adam turned to where he'd last seen Remington. "Didn't he come here *with* you?"

"No. He tied me up, but I got loose. I get the feeling that FBI agent you trusted so much is actually after the ledger himself."

Adam whirled and searched for Mason. He'd had the ledger last. He retraced the man's steps, remembering how he'd been standing at the outside corner of the conservatory. A few feet away was a row of thick bushes. As he approached, he heard a moan and found Mason holding his head, trying to sit up.

"He hit me," Mason said. "The bastard hit me."

"Who?" But Adam knew who the attacker was. And he'd bet Remington was long gone.

"Remington." Mason looked around suddenly. "The ledger. It's gone."

Adam ran to the gate and then the front of the house, Tanner by his side, but there was no sign of Remington or Brenda. He tried calling the agent's cell number, but there was no answer. He tried the FBI offices and, after a few minutes, got the supervisor. "He's taking a couple weeks off" was the man's answer.

That couldn't be right. Unless Remington had been playing them all along. But why would he take Brenda?

Remembering something, he pulled a paper out of his pocket, the page he'd torn from the ledger when he'd been with Tanner earlier, in his suite. He'd planned to give Emily the answers she wanted—after this was all over. He found his father's entry and his eyes shot across to the notations that indicated the Club member who'd carried out the dark deed. *Remy Langston.*

Remington.

Shit.

Remington had been right about there being a mole who was manipulating things behind the scenes so that the authorities couldn't get too close to the truth, to the ledger. He'd been the mole and Brenda had been his accomplice. He'd wanted to get rid of Ryan and the evidence of Remy Langston's crimes, as well as whatever crime he'd gone into debt for.

And of course, the ledger had that information. And Remington had the ledger.

"Leaving me out of this was a dick move," Tanner said when the police had received their statements and cleared them to leave a couple hours later. "But I understand why you did it."

Thanks to Mason helping explain the events of tonight and the past week, they'd been processed quickly. Now, Adam and Tanner were driving together, following Emily's car back to her apartment to ensure she arrived home safely.

"Oh, and I haven't been the victim of one or two of your *dick moves* in the past?" Adam shot back at him.

Tanner sent him an unrepentant grin. "I suppose we're even, then?"

"Hardly. But I'll let the past go if you will." Adam pulled into Emily's parking lot. "However, I'll still be looking out for you."

"From Phoenix?" Tanner laughed. "Good luck with that."

"From here. I'm staying."

Tanner's eyes widened as he studied Adam's serious expression. "No shit." He grinned. "It'll be good to have my brother back."

"Ditto. And we'll put the past behind us." And he hoped to do the same with Emily. He only wanted to think about the future—and the present.

As he turned off the car, Tanner stuck out his hand. "Deal." They shook on it, but Tanner kept his hand out, turning it over so his palm faced up.

Adam stared at it, confused. "What?"

"I think you and Em have some talking to do. I can drive myself home. Fork over the keys."

Adam *would* like some time with Emily to sort out what had happened. She seemed to have forgiven him for the handcuffing to the bed, but he wanted to make sure she was truly okay. That *they* were okay.

He dropped the keys into Tanner's outstretched hand.

After putting her car in Park, Emily sat, staring out the window, wondering how she could ask Adam to come back to her place tonight. There was so much she wanted to say to him. But he and Tanner needed time together, too. Maybe he could come over first thing in the morning.

She looked toward Adam's car. He climbed out and began walking toward her as Tanner got out and went to the driver's side. He sent her a little wave and a big grin. What did he have up his sleeve now?

Adam looked surprisingly uncertain as they met up on the sidewalk. "Mind if I come up for a bit?"

"Not at all." Her heart beat so hard she thought he ought to be able to hear it. He looked so serious. Was he here to talk about their future, or to say good-bye? Once inside, she set her keys and purse down and kicked off her shoes, surprised when Adam still looked nervous. "Do you want a drink?"

"No, thank you. Besides, you may want me to leave when you see what I have to tell you."

"That sounds serious." So, it was to be a good-bye then. A frisson of alarm went through her, and she thought she might split in two, right through the middle. "What's this about?"

He pulled her down beside him on the couch and pulled a folded paper from his pocket. "Read this."

She unfolded the paper and sat, stunned. "Is this...?" She was looking at the only evidence that her mother's accident had been the result of foul play. "You knew? For how long?"

Adam held her gaze. "Tanner and I decided to remove it from the ledger when we had our private chat, before you came in with the room service cart this morning."

Her hand went to her mouth as she read the name of the man who'd put a hit out on her mother. Frank Wilde. Only, it wasn't her mother who was supposed to be harmed. He'd ordered the hit on her father. Her mother's mistaken involvement in this had been the true tragedy.

Waves of emotion—relief that she'd found answers, anger at Frank Wilde, frustration and grief at what her family had endured—threatened to tug her under and drown her, but Adam was a rock she could cling to.

"It seems the Wilde family is doomed to hurt you," Adam said. "I intend to make up for that, if you'll let me."

"Your father already paid for his mistakes," she said. "And I realize they were *his* mistakes, not yours. Our parents made their own decisions."

"You knew about the affair?"

She pressed her fingers to her mouth for a long moment, afraid her feelings would sweep her away. "I suspected. I'd overheard a few arguments back when I was seventeen and my father first returned to town after being gone for a year. And after the accident, my mom said his name a couple times. Just enough to make me wonder. When your dad used to come by the hospital to visit Mom after the accident, he always looked so shaken by the whole thing, but I never realized that it was guilt."

"And love, I suppose," Adam said. "I just found out about all of this. Apparently, Tanner saw it in the ledger a few weeks ago. He said it was one of the reasons he started pulling away from you. He wasn't sure how to handle this. I'm so sorry, Em."

"It was your father's actions, not yours, so there's no apology to be made. Not by you, anyway. Besides, the punishment should fit the crime, and if my mother and your father had an affair, I think they've paid for their sins, several times over." Karen Moore would forever be marked by the choice she'd made, and Frank Wilde had been miserable, haunted by guilt until the day he died. It was tragic and sad for both families.

"And my crimes? How should I pay for them?" He took her hand and kissed the bruise on her wrist, then took her other hand to kiss her bandaged fingertips. He examined them, a frown marring his brow. "How did you get loose, by the way? It looks like you clawed your way out."

She huffed. "Like I'd tell you my trade secrets."

"I'm sorry I hurt you. Then, and now."

"No, you're not." When he opened his mouth to argue, she put a finger against his lips to silence him. "If it were up to you, I'd still be chained to the bed." A thrill of anticipation ran through her as a wicked grin curved his lips.

"If it were up to me, you'd always be chained to our bed."

Our bed. She loved the sound of that.

"But that's not something a man of the law would do." She cupped his face as a smile tugged at her lips. "I'm wondering what the punishment should be for chaining a woman who loves you to the bed you'd just made love to her in?"

He pretended to consider it. "If the punishment should fit the crime, I'd suggest she drag the perpetrator right back to that bed and give him no choice but to stay there with her."

"And sentence him to a lifetime of servitude."

"Sounds fair." He bent forward to kiss her lips.

"Except no chains," she said, pulling back before he could seal the deal. She didn't want him to feel trapped. She never wanted to know the pain of him leaving again. He needed to be free to pursue his career, to seek justice for others. "You're free to go wherever and do whatever you need to do to be you."

"I love you, Emily Moore. And I'm staying this time. Besides, Mason owes me a job and I intend to collect on that debt."

Her eyes widened. "DEA?"

"I made a vow when I came to town that I'd be here until I got things done. The Redemption Club isn't officially over until we find that ledger. And Remington and Brenda will have to face justice." He'd told her how Remington was quite possibly Remy Langston, and that the man Legacy security had detained in connection with her attack in their parking lot had finally confessed that he'd been hired by a man with that name. "So much to do around here."

She grinned. "And you sound excited to be doing it."

"But there's other unfinished business. Loving you. I'll never be done with that."

"And I'm never letting you walk away again, Adam Wilde. I finally have you right where I want you."

"You won't even need those handcuffs anymore."

She looked at him from beneath her lashes. "Doesn't mean we have to let them go to waste."

He laughed. "I'm pretty sure I'm the winner here, even if it did require a little sleight of hand."

EPILOGUE

Three months later

Robert Stone looked the duo over and decided he could do business with them. His ire had cooled and, with distance, he could see their usefulness.

Remington had taken on a false identity years ago and carved out a respectable job with the FBI. He'd conned the government agency for years. He was a man who could get things done.

Still, Stone had been extra cautious about who he'd trust after his son's unfaithfulness.

"You brought the item?" he asked Remington.

Brenda set the backpack on the table. She'd toned down her looks and died her blonde hair dark brown to disguise her identity. He wanted to strangle her barehanded for what she'd done to his son, but this was business. Still, she'd have to pay for her infraction someday. His revenge would be served ice-cold.

"We had to wait until the heat died down to travel," Remington said. "Wilde's got more resources now that he's heading up the new interagency task force, and he's been gunning for us. I had to get new papers, new identities."

Stone grunted. "He's doing his job." And he had to respect that. He set a briefcase on the table and opened it to show the cash.

At Remington's nod, Brenda opened her backpack and removed the red book.

Stone stroked its surface, the memories of his time with the Redemption Club flooding back to him. He flipped to the first page and verified its authenticity, his gaze landing on his name, and those of his two co-conspirators who'd founded Redemption Club with him. They'd been the first to trade favors, and their Club had grown into a beautiful, dark thing.

"I have to admit that the Cayman Islands are a great place to escape to." Remington glanced at the beach beyond Stone's back porch. It was only steps away.

Stone flipped through the book. "Some of it's missing."

"Just a few pages. We needed to sell them to pay for our new documentation and a safe way out of town."

"A necessary cost, I suppose." Stone smirked. "I see the page with your debt is missing."

Remington shrugged. "The bank heist didn't work out, anyway."

"Nor did the car accident, if I hear correctly. But it sounds like you got what you needed in the end."

Remington shrugged. "I'm satisfied. What are you planning to do with this, if I may ask? Will there still be a Redemption Club? I may be interested in contracting its services again someday."

"That's my business. But let's just say, if you need a gun for hire, or someone to do your dirty work in the future, you can contact me."

His number one rule was: *Be true to yourself.* And he was a ruthless businessman at heart.

If you missed Book 1...

STACKING THE DECK
(Redemption Club, Book 1)

In a city built for sin, the Redemption Club is a secret society that exists to fulfill a person's darkest desires—including murder games—for a price.

Raised off the grid by an anti-government group, Skye Hamilton puts her resourcefulness and survival training to good use taking the dangerous tasks nobody else wants. When a job searching for a runaway teen brings Redemption Club members gunning for her, putting those she cares about in danger, she'll risk everything to fight the enemy. Including her heart.

Jared Bennigan, Las Vegas bodyguard to the elite, accepted his latest job hoping it would lead to his missing sister. All evidence points to his client as the last person to have seen her, but he's not the only one looking for a woman who disappeared. Skye's enticing blue eyes contradict her tough, distrusting exterior, revealing an intriguing combination of vulnerability and intelligence. But those eyes are watching his client—through her rifle's scope.

To find both missing women, Jared will need to convince Skye—who plays a wicked game of hard-to-get—to be his partner. And with the Redemption Club intent on making Skye the prey in a human hunting expedition, her skills, and her trust in Jared, will be put to the test. It's the ultimate game of survival of the fittest. But who will win?

And coming Spring of 2016...

RAISING THE STAKES
(Redemption Club, Book 3)

Don't miss Ivy Stone's story. Can Devlin Grimm thaw the reputed ice queen's heart? Ivy's tempted to let him see the real her, but keeping her defenses up may just save her life.

Sign up for Anne Marie's newsletter at www.AnneMarieBecker.com for the latest news regarding releases and special deals.

ABOUT THE AUTHOR

Anne Marie has always been fascinated by people—inside and out—which led to degrees in Biology, Chemistry, Psychology, and Counseling. Her passion for understanding the human race is now satisfied by her roles as mother, wife, daughter, sister, and award-winning author of romantic suspense.

She writes to reclaim her sanity.

Find ways to connect with Anne Marie at www.AnneMarieBecker.com. There, sign up for her newsletter to receive the latest information regarding books, appearances, and giveaways.